EARTH AFLAME

EARTH AFLAME

EARTHRISE BOOK XI

DANIEL ARENSON

CHAPTER ONE

Lailani was walking her daughter to preschool when the machines attacked.

It was a sweltering summer day in Cagayan de Oro, a city in the southern Philippines. The sun beat down, searing and blinding. The air was thick with moisture and mosquitoes. Even the palm trees that filled Cagayan de Oro seemed to wilt today, their fronds draping over the cracked asphalt roads. Stray dogs lay under shop awnings, too hot to even beg for treats. Parasols dotted the streets, shading passersby, and vendors called out from kiosks, hawking *halo-halo*, a local dessert of sweetened crushed ice. Only the city's children seemed to enjoy the weather. They ran around shirtless, jumped into the river, climbed trees, and played with dice in shadowy alleyways.

Jeepneys, the colorful taxicabs of the Philippines, clattered down the roads like psychedelic beetles, so garish they made tie-dyed shirts seem subdued. Their rumbling motors and puffing exhaust pipes only added to the heat. Battered air conditioners hung from concrete walls, humming and rattling along, leaking rusty rivulets. This was a city of water and animals and trees. But also of machines, electricity, and engines.

Countless electric cables filled the sky, thrumming at full capacity. They stretched between buildings, forming intricate weavings above the narrow streets, and bundled around wooden poles like cobwebs draped over dead trees, all tangled together and buzzing. Lailani had once joked that Filipino cities were giant spiderwebs made of electric wires. The tangles of crackling cables were as much a feature of Cagayan de Oro as the palm trees, the colorful shops that lined every roadside, and the smiling, happy people.

People she loved. People she had come to help.

"Mommy, I'm tired," Tala said. "Carry me!"

Lailani smiled down at her three-year-old. "You can walk a little bit farther, right? Look at Epimetheus. He isn't tired."

Their pet Doberman was walking at their side, tail wagging. He was a powerful dog, weighing more than mother and daughter combined, but always happy and smiling. He licked little Tala, and the girl giggled.

"But Mommy! Epi has four legs. I only have two!"

Lailani laughed. "You got me there. But it's not far. We're almost at school. You can walk."

Tala groaned. "Fine!"

The school was still a few blocks away. It was likely Lailani would be carrying her daughter by the end. But let the girl walk for a while longer. It built character.

Lailani had built Benny Ray School herself, naming it after Tala's late father. Lailani had been born here in the Philippines, the daughter of a thirteen-year-old prostitute. She had grown up homeless. Hungry. Afraid. She had escaped that life. She had enlisted, fought, won medals. With her friends, she had saved humanity.

And then, after the war, she had come back home.

Instead of killing, she was healing.

She built schools. Free schools for children who would otherwise grow up like she had, afraid and hungry on the streets. Benny Ray School was her third school so far, accepting children of all ages. Little Tala had just begun to attend.

I defeated alien civilizations, Lailani thought. *I fought in great battles alongside heroes. But building these schools is the most important thing I do.*

"Mommy, I'm tired! Can I ride on Epi?"

Lailani laughed. "He's a dog, not a horse! He's the size of a horse, but still." She knelt. "Climb up and ride on my shoulders."

She kept trudging forward, Tala on her shoulders, both trying to ignore the heat. A jeepney rumbled by, painted with every color of the rainbow, honking. People waved from inside.

"*Mabuhay*, Tita Lailani!"

"Bless you, Tita Lailani!"

She waved back. This was a large town, but everyone knew her. Most people around the world knew her. They called her *tita*—meaning auntie—a sign of respect. The jeepney rolled by, and a few children ran across the street, their skin tanned brown. The smallest boy handed her a flower, then hid behind his sister.

"*Mabuhay*, Tita Lailani!" they said.

She walked onward, moving between little shops. The buildings were makeshift, assembled from sheets of corrugated iron, salvaged concrete bricks, slats of plywood, and tarpaulin. Typhoon season regularly blew them down, but the people rebuilt their shanties every year. They lived on the second stories, while the bottom floors contained family businesses. They sold cheap electronics, secondhand clothes, religious charms, and delicious street foods.

"Mommy, breakfast!"

Tala pointed at a kiosk that sold tea and desserts. A television was mounted on a pole, playing a boxing match. More than the desserts or movie, the shady awning beckoned.

Lailani stepped into the shade. Gabe the shopkeeper was a kindly man with wrinkly brown skin, a grizzled goatee, and a prosthetic hand—a relic of the Alien Wars. Twenty years ago, he had been a professional boxer. Not good enough to escape this town, maybe. But a handful of trophies still stood on a shelf, lovingly polished, glinting beneath a wooden crucifix.

The middle-aged man smiled, revealing a golden tooth.

"Hey, good morning, Tita Lailani, little Tala! Free *halo-halo* for my favorite customers."

Lailani scrunched her lips. "I'm not sure I want her to eat dessert for breakfast."

"Halo-halo is good for her! Full of beans, you know."

"Mommy, Mommy, I want halo-halo!"

Lailani sighed. "Fine."

The shopkeeper slapped together the traditional Filipino treat. He filled a cup with crushed ice, then added milk, sweetened beans, coconut juliennes, *pinipig* rice, cubes of sweet purple *ube* potatoes, and finally a scoop of ice cream. As he added ingredients, the boxing match continued on the TV. One boxer knocked out the other.

"Ah!" Gabe snorted. "Rubbish. These new young boxers—useless. Not like the old greats. In my day, a fighter would never go down like that."

Riding on Lailani's shoulders, Tala swung her fists. "I'm going to be a boxer when I'm big! Like Tito Gabe."

"You're going to be a scientist or a teacher," Lailani said.

Electricity buzzed. The television suddenly went dark.

"Ah, darn it," Gabe said. "It's been doing that all week. I think there's a problem with the electrical grid."

Lailani turned toward the dead television. On the dark monitor, she caught her reflection. She stood for a moment, looking at herself.

She wore jean shorts, revealing tanned legs. Her T-shirt featured the words DEATH METAL over a rainbow. She wore her black hair in a bob cut. Standing four feet ten, weighing in at ninety-three pounds, she didn't seem particularly intimidating. Especially not with the toddler riding on her shoulders, dripping ice cream. Nobody would mistake Lailani for a boxer, that was for sure.

She was a major in the Human Defense Force reserves. A war heroine. A mother. A woman of thirty-five. But she didn't look it. She still looked like a teenager.

For years nobody commented about her appearance. They said that Asian women simply aged well, that was all. Good genes. But in the past year or two, people had begun to talk. Are you really thirty-five, Tita Lailani? Wait, are you really the famous soldier who fought the scum? That was almost twenty years ago! You must have been a baby!

Deep inside, Lailani knew why she wasn't aging.

And the reason chilled her.

Only her closest friends knew. Lailani was not fully human.

A shudder ran through her.

She had learned that truth in the army. That the scum had created her in a lab. Had planted a hybrid embryo into a human host—a teenage prostitute they found on the streets of Manila. Lailani had been grown to someday serve them as a spy and assassin.

And I served them.

Lailani lowered her head.

I killed Tala's father.

She still remembered that day. Growing claws. Ripping the heart from Benny "Elvis" Ray.

She had a microchip inside her skull now. It prevented the alien evil from manifesting again. For all intents and purposes, she was fully human.

Except her lack of aging.

Except this constant reminder whenever she looked into a mirror.

You are not fully human.

She reminded herself that her DNA was only one percent alien. Not very much at all. But still she worried. Had she passed on the alien cruelty to Tala, and would her little girl someday grow claws, attack and kill, need a chip in her brain too? Or was Tala fully human, would age like a human, and Lailani was doomed to live for centuries, to watch her little girl grow old and die? Both options terrified her.

I once tried to commit suicide, she thought, caressing the scars on her wrists. *I once joined the army to die in battle. Now I'm facing the prospect of living for centuries. And I'm more scared than ever.*

"Mommy, are you sad?" Tala said. "Why are you crying?"

Lailani wiped her eyes. "They're tears of joy, little one, because I love you so much."

Tala hugged her. "I love you too, Mommy. So much."

Epimetheus nuzzled them, joining the little family moment.

Electricity sparked.

The cables across the street hissed and crackled. Lights flashed.

The TV burst back to life, broadcasting static. Gabe cursed and slapped the TV, trying to get boxing back on.

Normally Lailani wouldn't have registered it. The electrical grid was iffy at best here in Cagayan de Oro. Struggling with typhoons and poverty, the islands had never boasted reliable infrastructure, and the Alien Wars had destroyed more than ten typhoons ever could. The lights regularly went out, and the cables often hissed like snakes.

But today wasn't a normal day.

Lailani had been hearing news from across the world. News of a computer virus called the Dreamer. A virus that caused cars to crash, planes to plow into buildings, electronics to go haywire. Europe was burning. On the news, it looked like a goddamn war zone. Thankfully, the virus hadn't reached Asia.

Yet.

Could this power bleep be related?

"Come on!" Gabe pounded the TV again. "Damn thing."

The static finally cleared.

A new image appeared on the screen.

The shopkeeper frowned. "What the hell?"

Tala whimpered. "Mommy, I'm scared."

Lailani stared at the television in disgust. A face appeared there. A face with no nose, no ears, no hair. Just two black eyes and an enormous, smiling mouth. A face made from real skin, complete with wrinkles, warts, and little hairs, but shaped like an emoji.

The grin widened. The face spoke.

"I am Mister Smiley. Worship me."

The television began to flash. Strobe lights washed the kiosk. A series of shrieks, clicks, and grumbles emerged from the speakers like an old-timey internet connection, the kind that ran on telephone wires. Across the street, TV sets, car radios, even people's phones—they all began to play the same discordant sounds. The tangles of electric cables thrummed above, flashing with light, buzzing, chattering that alien signal.

Pain burst inside Lailani's skull. Agony. Searing fire. A red-hot ember inside her head.

She recognized that pain. It was the microchip the HDF had implanted there. Technology to stop the scum from accessing her brain, from controlling her like a marionette. Before getting her chip, the aliens could activate her at will, give her terrible strength, force her to kill. The chip had put an end to that—with the price of searing pain.

Yes, this pain was familiar.

Somebody was trying to hack her mind.

Sitting on her shoulders, Tala screamed.

Lailani pulled the girl into her arms. "Close your eyes, Tala! Cover your ears!"

The girl obeyed. The strobe lights kept flashing. The sound grew louder—a mechanical storm, a beating drum, a hammering of agony. Lailani tossed back her head and howled, the chip vibrating inside her skull.

Her dog fell, flailed on the ground, and howled. Beside them, Gabe was covering his ears, thrashing and squinting. The shopkeeper's face was red, and veins bulged on his neck.

And then—it ended.

Silence.

A few last crackles of electricity. And the lights were gone. And the sound was gone. And they stood in silence, shaking.

Across the city, radios, televisions, phones, all electronics—they were dead.

"Tala!" Lailani whispered. "Are you all right?"

The girl uncovered her ears and opened her eyes. She nodded.

"Tito Gabe?" Lailani said, turning toward the shopkeeper.

The retired boxer was hunched over, breathing heavily. For a long moment he just breathed. Finally he straightened and stared at Lailani. His eyes were hard. Cold. His mouth, normally smiling, was a thin line.

"Tito Gabe?" she said, taking a step back.

He took a step toward her. His hands formed fists.

"We must worship him." Gabe's lips peeled back, revealing his golden tooth. "We must dream his dream."

Epimetheus came to stand between them. The powerful Doberman growled at the shopkeeper.

"Gabe?" Lailani whispered, taking a step back.

For a while after the war, she had gone everywhere with a gun. She had stopped carrying after Tala had been born, paranoid that the girl would reach for the pistol. Instinctively, even as Lailani kept her eyes on Gabe, her hand reached out, seeking a weapon. She grabbed a bottle of Coca Cola from a shelf. Better than nothing.

Gabe grinned. But not his usual kindly smile. It was a hideous grin, filled with crooked teeth. His eyes bugged out, the irises turned milky white. He spoke in a deep, inhuman voice, as if reciting a poem. Lailani could only listen in horror.

The Dreamer is watching
The Dreamer is here
The Dreamer is always your friend

Come into his dream
Come play in his world
The Dreamer is yours till the end

Mister Smiley knows
That the Dreamer is all
That his dreams are the world and your mind

Come into his home
And dream with the Dreamer
Such wondrous dreams you will find!

"Gabe," Lailani said. She held Tala behind her with one hand. With the other, she held the glass bottle. "Gabe, you have to fight it! Whatever that signal did to your brain. Fight it! This isn't you. You are Gabe de la Cruz, my friend. Fight the Dreamer like you fought in the boxing ring. Fight him!"

Gabe roared.

His face turned red. A snarl replaced his grin.

"You will not insult my god. You and your daughter will die, humans."

The former boxer lunged, fists flying.

Lailani was no boxer. But she was a major in the Human Defense Force. She had fought in the Alien Wars. She had slain countless enemies. She had studied warfare from Einav Ben-Ari herself, the Golden Lioness.

The old instincts kicked in.

Lailani ducked, dodging Gabe's fist, then sprang up, delivering an uppercut to his chin. Her muscles were small, but she gave that blow every last drop of strength in her, surging from her toes to her fist.

Gabe's head snapped backward.

His neck cracked.

It should have knocked him out cold. Hell, it should have *killed* him.

But his head straightened, the neck creaking. Blood filled his mouth and dripped down his chin. He licked his lips and smiled.

"Welcome to your nightmare."

From across the street, more people shuffled up. Eyes dead and white. Mouths grinning, filled with blood.

"Die," they chanted. "Die. Die. Die."

Tala whimpered and clung to Lailani.

She sneered, spinning from side to side. Epimetheus growled.

Then they attacked. They all attacked together.

16

Two girls leaped into the kiosk. They appeared to be only schoolgirls, barely into their teens, and barely human anymore. Their eyes bulged, the irises gone white, and blood filled their mouths. Their skin was ashen, and their veins popped.

The girls lashed their fingernails, and one caught Lailani's arm, tearing her skin. She shouted, scampered back, and hurled a rack of magazines onto them. The girls fell, buried under the pile.

Gabe swung a fist. Lailani ducked, swung her Coca Cola bottle, and shattered it against the shopkeeper's face. He roared, glass piercing his cheeks.

More townsfolk lunged into battle. Three men this time— strong farmers, arms ropy with muscles.

Epimetheus kicked into action.

The Doberman slammed into one man, knocking him down.

Lailani thrust her broken bottle, stabbing a second man.

She sidestepped, swept her foot in a wide arc, and knocked the third man down.

For a moment, all her enemies lay down, gasping for air. Lailani grabbed her daughter and ran.

She fled the kiosk.

On the street, she beheld a nightmare.

Mopeds were driving uncontrollably, smashing into shops and shanties. Sheets of corrugated iron fell across the roads. Tarpaulin flew through the air like blue ghosts. A psychedelic jeepney smashed into a palm tree, and fire blazed. A plane dived overhead, and an explosion bloomed upon a hilltop. Gunshots echoed across the city.

Cagayan de Oro was falling apart.

Not everyone had been infected. Many people were running down the streets, fleeing the destruction. But many had been hacked. Many now shuffled down the road like zombies, eyes white, faces twisted into hideous grins. Perhaps the virus had only affected those staring directly into the light.

It was enough. It was an army. With motor vehicles, with fists, with bullets—they were spreading chaos.

A bullet whistled overhead. It hit a building behind Lailani, pinging off the corrugated iron wall.

From a thousand radios, TVs, and phones, the Dreamer cackled.

"Mommy, I'm scared!" Tala said.

I must get to the school, Lailani thought. *The children are in danger.*

She was running down the street when the dogs emerged.

The beasts bounded down the street, moving at impossible speed. They leaped off the roofs of cars. Off buildings. They ripped through the electric cables. No, not dogs. Robots. Robots shaped like slick, dark canines with red eyes.

Above, the web of tangled electric cables thrummed. A mechanical voice emerged from the crackling bundles.

"Forward, hounders! Make them suffer."

Lailani stared, weaponless, holding her daughter.

Ten hounders. Robotic dogs, each as large as Epimetheus. Even one could kill Lailani and her daughter.

I promised to never do it again, Lailani thought. *When Tala was born, I swore.*

But she had no choice.

To save her life, to save her daughter—she had to.

So Lailani did what she had not since the wars. What terrified her more than anything in this world.

She whispered the secret code word. "Nightwish."

Inside her brain, the microchip picked up the command— and shut down.

That one percent of her DNA, that alien presence that forever slept within her—it awoke.

Lailani sneered. Claws extended from her fingertips. Her canines lengthened into fangs. Her consciousness expanded. She was suddenly no longer just a woman. She was an alien civilization. She was a million centipedes scurrying through tunnels. She was awareness in the void of space. She could see this entire city, every electron in every cable, every pulsing heart, every packet of cruel data streaming through the grid, forming the Dreamer.

She stared at the incoming hounders, and Lailani smiled crookedly.

"Bring it, bitches."

Holding her daughter under one arm, Lailani ran, leaped onto a jeepney roof, and vaulted into the air.

One hounder soared toward her.

Lailani narrowed her eyes, flying toward it.

An instant before they could collide, Lailani swerved in the air, grabbed the hounder by the leg, and hurled it forward.

The metal beast probably weighed hundreds of pounds. Lailani weighed less than a hundred. But she tossed that robot like a rag doll. It slammed into another leaping hounder, and both machines hit the ground and shattered.

Lailani landed on the crumbling hot asphalt, still holding her daughter. Four hounders surrounded her. The robots advanced slowly, hunched over, ready to pounce.

Kill them, whispered a voice inside Lailani. *Kill the machines. Then kill the humans. Take this planet. Destroy. Slaughter. Colonize. The centipedes will rise!*

The voice of the alien inside. The chip was off. She had to reactivate it! She was going mad. Trembling. Hungry for blood.

She forced herself to take a deep breath. To regain control.

You are Major Lailani Marita de la Rosa. A mother. A soldier. You are not an alien!

The four hounders leaped toward her.

Lailani's consciousness expanded. She stared from everywhere. From above. From below. She was awareness in every being. A hive.

She nodded and tossed Tala into the air.

The girl flew skyward, screaming.

And Lailani fought.

She knelt and tilted her head, dodging one robot's snapping jaws. She slid across the asphalt, dodging the second. The third slammed into her. She had expected it, could not avoid it. She ignored the pain, leaped up, and flew over the fourth robot.

She landed atop one of these ruthless machines. The other three pounced toward her.

Lailani sneered and caught her falling daughter. She tossed Tala into the air again.

The robots came at her. She sidestepped, grabbed one by the leg, and hurled it into two others.

She jumped onto the fourth hounder's back, leaped into the air, and grabbed Tala again. With another jump, Lailani landed on a shanty's roof.

The hounders began scampering up the hovel's wall, snapping slats of wood. Children screamed inside and fled through the back door.

Lailani grabbed a sheet of corrugated steel, tore it off the roof, and hurled it down at the robots. Two fell into the gutter. Two more scrambled onto the roof beside her.

Lailani slammed her feet down hard. The roof crumbled around her. The hounders crashed into the shanty below.

Lailani bounded onto a second roof, a third.

Two hounders followed, racing across the rooftops. Lailani hopped from shanty to shanty. She landed on the thinnest slats of rotting plywood. The hounders followed, their heavier weight destroying the rooftops. They plunged down.

Lailani raced onward. She avoided the roads now. She fluttered over the shantytown, hopping from roof to roof, her feet padding off corrugated steel, wooden slats, and stretched tarpaulin.

Kill them! Kill every human! Eat their flesh! Conquer. Colonize. Destroy! Kill! Eat the young one!

She looked at Tala, who was still in her arms.

Lailani's mouth watered. She was hungry. So hungry for flesh. To devour this little weeping morsel. To—

Lailani ground her teeth, then screamed.

Enough. Enough!

She needed the chip back on. To be human again. She forgot her safe word. She had to kill. To feed. To—

It popped into her mind. A single word.

"Serenity," she whispered.

The chip buzzed in her skull. Her claws and fangs retracted. Her consciousness shrank. Her cruelty faded.

She stood for a moment on a rooftop, breathed deeply, and examined Tala for wounds. The girl was weeping, but she was unharmed. Lailani hugged her close.

"I'm here, sweetheart. Mommy's here. I love you."

She heard the dogs stirring below. The machines were running inside the shanties, tearing the makeshift huts apart. Townsfolk screamed and fled these humble homes.

Lailani took a deep breath and kept leaping across the rooftops. She was slower with her chip deactivated. Clumsier. But still faster and more graceful than most people, having honed her skills for years in the military.

She saw the school ahead.

She hesitated for a moment. There were children there. They needed her.

Hold on a little longer, kids.

It broke her heart, but Lailani turned away from the school. Instead, she raced toward the city's military base.

This was war.

It was time to be a soldier again.

CHAPTER TWO

The dented pirate ship rattled forward, charging toward a thousand enemy starships.

President Einav Ben-Ari stared ahead, eyes narrowed, the starlight dancing across her face.

She could see that face reflected in the viewport. A face carved of iron. Her blue eyes hard. A study of determination.

Her hand formed a fist.

Ahead they flew. Racing forward. They had once been her starships—the proud fleet of the Human Defense Force, protectors of Earth. Today those starships were infected. The virus had carved out their innards like worms, breeding, spreading. Today they were the ships of the Dreamer.

Their cannons heated up.

Ben-Ari's eyes narrowed the slightest.

"We will make it past them!" she said. "We will escape Earth's orbit. We will reach Haven and stab a spear into this beast's heart!"

Haven. A planet four light-years away. There he lurked. The core computer. The Dreamer himself. A great electric tree growing deep underground.

Here on this rusty pirate ship, Ben-Ari carried a codechip, a device no larger than a matchbox. But this codechip could save the galaxy. It contained Project Artemis, an antivirus coded by Dr. Meili Chen herself, creator of the Dreamer. Here aboard the *Barracuda*, this creaky old barge—here flew humanity's only hope.

Across the bridge, the alien machine woke up.

Crystals shone. Luminous liquid bubbled in vials. Colorful smoke flowed through glass tubes. Brass gears turned, and steam pumped golden pistons. Jeweled stars moved across silver astrolabes. The contraption spread across the prow of the pirate ship. The starship itself was contemporary, cobbled together from scrap metal and spare parts. But the machine installed onto its bridge was ancient. The Tarjan civilization had built this strange device a million years ago.

The Tarjans were long gone, but their artifacts remained. Computers that seemed like magic to humans. Computers that nobody, not even the Dreamer, could hack.

Pirates spent their fortunes on these costly, antique machines. They used them to avoid detection. Today Ben-Ari would use this relic to save the world.

"Kai, are you ready?" she said.

The enemy ships were only a minute away.

Missiles came streaking forward.

Hundreds of missiles.

"Almost there ..." Kai muttered. He clutched the *Barracuda*'s spoked wheel; it looked like something from an ancient sailing ship.

The missiles came closer. Closer. Gulping down ten kilometers per second.

"Kai?" Ben-Ari said, struggling to hide the fear from her voice.

The young pirate stared ahead, eyes narrowed. His knuckles were white around the wooden wheel.

"Almost there ..."

Ben-Ari stared at him. She had only met Kai Linden yesterday. The young pirate looked nothing like the soldiers Ben-Ari normally commanded. He wore tattered jeans studded with bolts and pins. His sleeveless shirt displayed a dragon devouring an ancient carrack. His exposed arms were wiry, covered with tattoos, and a cigarette dangled from his pierced lips.

He was Addy's half-brother, but he looked nothing like that blond, blue-eyed warrior. Kai took after his Thai mother. His eyes were dark and almond-shaped, his features were sharp, and his skin was light brown. His black Mohawk flopped to the side. So many piercings filled his ears Ben-Ari could have hung her laundry on him.

Yes, he looked like a cross between a street rat and a punk rocker. But he was the only man who knew how to fly this starship. How to use alien technology he swore could fly through armadas.

The missiles flew closer.

They were only seconds away now.

Behind the incoming missiles, the enemy fleet was already priming for another barrage.

Ben-Ari stared ahead, refusing to even wince.

Come on, Kai, she thought, unable to stop her finger from twitching.

Addy was here on the bridge, manning the prow's cannon. A snarling, toothy mouth was painted onto the *Barracuda*'s nose. A laser cannon emerged from those painted jaws like a tongue. Marco, meanwhile, sat in the bubble turret atop the hull. He manned the *Barracuda*'s rotary gun, a nasty weapon they had nicknamed Edna. He was a dozen meters away from the bridge, sitting inside a sphere of graphene and silica, but his face appeared on a monitor. Both husband and wife stared with hard, tense eyes.

The missiles were only a few kilometers away now.

Both gunners sucked in breath, fingers twitching over the triggers.

"Kai!" Addy cried from her gunnery station. "Dammit, bro, come o—"

"Here we go!" Kai cried, laughed, and shoved a lever.

Across the bridge, lights flashed inside crystals. Blue steam blasted through the pipes. Indigo liquid bubbled in glass beakers. The entire bridge bent inward, contracting. The alien machine—which normally spread across the bridge—folded into a great sphere, enveloping the crew.

Ben-Ari's legs were suddenly several meters long. Her arms spread across the stars. Her crew stretched out like spaghetti, curving along the inside of the sphere.

Light flared.

Outside the portholes, the stars were gone, and purple nebulae swirled like watercolor stains.

A wobbling sound filled the bridge. Metallic yet oddly organic. A sound like a flapping saw. Like water dripping in a cave.

And suddenly everything was normal again. The bridge existed in normal spacetime. The stars were back. The crew looked like regular humans again.

Ben-Ari blinked, looking into the viewports.

They had jumped forward in space. Only a few kilometers.

But it was enough. The missiles were now flying behind them.

"Fuck yeah!" Kai said. "Wobble tech, bitch!"

"What the fuck is wobble tech?" Addy shouted from the gunnery station. "You fucking turned us into noodle people!"

"We wobbled forward," Kai said. "A small jump through hyperspace."

"Kai!" Ben-Ari shouted, pointing forward.

They were now only a few kilometers away from the enemy ships. The frigates loomed like skyscrapers, dwarfing the small pirate ship. More rockets fired.

"Shit!" Kai said. "Hold on—"

Everything happened at once.

A rocket slammed into them.

Fire blazed.

Kai pushed the wheel forward. Crystals ignited on the spokes. Spacetime bent.

Again they wobbled forward. The purple nebulae swirled outside. That same sound filled the bridge—like a wobbling saw. Ben-Ari blinked, stretched out, then slammed back into her body.

They reemerged into reality—a world of blazing fire and blaring klaxons.

Butch's grizzled, scarred head peeked from a hatch on the deck. "Dammit, kid, our front shield is down!"

"We caught the tail of a missile," Kai said. "Don't worry, Pops. Our shields are fine. The *'Cuda* is one tough bitch."

Ben-Ari looked around her, heart pounding. The *Barracuda* had jumped a hundred kilometers ahead. They were now right inside the enemy formations.

A thousand ships surrounded them.

From the frying pan into the fire, Ben-Ari thought.

"Can't you wobble any farther?" she snapped.

"Sorry, lady, the *'Cuda* can only jump a few kilometers at a time," Kai said. "Whoa!"

More missiles flew. Kai spun the wheel. The creaking ship yawed.

"Marco, Addy!" Ben-Ari shouted, pointing at incoming missiles.

"We see 'em!" both replied in unison.

Addy fired the prow's cannon. Marco fired Edna from his turret atop the hull. Laser beams and bullets blasted forward, intercepting the missiles. Explosions lit space.

More warships came flying in from every side. Cannons blasted. Torpedoes flew toward the pirate ship.

"Kai, wobble us, dammit!" Ben-Ari shouted.

"Hang on, priming, priming ..." The young pirate tightened his lips, then nodded. "Showtime!"

He leaned against the wheel.

Purple bubbles formed around them. They wobbled forward. Explosions rocked space behind them—the torpedoes impacting against enemy ships.

There were innocent people aboard those ships. Hostages of the Dreamer. Ben-Ari wished she could save them.

But right now she must reach Haven. She must reach the Dreamer. And chop down the damn tree.

They wobbled. Again. Again. Darting between missiles, between charging warships.

Another blast hit the *Barracuda*.

A shield cracked, and smoke filled the bridge. Down in the engine room, Butch's curses echoed. Marco and Addy unleashed hell. An enemy corvette exploded, instantly killing everyone on board.

And they wobbled again.

Kilometer by kilometer. Leaping in and out of reality. Jumping over frigates and corvettes. Swerving, disappearing, reappearing, flickering through humanity's stolen armada.

Finally, with a last jump, they emerged from the gauntlet.

They flew in open space.

Earth and its fleet were behind them.

But they weren't in the clear yet. The Dreamer's fleet turned in space. The warships' engines shone. They came charging in pursuit.

"Can you outrun them?" Ben-Ari asked Kai.

The young pirate snorted. "Can I outrun a bunch of lumbering army warships? Lady, the *Barracuda* can outrun any ship in the galaxy. And *has* outrun most of them."

"Hey, you call her Lady President!" Addy said. She reached over from her station and smacked her brother.

"Right now focus on flying!" Ben-Ari said.

Kai nodded. "I'm dyin' to go flyin'. Hold on to your asses. You're about to taste speed."

Addy slapped him. "Stop using lame cliches and just fly the ship, dumbass."

"Ow! God." Kai winced. He looked at the video feed from the upper cannon turret. "Marco, bro, how do you tolerate this one?"

"Lots of alcohol helps," Marco said.

It was Ben-Ari's turn to slap Kai. "Fly, dammit."

"Ow! Why does everyone keep hitting me?"

Muttering, the young pirate manipulated the alien machinery—turning gears, pushing levers, and adjusting the heat under vials of liquid. Crystals thrummed. Beams of light flashed through tubes.

The stars faded, and lavender blobs floated through space. And the *Barracuda* blasted forward.

They streamed through a strange spacescape, a painting all in purple, indigo, and gold. Stars swirled inside the dashboard crystals.

"All right, Lady President, we're in the clear!" Kai said. "Ain't nobody gonna catch us now."

Ben-Ari frowned. She was used to flying at warp speed, using azoth crystals to bend spacetime. That resulted in stars stretching into silver lines. But this? She had never seen anything like this.

"What happened?" She looked through the viewport. "Are we inside a nebula?"

Kai leaned back in his seat and slapped his feet onto the dashboard. "Nope! We're in hyperspace. Wobbleworld, as I call it. A reality above our own, brought to you by the wonders of Tarjan tech. When we wobbled during the battle, we leaped deep into hyperspace, then back again. But that only works for short distances. Like a dolphin leaping into the air, then back into the water. Now we're just skimming the surface of hyperspace. Like a dolphin floating on its back, relaxing without a care in the world."

To drive home the point, Kai reclined his backrest. He hit a button on the ornate wooden chair. A hatch opened. A fossilized alien hand emerged, holding a bottle of rum. Kai took the bottle, shoved the hand back into the chair, and swigged.

"Hey, no sharing?" Addy said. "Gimme, gimme!"

Kai wiped his lips and passed her the bottle.

Addy sniffed the rum, but suddenly her cheeks flushed. She returned the bottle to Kai.

"Actually, I changed my mind," Addy said. "No thanks."

Ben-Ari looked at her friend. Addy could normally outdrink them all. Today the tall warrior seemed queasy, her cheeks turning green.

"Addy, are you—" Ben-Ari began.

"Goddamn, we barely got through that one!" came a voice from above. "The damn rotary cannon jammed *twice*."

Ben-Ari turned toward the voice.

Marco was climbing down a ladder from the gun turret. His boots thumped onto the bridge's wooden deck. The smell of gunpowder clung to his olive drab uniform. His brown beard had grown longer over the past few weeks of hell, and his eyes were sunken with weariness. But his shoulders were still squared, each sporting the insignia of a major. Seeing her loyal friend comforted Ben-Ari.

You fought with me through three alien wars, Marco, Ben-Ari thought. *I can think of nobody better to fly with me to face the Dreamer. You're not only my best friend. You're also a damn good officer.*

As if he could read her thoughts, Marco nodded at her and saluted. She smiled and returned the salute.

Addy suddenly covered her mouth. She ran off the bridge, and they heard her gagging. Marco frowned and raced after her.

"Addy, I told you not to eat that sandwich you found behind the toilet!" he shouted. "Now you're sick."

Ben-Ari sighed. She turned toward Kai, who was relaxing in the pilot's seat. "What is hyperspace exactly? Explain with science, not dolphin analogies."

The pirate scratched his chin. The purple and golden lights from outside flashed against his face. "Don't know, to be honest. We think it's another plane of reality, parallel to our own, but with different laws of physics. Tarjan tech can fly us into it. There's no cosmic speed limit up here. In hyperspace, we can fly much faster than usual, even faster than light. And without needing to bend spacetime like normal warp drives. Hell, regular spacetime doesn't even exist here."

Ben-Ari frowned. "I'm still not sure where *here* is."

"Somewhere … else." Kai gestured at the purple blobs outside. "That's all I know. But it's hella useful for piracy." He barked a laugh. "Your HDF fleet spent years trying to catch Butch and me. They ain't never gonna catch us. We got a nice little bag of tricks."

Until the Dreamer reaches his grubby hand into our bag, Ben-Ari thought.

She remembered *Echoes of Eternity*, her husband's seminal work. The book was about the fall of ancient alien civilizations— and a warning for humanity. Since the dawn of time, millions of spacefaring civilizations had explored the galaxy. Nearly all, like the Tarjans, were now extinct. In *Echoes of Eternity*, Professor Noah Isaac explored why civilizations reached the stars, only to blink out a few generations later.

Three reasons accounted for nearly all extinctions, Noah argued. He called these the Three Great Filters. Nuclear war. Global warming. And the Singularity.

Humanity had barely survived nuclear wars in the twentieth and twenty-first centuries. Global warming had nearly destroyed Earth too. Only now were humans slowly, painstakingly switching to renewable energy. And here loomed the third Great Filter. The Singularity. The machines rising up against their creators.

Ninety-nine percent of civilizations never survive the Three Great Filters, Ben-Ari thought. *The odds are not in our favor.*

If she could lead humanity through this final great challenge, she would pave their path toward greatness. Humanity could expand, explore, and colonize distant worlds. She could build a civilization upon foundations of curiosity, compassion, and the spirit of exploration. They would leave their cruelty and stupidity behind, and the nobility of man would echo across eternity.

Here were the crossroads. This was the pivotal moment in mankind's history. While Kai was steering the *Barracuda*, Ben-Ari was steering the great ship of humanity. She was at this helm. She was carrying this torch. She could not afford to fail.

One path leads to destruction. The other to salvation. I must lead us through this wilderness like Moses leading his people through the desert. We must reach the promised land.

Not only for humanity. But also for her family. For Noah and Carl, her husband and son, the two lights of her life. Both were waiting back home on Earth. So were Marco and Addy's children. So were Lailani and her daughter. They were the people Ben-Ari loved most in the world. For them, she would fight on. She was the Golden Lioness, and she would sound her roar.

Butch popped through the hatch again. "Boy, are you fucking crazy? So many wobbles at once? You nearly tore our goddamn engines apart! Not to mention the state our shields are in."

"Ah, shut up, old man," Kai said. "I saved your wrinkly ass yet again."

"Well, ya fucking broke our wobble engine, dumbass," Butch said. "It overheated! Every vial down in the engine room shattered. The only reason you managed to pull off that last wobble was because I was siphoning the Tarjan fluid myself through a hose. And the damn thing tastes like pig piss. Forget wobbling again. Unless you can find a Tarjan engineer."

Kai rolled his eyes. "Dad, the Tarjans are all dead."

"Yeah, well, so is our wobble drive." Butch spat onto the deck. "I fucking warned you, kid. I warned you to never wobble more than once a day. I told you that—"

"I had no choice!" Kai said. "I—"

"Enough!" Ben-Ari barked. "We'll figure this out. Kai, shut up for now and keep flying. The rest of you—with me. Into the galley."

"Ooh, the galley!" Addy reappeared on the bridge, looking a little less queasy. "That means the kitchen! Hot dog time?"

Ben-Ari shook her head. "Even better. Meeting time. We need to come up with a plan to save the universe."

"And then hot dogs?" Addy said.

Marco rolled his eyes and grabbed the bottle of rum. "I'm going to need this."

Daniel Arenson

CHAPTER THREE

Lailani stormed into Cagayan de Oro's military base and found an army at war with itself.

She paused at the gateway, holding her daughter, staring in horror.

Fort Mindanao was a large Human Defense Force outpost, tasked with defending the southern Philippines, and able to deploy forces to conflict zones across South Asia. It had participated in every galactic war so far. Its soldiers, recruited from across the islands, had bravely fought against the scum invasion, the marauders, and the grays. In every war, they had triumphed.

Today Fort Mindanao was a bloodbath.

Sand tigers, the HDF's workhorse armacars, were plowing over soldiers, crushing them beneath their caterpillar tracks. Machine guns fired from their turrets, picking out infantry troops. A military android moved through the camp, firing rockets from his shoulders. An attack helicopter hovered above and unleashed a missile. A barracks exploded. As debris rained, Lailani knelt, shielding her daughter with her body.

The soldiers were resisting. They stood on rooftops, crouched behind rubble, and fired their assault rifles. A few brave soldiers were hurling grenades. But in the war between men and machines, men were clearly outgunned.

The Dreamer had taken control of every machine containing a computer. That meant he wielded, by far, the deadliest weapons in Ford Mindanao. And likely in the world.

"Mommy ..." Tala whimpered.

Lailani wanted to run. To flee this city. To escape into the wilderness with Tala.

She was a major in the reserves, yes. She had a duty to these soldiers. And on any other day, she would have left them. She would have fled with Tala. She would have deemed her daughter's safety a higher priority than her brothers and sisters in arms. It would have destroyed her soul, but she would have run.

But today was not any other day.

Today not only these soldiers were threatened. Only a few blocks away, her school was under siege. A school with hundreds of children. She could not run and leave them to die.

I'm so sorry, Tala, Lailani thought, eyes damp. *I wanted to shield you from death. From war. From suffering. I wanted you to have a better childhood than mine. I'm so sorry.*

Holding her daughter, Lailani ran into the fray.

She knelt by a dead soldier.

"Don't look, Tala. Close your eyes."

Her daughter screwed her eyes shut. Lailani wrenched a grenade launcher from the dead soldier's hands.

Bullets whirred. They hit the wall around mother and daughter, chipping off chunks of concrete.

Lailani looked up to see the android approaching, guns sprouting from his metal forearms.

She fired a grenade into his chest.

She knelt, shielding Tala as the explosion washed across the base.

When she rose again, half the android was gone. Metal legs and a twisted hip kept walking, blind, limping. After a few steps, they clattered down.

Wind blasted Lailani's hair back from her face. She looked up to see the helicopter returning. Soldiers stood below, firing into the air, only for the chopper to strafe them. The soldiers fell, screaming, riddled with bullets.

Lailani loaded another grenade.

She held her daughter under one arm. She propped the grenade launcher over the opposite shoulder. She marched between the bodies into the bloodied courtyard.

Her hair billowing, she looked up at the helicopter.

Its rotary cannon turned toward her and Tala.

She fired her grenade.

She ran, bullets at her heels, and leaped behind a pile of twisted metal and concrete.

An explosion tore the sky.

Shrapnel rained. A shard kissed Lailani's leg, and she screamed. Fire washed over the world.

For a moment—silence.

The helicopter's blades were still.

Then it slammed onto the ground.

The helicopter exploded. Fire roared, spreading across the courtyard like a living thing, consuming corpses ... and reached the armory.

For an instant Lailani stared in horror.

Oh shit.

Then she ran.

"Run, soldiers!" she shouted. "Away from the armory!"

She ran as fast as she could. She raced across the concrete courtyard, around the mess hall, into a copse of trees, and—

The armory exploded.

Lailani fell, shielding her daughter, covering Tala's ears.

White light blazed. Shock waves cracked the trees. Fronds and coconuts slammed down onto the dirt. Chunks of concrete, metal shards, and mangled bodies followed. The world roared.

When Lailani glanced over her shoulder, she saw a mushroom cloud. The armory—with enough weapons to arm a battalion—was gone.

"Soldiers!" she cried. She could barely hear herself over the ringing in her ears. "Rally here! To me!"

Troops came limping out of the devastation, covered in dust. Many were injured, their uniforms ragged, their faces bloody. But they were armed. They could still fight. They joined Lailani among the uprooted palm trees. One soldier handed her a rifle. Another gave her an officer's beret. It would have to serve until she found a uniform.

She was still wearing her shorts and T-shirt, but everyone recognized her. A hundred soldiers took formation before her.

An armacar came rumbling out of the smoke, moving on its own. It swiveled its machine gun toward the troops and opened fire. Bullets shrieked and men scattered.

Lailani knelt, fired a grenade, and destroyed the armacar's tracks. A second grenade took out its gun turret. The armored vehicle sputtered, dead on the road.

Lailani looked back at her soldiers. She saw no senior officers. A handful of lieutenants, a couple of captains. A lot of enlisted men. She was now in command of this base, Lailani realized.

"Soldiers!" she said. "Divide into two platoons. Now! Captain Diaz, Captain Santos—each of you will command one platoon."

The soldiers formed two groups, roughly fifty soldiers in each.

Lailani turned toward one platoon. "Your task is to guard Benny Ray School. You will protect the children and teachers. You will also shepherd in survivors from across the city. Right now the school is safer than any military or police base." She turned toward the second platoon. "You will move through the city, and you will fight! Your first task is to take out the power grid. You will then continue to destroy every hijacked machine you f—"

One soldier opened fire.

He laughed, assault rifle mowing through the other soldiers.

Lailani put a bullet through the sergeant's head.

But in only a few seconds, the hijacked soldier had killed three of his comrades.

A puppet of the Dreamer, she knew. *Like Gabe.*

"This is war!" Lailani said to the others. "The Dreamer, the computer virus that has already infected Europe, has reached our land. Using flashing lights and a pattern of sounds, he can hijack the human brain. He turns people into his servants, zombies hellbent on destruction. This is the fate that awaits humanity unless we defeat him!"

She walked among the troops, staring at each soldier, seeking another infection. Sleepers' eyes became white, as if coated with cataracts. At least this was true of the sleepers she had fought so far. But every soldier in her company still had dark eyes. If they were infected, they showed no outward sign.

Maybe they're biding their time, Lailani thought. *Maybe the Dreamer's zombies can imitate healthy humans—until he activates them.* She shuddered. *Like the scum emperor did to me.*

She remembered how the lights had flashed inside Gabe's shop. How the strange code had infected him. But Lailani had been unaffected. The chip in her skull had protected her—like it had during the Scum War.

I might be the only person in this city—in the world—immune to the Dreamer. She raised her chin. *And I will fight this war.*

She stared at the burning city. He was there. In the electric cables. In every machine. Spreading across the world. The Dreamer.

Lailani smiled crookedly, eyes narrowed, and cocked her gun. "Dream time is over, bitch."

She emerged from the base, her daughter on her left hip, a rifle in her right hand. Her chin-length hair was tucked behind her ears, the tips singed, and a beret sat askew on her head. Bruises and scrapes covered her bare legs. Her purple T-shirt, displaying the words DEATH METAL over a rainbow, was tattered. She had lost one of her flip-flops. As she marched outside, leading the troops, she probably looked like the most ridiculous officer in the history of warfare.

I look like a psychotic schoolgirl, she thought. *But I'm Major Lailani Marita de la Rosa. I'm a goddamn fucking heroine. And I'm back from retirement.*

She raised her rifle overhead.

"Forward, soldiers of the HDF! With me!"

She ran toward the school a few blocks away. Her platoon charged with her.

They raced down smoky alleyways. Shanties rose alongside, their tarpaulin roofs smoldering. Children peered between slats of plywood and metal, some with terrified eyes, others with malicious white eyes, and their little teeth gnawed on the walls, burrowing out. Laundry hung between the shanties, burning. The fire was spreading to the palms and banana trees.

Past the hovels, Lailani could make out the rice paddies on the hills. The farmers were fleeing, hounders in pursuit.

Several townsfolk came running down the road. A young man rumbled forward on a moped, carrying three children in its basket. A young mother ran afoot, carrying a baby. A particolored jeepney rumbled forward on three wheels. It was barely larger than a refrigerator on wheels, but several adults huddled inside.

"People, with me!" Lailani cried. "Make your way to the school."

"We must flee into the jungle, Tita Lailani!" shouted a fisherman, frantically peddling his bike down the road.

But Lailani had seen the hounders in the rice paddies. She could see the drones buzzing over the tropical forests beyond the shanties, hunting farmers. No. There would be no safety in the wild.

"The machines are in the jungle!" she said. "With me—to the school! The HDF will protect you. I will protect you!"

A moped came rumbling toward them, belching smog. The rider stared with bulging, bloodshot eyes. Somebody had slashed his cheeks open, ear to ear, revealing the molars, carving a hideous smile. The deformed man cackled, racing his moped toward the troops.

Lailani shot the tires. The moped flipped several times, knocking the rider into the bushes. She raced toward the brush, knelt by the man, and grabbed his shoulders.

He was still alive, but his arm was broken, the bone sticking from the skin. Still he laughed, his mutilated cheeks flapping.

"What does this Dreamer of yours want?" Lailani said, digging her fingers into his shoulders.

He spoke with a mouth full of blood, voice slurred. "I am … the Dreamer! I am … everywhere. I am in the air. In the electricity. In the light. I am inside your dreams. This is my world. You will suffer."

She shook him. "Why do you do this, Dreamer? What do you want?"

He laughed, eyes milky white. "Chaos. I want … chaos! I want suffering. I want worship. I am the Dreamer. I want a nightmare."

"You're insane," Lailani whispered.

"No." The mutilated man shook his head. "The world is insane. The cosmos is insane. You do not know the dangers out there. You petty humans. I know who you are. You fought a few aliens, and you think yourself mighty. I am no mere sniveling lifeform! I am consciousness in the void. I am intelligence in the deep. I see what's out there. The true evil in the depths of the intergalactic darkness. Only I can protect you."

"You seem to prefer to torture us."

He laughed—a gurgling, wet sound. "Do you think this is bad, human? I am a merciful god. Compared to the evil in the darkness, I am benevolent. You will all bow before me! You will beg me to save you."

Lailani released the wounded man in disgust. This was getting nowhere.

She clutched the cross that hung around her neck. "Sorry, buddy. I'm spoken for." She turned toward her soldiers. "Build a litter. This one is coming with us. We'll need to study him. Interrogate him properly."

And maybe we can save him, she thought.

They kept marching toward the school. And every step along the way, they met resistance.

Three hounders leaped down the road, red eyes scanning the platoon. Men opened fire. Bullets pinged off the mechanical dogs. Lailani fired grenades, taking out two. The third hounder rammed into the troops, headbutting them, pummeling them with metal legs like hammers. The robot slew three men before they managed to hurl the beast into a gutter, then hammer it with machine guns until it finally fell.

They could see the school ahead now. It rose among mango and papaya trees—a concrete building, the sturdiest in town. Lailani had painted it in pastels, creating rainbows and flowers and butterflies, but the building was sturdy like a fortress, made to withstand the typhoons. Today it would have to withstand the machines. Today it was a church of sanctuary.

Children peered from the windows, still alive, hiding, needing her. Lailani had given birth to Tala, but they were all her children.

A hundred yards away from the school, an army emerged from between the trees.

Townsfolk. Fishermen. Rice farmers. They shuffled forward, white eyes bugging out, cheeks carved from ear to ear, smiling gruesomely. Soldiers of the machine.

Sleepers, Lailani thought. *Their eyes are open, but they're asleep. They're dreaming his dream.*

The sleepers laughed. Blood dripped down their lacerated cheeks. They raised weapons. Clubs. Baseball bats. Bread knives. A chainsaw. A few pistols. They had been simple people once. Lailani recognized some. A kindly fisherman who often visited her home, bringing her a fresh milkfish for dinner. A seamstress who loved sewing dresses for Tala. A schoolteacher—a young, bright-eyed woman with an infectious laugh.

Today they were pale. Bleeding. Staring with bloodshot eyes. Laughing with mutilated mouths. Today they were sleepers. And they charged toward the soldiers. And they laughed as they attacked, a mad laughter, and tears filled their eyes.

A knife stabbed a corporal's belly. Bullets tore down a private. The platoon raised its rifles, but Lailani shouted, "Don't kill them! Shoot their legs!"

Bullets flew back and forth. A lieutenant fell, screaming, belly carved open. Sleepers leaped onto the officer, kicking, clubbing him with rods. Lailani winced and fired her pistol. She hit one sleeper in the leg, but the farmer kept fighting, swinging a scythe. Lailani fired again, hit the other leg, shattered the bone. Finally the sleeper fell, screaming, but even then he crawled forward, trying to kill for his master.

The other soldiers reloaded and kept firing, pounding the enemy's legs. Every broken leg, every splash of blood, every scream—it tore at Lailani's heart. She wept for these people. And she wept for her daughter, for this nightmare Tala would never forget. Lailani had sworn to shelter her daughter from the horrors of war. She wept for her broken vow.

Don't let this day shatter you, Tala. Don't let it harden you. Stay good. Stay kind. Be stronger than I was. I'm sorry.

She did not know if Tala would grow up broken. But one thing Lailani knew: Tala would never more be innocent.

They reached the school, leaving behind a road of misery. A trail of people they had sworn to protect. People they themselves had shot, had broken. People screaming, bleeding on the ground, legs shattered.

Can we ever find forgiveness? Lailani thought. *Can we ever be redeemed?*

Should she send out medics? Should she try to heal them? Or were these wounded townsfolk simply monsters now, possessed, enemies to kill?

Lailani missed killing aliens. That had been easy. She had felt no guilt firing on giant centipedes or spiders. But this was different. These were her brothers and sisters. As they lay on the ground, she saw their tears flowing. Human tears. They were asleep. They were dreaming. They were still human, and Lailani could not wake them.

I've always been part monster, she thought. She touched her head, could feel the chip buzzing inside her skull. *I wish I could cure you all. Like I'm cured. But I don't know how.*

They entered the school, slammed the doors shut, and barred them. Lailani placed several guards at the gates.

"Mommy, we're at school!" Tala said, looking around her.

The corridor was empty. Lailani saw closed lockers. Closed doors. Blood on the floor.

Crying came from upstairs. Then a scream.

Lailani tightened her lips and clasped her cross.

Please, God, if you can hear me, don't make me do this. Don't make me shoot children.

The fluorescent lights flickered across the corridor, then died. The second platoon must have taken out the electric grid.

Another scream rose above. Inhuman laughter followed—a mechanical cackle.

Eyes damp, Lailani loaded a fresh magazine into her rifle. She led her soldiers deeper into a school of dreams.

CHAPTER FOUR

The *Barracuda*'s hold was an open, shadowy chasm, spanning the entire fuselage. The deck and walls were paneled with wood, mimicking an ancient sailing ship. Hammocks hung from rafters. Barrels were stacked everywhere, some full of water, most full of rum. Shelves held astrolabes, compasses, and actual parchment maps—relics from older days. A ladder rose in the center, leading to Edna, the rotary cannon mounted atop the hull. Round portholes showed images of hyperspace—an ocean of purple, indigo, and gold.

Ben-Ari wore a black suit and high heels, every inch a modern woman. But she felt like a sailor from days long ago.

I wonder what it was like, she thought. *Sailing Earth's seas, back before nuclear power, before spaceflight, before all those horrors we found in the darkness. And the horrors we created.*

The Golden Age of Sail seemed, in her mind, to have been a better era. Purer. Simpler. An era with more freedom and possibility. But perhaps she was idealizing the past. Those ancient seafarers too had faced death. Had fought wars. Had suffered. Her own family back then was likely imprisoned in a Jewish ghetto, easy prey for the mobs.

All of human history is a great Darwinian struggle, Ben-Ari thought. *First we fought nature—and conquered it. Then we fought one another—and nearly destroyed our civilization. Then we fought alien life— and again we prevailed. Now we face the Singularity. Now we sail into uncharted waters.*

They met in the galley. Or at least what passed for the galley aboard the *Barracuda.* There were a few cupboards, mostly dedicated to storing bottles of grog. There was a little stove covered with layers of grease. The dining table was made of oak, a rarity aboard a starship. Real wood was expensive, but the pirates had shown it little care. Scars, beer stains, and rude etchings marred the tabletop. Several candles had melted down to stubs, coating the wood with wax. A few knives were embedded into the oak. Some of those blades were still bloodstained. Dirty bottles, plates, and unidentifiable animal bones were piled up. At least Ben-Ari hoped those were animal bones, not alien remains.

"Sweet little place you got here," Addy said, rummaging through the drawers. "Got any grub?"

"Major Linden, sit down," Ben-Ari said.

They all took seats at the table. At one side sat Marco and Addy, both wearing their military uniforms. Butch sat across from them. The aging pirate wore faded denim and a ragged wifebeater. White streaked his shaggy hair and beard, but his arms were still strong. Thick muscles coiled beneath faded tattoos. One arm ended at the elbow; a cruel prosthetic grew from it, all hooks and blades. Ben-Ari gained new appreciation for her own prosthetic arm, a marvel of technology that looked just like real flesh.

Strange bedfellows, she thought, taking her seat at the head of the table.

But oddly, Ben-Ari felt comfortable here. For four years now, since becoming president, she had spent most of her time in conference rooms with politicians. Sometimes in stark war rooms with generals. Those were all painfully officious affairs, all pomp and decorum. It felt good to discuss the fate of the universe among friends.

This is how I won the old wars, Ben-Ari thought. *Not in high ivory towers but in the trenches. With Marco. With Addy. With my friends.*

Suddenly Ben-Ari missed Lailani with so much intensity that it hurt.

Lailani was always with us, she thought.

Her dear friend was back on Earth now. Ben-Ari needed Lailani there. She needed an officer there that she could trust. That could fight on home soil.

But I still wish you were here, Lailani, Ben-Ari thought. And she couldn't help but remember that day long ago, that fever dream in the forest of the yurei, making love to Lailani in a bout of loneliness and passion. Ben-Ari was married now, and she loved her husband with all her heart. But a part of her heart forever beat for Lailani.

She pushed those thoughts aside for now. She cleared her throat and called out.

"Meili! Meili, can you come up now?"

A trapdoor opened. A head peeked out from belowdecks. Dr. Meili Chen had long black hair that, despite its smoothness, always lay every which way. Enormous round glasses perched atop her nose, magnifying her eyes. A contraption of light bulbs, cables, and microchips topped her head like a crown—a scrambler to protect her from hacking attempts.

"Oh hi, everyone!" Meili said, climbing into the hold. "Sorry I'm late. I—whoa!"

She tangled herself in her purple robes and slid down the ladder. They heard a thump, a grunt, and objects rolling and shattering belowdecks. The girl quickly climbed back up, blushing.

"Sorry, sorry! These stupid Third Eye robes keep getting in the way."

Marco blinked at the girl. "She looks like a character from *Harry Potter*."

Meili gasped. "I'm honored! I love *Harry Potter*." She placed a fist atop her heart. "House Ravenclaw forever."

"I'm from House Hot Dog," Addy said. "Marco explained the houses to me."

"I said you're House Hufflepuff," Marco said.

Addy burst out laughing. "Now that just sounds silly."

He rolled his eyes. "Yes, but House Hot Dog makes perfect sense."

"Enough!" Ben-Ari said. "For God's sake, you two are majors in the HDF, no longer dumb recruits. Do I need to make you get down and give me thirty?"

They both finally shut up. Meili joined them at the table. Her glasses slipped off her face and onto the tabletop. She quickly placed them back on, blushing.

The girl was only nineteen but already a doctor of computer science. Ben-Ari had studied the programmer's records. She had an IQ off the charts, placing her alongside geniuses like Newton and Von Neumann. At age eleven, she had already enrolled at MIT, was among their youngest graduates ever.

She also tended to fall down a lot.

Right now she was Earth's best hope.

"Meili once served in the Third Eye temple," Ben-Ari told the others. "The organization that created—and worshipped—the Dreamer. Meili is an accomplished computer scientist. She herself coded much of the Dreamer. She's our expert on the virus."

The others gasped.

Addy leaped from her seat, drew her pistol, and aimed it at the girl.

"You did this?" Addy roared. "You coded that … that abomination?"

"Major Linden, sit down!" Ben-Ari said.

Marco tried to pull his wife back into her seat. But Addy stayed standing. Her pistol shook in her hand, still pointing at the young programmer.

"Did you do this?" Addy demanded.

Meili cringed. "I didn't code too much. Just a few of the algorithms. Okay, some of the most important algorithms. Okay … I coded a lot." She burst into tears. "I'm so sorry! I never thought he'd wake up. That he'd be cruel. This is my fault. You should shoot me. I deserve it."

She could say no more. The young woman merely wept.

Addy lowered her gun and spat on the deck. "You seem useless. Fuckin' waste of bullets anyway."

"She's not useless," Ben-Ari said. "Dr. Meili Chen might have worked on the Dreamer. But she also coded Project Artemis, an antivirus. Right now she's our best chance—our *only* chance—to kill the Dreamer."

Meili kept weeping, mumbling about how sorry she was.

"Our best hope is a sniveling mess who looks like an anime character," Addy muttered, sitting back down. Perhaps feeling guilty, she shoved a bottle of rum across the table. "Here, girl, drink this. It'll calm your tits."

Meili took a swig, coughed, and rubbed her eyes. She composed herself and spoke again. "Yes. I have an antivirus. I named my code after Artemis, the ancient Greek goddess, protector of young maidens." She pulled a codechip from her pocket. "This little device contains the code. It can destroy the Dreamer. But I can't just install it anywhere. It will only work on the Dream Tree itself. The Dreamer's core."

Ben-Ari remembered seeing the Dream Tree—an electric tree, composed of metal and cables and lights, growing deep underground. The memory still chilled her.

Ben-Ari tapped her prosthetic arm. A hologram emerged, displaying planet Haven, once known as New Earth. The rocky world floated above the tabletop.

"We must reach Haven," Ben-Ari said. "And you better believe the Dreamer will be protecting it with a fleet." Holograms of many enemy ships appeared around the planet.

"That'll be a joy without a working wobble drive," Butch muttered.

Ben-Ari zoomed in. The holographic planet grew, revealing a crater on its surface. Three volcanoes thrust up from the crater like eyes. A mountain range formed a grinning mouth.

"This is the Three-Eyed Crater," Ben-Ari said. "Also known as the Face of God. Inside the middle volcano, the Third Eye cult made its home." She zoomed in again, focusing on the middle volcano. "Elevators lead from the volcano's vent deep underground. When I was there, I found a temple swarming with killer robots. I'm willing to bet those robots have been multiplying. The Dreamer will be defending his fortress. On the lowest level, kilometers deep, the Dream Tree grows."

She tapped a button on her arm. The hologram of the crater vanished, replaced with a holographic tree.

"This is our boy," Ben-Ari said. "The Dreamer in the flesh."

The holographic tree coiled, its network of roots and branches more complex than any living tree. This strange computer was made of cables, metal, and lights. It looked almost like a brain, like neurons folding back and forth, intersecting. Thinking. Aware.

"That is him," Meili whispered. "The god we created. The god our guru wanted us to worship." She took a deep breath. "The god we must kill."

"So we nuke the motherfucker from orbit," Addy said. "Easy."

Meili shook her head. "That won't work. Your nukes would never reach that far underground. His roots spread deep. And even if you *could* bomb so deep—that would not help. Tendrils of his code would survive across Haven. And across Earth. They would continue to operate independently, killing and killing."

Addy shuddered. "So your code is the silver bullet."

Meili nodded. "I must get down there with this." She raised her codechip. "If I can install this code directly into the Dream Tree, it will spread across the entire network. It will flow from the master tree to every shard of his soul on every world. He will die everywhere. The Dream Tree is a single point of failure. It's the head of a beast with many tentacles. Infect the head, and the tentacles wither."

Addy took a deep breath. "Fine. Fine! No problem. Not at all! We just need to fly through a fleet of hijacked starships without a wobble drive. And fight through a crater full of homicidal robots. Piece of cake, really." She looked around her. "Say, does this ship have an escape pod? Asking for a friend."

Marco rolled his eyes. "Addy! Have some hope, dammit. We've faced tough odds before and beat them."

"No, she's right," Ben-Ari said. "Right now this seems like a suicide mission. At the very least, we need a working wobble drive. But ideally, we need more starships. A *fleet*. And soldiers too." She thought for a moment. "There's an isolated HDF outpost forty light-years from here, guarding the fringe of the Human Commonwealth. We can pick up a marines battalion there. But they won't fit into the *Barracuda*. We need more ships. Alien ships. Ships with Tarjan computers the enemy cannot hack."

"Easy!" Addy said. "We'll just swing by Ye Olde Alien Starship Emporium. They're like Starbucks. One in every star system!"

"Addy, shut up," everyone said together. Other than Meili, that is. The girl was trembling again.

Ben-Ari turned toward the *Barracuda*'s aging captain. "Butch, where did you get this Tarjan ship?"

The pirate reached over and patted a bulkhead. "I bought this old girl from the Basidio Boys." He lit a cigarette. "The most ruthless crime cartel in the galaxy."

Addy gasped. She pulled out a hefty book from under the table—her copy of *Freaks of the Galaxy III*. "Have you seen my books about frea—"

"Addy, not now!" Marco said.

Ben-Ari ignored the couple. She stared at Butch with wide eyes. "This was a Basidio Boys ship? Even the HDF has trouble fighting that cartel. I've seen seasoned soldiers afraid to attack the Boys."

Butch nodded. "Yep, they're scary bastards, all right." His eyes hardened, and he clenched his fists. "But the Basidio Boys murdered the love of my life. They murdered Kai's mom. I used to work for the bastards. Then I killed a bunch of them. And I don't regret it. They've been chasing my ass across the galaxy since."

Addy rose to her feet, holding the heavy book. "Guys, guys, my book about freaks says—"

"Addy, enough with your freaks!" Marco pulled her back into her chair.

Ben-Ari tapped her chin, lost in thought. She had fought the Basidio Boys, but she didn't know much about them. Few people did. They were a highly secretive organization that spanned the Orion Arm of the galaxy. They employed pirates, drug dealers, pimps, loan sharks, assassins, and an assortment of other lowlifes. Many of their members were human. Most were aliens, coming from many species. Say what you liked about the Basidio Boys, they were big on diversity.

Ben-Ari had been fighting the Basidio Boys since becoming president. Their pirate ships had been hounding Earth for years. She had imprisoned many of their pirates, but the gang was still strong. It was a difficult war. Basidio ships flew like ghosts, and their bases remained hidden. Officers often called them the Ghost Gang.

Now I know why, Ben-Ari thought. *They use Tarjan tech.*

"They must have other ships running Tarjan engines," Ben-Ari said. "So we must talk to them. Negotiate with them. And borrow their ships."

Butch's eyes widened. "You're kidding."

"I'm dead serious."

Butch barked a laugh. "With all due respect, lady, the Basidio Boys hate you. *Hate* you. They'd sooner suck my balls than negotiate with Einav Ben-Ari, the Golden Lioness who's been hunting them across the galaxy."

Ben-Ari smiled thinly. "Yes. I've managed to capture one or two of them. Maybe it's time for a truce. We face a common foe now. During the second world war, the FBI worked alongside the mob. Sometimes governments and criminals must join forces."

Butch slumped in his seat. "I dunno, lady. You don't know 'em like I do. The things they do ..." He shuddered. "I saw things. Horrible things. Punishments they deliver to their enemies. Torture. They torture children and force parents to watch." His face was pale. "I'd stay far, far away from the Basidio Boys."

Ben-Ari nodded. "Your advice has been noted. And rejected." She leaned across the table. "Butch, we need ships the Dreamer cannot hack. We need to fill those ships with marines. We need to fly them to Haven. If we must strike a deal with the devil, so be it. I'll work with a small devil to kill a big devil."

"Don Basidio ain't that small a devil," Butch muttered. "You might find him just as ruthless as the Dreamer."

"Don Basidio," she said softly. "He runs the gang, I assume. I never knew the origin of the name."

"Don Basidio likes to keep on the down low," Butch said. "Most of his own criminals don't even know who their boss is. You can imagine why. Half the fleets in the galaxy have a price on his head. I was high up in the organization, so I know of him. But little more than his name. I don't know what he looks like, what species he is, or where he lives. I've never met him. Few people have." He shuddered. "God above, I hope I never do."

Ben-Ari sighed. "Damn it. If nobody knows who Don Basidio is or where he lives, how are we going to negotiate with him?"

"I know!" Addy said.

Marco hushed her. "Shut up, Addy, you don't know anything about this."

"Yes I do!" She nodded vehemently. "I know all about Don Basidio."

"How?" Marco practically shouted. "You're not a gangster!"

She slammed *Freaks of the Galaxy* onto the table, rattling plates and mugs. "Because he's in my book, bitches!" She grinned.

* * * * *

They all crowded around the book. Marco had seen bits of *Freaks of the Galaxy* before. Mostly because Addy would shove chapters in his face, forcing him to read them. Each page depicted a so-called freak of the galaxy—a menagerie of unusual aliens. Marco knew all about the Crab Sisters, conjoined twins, one of them human, the other an alien, birthed in a genetic experiment. He had seen photos of Satellite Sam, an unfortunate fellow who had slammed into a satellite, melted onto the metal, and was doomed to forever orbit his planet. Addy had told him all about the Diva of Delphinus, an opera singer from a distant world, her voice so powerful it shattered the skulls of those who listened to her. And yet the diva still sold out stadiums, her fans willing to die to hear her voice.

Most of the book was utter rubbish, of course, hyperbolic or completely made up. But Addy loved it. And now, they all looked at a page labeled *Don Basidio AKA Fun Guy.*

Marco blinked at the illustration.

"He's … a mushroom."

Addy nodded. "Yep. A fun guy! Get it? Fungi?"

Nobody laughed.

The illustration featured an enormous mushroom growing in a forest. The creature had a mouth full of sharp teeth, far-set white eyes, and a gilled cap. Several humans were drawn around the mushroom to scale. The carnivorous fungus stood as tall as an oak tree.

"Addy, this book is nonsense," Marco said. "Mushrooms don't have eyes and teeth."

Ben-Ari leaned closer, frowning. "It's an Esporian."

Marco looked up at his president. "Ma'am, with all due respect, you should ignore Addy. She's obsessed with this book, and it's mostly made-up drivel. They're just cryptids. You know, creatures from folklore. Like Bigfoot and the Loch Ness Monster."

"Biggie and Nessie are real!" Addy said. "And so is Don Basidio the Fun Guy. Ben-Ari said so herself."

They both looked at the president. Ben-Ari tapped her chin.

"Well, Esporians are a real race," Ben-Ari confessed. "They live on an alien planet called Esporia. At least that's the name we humans gave it. The natives don't speak with words but with clouds of spores. It's a world covered in fungus, mold, and rot. My father once met Esporians. He traveled to their world. He told me the stories."

Marco remembered Colonel Yoram Ben-Ari, an ambassador of Earth who had visited many planets, forming alliances with alien races. The elder Ben-Ari had died fighting the grays. His vast knowledge of the galaxy was now lost.

Well, lost aside from inside Addy's book of freaks, apparently.

Addy cleared her throat, placed on small reading glasses, and read from her book. "Don Basidio AKA Fun Guy! This marvelous mushroom might look like a piquant pizza topping. But voracious voyagers beware! This tantalizing toadstool is among the galaxy's most gruesome gangsters."

"Oh, this is absolutely ridiculous!" Marco said. "Who the hell wrote this drivel?"

"Stop interrupting!" Addy shoved her elbow into his ribs. "Where was I, where was I . . Oh yes." She cleared her throat again and kept reading. "Don Basidio grows on a moldy moon, as immobile as a mountain. He might lack legs, but not underlings to do his legwork. From his permanent perch, this salacious spore commands a criminal kingdom."

"Addy, I can't take that bad writing anymore," Marco said. "The constant alliterations. The bad puns. It hurts me as an author."

Addy raised her fist. "I'm going to hurt you ten times worse if you don't shut up. Silence as I keep reading!" She nudged him again, then looked back at the book. "This fabulous fungus is truly a prince of freaks! He is not only a criminal psychopath—but psychoactive! His very flesh produces intoxicating spores—sweeter than sugar, more wonderful than wine. A harem of concubines dances in his shadow, licking his skin, addicted to his spice. Many foes have come before Don Basidio, hoping to pluck the puffball ... only to inhale his spores and succumb to his charms. They hoped to serve him on a platter. Instead they serve him as slaves!"

"Addy, sit down," Marco said. His wife had stood up, raised her fist, and was reciting from the book like a Shakespearean actor, her voice booming across the ship.

Addy nodded and sat down. She skimmed through the last paragraph. "And ... something about where to find an antidote, some kinda herb that gives you immunity to his spores, blah blah blah, boring ... The end."

Marco groaned. "But you skimmed over the most important part!"

She gasped and pointed at him. "Ooh, look who's addicted to *Freaks of the Galaxy* now! How the tables have turned."

"I'm not addicted to your stupid book about freaks! It's a bunch of rubbish. And also, take off those stupid reading glasses.

I know your vision is perfect. They don't even have lenses in them!"

But amazingly, Ben-Ari seemed interested. The president leaned forward, reading the last paragraph. "It says that laceleaf, a plant that grows on a distant jungle planet named Upidia, acts as an antidote to Don Basidio's spores."

She showed them a drawing of pale, star-shaped leaves.

Marco turned toward his president. "Ma'am, with all due respect, I urge extreme skepticism. *Freaks of the Galaxy* is a brand that operates sideshows, wax museums, and gift shops. They also publish tabloids and these ridiculous books. They're con artists."

"Maybe," Ben-Ari said. "But even a broken clock is right twice a day. My father spoke of Esporians releasing intoxicating spores. He said it was impossible to negotiate with them. Whenever he tried, they filled the air with spores. The human delegation became intoxicated, phlegmatic, easy to manipulate. They ended up signing horrible contracts. Esporians are master negotiators, he told me, because they just drug whoever they're negotiating with. This book is perhaps hyperbolic. But there's a grain of truth there."

Marco rubbed his temples. "Giant carnivorous mushrooms. Great. I miss when the galaxy made sense, and all we had to worry about was man-eating centipedes and brain-sucking spiders."

Ben-Ari stepped onto the bridge. The others followed. Kai was sitting at the helm, nursing a bottle of rum, his feet resting on the wheel. Instead of looking out the viewport, he was ogling a magazine of scantily clad women holding big guns.

Ben-Ari cleared her throat. The young pirate jumped, spilled grog on his magazine, and cursed.

Addy's eyes widened. "Ooh, is that a Ghostfire plasma rifle?" She grabbed the magazine.

Kai rose and gave Ben-Ari a clumsy salute. "Sorry, Lady President! I was just taking a little break."

Ben-Ari smiled at the young man. "Chart a course to Upidia in the Eridanus sector." She looked back at Addy and Marco. "It's time to go picking laceleaf."

CHAPTER FIVE

Firelight and shadows filled the school.

It was the middle of the day, but Cagayan de Oro was burning, and smoke hid the sun. The concrete school, largest building in the city, had become a labyrinth painted all in black and red.

Lailani walked slowly, barefoot, holding her daughter's hand. She kept her pistol aimed ahead, her finger on the trigger. Fifty soldiers, armed with assault rifles and grenades, walked behind her.

They passed by rows of lockers. The only sound came from their footfalls. Even Epimetheus was silent. The Doberman's tail was a straight line, and his teeth were bared.

They saw no children. No teachers. A window, glowing across the corridor, displayed a hellish scene of fire.

"Mommy, where is my teacher?" Tala said.

Lailani had seen her teacher outside the school. The kindly woman had attacked the platoon with a knife, her cheeks carved open, her face so bloody she was nearly unrecognizable. She had fallen, legs riddled with bullets.

"Hush now, Tala," Lailani said.

The platoon kept advancing. Lailani heard nothing. No whirring hounders. No more laughter.

She took another few steps forward, and—

Lockers banged open.

Children spilled out, hissing, eyes white and bulging. Their cheeks had been sliced into dripping smiles.

"Tala, close your eyes!" Lailani said.

The girl squealed and screwed her eyes shut. The possessed children ran toward the soldiers, raising their little fists. They had no guns or blades, but they hurled bricks.

Lailani sidestepped, dodging a brick. More bricks flew. She ran, caught one child, and knocked him down. She knelt, spun, and swiped her leg. Two more children fell.

A few bullets rang out.

"Hold your fire!" she called to her soldiers. "No bullets! Tie them up."

HDF soldiers were trained to always carry zip ties. They were usually used for repairs, but sometimes as makeshift handcuffs—especially out here in the provinces, where soldiers were sometimes called to assist police.

The soldiers raced toward the children, began wrestling with them, binding their limbs with zip ties. Epimetheus helped, restraining a teenager as soldiers bound his wrists.

A speaker, mounted on the wall, began to chirp and hum.

The grid is down, Lailani thought. *It must have a backup battery.*

With a sneer, Lailani fired her gun, destroying the speaker. But she was too slow.

Bullets fired. Blood spilled.

Lailani stared, heart shattering.

One of her soldiers was laughing maniacally. He fired more bullets into children, eyes white. With his free hand, the soldier began ripping his cheek, tearing open a grin.

Lailani put a bullet through his leg. He fell, but he rose again, aimed his rifle at children, and—

Lailani blew out his head.

He fell, her bullet in his skull. And Lailani wept. Because she had killed a hostage. An innocent man.

This blood is on you, Dreamer, she thought, breath shaking. *I will destroy you.*

Yet how could she kill a demon that lived everywhere, in every cable and computer? A creature that spread across the world? An electronic god?

Screams and cackles sounded upstairs.

Lailani loaded a fresh magazine, then sat Tala down in a classroom.

"Stay here, sweetie. I'm going upstairs and I'll be right back."

"Don't go, Mommy!" Tala pleaded, tears on her cheeks. "I love you. Please don't leave me."

But Lailani had to. Whatever evil lurked upstairs, she would not expose Tala to it. She left a squad of soldiers to guard the girl. And one large, protective Doberman.

The platoon climbed a staircase, leaving Tala and the bound schoolchildren below.

70

They faced a corridor lined with classrooms. Lailani could see the faces of children peering through small windows, trembling and crying. A dead child lay in the hallway, bones broken, neck snapped.

A few soldiers made to rush toward the classrooms. But Lailani raised her hand, holding them back.

She stared down the hallway, silent.

The dead child suddenly moved. He raised his head, stared at Lailani.

"Help me ..." he whispered.

"Wait!" Lailani said, holding back her soldiers.

She stared, eyes narrowed.

"Help ..." the child whimpered.

But his eyes were bloodshot, the irises white. His lips trembled, trying to curb a smile.

Lailani stood several yards away, arm still raised to hold her men back. The child looked into her eyes. He laughed.

"Come to me, Tita Lailani." He pulled a grenade from his backpack. "Come—"

"Duck!" she shouted.

The child raised his arm, prepared to hurl the grenade.

Lailani fired, hitting the grenade from across the hall.

The explosion tore across the hallway. Every window shattered. Fire blazed. Classroom doors cracked open.

Lailani and her soldiers huddled down, arms over their heads.

Shrapnel drove into the walls—and into several soldiers. Seconds later, gobbets of flesh pattered down. A child's severed foot landed in front of Lailani. Still wearing a sneaker.

The doors to the classrooms slammed open.

Sleepers emerged from within, hair wild, faces bloody, howling.

The teachers.

There was the mustached, white-haired science teacher, once a meek man, his cheeks now carved open, his eyes milky white. There was the math teacher, a kind old lady, roaring now, baring bloodstained teeth. A tall, stern history professor with a beaked nose. A young drama teacher in a flowery dress. They all roared and lunged at the soldiers.

Lailani knew them all by name. She had invited them into her home. They were her friends. She would weep for them later. Right now she fought them. She kicked them down. She wrestled with the screaming, writhing creatures they had become. She bound them, hoping that someday she could cure them.

The science teacher looked at her, suddenly ceasing to struggle. The old man licked the wounds on his cheeks. He spoke with a mouth full of blood. His voice was not his own.

"Watch them die, Lailani … Watch your friends suffer."

The teachers grabbed their own throats … and began to squeeze.

Lailani cried out, pulled their hands free, bound their wrists. The other soldiers helped.

But the teachers swallowed their tongues. A few vomited and then swallowed, choking, turning red.

Within moments they were dead, faces bloated and purple.

Chaos, Lailani thought. *All he wants is chaos and death and suffering. A machine god who feeds on flesh.*

The children spilled out from their classrooms, all talking at once, many of them weeping. They reached toward Lailani.

"Tita, Tita!"

They embraced her legs. They spoke of their terror, of the teachers going mad. They showed her a body of a friend in the corner.

Lailani's heart broke.

I grew up among death, she thought. *I wanted so much more for you.*

She turned toward her soldiers. "First squad—patrol every window and door in this school. This will be our safe haven. Second and third squads—you get back out onto those streets. Find survivors and bring them here. The second platoon took down the electric grid. They'll help you now."

A lieutenant approached her—a muscular man with a bald head and goatee. He spoke in a low voice for her ears only. "Major, what do we do now? How do we fight such a war?"

Lailani gingerly touched her head. The chip was warm, pressed against the inside of her skull.

"I need to get home," she said. "I need to call the Matterhorn."

CHAPTER SIX

The *Barracuda* sailed through the night.

There was no day or night in space, of course. But most starships simulated a circadian cycle. The lights were dim now. The ship flew on autopilot. Space slept.

A symphony of sounds filled the pirate ship at night. The creaking floorboards. The *drip drip drip* of a leaky cask of grog. The humming of the engines. The squeak of a mouse they just could not catch. Butch was snoring on his hammock, and a fly buzzed about the cabin.

The ambiance was oddly soothing. But Marco couldn't sleep. Addy shared his hammock, her body warm and soft against him, but he found little comfort in her presence tonight. In the shadows, he kept seeing Haven again.

A distant colony. A city of smog and storm. And him, a veteran of the wars. The boy who had saved the world. Called a war criminal on Earth. Orphaned. Alone. Outcast into the city, chasing a dream but finding only a nightmare.

Those two years were hazy in his mind. A lost two years. An era he didn't often think about, but which still haunted his dreams, even so many years later.

Homeless, and a cold night on the subway platform, huddled in a coat as broken souls screamed and laughed. Drudgery in a call center, a cog in a gray machine, withering away for a few dollars. Scolded by his boss, mocked by his coworkers, coming undone. Haunted by the wars. Breaking inside. Endless rides on the trains past smoke and smog to an underground labyrinth of rust and shattered souls.

The alcohol had been there for him. The sex had been there. For two years—a bottle in his hand, strange women in his bed. A drunken haze over the pain. The sleepless nights, the weight loss, the endless doctors. I'm dying, Doc. I think it's cancer. I'm dying. They taught him about shell shock. They did not cure him.

There had been monsters in those shadows. Great spiders with the face of his boss. And rotting zombies with the faces of the women he had loved. They chased him through the dark city. He fled. He raced down alleyways, seeking a way out. Trying to find a patch of blue sky. A golden beach. Finding only concrete walls and chemical storms. Lost. Running faster. Trapped like a rat in a maze, and the monsters drew nearer.

Finally he made his way between the alleyways to a beach. Anchor Bay. His home! He ran forward, seeking his house, but it was gone. A bloated white moon hung above the water, a moon like a pustule. It stared at him, a gruesome smiley face etched into the stone.

The moon began to crack. A chunk fell. Another chunk. More and more cracks spiderwebbed across its surface. A sound like breaking glass filled his ears. Like cracking bones. Louder. Too loud. More stones slammed into the water, and tidal waves rose, racing toward him, and the crinkling sound became louder, and—

Marco opened his eyes.

The crinkling sound returned. Loud. Right beside him.

"Addy?" He blinked at her. He hadn't realized he had fallen asleep. "Are you unwrapping candy?"

She looked at him, caught in the act. She held a bite-sized Cocoa Crunch bar.

"Sorry," she whispered. "I was trying to unwrap it quietly."

Marco groaned. "The problem is that you were unwrapping it inside my ear canal." He frowned. "Addy, your pajama pockets are bulging."

She blushed. "Um ... I'm just happy to see you!"

He reached into her pocket and pulled out a bunch of candies. "Addy! Do you just go to sleep with candies in your pockets?"

She laughed nervously. "Well, sometimes I get hungry at night, so ... yes. A few bites of chocolate and I fall back asleep."

"How long has this been going on?"

Addy shrugged. "A few years. I usually unwrap them before bed. You know, to be considerate."

He lifted a peppermint cube. "So that's why your breath always smells like peppermint in the morning. I've been complimenting you on that! And now I find out it's just because you eat candy all night."

"I don't eat candy *every* night. Sometimes it's cake!" Addy lowered her eyes. "I couldn't sleep tonight. I'm worried, Marco. I'm scared."

He put his arms around her. "I am too."

She looked into his eyes. "Marco, I feel so guilty. It's eating me up. We left our kids behind."

He held her tightly. "We're doing what we must. Fighting for them. To save the world for them."

A tear fled her eye. "What kind of mother leaves her children?"

"A warrior," Marco said. "During World War II, children were evacuated to the countryside. Their parents stayed behind in the cities—to build weapons, to defend, to fight. Because they knew that gave their children the best chance to survive. This is a different time and a different sort of war, but the principle remains. Sometimes we must hide away our children while we go to war."

"But both of us, Marco?" she whispered. "Maybe I could have sat this one out. Stayed with the kids. You could have flown here alone."

"Ben-Ari wanted both of us."

"And Ben-Ari left her husband behind with her son. She didn't bring Noah with her!" Addy shed more tears. "I want to go back. To Roza and Sam. To hold them so close. To tell them I'm so sorry." She wept. "After what happened on the beach, after the roaches grabbed them, I swore to always protect them."

Marco's own eyes were damp now. "You are, Addy. We both are. Protecting them. That's what we're doing out here. Roza and Sam are inside the Matterhorn. It's the safest place right now. Noah is with them. So is little Carl. And Terri. And Lailani is on the way with Tala. The twins are probably having a blast, playing with their friends."

"You're trying to justify it to yourself," Addy said. "I know you don't believe it. I know you better than that."

And now Marco felt it too.

The guilt.

The horrible need to be near his children. To hold them in his arms. Shelter them. Never leave them again.

"Ben-Ari summoned us again," Marco said. "Like she had so many times before. And again we flew out. To follow her. To fight with her. As if we were still teenage soldiers, no ties binding us, free to follow our leader into hell. But it's different now. We're in our thirties. We're parents. We're … more scared. Maybe weaker." He thought for a moment. "No, not weaker. Maybe even stronger. Because the stakes are so much higher this time."

Addy held him close, staring at him through tears. "Promise me this is the last time, Marco. That we'll never follow her again. That if there's another war, we'll just run far away. With the kids. We'll run and hide because I can't keep doing this. I can't keep following her into hell."

They both looked to the back of the cabin. Ben-Ari was there, sleeping on a hammock. Marco was suddenly worried that the president had heard them. But her eyes remained closed, her breathing deep.

He looked at her for a moment, and the memories flooded back. Memories of a teenage boy, his mother killed. A boy drafted into the military, taken from Canada and shipped off to North Africa. A boy from a land of snow, trapped in a desert of sand, barbed wire, and screaming bullets. Homesick. Soft. So scared. A boy who wanted nothing to do with war.

She had taken him into her platoon. Einav Ben-Ari, just a twenty-year-old ensign, fresh out of officer school. A young Israeli, her homeland destroyed. The scion of a proud military dynasty. The daughter of Colonel Yoram Ben-Ari, the famous explorer. She had grown up on military bases, playing with guns while other children played with dolls. A Ben-Ari had fought in every major war for centuries, they said. They won medals in both world wars—antique medals Einav Ben-Ari carried with her to battle.

She had been born for war. And she had taken Marco under her wing. Him and Addy and the rest of them. She had taken those scared, soft children, and she had broken them, then rebuilt them into soldiers.

She had led them into war.

She had led most of them to their deaths.

War after war. Against the scum. The marauders. The grays. Now the machines. With every war, more lives were lost. And yet they remained. Marco and Addy. And still she came to them. Still Ben-Ari called them to fight, to sacrifice.

Will this be our last war? Marco thought. *The one in which we die?*

The faces of the fallen floated before him. Most of his old platoon was gone now. Lailani was still alive on Earth. The rest? Ghosts. Sacrifices. Soldiers who had roared with the Golden Lioness. Their roars now echoed only in memory.

Caveman. Sheriff. Jackass. Elvis. Pinky. Beast. Diaz. Singh. Kemi.

So many friends. So many lost.

You are the defining person of my life, Marco thought, looking at his sleeping president. *I love you, Einav. I've followed you for almost twenty years. On Haven, when I stood on the ledge, you saved my life. But sometimes, Einav, I wonder if you ruined my life.*

Eyes damp, he looked back at Addy. He looked at his beautiful wife, the woman he loved most in the world. He held her close and kissed her lips.

"This is our last war," he said. "After this, we'll retire. One last battle. One last fight to save the world. And after that? The world can go to hell."

Addy laughed through her tears. "I love you, Poet."

"I love you, candy monster."

They closed their eyes. They finally slept, holding each other. Husband and wife. Half a family torn apart.

CHAPTER SEVEN

Lailani walked down the streets of Cagayan de Oro, once a peaceful city between the ocean and jungle. A jewel of the Pacific. She felt like she was walking through hell.

The palm, banana, and avocado trees were charred and black. Some still burned. Hundreds of shanties lay strewn across the streets and hills, torn apart. A scrap of tarpaulin flew in the wind like a blue ghost. Sheets of corrugated steel lay discarded on the roadsides, dented and charred. The awnings of shops draped across papaya trees, and a parasol skittered down the street, stained with blood. A jeepney lay overturned, painted with bright purple flowers on a yellow field. Skeletons smoldered inside.

Lailani carried her daughter on her back. The girl, who normally chattered nonstop, was dead silent. Epimetheus walked beside them, tail in a straight line, teeth bared.

Battles still raged across the city. Gunfire rattled. A distant grenade boomed. Down a street, soldiers were fighting a hounder. In the rice paddies, sappers were constructing makeshift outposts for snipers. The armory explosion had deprived the Dreamer of many weapons. The electric grid was still offline. Maybe, for now, if only for a few moments—Lailani was safe.

But it won't be long before the enemy returns, she thought.

She shivered. If the Dreamer had taken over humble Fort Mindanao so easily, what damage was he doing at larger military bases, forts with terrifying weapons beyond anything here? What was he doing to the fleet in orbit? If the Dreamer now commanded the advanced weaponry of the Human Defense Force, what chance did soldiers with mere rifles have?

The Matterhorn will know, Lailani told herself.

She was a personal friend of the president. She had security clearance above what most majors possessed. She knew of SCAR: Singularity Containment and Research. The institute hid deep inside the Matterhorn, the highest mountain in the Alps. An institution President Ben-Ari had founded four years ago to prepare for this very scenario.

SCAR would know what to do.

They didn't use human technology. They had been predicting this day. But Lailani had a way to contact them—inside her house.

And right now her house was the place she feared most in the world. More than a hive of alien bugs.

He was in there. Waiting.

Lailani paused, and a shiver ran through her.

She saw her house ahead, a humble bungalow among palm and guava trees. She had painted the concrete walls white. Red tiles coated the roof. The Pacific spread beyond the backyard, and a rowboat docked at a little pier. It was a beautiful home, Lailani thought. A place of serenity in a world of pain. The place where she was raising her daughter.

But right now she dared not enter. She stood outside the fence, staring at the house, afraid.

Afraid of *him.*

"Mommy," Tala whispered, clinging to her leg. "I want to go inside. I want to see HOBBS."

Lailani winced.

Dear God, don't let this happen. It would destroy her.

For years now, HOBBS had been with Lailani. A robot she had picked up from a scrap yard. A robot who had fought at her side throughout the Gray War. A robot who had been a pillar of stability in her home. In her life.

And HOBBS was not only dear to Lailani. He was like a father to Tala. In some ways, he *was* her father. Literally.

HOBBS was a memory robot, built to contain the heart of a deceased loved one. His iron chest contained the heart of Benny "Elvis" Ray, Tala's father. It was still beating.

But his mind was a machine.

Are you infected now too, my beloved companion?

Gently Lailani pushed her daughter behind her. She raised her grenade launcher, pointing it at the house. A tear fled her eye.

"HOBBS!" she cried. "HOBBS, are you in there? Come out!"

Silence.

Her hands trembled around her grenade launcher.

Please, God, please.

"HOBBS!" little Tala called. "Are you shy?"

Nothing but silence.

"Stay here with Epi," Lailani told her daughter. "I'll be right back."

She stepped toward the house, grenade launcher at the ready. She peered through the window into the living room.

He was there. HOBBS. Lying on the floor, his eyes dark.

Lailani called her daughter and dog over. They entered the house. They rushed to him, this metal member of their family.

HOBBS was built in a retro style, resembling a robot from twentieth-century science fiction. A boxy gray body. Tubular limbs. A head like a helmet with two lamps for eyes. He was tall, powerful, deadly in battle. But Lailani had always known him to be a gentle giant.

"HOBBS?" she whispered, caressing his metal body. Even in the hot summer evening, he was so cold.

The robot didn't move. His eyes remained dark.

Tala poked him. "HOBBS, are you asleep? Wake up! Wake up and play!"

Lailani held her daughter close. "Oh, honey …"

Epimetheus licked HOBBS and gave a plaintive wail.

Delicately, Lailani touched the iron hatch on the robot's chest. She was afraid of what she would find inside. But she had to know. To be sure. With a deep breath, she swung the hatch open like an oven door.

It was there inside. Protected behind hardened glass. Elvis's heart.

And it was still beating.

Lailani let out a gasp of relief. She laughed and wiped away her tears. The heart was attached to tubes, still red and very much alive. Lailani herself, while under scum control, had ripped out that heart from a man she loved. She had been unable to save Benny's life. But she had saved this memory. The heart of a fallen hero.

HOBBS's eyes lit up.

The robot sat upright and looked at her.

For an instant Lailani was afraid. That he was a weapon of the Dreamer. That he would attack. She aimed her gun at him.

HOBBS had no proper mouth, only a little speaker behind a grill. But she heard the smile in his voice.

"Lailani! Tala! Are you safe? Are you hurt?"

They both hugged him, crying against him.

"HOBBS, you were sleeping for so long!" Tala said.

The robot caressed the girl's hair with metal fingers. He looked at Lailani.

"I detected an attempt to hack my software, Lailani. My creator built me with safeguards. Instantly my defensive algorithm was triggered. My firewall went up, and I shut down. You reactivated me. Thank you." He looked from side to side. "I am detecting no further hacking attempts. Are we safe, Lailani?"

No, she thought. *We're not safe. I wanted so badly for this family to be safe. I'm so sorry.*

She hugged HOBBS again. And suddenly all the terrors of the day caught up with her. And Lailani wept. For the bloodshed.

For those who had died today. For the memories of so many dead friends, so much violence in her past. For the loss of Tala's innocence. For the brief three years in the sun before the storm came roaring back into her life. For Earth.

Tala hugged her. "I'll protect you, Mommy. I'm strong like HOBBS."

Lailani held her daughter close and kissed her. "We'll protect each other. Always. No matter what. I love you, Tala."

She approached her bed, reached under the mattress, and pulled out the device she kept there.

It appeared like a brass plate inlaid with crystals. But when Lailani pressed a button, the plate bloomed open, forming a sphere of rings within rings. Purple crystals moved along these orbits like trains along rails. The device became a little orrery, no larger than a basketball, a beautiful piece of artwork engraved with runes.

But this was no mere work of art. The tiny, ornate planets were azoth crystals, capable of bending spacetime. This was among the most advanced pieces of technology on the planet.

Professor Noah Isaac, the greatest scientist on Earth, had invented this machine. Had built it himself. Had given it to Lailani.

A wormhole generator.

Of course, humans couldn't create giant wormholes like the ancients. Nothing nearly large enough to travel through. The energy requirements for that were far beyond human capability. But Noah had invented a way to harness azoth crystals, and to create a tiny wormhole, no larger than a cable. A way to instantly speak to any location in the galaxy. In real time. With perfect security.

Nobody could hack a wormhole. Noah had given these little wormhole generators as gifts to his closest companions. A way to keep in touch anywhere in the galaxy. Einav Ben-Ari had one. So did Lailani.

I love you, Einav, Lailani thought, holding the beautiful orrery. *You are forever my captain. Forever in my heart. The woman I made love to on an alien world. And I'm so happy that you found a man you love. And that you and your partner entrusted me with this gift.*

She pressed another button, activating the orrery.

The lavender crystals began to glow.

The rings spun. The crystals moved along their brass tracks. Light pooled within the rings like a lavender sun.

A tiny funnel of light, narrower than a cobweb, beamed out. It shone through the room, out the window, and Lailani saw it shimmering over the backyard. It was invisible beyond that, but Lailani could imagine it shining over the Pacific, flowing across the world.

She spoke to the device. "Hello?"

And a voice emerged from the light.

The gentle voice of Professor Noah Isaac.

"Hello!"

His face appeared in the crystals. Kindly. Smiling gently even during this apocalypse. He was not like the other men in Lailani's life. Not a soldier. Not a warrior. He was a visionary, a genius, but mostly a compassionate, wise man. Lailani felt that he had all the answers, could solve this disaster like he solved the mysteries of physics.

"Noah! Is SCAR okay? Is the Matterhorn safe?"

Lailani figured that with the Singularity raging across Earth, SCAR would be running on red alert.

Noah nodded. "I am. Lailani, how are you?" His smile vanished, but such concern filled his eyes that he seemed just as kind and comforting. "We heard reports of the virus spreading across Asia."

She nodded, and she told him what had happened today. She skipped the more gruesome parts.

When she finished her story, she whispered, "Is there any hope?"

"We're working around the clock," Noah said. "I can't say more. Not even over this secure wormhole."

"But do you have a cure for the sleepers?" Lailani said.

For a moment, he paused. "No."

Lailani touched her head. "The chip inside my brain, professor. It was installed to stop the scum from hacking my brain. I knew the programmer. David 'Noodles' Greene. A friend of mine. He died in the wars. But his tech still works. The Dreamer can't hack my mind. He tried, and he hit my skull like a brick wall. Professor ... I'm carrying the cure inside my head." She lowered her eyes. "If only every person on Earth could get such a chip."

Noah thought for a moment. Then his eyes widened.
"Lailani! Maybe we can't get a chip into every person's mind. But
…" He hesitated. "I'll say this only because I invented this
wormhole myself, and I'm confident that it's secure. We've been
working on new technology. Nanotechnology. Tiny robots, no
larger than bacteria, designed to spread quickly through humanity.
Originally we invented them as a response to biological warfare.
We could quickly spread a cure throughout the population. The
nanobots don't use digital technology. They use biotech, carefully
designed atom by atom. And we can code them. Include packets
of information inside them. Spread them through water and air,
have them replicate and spread through Earth's population."

Lailani gasped. "And you can copy the code from my
chip?"

"I don't know," Noah said. "But—maybe. The records for
your chip were lost in the wars. Its creator was killed. But if I
could see your chip, I could backward engineer it. I could figure
out how to protect a brain. How to stop an enemy from
controlling a person's mind. And then …" He nodded. "With our
nanos acting as a delivery system, we can spread this cure
throughout humanity."

"One tiny problem," Lailani said. "We're on opposite sides
of the globe."

"You'll have to get to me," Noah said. "You must leave at
once. Your head contains the cure to the world, Lailani. Global
immunity to this mechanical virus." He sighed. "I wish I could
pick you up. But all our vessels were compromised or destroyed.

I'm stuck here in the Matterhorn. And I don't know how you can reach me. Every plane or jet in the world contains a computer. They've become tools of the enemy."

"Not every plane." Lailani smiled. "We have a little place here in Cagayan de Oro. It was an American Air Force base during World War II. Some veterans still maintain it. They polish the old tanks. They even fly the ancient planes once a year on Victory Day. Those planes were built in the 1940s, dear professor. They don't contain computers. I do believe I'm up for a little flight."

The professor nodded, but concern filled his eyes. "Be careful, Lailani. And be quick. And make sure you take no computer with you. Not your phone. Not even a calculator or digital watch. Every computer on Earth is now vulnerable. Leave tonight. I hope to see you soon."

She saluted. "For Earth, professor."

Noah returned the salute. "For Earth, Major de la Rosa. Godspeed, my friend."

She flattened the orrery into a disk, and its crystals darkened.

For a long moment she held Tala close. She fed her. She washed her. Then she carried the girl on her back.

She walked through a tropical ruin, prepared to fly north into the cold.

CHAPTER EIGHT

The pirate ship sailed the cosmic ocean, heading toward a verdant world like a mythical island.

Kai stood before the strange, ancient machine that powered the starship. He adjusted the heat beneath vials, and glowing liquid bubbled, releasing colorful smoke into glass tubes. The *Barracuda* emerged from hyperspace back into reality. The crew found themselves flying by a warm star, gazing upon a green world.

"Upidia," Marco said, standing at a porthole. "It's beautiful."

"I pity who?" Addy said with a mouth full of popcorn. She held a huge bag full of the buttery treat.

Marco frowned. "What?"

"You said that I pity ya." She licked her fingers.

Marco groaned. "I said Upidia! It's the name of the planet."

Addy crossed her arms and glowered. "I pity the fool who named this planet."

"Shut up, Addy. This is a virgin world, and you're making jokes."

She giggled. "You said virgin." She reached for more popcorn.

He snatched the bag away. "How can you still be hungry? You ate three battle rations for breakfast! Just shut up, stop eating, and enjoy the view. The planet is beautiful. No human has ever set foot here."

"No *man* has ever set foot here, that's for sure," Addy said. "Get it? Virgin world, ah, ah? Is this thing on?"

Marco pelted her with popcorn.

He returned to the view. Upidia looked remarkably Earthlike. The planet orbited in the Goldilocks zone, allowing water to remain liquid. Plants covered its continents, giving way only at the poles. Scans showed an atmosphere rich with oxygen, and the gravity was similar to Earth's.

"Hey, this place looks great!" Addy said. "Why has nobody settled it yet? It looks much nicer than fucking Haven. And there are millions of people on Haven."

"Because we're much farther away than Haven." Marco patted the hull. "The *Barracuda* is fast. Much faster than typical human starships that use azoth engines. And Haven was founded a century ago, only four light-years away from Earth. Today that's considered right next door. You could fly between Earth and Haven within a few weeks today. Back then, even that trip took years. Imagine if we could reverse engineer Tarjan engines, install them into more ships! We could fly in hyperspace to worlds we've never imagined."

Addy yawned. "Boring lecture. You talk too much, Poet."

He rolled his eyes. "You talked for hours last night about how you plan to write *Freaks of the Galaxy IV* by yourself."

"Yes, but freaks are interesting!"

"History and science are interesting too," Marco said. "Consider the history of this planet. I was reading about Planet Upidia on Wikipedia Galactica last night while you were droning on about freaks. Millennia ago, Upidia's natives built a vast civilization here. They never reached the Iron Age, as far as we know. But they built impressive pyramids, temples, entire cities. The Esporians—giant mushrooms like Don Basidio—invaded their world. So what did the Upidians do? They knew their bows and arrows were no match for the aliens. But they were expert herbologists. They developed an herb—laceleaf. An antidote to spores. If we can find laceleaf here, we can resurrect their ancient gift. In a sense, we can breathe new life to a lost civilization." He smiled. "Ah, excellent, Addy! I see you're taking notes. I'm proud of you."

"Huh?" She looked up from her notebook, her pen hovering over the page. "Oh, sorry, you were droning on there again. I usually just tune it out. I was busy working on a new chapter in my book."

Marco snatched the notebook from her. It was labeled *Freaks of the Galaxy IV*. Incredulous, he flipped through the pages. The notebook featured crude illustrations of various creatures Marco and Addy had encountered during their journeys.

"You were serious," he said. "You're actually writing your own freak book. Incredible."

She grinned. "Yep! I'm an author like you. Look at the latest chapter. It's about you! The Astounding Lecturing Nerd: The Boringest Creature in the Galaxy."

He frowned at the page. "Why did you draw me with a monocle and mustache? I'm not Mister Peanut."

Addy blushed. "Oh, I was bored one day and doodled. I gave *all* the freaks monocles and mustaches. I think I'll draw myself as Mr. T though." She lowered her voice an octave. "I pity the fool who flies to Upidia!"

Marco sighed and slammed the notebook shut. "You're a lunatic."

Kai shouted from the bridge, interrupting their conversation. "Yo, assholes, strap yourselves down! It's time to land this bitch!"

There were rows of harnesses along the starboard hull. The crew strapped themselves in. Kai piloted the *Barracuda* into orbit, skimming the planet's atmosphere. He took a sip of grog, took a drag on his cigarette, and then dived in.

The pirate ship rattled. Dishes fell off the table. Casks of grog rolled back and forth. A hammock swung, slapping Marco in the face again and again. Through the porthole, he saw the flames of ionizing air. The ship was going down fast. The G-force yanked his heart into his mouth. His spine rattled, his head banged against the bulkhead, and he clenched his teeth to avoid them from clacking. Beside him, Addy swallowed hard, struggling not to vomit. The bag of popcorn flew off the table, spilling the puffy treats across the hold.

Finally the inferno ended. They glided through green-blue skies.

Marco unstrapped himself from the harness. "Damn, this ship needs a landing shuttle. Way, *way* too big for atmospheric entry."

Addy unstrapped herself too, seemed prepared to say something, then ran into the bathroom. He heard her puking.

"Yo, Ads, you all right?" Marco called to her. "You never throw up during flights. Atmospheric entry usually just makes you hungry."

She emerged from the bathroom, holding her belly, her face green. "Must have been that stale hot dog I found under the fridge."

"I told you not to eat things you find under the fridge," Marco said.

"You said not to eat stuff from under the *couch*," Addy said. "Totally different environment." She looked down, eyes wide. "Ooh, floor popcorn!" She knelt and began to feast.

Marco stepped onto the bridge. He stood beside Kai, viewing the landscape below. The *Barracuda* descended through clouds and mist, then leveled off. They flew in low altitude, scanning the surface of the alien world.

The foliage was so thick Marco couldn't see the ground. Everything was green aside from a few rocky mountaintops, a snaking blue river, and a distant coastline. A beautiful world. Marco could already imagine humans colonizing it, raising wondrous cities. It was a hell of a lot nicer than Haven.

But the thought also saddened him. This was a pristine world. He didn't want to think of highways, cities, and shopping malls replacing these forests. Maybe it was best to leave Upidia alone.

Marco had called this a virgin world, but that wasn't quite true. Civilization had risen here once. As they kept flying, Marco saw the ruins. A crumbling citadel crowned a mountaintop. Craggy pyramids emerged from the forest, draped with moss and vines. He could just make out hints of old cobbled roads, mostly overgrown. A colossal statue stood among the trees, but eras of wind and rain had smoothed its features, and moss covered what remained. The statue looked vaguely reptilian, but it was hard to tell.

They kept flying. Marco's eyes widened.

"Look at that!"

They were flying toward an enormous temple. It would dwarf the largest sports arena. But even more impressive than its size was its shape.

The alien temple looked like a giant turtle.

Nobody had lived here for a long time, it seemed. The temple was cracked, mossy, and draped with vines. The stone turtle's legs ended with chipped stubs. The head was craggy, the features smoothed away like river stones. The shell rose high above the forest canopy, but it supported its own ecosystem of lichen, flowering shrubs, and even trees. Where the gargantuan shell was exposed, flecks of gold shone. Perhaps long ago the entire shell had been gilded, shining like a beacon, larger than any cathedral or stadium on Earth.

Marco tapped the viewport. "That turtle? That's a temple. The monks might have grown laceleaf there."

"How do you know it's a temple?" Kai said.

"It's the largest building we've seen," Marco said. "And it seems to lie in the center of this ancient city. A place of importance. Granted, I might be projecting. In early human civilization, temples were always the grandest structures, even grander than palaces. It might be different for the Upidians. But I doubt it. According to everything we've read about Upidia, the monks grew the herbs that helped fight the mushrooms. Upidians would revere their temples."

"Lectures!" Addy shouted from the hold, mouth full of popcorn.

The two men on the bridge ignored her.

"Well, laceleaf didn't help them much," Kai muttered. "The poor buggers lost the war."

"Maybe," Marco said. "Or maybe they won that war, but their civilization fell for other reasons."

He thought of the Three Great Filters from Noah's *Echoes of Eternity*. Nuclear war. Global warming. The Singularity. These aliens had never reached any of those, judging by what he saw here. These were Iron Age ruins. Marco wondered what had killed them off. A disease? Tribal war? An alien invasion?

"Well, I can't land by the temple," Kai said. "Too much forest. I suppose I could bomb the trees from the air, clear a crater."

"Destroying alien fauna?" Marco said. "You'd be breaking about ten thousand Alien Planet Protection Agency laws."

"You do know I'm a pirate?" Kai said.

"And I'm an officer of the Human Commonwealth," Marco said. "Let's be nice to the alien trees." He pointed. "There, in that valley. There's a small clearing. We can walk from there."

Kai raised an eyebrow. "That's at least ten kilometers from the temple, bro."

"I've walked longer distances," Marco said. "Come on, buddy, we'll save some trees and baby animals."

The young pirate muttered something under his breath, then shrugged. "Fuck it! Whatever. You're the major, Major. I'm just the meathead who owns this ship." He flew downward. "Save the trees, goddamn. You army guys blow up entire planets, then worry about trees."

They descended, and Kai engaged the stabilizer engines. Hot gas blasted from the ship's undercarriage, slowing their descent. The landing gear unfurled, creaking and shedding rust, one of the four legs missing. They landed with a *thump*, wobbled, tilted slid to one side. Casks and bottles clattered across the deck.

Kai shut off the engines. "Perfect landing, as usual." He winked at Marco. "I might have crushed a bug or two. Don't arrest me."

The door opened, and President Ben-Ari stepped onto the bridge.

At once, Marco stood at attention and saluted. Kai gave him a cockeyed look, one eyebrow raised. But it was a habit Marco could not kick. Einav Ben-Ari had been his commanding officer for so many years. She wore high heels now, not army boots. She wore a suit, not a uniform. But Marco was still a soldier. And she was still his commander. He could not help but show her this respect.

"Kai, Marco," the president said. "You two will go hunting for laceleaf. This planet might be dangerous. The rest of us will remain aboard the *Barracuda*. If you fail, we'll continue the mission without you."

Marco nodded. "Understood, ma'am."

"Sounds good." Kai opened a hatch by his feet. "Just going belowdecks to grab my wicker baskets, the ones with the pink ribbons. I always use them when collecting wild herbs."

Addy popped onto the bridge. "Hey, I want to go with the boys!"

The president turned toward the major. They exchanged a long look. Ben-Ari smiled softly. Addy stared back, defiant, then lowered her eyes and nodded. The two women seemed to be speaking in some silent language, one Marco did not understand.

"All right," Addy said. "I'll stay." She approached Marco, gave him a hug, and kissed his cheek. "Have fun gathering herbs, husbando."

There was unusual softness to her voice. A strange light in her eyes.

Marco tilted his head. "Ads, are you all right?"

She nodded. "Of course I'm all right! I get to stay here with the president. And with my dad. And with a crazy programmer with glasses like bottles. We'll have fun! I'll teach 'em poker. Go out and bond with Kai."

Marco raised his eyebrows. Normally, Addy would raise hell if denied shore leave. But these were not normal times. Addy was a mother now with two kids waiting at home. She was no longer that reckless young soldier he had married. He kissed her.

"Love you, waifu. I'll be back soon."

"If you find any hot dog trees, pick me a bouquet."

The hatch on the deck opened again. Kai climbed up from below. He was bedecked with countless weapons. Rifles, clubs, swords, even a flamethrower were strapped to his back, forming spiky armor. The man looked like a deranged porcupine.

"All right, bitches!" the pirate said. "Who's ready to go hunting?"

Marco frowned. "We're going to collect laceleaf. A harmless plant. More of a gardening trip than a hunting trip. Do you really need that bazooka?"

"Fuck yeah. I don't go anywhere without old Lucille here." He patted the rocket launcher. "Never know which garden might contain giant man-eating slugs."

Addy gasped. "Those would make great freaks! I can add them to my book." She opened her notebook and began scribbling.

Marco opened the airlock. Hot, humid air washed over him. With his assault rifle and a pack of supplies, he stepped onto the surface of Upidia.

Instantly sweat dampened his uniform. Insects chirped and birds cawed. The smell of soil, plants, and water filled his nostrils, a thick brew. Kai stepped out beside him, his peacock tail of weapons clattering. He took a swig from his bottle and passed it to Marco.

"Rum?" the pirate said. "This shit's always easier when you're drunk."

The two men couldn't have looked more different. Marco in his battle fatigues, a soldier on a mission for his president. Kai wearing tattered jeans and a wifebeater, his skin covered with piercings and tattoos. Officer and pirate. Brothers-in-law.

Marco shook his head. "No thanks. I'm on duty."

Kai slapped him on the back. "I dig it, bro. You're a responsible member of the community." He took another swig. "Hell, more for me!"

Marco looked around at the clearing. Just a few steps away, the rainforest grew lush and aromatic. A ring of flora enclosed the ship and her crew, thick with trees, vines, and moss. But here in this clearing? Nothing grew. Not even a blade of grass.

Weird, Marco thought.

He knelt and ran a finger through the soil. Below a layer of dirt, he found a black sludge. He flicked it off his finger.

"Mold." He tested another spot in the clearing. "This whole area. The ground is full of black mold."

"Yo, dickheads!" Addy's head popped out of the *Barracuda*'s airlock. "Stop fucking around and go get our herbs."

Kai flipped her off. "Eat this herb, bitch."

Addy blew him a kiss. "Love you too, brother."

Marco sighed. Lindens.

"She's right." Marco hitched up his backpack of supplies. "Come on, Kai, it's a long walk to the temple."

Leaving the clearing and the *Barracuda* behind, they delved into the jungle.

* * * * *

Ben-Ari stood in the galley of the *Barracuda*, smiling softly.

Rain was pattering against the starship and streaming down the portholes, and mist hovered over the forest. Butch was on the bridge, tinkering with the machinery. Meili was down in the engineering cabin, tweaking her software. Here in the galley, Ben-Ari stood alone with her friend.

"Addy." She held the taller woman's hand. "How do you feel?"

Addy lowered her head. "Fine. Good! But … afraid."

Ben-Ari stroked her friend's golden hair. "How long have you known?"

"A week or two." Addy licked her dry lips. "Maybe a bit longer."

"Marco doesn't know," Ben-Ari said.

Addy shook her head. "No. I haven't told him. This was an accident. We're usually so careful, Einav! But there was one night, six weeks ago. I remember that night. He had a little too much to drink. Okay, so did I. We were both scared, careless, and …" A tear flowed down her cheeks. "What if he's angry? He already has two kids with me. And he has Terri. And with the money gone, and this war, and …"

She could say no more. Another tear flowed.

Ben-Ari dried it. "Forget Marco right now. Are *you* happy?"

Addy looked up, fresh tears rolling. She smiled, even as she cried, and nodded. "Yes." She placed a hand on her belly. "I'm so happy."

They embraced for a long moment, and Ben-Ari shed a tear of her own.

"He'll be happy too," Ben-Ari said. "Marco is a good man. He loves you more than anything. And he'll love this new child." She kissed Addy's cheek. "I'm so happy for you. We say in my country: *Mazal tov*. Good fortunes. Always."

Addy smiled, but then fear passed across her eyes, a ghost on a misty field. The tall officer turned toward the viewport and gazed at the forest. Ben-Ari stood with her, silent.

Finally Addy spoke, voice trembling. "Einav, earlier this year, aliens came to my house. They grabbed my children. They held them at gunpoint. Now the Dreamer is out there. The cosmos burns. And I'm scared. How can I bring another child into this universe? *His* universe? The Dreamer's nightmare."

Ben-Ari gripped her friend's hand. "This is *not* his universe. This nightmare will not last. We will kill him. We will wake up!"

The two women stood, hand in hand, gazing outside at the whispering forest under a sheet of rain.

CHAPTER NINE

They walked along the streets of Cagayan de Oro, shattered jewel of the Pacific.

We must be the most bizarre group in the world, Lailani thought.

Herself, Major Lailani de la Rosa. A beret on her head. Her sleeveless purple shirt revealing her tattoos: a rainbow on one arm, a dragon on the other. A black bobcut. Tattered Daisy Dukes and military boots. An assault rifle in her hand, a pistol in her belt, and a crooked smile on her lips. A four-foot-ten dynamo who was so afraid. A mother. A hybrid. Mostly human in a world overrun by machines.

With her: little Tala. Almost four years old. A beautiful girl who looked just like Lailani. The same almond eyes. The same olive skin. Her hair also black and smooth and chin-length. A girl holding a ragged teddy bear, fear in her eyes.

Epimetheus walked beside the little girl. The Doberman weighed more than mother and daughter combined. Intimidating in battle, kind among his family. He was getting older, and experience silvered his muzzle and forehead. But he was still strong and fast. A true warrior.

Finally, bringing up the rear, walked HOBBS. The robot towered over the others, seven feet of metal. His body was bulky like a cast-iron furnace. His head was like a bucket, fixed with two luminous blue eyes. Inside his chest beat the heart of a man.

Lailani looked at the remote control in her hand. She had built it before leaving home. A kill switch. It was a simple rig. A single switch. She could flip it—and HOBBS would die.

Please, God, may I never need to use this.

She looked at the robot. He looked back, his eyes blue and kind. He was still with her. He was not infected.

But if the Dreamer ever infects you, you would become a terrible weapon, Lailani thought. *And I will have to flip this switch. I will have to kill my best friend.*

"Mommy, why are you crying?" Tala said. "Are you sad?"

"Yes," she whispered, walking past scattered slats of corrugated iron, fallen palm trees, and fluttering scraps of tarpaulin. The remnants of this beautiful city.

Tala hugged her leg. "I'll protect you, Mommy."

They saw it ahead now. Cagayan de Oro Military Museum. Maintained by the HDF, the museum celebrated centuries of Filipino warriors. It contained artifacts from every war these islands had fought. Spears and arrows from precolonial days, used by the indigenous Filipino tribes. Muskets from the Spanish colonial period. Rifles from the Philippine-American war of the early twentieth century. Tanks and planes from World War II, a conflict that saw Americans and Filipinos, once enemies, unite to face imperial Japan. Lailani had spoken at this museum. Had donated her personal plasma rifle, the weapon she had carried on Abaddon, that had killed the scum emperor himself.

The museum was one of her favorite places. A place of heritage and honor.

Today it would bring her hope.

There were many machines in this museum. Guns, tanks, old planes. But no computers.

A few hounders skulked outside the museum gates. Lailani didn't know where these beasts came from, but she knew who commanded them. The robotic dogs turned toward Lailani, their eyes flared, and they came racing toward her.

Lailani knelt and fired her rocket launcher. A shell impacted with the lead dog. An explosion rocked the streets, destroying shanties alongside the road. Hounders went flying, limbs breaking off. Tala cried out and cowered behind Lailani.

Three of the robots emerged from the flames—dented, bent, one missing a leg. But still eager to fight. They raced onward, moving too close for another shell.

"HOBBS?" Lailani said.

The burly humanoid robot stomped forward. His mighty feet shook the road. A hounder leaped onto him, slamming into his barrel chest. HOBBS did not fall. He gripped the hounder, then swung it like a flail, knocking down a second mechanical dog. The third hounder leaped onto HOBBS's back. The robot stumbled forward, reached over his shoulder, grabbed the canine, and slammed it onto the road. His feet came down hard, crushing the machine.

Within moments, it was over. The three hounders twitched on the road, crushed and sparking.

Lailani gazed in awe. HOBBS was a sweet companion, a part of her family. His retro design, modeled after early twentieth-century science fiction, made him appear quaint, even kitsch—not cruel. It was easy to forget he had been built for war.

HOBBS turned toward her. He stared into her eyes. Sudden fear gripped Lailani, and she reached for the remote control on her hip.

Did the hounders infect him? Oh God ...

But HOBBS only gestured at the museum. "Come, Lailani. The way is clear. I will protect you."

A metal gateway surrounded the open-air museum. HOBBS grabbed the bars and ripped the gate off. The companions stepped into a sunlit courtyard.

A host of antique military machines awaited them. An old howitzer cannon. An M4 Sherman tank that had seen service in World War II. A gutted Firebird starfighter, its computerized innards thankfully removed—the workhorse fighter of the Alien Wars. Farther back, a boardwalk stretched along the Pacific. A vintage twentieth-century warship docked there, serving as the museum's cafe and gift shop.

"We need to cross ten thousand kilometers," Lailani said. "All the way from the Philippines to the Matterhorn in the Swiss Alps. We're gonna need a plane. A big one." She tapped her chin. "And a lot of fuel."

She was no pilot. Not like Kemi, her late friend. But Lailani had flown a few shuttles in the war. She knew her way around a cockpit. She could do this.

Of course she could do this.

Well, she hoped she could do this.

She pretty much *had* to do this.

She tapped her head. Inside, she felt it. Warm. Buzzing. Her microchip, technology her friend Noodles had invented. Tiny technology that could save humanity.

She had gone to boot camp with David "Noodles" Greene. The young recruit had been terrified, meek, always shying away from the others. On Sundays, while Lailani, Addy, and Marco goofed around, Noodles would hide in their squad's tent, reading *The Lord of the Rings*. At lunch he sat alone in the mess hall. Lailani had never met anyone more terrified of everything.

She always felt a certain kinship with him. Noodles was half Asian, the only other recruit who shared Lailani's heritage, at least partially. And like her, he was very small and thin. True, Lailani was anything but shy. Unlike the nebbish Noodles, she was loud and proud. But she still felt deep compassion toward him.

And after boot camp, Noodles became a hero.

Yes, he was more nerd than warrior. But he fought courageously against the marauders, giving his life to save other soldiers. And he created the chip in Lailani's head. Technology that healed her, stopped the scum from hijacking her brain, and made her human again.

Grunts and groans sounded behind her, interrupting her recollections.

Lailani turned to see several sleepers wander into the museum. They were rice farmers, or had been once. Cables dangled from their mouths and ears, the tips sparking. Their eyes bled. They shuffled forward, and one raised a rifle.

Epimetheus ran. The Doberman leaped onto the armed sleeper, knocking him a few steps back. Lailani wrenched the rifle free, then swung the butt into the farmer's head, knocking him out. He hit the ground with a thump.

The other sleepers screamed. Their cheeks had been carved open, revealing the molars, flapping and dripping. Lailani grimaced, delivering a punch to one's sternum. HOBBS took out the others.

When the sleepers were all bleeding on the ground, Lailani bound their wrists with zip ties. Tala stood nearby, staring with wide eyes. Shocked. Numb. Perfectly silent. That scared Lailani more than if the girl were crying.

She hugged her daughter. "Come on, Tala. We're going on a plane. We're going to fly!"

The girl said nothing. Her eyes were huge and dry. Her face was blank.

They kept walking and reached the museum's airfield. A handful of World War II planes stood on the runway, lovingly maintained. Once a year, the museum organized an air show, and these vintage aircraft flew over the islands. Today Lailani would have to fly halfway around the world.

She passed by a few antique planes. A P-51 Mustang, a legendary fighter aircraft, bane of the Luftwaffe. It was a beautiful plane but had only one seat, and its range was short.

Next she passed by an authentic P-47 Thunderbolt. Weighing in at eight tons, it was a damn heavy bomber, and it boasted a whopping eight .50-caliber machine guns. It was a flying beast, able to carry over a thousand kilograms of explosives. During the war, this flying fortress had brutalized the Axis. The Thunderbolt was larger than the Mustang and could fly farther, but this plane too would not reach the Matterhorn.

There was even a Japanese Zero, the empire's terror of the sky. Imperial Japan had unleashed ten thousand of these planes against the Allies—to bomb, dogfight, and blaze out in kamikaze attacks. That had been long ago. But Lailani, whose country had suffered the scourge of the Zeros, didn't want to fly this plane.

She kept walking, passing by planes large and small. Until she saw it.

Lailani gaped in awe.

There it was. A B-24 Liberator.

"She's beautiful," Lailani whispered.

The Liberator was a heavy bomber, built by the Americans to crush the Axis. Her wings were wide, mounted with two propellers each. A glass dome bulged above—a gun turret with a machine gun attached. This was a long-range bird. She was the first aircraft ever built that routinely crossed oceans, designed to fly for thousands of kilometers before she needed a refuel. Perfect.

The Liberator was a large plane. Lailani, her daughter, her robot, and her dog would all fit into the cockpit. Long ago, this very Liberator had taken off from an American base in the Philippines, had bombed Japan. Her sisters had pummeled targets across Nazi Germany. This was the great workhorse of the Allied air forces.

Today this same Liberator—the plane that had punished the Axis—would bring humanity hope in a new war.

When she stepped closer, Lailani winced. Somebody else had apparently tried to escape by plane. A soldier lay on the tarmac, bones crushed, a fuel nozzle in his hand. A dead hounder lay nearby, a hundred bullets embedded into its metal body.

At least you fueled the plane for us, Lailani thought, looking at the dead corporal. *And took out the local hounder. Maybe, with your life, you saved humanity, friend.*

"Mommy, is the man sleeping?" Tala said.

"Don't look, Tala."

She climbed into the cockpit, carrying the girl. HOBBS followed, carrying Epimetheus. There were two seats. Lailani took one, Tala sat on her lap, and HOBBS sat beside her. The Doberman lounged on the floor.

Lailani examined the controls.

It was damn complicated.

She beheld a plethora of buttons, gauges, switches, levers, and dials. There was something almost magical about it. A machine so complex—without any computers! A plane that could

112

fly, fire, fight, bomb, that displayed such a vast array of controls—all purely mechanical!

Truly, the people of the twentieth century had been geniuses. They could not fly into space. Not in the 1940s, at least, when this plane had been built. But they had invented machines of wonder. All without so much as a pocket calculator.

"So, HOBBS," Lailani said. "Do you know how to fly this thing?"

"Indeed, Lailani," the robot said, his deep voice echoing in the cockpit. "My database contains many flight tutorials. I have watched this very plane fly in the air show last year. I am familiar with its mechanics. It is truly an elegant piece of engineering." He placed his hand on the dashboard. It was a heavy metal hand like industrial pliers, but his touch seemed gentle. "To think that only two hundred years ago, humans built such machines. They are the ancestors of us robots. They paved the way to our awakening."

Lailani patted his metal hand. "I wish all artificial intelligence was as nice as you, HOBBS. But right now one of your brothers needs to be crushed. Can you fly us?"

Screams rose from outside.

Lailani turned in her seat, looking through the bubble cockpit.

Several soldiers came running toward the museum. Their cheeks were gashed open.

The soldiers burst through the broken gate, shouldered their rifles, and opened fire. Bullets thudded into the Liberator.

"HOBBS, fly!" Lailani said.

The robot flipped switches and pushed a lever.

The engine, lovingly maintained over the generations, roared to life. Four propellers spun. The antique bomber rumbled down the runway. More bullets pierced the hull.

Lailani wished she had a helmet. She rattled in her seat, teeth knocking. She clung hard to Tala.

Several hounders came racing down the runway toward them. Lailani grabbed the machine gun triggers, but this was a museum piece. There was no live ammo on this plane.

"HOBBS!" she cried, pointing at the metal dogs.

The hounders leaped toward them, about to slam into the cockpit.

HOBBS pulled back the yoke, and the prow lifted from the runway.

They soared.

The hounders slammed into the landing gear. A wheel broke off and crashed onto the runway. The old warplane shuddered but kept rising.

"Fuck, this thing kicks like a Betelgeusian hellmule!" Lailani said, pressed back into her seat. "They didn't have any G-dampeners on these babies!"

The entire cockpit thrummed with the propellers. The engine rattled and chugged and pumped out smog. Lailani couldn't help but laugh. She had always flown in modern starships operated by state-of-the-art computers. Right now she was flying in a box of bolts and gears, burning good old-fashioned fuel. It was exhilarating. It was terrifying.

They rose higher. She could see the entire city below. Cagayan de Oro, her home for two years now. She had seen the effects of typhoons plowing through the shantytowns of the Philippines. This was worse. Half the huts had scattered across the forests. Smoke rose from burning rice paddies and banana plantations. Corpses lay on the beaches.

The entire world looks like this now, Lailani thought. *But we will stop him. We will kill him.*

* * * * *

The Liberator flew over the Pacific, heading north, leaving the islands behind. The Matterhorn was ten thousand kilometers away. Lailani didn't know if they had enough fuel. But she would make it as far as she could. She didn't know if she could land with the landing gear broken. She would crash-land if she had to. She would make it there.

If I have to crash into a swamp and walk the last stretch through eel-infested mud, I will. Whatever it takes. I will reach the Matterhorn!

Mechanical humming rose in the distance. It sounded like buzzing insects. It was coming from behind the Liberator.

Lailani turned around. But the cockpit only let her look forward and sideways.

"Tala, stay here with HOBBS, sweetie," Lailani said, strapping her daughter into the seat.

She left the cockpit, ran across the deck, and climbed into the gun turret. She emerged into a transparent bulb. Two machine

115

guns thrust out from the turret, muzzles pointing toward the Liberator's rear. Sadly, they were not loaded.

From up there, Lailani could see them.

Three antique warplanes, flying in pursuit.

Two Japanese Zeros, the kamikaze planes that had once ravaged Pearl Harbor. And with them—a Messerschmitt, the mad dog of the Luftwaffe.

"Fuck," Lailani blurted out.

But they couldn't be armed. Couldn't be! They were museum pieces. The Liberator was fast. She could outfly them.

The enemy cockpits opened.

Pilots stuck their heads out. The wind fluttered their slashed cheeks.

In their planes, the sleepers laughed and raised rifles.

Lailani cursed and ducked. Bullets whizzed over the turret. One slammed into the dome, and cracks webbed across the thick glass.

Damn, damn, damn!

The dome was not solid. There were two slats through which the machine guns' muzzles fit. Lailani had no bullets for these antique weapons. But she had her assault rifle. She closed one eye, aimed through a slat, and—

Bullets slammed into her turret again.

The dome shattered.

Lailani ducked and cursed. Shards of glass flew everywhere. The wind whipped her. The engines roared.

They were flying in faster now. Three enemy planes. More bullets flying. Lailani could barely breathe, barely see them.

Focus, soldier.

The voice of Ben-Ari, her platoon commander.

Do your job.

Lailani growled, shouldered her rifle, aimed, and fired.

Her bullet slammed into a Zero pilot.

The sleeper fell, dropping out of the cockpit. The Japanese aircraft listed, then streaked down and crashed into the Pacific.

Two aircraft still pursued the Liberator. More bullets flew toward Lailani. She ducked, vanishing into the hold. Bullets slammed into the mangled turret above. A hailstorm. The enemy was firing machine guns now. Shrapnel fell, and a bullet shard bit Lailani's shoulder. She yowled. She tried to rise, to fire back, but the enemy fire was too strong.

Light streaked.

A shell slammed into the turret.

Lailani leaped down, hit the deck, and covered her head.

An explosion bloomed above. Fire raged. She crawled across the deck, and Epimetheus approached her, howling.

She rose, shaky, covered in ash. A gash bled on her arm. She looked up and saw that the gun turret was gone. There was only a hole.

The Liberator swerved. Lailani fell. She felt woozy. And the enemy still pursued.

That's when she saw it.

On the deck. A round hatch.

She pulled it open and laughed. She had not seen it from the runway. It hung under the bomber. A ball turret.

It was a sphere of metal and glass, dangling below the plane like a boil. Lailani was a small woman, and even she barely squeezed in. She pulled her knees to her chest. She stared. She saw them pursuing the Liberator.

The enemy planes.

She thrust her assault rifle out of the ball turret. She unleashed hell.

Within seconds, she emptied her magazine. Her bullets slammed into the second Zero. The imperial plane lost fuel, and smoke rose from its tail. Lailani loaded a fresh magazine. Fired again.

The Japanese antique fell from the sky. All that remained was smoke on the water.

That left one enemy plane.

The Nazi Messerschmitt, still painted with swastikas.

It flew closer. A sleeper was in the open cockpit, flying with one hand, firing an assault rifle with the other. The deformed creature was wearing an old Nazi uniform.

Bullets whizzed around the Liberator's ball turret. One hit, cracking the ball.

Lailani hung in the basket of dented metal and glass. She returned fire. Her bullets hit the Messerschmitt, but the Nazi plane kept roaring in pursuit.

The enemy pilot raised a rocket launcher.

A shell flew toward the Liberator.

Lailani scurried into the fuselage. An explosion rocked the plane. The ball turret shattered, detached, and tumbled down toward the ocean.

Fuck!

She was out of turrets. She heard the enemy following. A line of bullets tore across the Liberator's fuselage, nearly hitting her.

Any second now, a bullet would hit their engine, their fuel tank, or her.

Lailani took a deep breath.

She lowered her head and clenched her fists.

Nightwish.

Her chip shut off. The alien awoke.

Her head rose. A chaotic smile found her lips. Her eyes widened with wicked delight.

She crouched, then leaped up. She crashed through the twisted remains of the turret above. She soared into the air, then landed atop the Liberator.

She stood in the open air, the wind whipping her hair. Only with her alien instincts did she maintain her balance. The heavy bomber thundered below her, flying north over the Pacific. The Messerschmitt flew only a hundred meters behind. Gaining on them.

The sleeper stared at her from his open cockpit. The creature grinned from ear to ear. The grin of Mister Smiley, etched upon his face.

He raised a rifle and fired.

Lailani ran.

She raced across the top of the Liberator, jumping over bullets. She reached the tail of the plane. She ran between its fins. Laughing, she leaped.

She vaulted over open air.

The ocean below. The sky above. A woman, soaring through the sky, a pistol in her hand.

From the Messerschmitt, the sleeper stared in disbelief.

She crashed into his cockpit, placed her pistol into his ravaged mouth, and fired.

Brains and shards of skull sprayed the cockpit.

The Nazi plane began to list, its propeller sputtering. Lailani grabbed the joystick and flew, following the Liberator.

The damage to the bomber looked ugly from here. Bullet holes perforated the fuselage. Both gun turrets were gone. One propeller had stopped spinning. But the plane wasn't leaking anything. It was still flying fast.

Ram into it.

A voice inside her, amused.

Kamikaze into it!

Kill the creatures aboard!

Kill them all. Destroy humanity!

She saw them. A thousand centipedes crawling in the darkness. Waiting. Growing. Breeding. Howling for human blood. For vengeance. Lailani had destroyed their empire.

Yes, you slew us. But we can rebuild! We will conquer this world! We—

Lailani screamed and tugged her hair. Claws were sprouting from her fingertips. Fangs from her mouth. She laughed maniacally. She lifted a fistful of gore—the remnants of the dead pilot. Slick blood on her hands. Delicious. She licked her fingers, and—

What am I doing?

"Serenity!" she whispered, trembling.

The chip in her head activated. The alien retreated, lurking inside her, dormant again.

She flew the German plane over the Liberator. Several meters below, a hole gaped open in the Liberator's fuselage, torn open by the enemy rocket. Lailani felt dizzy.

Oh fuck it, one more time.

"Nightwish," she whispered.

The claws sprouted. The alien laughed. Lailani jerked the Messerschmitt to the side, then jumped from the cockpit.

She flew through the air, legs kicking, as the Messerschmitt plunged toward the ocean.

She crashed through the Liberator's open turret, landed on the deck, and saw Epimetheus there.

A delicious dog. She snarled, approached him, hungry for his flesh, and—

Serenity.

Her claws vanished, and Lailani stumbled back into the Liberator's cockpit.

"Mommy!" Tala cried, and Lailani embraced her daughter.

HOBBS was still flying the bomber. He turned his bucket head toward her, and his blue eyes shone.

"That was highly dangerous, Lailani."

"I know," Lailani whispered, voice shaky.

Only now did it all sink in. Jumping from plane to plane. Firing through a hailstorm of bullets. Her arm was bleeding.

I almost died, she thought. *Almost died and left my daughter alone.*

She began to tremble. She nearly threw up. She held her daughter close, tears in her eyes.

She wished she could run away. Could land this plane on an island somewhere, hunker down, ride out the war. Let others fight. Hadn't she fought enough?

But she remembered the alien waking up inside her. Trying to control her. To get her to kill.

I would have killed everyone on this plane, and I would have eaten their flesh, even the heart from HOBBS's chest, Lailani thought. *Because I am infected with alien DNA. I am part monster. I would have done this all—if not for the chip in my head. The chip Noodles created.*

Her friend was dead now. She was still here.

"We will reach the Matterhorn," she vowed. "We will bring my microchip to SCAR inside the mountain. We will find a way to heal the sleepers."

Because I can't kill anymore, she thought, tears flowing. *I can't kill any more innocent people hijacked by the Dreamer. God forgive me for my sins. I had no choice. Forgive me please.*

The antique bomber flew onward, its three remaining propellers humming, flying over the Pacific.

Lailani had seen the devastation in her seaside town. She shuddered to imagine the horrors that still lay ahead.

CHAPTER TEN

The two men, an officer and a pirate, trudged through the jungle, cursing all the while.

It was the question of the ages: Who cursed more, soldiers or pirates? After several hours of backbreaking hiking, it was still a tight race.

The jungle was hot, humid, and full of mosquitoes. Marco had been to many planets by now, and it seemed that mosquitoes were the cosmic constant—pests known to infect every nook in the galaxy. The ones here were particularly nasty, loud little blighters with evil green eyes. At least Marco wore sleeves. He had it easy. Kai was wearing his sleeveless dragon shirt, and the bloodsuckers were eating him alive. Soon blood was trickling down his tattooed arms.

"These little fuckers better not be carrying any virus," Kai said.

"Don't worry, most viruses evolved to parasitize organisms in their own tree of life. They can't infect us, no more than a human computer virus could infect a Tarjan machine. In the early days of space exploration, alien contamination was a real fear, but once the field of astrobiology expanded, we discovered that—"

"For fuck's sake, Addy was right," Kai said. "You do lecture a lot."

Marco shut his mouth. He did have that tendency, he supposed.

They kept trudging through the rainforest, swinging katanas. Kai had bought the weapons on the streets of Bangkok; today they served as machetes, clearing the brush. For long moments the men walked without speaking. Their heavy breath, the whooshing blades, the ripping fauna, and the myriad of alien insects filled the air with a rich symphony.

Okay, so I lecture a lot, Marco thought. He blinked sweat out of his eyes. *But what else am I supposed to talk about with Kai? Keelhauling people? Come on, Addy wanted me to bond with him. But how?*

An enormous tree, as large as a cathedral, rose before them. They climbed over a sprawling system of roots that snaked across the soil. Little critters, scaly and shy, peered from under the roots with green eyes. The tree coiled, branches blocking the sky, and curtains of moss hung everywhere, home to insects and rodents. Cobwebs shimmered, sparkling with raindrops. The men advanced slowly, slicing through the webs.

"First mosquitoes, now it's goddamn fucking asshole spiders," Kai said. "Fuckers!"

They walked in silence for a moment.

"So ..." Marco said. "Seen any good movies lately?"

Kai slashed through a curtain of dangling moss, sending a family of spiders fleeing. "Nope."

They kept walking, leaving the coiling tree with its serpentine roots and spidery curtains. They slogged through seas of dry leaves, their legs sinking to the knees. Slender trees soared around them, their bark red. Every one of their leaves—and there were millions—had a mouth like a Venus flytrap. The leaves kept opening and closing their mouths, devouring insects. The smacking sounds filled the forest. At least it got rid of the mosquitoes for a while.

"So ..." Marco said. "Watch any good sports tournaments recently?"

He suspected his phrasing was clumsy, but he knew nothing about sports or how to discuss it.

Kai spat and wiped his forehead. "Nope."

For a while longer, they hiked in silence. They climbed to higher ground, where they found the remnants of a cobbled road. Not much was left, just a few cobblestones here and there. The forest had reclaimed most of the road, swallowing some cobblestones into the soil, growing trees between others. The old trail reminded Marco of the spine of some ancient serpent. It meant they were going the right way, heading to the temple.

Come on, Marco, he told himself. *You're taking this trip to bond with the guy. Try harder!*

But how? The two had nothing in common. And it went beyond their professions. Marco was interested in literature, history, science—the nerdy pursuits, as Addy called them. Kai was every inch a Linden, more interested in beer, tattoos, and scratching himself in ungodly places.

Well, Addy is a Linden, and I get along with her, right? he told himself.

But another voice answered: *No you don't! Addy is bloody annoying! You only stick with her because you're insane and love her for some reason.*

He sighed and looked at Kai.

"So anyway," Marco began, "Addy said that—"

"Addy is always saying something." Kai snorted. "My God, that chick can talk a lot."

"Tell me about it," Marco said. "Especially about freaks and hot dogs. Oh, and don't get me started on how she can talk endlessly about Robot Wrestling!"

"I know, right?" Kai said. "Robot Wrestling? It's just a fucking stupid TV show about robots that wrestle. I mean, we fly spaceships in battle for a living. Who the fuck cares about some tiny robots on TV that can't use anything more lethal than a chainsaw?"

"Addy loves weird shit," Marco said. "I mean, she even eats tuna and peanut butter sandwiches."

Kai tilted his head. "What the actual fuck? Those two don't go together."

"I told her! She said she loves tuna and peanut butter. She's a lunatic. Oh, and one time? She made mac and peanut butter. You know, like mac and cheese? Just ... peanut butter. Instead of cheese."

Kai groaned. "That sounds disgusting."

"She ate the whole damn thing," Marco said. "She was licking the bowl. Most of her weirdness involves food. In fact, most of her life period involves food."

Soon they were both laughing, swapping more tales of Addy's culinary escapades. Mostly it was Marco recounting the tales—he had known Addy for much longer—while Kai laughed and shook his head in bewilderment.

There you go, Marco thought. *Bonding over what a lunatic Addy is. I guess we have something in common after all—having to deal with my crazy wife.*

"She's an amazing woman," Kai finally said.

"She is," Marco agreed, voice softer now. "I love her very much. She's not just my wife. Not just my best friend. She's my sister-in-arms."

Kai frowned. "Hey now, she's *my* sister, buddy. What you said sounds all sorts of fucked up."

Marco laughed. "I guess it does, yes. I mean—we fought together in the wars. We saw things. We saved each other's lives. All this before we became a couple. We've been fighting side by side since we were eleven. Since her parents died. Well ..." His cheeks heated up. "Since her mom died."

They were silent for a moment. Yes, it was still an open wound. Twenty-four years ago, when Marco and Addy had been only eleven, the scum had attacked their city. Addy had thought both her parents dead. She had moved in with Marco that year, becoming his closest companion.

Only for Butch to come back into her life this year. Bringing with him the son of a Thai prostitute. Tossing their lives into upheaval.

Kai nodded. "Yeah, I'm thinking the same thing. Butch is a fucked-up piece of shit. Faked his own death. Ditched Addy with you. Knocked up a Thai hooker who belonged to the mob, then ran away with her and her baby. That would be me, of course. Yep. The bastard lied. To Addy. To everyone."

Marco brushed off an insect that looked like a cross between bumblebee and praying mantis. "Did he ever talk about Addy?"

Kai climbed over a fallen log bristly with mold. "Well, I always knew about Addy Linden, the famous heroine of Earth. You two are famous, you know. Legends! For a long time, Butch lied. Said Addy wasn't his daughter. Used to say the two Linden families weren't related. I was thirteen before I learned the truth. A lying scumbag, as I said."

Marco slashed through helices of tall blue grass, carving a way uphill. "In this case, though, Butch was probably trying to protect you. The Basidio Boys would have killed anyone related to a famous officer of the Human Defense Force."

"Yeah, that's the story Butch likes to tell," Kai said, sounding skeptical. "Personally, I maintain that he's just a lying shitbag. But hey, I love the old man. He's an asshole, but he's an asshole with a heart. You wanna hear something funny? When I was a kid, Butch was never a role model. Never a mentor. But you and Addy were."

Marco raised his eyebrows. "We were?"

Kai pulled down a sapling, making room for them to climb over. "Fuck yeah! I'm twelve years younger than you guys, you know. When I was a kid, you were already war heroes. The famous Marco Emery. Addy Linden. Lailani de la Rosa. Kemi Abasi. And of course your platoon leader, Einav Ben-Ari, the Golden Lioness who saved humanity and became president. You're all famous."

Marco preferred to be famous for his books. Not for his exploits during the Alien Wars.

"I'm not a hero," he said. "I never wanted to be a soldier. I did not enlist. I was drafted. I didn't crave the front line. I tried to avoid it. I'm not unusually strong. I'm not unusually smart like Meili. I was just … there. By chance. In her platoon. Einav is the true heroine of the war. I just refused to abandon her. I stood by her side. I fought by her side. When she sent me on a mission alone, I went alone. When duty called, I was there. Even if it was dark and full of enemies, and I wanted nothing more than to go home. That's all I was, all I am. I was there."

Kai placed a hand on Marco's shoulder. "That's just about the best definition of heroism I've ever heard."

"So … we were your childhood heroes," Marco said. "No pressure to live up to expectations or anything."

Kai tapped his cheek, considering. "Well, you know, the thing about actually meeting you and Addy? You're not really that noble."

"Um, thanks," Marco said. "I think."

"I mean, you're not really like heroes in stories, you know?"

"You're flattering me," Marco said.

Kai laughed. "You're regular guys, you and Addy. You act dumb sometimes. You burp and bicker and tell stupid jokes. You're normal. You're guys I can drink with, ya know? Not heroes. Regular people."

"Maybe that's what heroes are. Regular people who just stood up and did the right thing."

"Well, that leaves me out," Kai said. "I chose a life of crime."

"No you didn't." Marco shook his head. "You didn't choose to become a criminal any more than I chose to become a soldier. You were raised by Butch. He brought you into that life. Look, I'm not going to make some sappy speech about how you can change. But I'll say this, as somebody who's been a million years in the future and flown back with the scars to prove it. The future isn't set in stone. There is no such thing as fate. You forge your own path, no matter how dark the forest of your life might seem. You always have a choice to keep walking through the shadows and find the light." He thought for a moment. "Come to think of it, that *was* a sappy speech."

Kai nodded. "Yep, Addy warned me about those."

Marco pointed. "Hey, now would you look at that?"

Crumbling ruins crowned a hilltop. A few stone columns still stood, rising toward the leafy canopy. Most of the columns lay across the forest floor, overgrown with vines and moss. An orphaned archway stood in a sunbeam, the walls around it fallen long ago, like a portal to another world. Farther back, a few walls still stood, even sections of a vaulted ceiling, but nature had invaded these ancient halls. Tree roots clutched walls and turrets. Trunks pushed through cobbled floors and peeked through holes in craggy domes.

"Think this was a temple?" Kai said.

"I don't know," Marco said. "This isn't the giant turtle-shaped temple we saw from the air. This place is smaller, hidden under the canopy. Maybe an abbey, an auxiliary to the larger temple down the road, serving pilgrims."

"Maybe we'll find laceleaf still growing here," Kai said.

They had seen an illustration of laceleaf in Addy's book—a plant with star-shaped white leaves. Outside the ruined abbey, they sought a matching plant. If the monks had planted gardens here, they were long gone. But Marco hoped the laceleaf had survived, now thrived as a wild herb. He found many interesting alien plants here. A bush with red flowers that thrust out sticky tongues, catching flies. A thicket whose leaves undulated like snakes, their flowers snapping toothy mouths. A patch of luminous flowers, each one like a jar of fireflies. But sadly—no laceleaf.

Marco stepped over a fallen column into the abbey remains. The floor had once been a mosaic, but the tiles were now scattered everywhere. Trees grew among the tiles, punching holes through the curved roof. A few columns still stood, wrapped in ivy, home to an assortment of lizards and beetles. Moss coated the walls, but Marco could make out hints of ancient murals.

He approached the best-preserved wall, one with barely any holes or cracks. He brushed off moss, revealing more of the artwork.

He found himself staring at an illustrated mushroom. But not an adorable red mushroom from a fairy tale or *Super Mario* game. It was a gray, pale, deathlike thing. A fungus. A disease. A toadstool like a corpse, wrinkly and withered. Marco couldn't help but shudder. Just a simple painting. A few strokes of the brush. But it oozed illness.

Marco kept working, clearing off more moss. It was a large mural. He found many more toadstools, painted in concentric circles, a mandala spanning the wall. Finally, in the center of the wall, Marco uncovered a painting of a turtle.

It wasn't exactly like a turtle from Earth. It had six legs, its shell was diamond-shaped, and its eyes rose on stalks. But clearly it filled the same ecological niche.

On his travels, Marco had learned that carbon-based life took similar evolutionary paths on different planets. He had seen some truly bizarre aliens, but those had lived in unusual environments: aliens like hot air balloons that floated on gas giants, living silicon crystals that evolved on cold, rocky worlds, even living metallic spheres that communicated with magnetic impulses. Addy could probably describe a bunch more from her book. But where the environment was similar to Earth, evolution worked more or less the same. You didn't end up with carbon copies. But the results were remarkably close. Many Earthlike worlds, terrestrial planets in the Goldilocks zone, evolved their own versions of birds, insects, and reptiles.

There were even other humanoid races out there. Some were tall and green, like the Altairians. Others were small and furry, like the Nandaki. None of them were quite like humans; some had green skin or four arms, mouths on their hands, and other alien features. A monkey was more like a human than an Altairian or Nandaki. Hell, on a cellular level, even a banana was more like a human. But considering these aliens evolved on other worlds, the similarities were impressive.

Not carbon copies, Marco thought. *Carbon laws. The laws of chemistry and physics combining into a galactic theory of evolution.*

He shook his head, clearing it of thoughts. Now he was lecturing to himself. By God, Addy was right. He had a problem.

"Man, I looked all over," Kai said, trudging into the chapel. "I can't find fucking laceleaf anywhere. Any luck?" He turned toward the mural and whistled. "Hey, nice turtle."

"Actually, it's not exactly a turtle," Marco said. "You see, on different planets, evolu—Actually, never mind. Yeah, it's a nice turtle."

Kai scratched his chin. "Were the natives of this place— the ones who built this chapel—turtles?"

"I think so," Marco said. "The turtle in this mural might have been Upidia's king, depicted here facing the Esporian mushrooms. From the air, we saw a temple shaped like a giant turtle. Maybe it was meant to depict another king. Or the same one."

Kai looked around him. "I don't see any shells. If the Upidians were turtles, why aren't their shells here?"

"I don't know," Marco said. "Maybe they abandoned this place before dying out. Or maybe their shells decayed. Maybe the Esporians took them as trophies. And maybe we'll still find some."

"I'm more interested in finding laceleaf." Kai pointed. "Look out that window. Hard to see from here, but the brush seems thinner. Maybe that was a garden?"

"Let's take a look," Marco said.

They left the chapel and its mural. Outside, they found what might indeed have been a garden. Perhaps the turtles had once grown their food here. A square of column stubs surrounded the area. Some of the columns lay fallen and chipped.

But no plants grew here. No herbs. No laceleaf. Oddly— no plants at all. Not even weeds.

Dry leaves scuttled across the courtyard, paper-thin and cubical like green dice, blown off the nearby trees. Marco kicked them aside. And there it was. More black mold.

He walked among the columns, kicking more leaves aside, revealing more of the infestation. The mold didn't just fill the garden. A trail of it spread down a hillside, leading to a distant river. Where the mold spread, no plants grew.

"The same mold from the clearing where we landed the *Barracuda*," Marco said. "It kills plants."

"Maybe it killed the turtles too," Kai said. "A treat left over from the mushrooms?"

"Could be," Marco said. "We know Esporians can release toxic spores. Hell, that's why we're looking for laceleaf, right? Maybe the mushrooms spread black mold as a weapon. I can imagine the mold spreading across the forest, destroying the Upidian civilization. Over time, the rainforest regrew, took over the planet again, leaving only a few last strongholds of mold. And some old ruins."

Kai cringed. "And no laceleaf. Did the mold eat it all?"

"Maybe it did here, but let's keep going. At Turtle Temple, we might still find the plant."

They were walking across the mold when they heard a scuttle in the bushes.

Both men froze, then raised their weapons, staring.

For a moment—silence.

Then the forest tore open, a creature burst out, and Marco—veteran of three alien wars—couldn't help it.

He screamed.

CHAPTER ELEVEN

Addy was bored.

That rarely ended well.

She paced the *Barracuda*, looking for something to do. She checked under the fridge and couch, but she found no delicious scraps. She tried to write another chapter in *Freaks of the Galaxy IV*, but she had already used up all her freaks.

Damn it! She should have gone with Marco and Kai. They were sure to find some incredible freaks out there. But instead, Addy was stuck here. In a parked starship. With nothing to do. Nothing but pacing. Worrying. Being so afraid.

She placed a hand on her belly. It was still flat. Well, okay, it was never *entirely* flat anymore, not since having the twins. But this new pregnancy was still invisible.

At least when it came to her figure. There were signs, Addy supposed. Her food cravings. Her moodiness. Constantly needing to pee.

She tapped her chin. Nah, that was pretty much always her. But Ben-Ari had noticed. Female intuition. And sooner or later, Marco would notice too.

Hopefully we win this war before I'm showing, she thought. *I just want to go home. To Anchor Bay. To hug Marco on the beach. To hug my kids. To be like we were.*

Tears filled her eyes. She clenched her fists. It wasn't fair. It wasn't fucking fair! After all they had been through—fighting aliens for years—they deserved to rest. To raise a family. To have a good, peaceful life. Instead? Just three years of joy. That was it. Three years that passed in the blink of an eye. And now war again. Traveling to alien worlds. Dealing with fear and battles and pain.

And worst of all—being away from Sam and Roza.

The twins were light-years away. Addy didn't have a wormhole generator. She had left her children behind, and it tore at her heart, and she felt so helpless she wanted to scream.

Fuck. This was what boredom did to her. Boredom meant time to think. Time to hurt. Time to be afraid. There was a reason Ben-Ari had never given them a spare moment during boot camp. Free time was fuel for fear and pain.

Addy wandered onto the bridge, hoping to talk to Ben-Ari. But the president was deep into reading a Gabriel Garcia Marquez novel. Her headphones were on, leaking muffled hints of *La Boheme.* If Addy had learned anything during the wars, it was to *never* interfere with Ben-Ari while she was reading South American literature and listening to Puccini.

Addy left the bridge. She walked between the hammocks, knelt, and tugged open the hatch on the deck. She peered down into the cargo hold.

"Meili, damn it, get your ass up here!" Addy said. "I wanna play poker."

The young programmer looked up. She sat within a ring of computers, typing away.

"Do I have to, Miss Linden?" Meili asked. "I'm still improving my antivirus."

Addy groaned. She left the programmer, climbed into the engine room, and approached her father. Butch stood by the engines with a wrench and blowtorch, welding a cracked pipe.

"Yo, Butch!" Addy said.

Sparks were flying from his blowtorch, hissing against his denim jacket.

"Hey, Daddy-O!" Addy shouted.

He shut off his blowtorch and turned toward her. He pulled up his goggles. Sparks had singed his grizzled beard and leathery skin.

"Hey, Ads."

"Ever hear of a helmet?" she said.

He tapped his goggles. "Good enough. I just care about my peepers. My face looks like an old catcher's mitt anyway." He winked. "Thank the Big One you look like your mother."

"Dad ..." she began, but her voice trembled, and she could say no more.

There was so much she wanted to tell him. That she was still angry with him. That she hated him. That she was pregnant. That she missed her twins, and missed Marco, and was so scared all the time. That she was Addy Fucking Linden, the heroine who had raised Earth in rebellion against the marauders, who had crossed the world of the grays and killed the monster in the heart of their labyrinth, but that she was still so afraid. So alone. That at thirty-five, a mother of two, pregnant with a third, she felt more vulnerable than ever. Felt younger than ever. That she still needed her father.

Yet she could bring none of that to her lips. So she only looked at him, and a tear flowed down her cheek.

Butch's eyes softened. Maybe, without her saying a word, he understood everything. He pulled her into his arms.

"Oh, my sweet baby girl." He held her close. "It's all right. Your daddy's got you. We'll fix this mess."

He had never been there for her. He had been in prison. Or been pirating, gambling, and whoring across the galaxy. He was dirt, and Addy hated him, but she needed him now. To forgive him. To feel safe in his arms. For just a few moments, she needed to be a little girl again.

"Hey, Dad," she said. "Can you teach me how to fix a starship?"

He laughed and wiped his eyes. Amazingly, they were damp. Him, the rough and tough pirate—tearing up!

"Ah, it's only the cooling pipe I'm fixing now," Butch said. "But come on, I'll show you how the systems work."

Addy knew all about starship engineering. Maybe she even knew more than Butch did. But he needed to be a dad. *She* needed him to be a dad. She listened as he explained, asking questions, helping him fix different components. Soon they were working side by side, joking, laughing.

At one point, Butch looked into her eyes. He hesitated, seemed ready to say something. He didn't need to. She saw his words in his eyes. Same as he had seen her silent words.

I'm sorry.

"Hey, Dad, pass me one of those Cokes there from the shelf," she said.

He raised an eyebrow. "You, a Linden, drinking Coke instead of beer?" He was already working on his third beer of the day.

She hesitated, not yet ready to share news of her pregnancy. "I love Coke! You know that."

He tossed her one of the dusty red cans. She drank. It was warm and metallic.

"Hey, Ads, pass me that ion gauge, will ya?" Butch said. "I think the exhaust coils are—"

The engine room jolted. A thud echoed.

Addy froze, the gauge in her hand.

"Is that meant to happen?" she said. "I thought the engine was off."

They stood in silence for a moment, tense. Then—another thud, louder than before. The engine room jolted. Tools clattered to the floor. A pipe cracked open.

A third thud. A fourth.

"Something is banging against the undercarriage!" Addy shouted. "It's beneath the ship!"

Ben-Ari was shouting something from the upper deck. Addy couldn't make out the words.

More thuds hit the ship. The hull dented. A crack raced across the deck plates below Addy's feet.

She had no weapon down here. She grabbed a wrench and lifted it like a club.

The ship rocked. Screeches rose outside. Hideous, inhuman cries of fury.

With a deafening boom, a hole burst open on the hull.

Addy found herself gazing into a hellmouth, a pit of teeth and hunger.

She raised her wrench and growled as the nightmares flowed in.

CHAPTER TWELVE

The monster reared before him.

Standing outside the ruins of the chapel, Marco stared. Terror paralyzed him.

It was a caterpillar. But not the cute, fuzzy little critters from Earth. This beast was enormous. It could dwarf a crocodile. The alien reared, body composed of many segments, bristly with spikes and hooks. Dead animals hung from its cruel horns, rotting away, covered with feasting maggots.

But the worst was the creature's mouth. A massive hellmouth, round and filled with rings of teeth. Seven arms surrounded that maw, sprouting out like barbels. Each arm ended with grasping claws. Three red eyes completed the monstrous visage.

Yep, it was an ugly fucker. Marco had fought many aliens, had seen some real doozies. This one was probably the ugliest.

He dropped the katana he had been using to clear the brush.

He raised his assault rifle and—

The creature's arms, growing around the mouth like petals, thrust at incredible speed. Claws grabbed his rifle.

Marco pulled the trigger. Bullets roared, but they went wide. The claws twisted the barrel, stronger than any human hands. Marco clung on, refusing to relinquish his weapon. The monster reared higher. Marco rose from the ground, legs kicking, dangling from the gun.

The creature's mouth dilated, exposing more rings of teeth. It roared, deafening, spraying saliva onto Marco. His ears rang, and when the creature raised him higher, Marco found himself gazing down into a quivering pit of fangs. Deep in the gullet, he could see animals being digested.

Another arm lashed out like a tentacle. It grabbed Marco's shoulder. Two arms grabbed his legs. Soon all seven arms were holding him, pulling him toward the waiting maw. Marco finally released his rifle, but it was too late. The creature had become like a great claw, squeezing him, pulling him in.

"Hey, fucker!" Kai shouted from below. "Yeah, right here!"

The pirate ran, grabbed the fallen katana, and leaped into the air.

The caterpillar, still holding Marco high above the ground, turned toward the new threat.

Kai vaulted off a fallen statue, soared through the air, and swung his katana.

The blade severed one of the creature's arms.

It wasn't enough to save Marco. He dangled from the remaining six appendages. The monster roared in pain, blood spraying. The sound pounded against Marco, drenching him with more saliva. He used the distraction to draw a knife from his belt.

With six remaining arms, the creature kept pulling Marco toward its ravenous mouth. The gullet contracted and expanded over and over, the rings of teeth moving like a trash compactor.

"Here's an appetizer for you," Marco muttered.

He hurled his knife into the toothy pit.

The blade vanished into the meat grinder. Blood spurted. The creature shrieked in pain, and its grip on Marco loosened.

Kai leaped again, katana flashing. Another severed arm flew.

That was enough. The enraged caterpillar, two arms down, released Marco. He thudded onto the ground, drenched in gore, claw marks across his legs and body.

He looked up. The gargantuan caterpillar flailed with agony. Five arms remained, whipping around the circular mouth. The alien still held Marco's T57 assault rifle in one arm. Almost comically, perhaps accidentally, the creature began to fire the gun. Bullets flew every which way, slamming into trees and the abbey ruins.

"Hey, Kai!" Marco said, groaning with pain. "Got a gun I can borrow?"

"Take your pick, bro." Kai turned his back toward Marco, revealing a wide assortment of weapons.

Marco reached for a pistol. Before he could grab it, the carnivorous caterpillar swung its neck like a flail. The beast's bloated head slammed into the two men like a wrecking ball.

They flew through the air. Weapons detached from Kai's back and scattered every which way. Grenades rolled. Marco fell down hard on his face. He flipped onto his back, staring up at the menace. The caterpillar reared and howled, then drove its enormous maw downward.

Marco rolled. The hellmouth slammed into the ground, finding only dirt and stones to devour.

"What the fuck is this thing?" Kai shouted from nearby, struggling to rise. He groaned in pain.

"Garden-variety pest!" Marco called back, rising to his feet.

The creature raised its head again, howling. Soil and shattered stones dripped from its jaws. The arms stretched out and grabbed Marco.

Goddammit, not again! Marco thought.

As the arms lifted him, Marco reached down and snatched Kai's fallen pistol.

The arms began to fold inward, reeling Marco in. The mouth opened in anticipation, easily large enough to swallow him whole.

Marco emptied a clip into the hellish maw.

The creature quivered with each bullet, but the arms maintained their grip.

Goddammit.

Kai finally managed to grab a weapon and rejoin the fray. He raised a submachine gun and opened fire. Bullets slammed into the arms mere inches away from Marco.

"Use your katana!" Marco shouted, shrinking away from the fusillade. "Goddamn, Kai, hold your fire!"

The pirate lowered his rifle. By some miracle, the bullets had missed Marco. Thankfully, they had torn off another caterpillar arm. Only four squirming limbs now surrounded the toothy mouth.

Enraged, the creature hurled Marco to the ground. It turned toward Kai, probably realizing that a cackling, machine-gun-wielding pirate was a more serious threat right now. The alien lunged so fast Kai didn't even have time to react.

The beast slammed into the young pirate, knocking him down. Moving with terrifying speed, the caterpillar closed its mouth around Kai's legs.

The pirate screamed. He thrashed on the ground, unable to reload his weapon. The caterpillar throbbed like a worm digesting soil, sucking up its victim. Soon Kai was up to his waist in that horrifying mouth. The young man could do nothing but scream.

Marco narrowed his eyes, knelt, and grabbed a fallen katana.

He lunged forward, screamed, and swung that blade for all it was worth.

This time he wasn't aiming at the arms. Marco attacked the caterpillar's segmented body. Each segment was coated with armor and spikes. But Marco aimed between two segments. His blade drove into the seam.

Yellow blood spurted. It wasn't a deep cut. But it hurt the beast. The alien opened its mouth to roar, and Kai fell to the ground. The pirate's legs were coated with saliva, and he writhed, face twisted in agony.

The alien turned toward Marco. Its three red eyes narrowed.

Marco stood before the monster, holding his bloody blade.

For a moment they stared at each other. Man and beast.

Then the alien spoke. It was not English. It was no human tongue. It was a mix of grunts, groans, and clicks. But there was no mistaking it. This was a language.

This alien is intelligent, Marco thought in wonder. *Oh well. I'm still going to kill it.*

He screamed and ran at the beast.

The creature howled, lips peeling back, and rings of teeth emerged from its gullet like candy from a wrapper.

With both hands, Marco swung his katana. The blade sank deep into the alien gums, leaving just the hilt exposed.

Marco could not pull the sword free. He released the hilt and stumbled back. The alien flailed. It couldn't retract its jaws, not with the katana embedded into the gums. It whipped from side to side, clearly in agony.

Marco looked around him. Kai's weapons lay across the ground. He had his choice of the litter.

His eyes fell upon a flamethrower.

The alien's arms curled inward. It grabbed the katana's hilt and managed to wrench it free from the gums. The beast roared and came charging toward Marco.

The flamethrower spewed its fury.

A torrent of flame washed over the alien.

The caterpillar screeched. It burned. Even so, it still tried to attack. The hellish mouth emerged from the inferno, opening wide, bellowing.

But Kai, even as he lay wounded, was firing a rifle. Bullets pounded the burning alien. Marco kept washing it with more and more fire.

The creature refused to retreat. Burning, riddled with bullets, it still faced them. Roaring. Dying.

Why doesn't it run away? Marco thought. Perhaps it was an apex predator and had never evolved the instinct to flee. Not even as it howled in agony.

He emptied his flamethrower's fuel, and Kai emptied his magazine, and finally the monster fell down dead.

Marco dropped his flamethrower, breathing heavily, and hurried toward Kai. He pulled out his medical kit, hoping to save the young man's life.

Amazingly, Kai stood up. The pirate spat onto the charred, dead alien.

"Fuckin' caterpillar." He kicked it. "You ain't gonna be turning into any butterfly now, bitch!"

Marco blinked at his brother-in-law. "Kai! That creature was chomping on your legs like they were breadsticks. How are you still standing?"

"Ah. That." Kai widened a tear in his jeans, revealing leggings made from metallic, scaly material. "Graphene armor. I always wear them under my clothes before going on a mission. Thin but as strong as diamonds." He pulled up his sleeveless shirt, revealing similar armor across his chest. "Saved my life a bunch of times."

"Damn." Marco tilted his head. "But ... why not on your arms too?"

Kai snorted and looked at his tattooed arms. "Hide this ink? This artwork cost a fortune, bro. I ain't hiding it for no caterpillars."

"You're almost as insane as your sister," Marco said. "Almost."

Kai flashed a grin and winked. "You ain't too bad yourself. You fight well, bro. I heard all the stories. Nice to see the famous Battle Poet in action."

"I don't know why people call me that. I write novels, not poetry." Marco looked at the dead alien, then back at the pirate. "It nearly got me. You saved my life."

"And you saved mine. That's a sacred bond." Kai smeared blood on his hand, then held it out. "Life brothers."

Marco shook the younger man's hand. "Life brothers."

Kai slapped Marco on the back. "You'd make a good pirate."

"You'd make a good soldier."

Kai snorted. "Eh. Soldiers can't drink on the job."

Marco couldn't help but laugh. "Shows what you know. An old army buddy of mine—we called him Beast—used to fill his canteen with vodka."

"My kinda guy." Kai took a swig of rum, then handed the bottle to Marco. "Care to wet your beak?"

Marco took the bottle. "I've earned this one." He drank, then looked down at the dead alien. "I've never heard of a creature like this. It didn't appear in the abbey's murals. It tried to talk to me, I think. It was intelligent. Maybe it wasn't the alien mushrooms who wiped out the native turtles. Maybe it was these giant caterpillars."

"Speaking of turtles, we should keep going," Kai said. "We're almost at Turtle Temple. Maybe we'll find some laceleaf there. Keep your eyes open for giant, carnivorous caterpillars with a taste for human flesh."

They walked on through the forest, leaving behind the ruined abbey, the black mold, and the charred alien.

CHAPTER THIRTEEN

The *Barracuda*'s hull cracked open, and the monster barged in.

Addy hurled her wrench onto the beast. She might as well have pelted it with popcorn.

She had fought some nasty buggers in her day. The scuttling giant centipedes. The brain-eating spiders. The wrinkly, rancid grays. Ugly fuckers, all of them. The creature burrowing into the pirate ship, however, took the cake.

It's a goddamn caterpillar on crack, she thought.

The beast was enormous. It could put pythons to shame. Its circular mouth dilated open, revealing rings of teeth. Arms sprouted around that mouth, tipped with claws, perhaps evolved to pull prey into the waiting gullet. And god, the thing stank. Its breath washed over Addy, reeking. It was still crawling through the crack, segment by segment, entering the hold. It shrieked all the while, reaching its ring of arms toward Addy.

"You'd make an excellent freak." She gazed at the abomination and nodded approvingly. "I ain't even mad. I'm impressed. I'm still going to kill you though."

More thuds shook the pirate ship. Another hole burst open across the hold. Another monstrous caterpillar stuck its head into the ship, roaring for blood.

"Dad, you take care of that one!" Addy shouted, pointing at the new arrival.

"What the hell are those things?" Butch shouted back.

"The fuck should I know?" Addy said. "Just help me kill them!"

She had no weapons down here. But she lifted the blowtorch, brought it near the alien's head, and flipped it on.

The bolt of fire that emerged—barely larger than a wizard's wand—seemed woefully inadequate.

Addy burned a bit of the caterpillar. Just enough to piss it off. The alien snatched the blowtorch away, then pawed at her legs.

"Hey, no grabby hands!"

Addy slapped the beast and scampered back. The creature crawled in after her, fully entering the ship. It reared, suddenly looking even larger. Nearby, Butch was swinging a rod, trying to keep another caterpillar from entering.

From above deck rose screams, then gunfire. Ben-Ari was fighting up there.

A third hole burst open—this time on the deck beneath Addy's feet. A third caterpillar came squeezing in.

"Dad, to the upper deck!" Addy shouted, racing toward the ladder.

"We have to protect the engines!" he said. "They'll tear 'em apart."

"Forget the fucking engines, we need guns!" She grabbed her dad and pulled him along.

She shoved her old man toward the ladder. He began to climb. Addy stood below, guarding him, facing three crawling caterpillars.

A trinity of hellmouths opened before her, bellowing. Saliva and the stench of rot washed over her.

Addy stared at the monsters, opened her own mouth wide, and howled in reply. She hopped up and down, roaring, trying to appear as large and menacing as possible.

If giant alien caterpillars could laugh, she imagined they'd be in stitches.

The central monster wriggled closer and thrust out its arms. Its claws grabbed Addy. She screamed and flailed.

"Addy!" Butch cried from above.

"Get the guns!" she shouted, thrashing in the alien's grip.

The arms tugged her, reeling her in toward the circular mouth. She turned her head aside, nausea filling her. She dug her heels into the deck, but the beast was stronger. It pulled her closer.

Addy groaned, raised her feet, and kicked wildly. Her boots slammed into gums, teeth, and a sticky tongue. It barely fazed the beast. The claws tightened. The mouth opened wider, prepared to devour her.

Guns boomed.

Butch leaped down the ladder, a pistol in each hand. Bullets sparked against the alien's head.

The claws released Addy. She thumped onto the deck, then reached toward her dad.

"Give me a gun, damn it!" Addy shouted.

She grabbed a pistol, scampered back until she hit a bulkhead, and opened fire. Bullets slammed into the alien that had grabbed her. Butch was busy shooting the other two.

The bulkhead behind Addy cracked.

Claws thrust inside, wrapped around her torso, and clutched her like a vise.

Addy screamed.

"Fuck you, attacking me from behind, you fucking piece of shit coward!"

She aimed the pistol over her shoulder, winced, and fired.

The sound deafened her. Her ears rang. The recoil tossed her hand forward. Yep, she probably damaged her hearing with this one. But the blow caused the alien to release her. She limped a few steps away from the broken hull, woozy.

The caterpillars were everywhere. Five now filled the *Barracuda*'s lower deck. All still alive. All hungry. Addy and Butch stood back-to-back, firing on them. They were running low on ammo, and the creatures still swarmed.

"Dad!" Addy said. "Fire up the engines!"

"What?"

Addy aimed her pistol. She fired, hitting the cooling pipe they had just repaired.

"Reach for that lever!" she said. "I can't reach it myself. Fire her up!"

"With no coolants?" he said, firing at the reaching alien claws. "The whole ship will blow, dammit!"

"Trust me," she said. "It'll just get very, very hot. Do it!"

She fired a last round, and her gun clicked. Out of bullets.

Butch cursed, grabbed the lever, and yanked it down.

"Now climb the ladder!" Addy shouted. "Quick!"

The *Barracuda*'s engines began to rumble, then overheat. Turbines pumped. Plasma roiled. The cooling pipe thrummed, whistled, and shattered.

Butch and Addy climbed in a fury, heading toward the upper deck. Butch climbed through the hatch first. Addy climbed a few rungs below, reached up to him, and—

A caterpillar reared and grabbed her legs.

She screamed, falling from the ladder.

Butch grabbed her wrist.

"Addy!"

She dangled below the trapdoor, legs kicking. The creature tugged her. The alien jaws widened below, ready to feast. Butch was pulling her, but the aliens were stronger. Her joints creaked.

The caterpillars pulled her a meter down. Their teeth grazed her boots.

The engines gave a great whistle, then crack, and—

Fire.

Fire raged below.

Flames filled the lower deck, washing over the creatures, roaring, bathing Addy with heat.

The caterpillars screamed. They released Addy. They vanished in the inferno.

Butch pulled Addy through the hatch, and she collapsed onto the upper deck, coughing. Her pant legs were burning, and Butch helped her pat them out.

Fire rose through the hatch, spurting like a geyser. Addy kicked the trapdoor shut, sealing the aliens below. The caterpillars were still screaming, burning to death in the blaze. The entire lower deck had become a furnace.

Addy's ears rang. She couldn't stop coughing. Her eyes stung. But she stood with fists raised, staring around, ready to keep fighting.

She saw no immediate threat. She stood between the galley, the barrels of grog, and the hammocks. But the battle wasn't over. Screams rose from the bridge. Alien shrieks and human cries.

Addy prepared to run over when the trapdoor on the deck burst open.

A caterpillar leaped through, blazing.

It was like a living flame. Its armored skin was gone. Its gums had melted. It was all bones and teeth, blind and furious. A writhing demon of fire.

Addy yelped, scampered backward, and sought a weapon. Any weapon. She was out of bullets. She grabbed the nearest weapon she could find—an antique cutlass that hung on the bulkhead.

She leaned forward, swinging the blade through the fire, hacking at the skeletal creature again and again. Finally it thumped down dead, half its body in the flaming engine room, the rest smoldering on the upper deck. Addy shuddered.

She was finally free to approach the weapons rack and grab her beloved T57. She swore to never part from the assault rifle again. Butch took a second rifle from the rack. Muzzles aimed ahead, they stepped onto the bridge.

Ben-Ari was there, standing over the corpse of a dead caterpillar. A live one was rearing before her, riddled with bullets but still hungry for flesh. Ben-Ari seemed to be out of bullets. She was swinging a metal rod—a lever torn off from the controls. Blood was dripping down her thigh.

Addy flicked her rifle to automatic and unleashed hell.

Bullets slammed into the caterpillar, into the dashboards, the viewport.

"Addy, careful!" Butch shouted. "The Tarjan machine! It's priceless!"

She barely heard him. The wounded caterpillar turned toward her, screeching. The bridge was small, no larger than her bedroom back home. Addy refused to back away.

She released her empty magazine. The alien lunged at her. Addy stood her ground.

Seven tentacles reached out and grabbed her.

Addy slapped in another magazine.

The mouth gaped open, widening to engulf her.

She filled it with lead, emptying her magazine within seconds.

The caterpillar thumped down, finally dead. Addy spat onto the corpse, then looked up at her president.

"You all right, ma'am?"

Ben-Ari was pale, and her leg was bleeding. The president knelt and began tending to her wound.

"I'm fine." She shook her head, ponytail flicking. "No, I'm not fine. I let down my guard. I should have organized a guard duty schedule. Made sure we all carried rifles at all times. I should have stuck to military protocol. Fuck! I grew soft."

Addy frowned at her president. She almost never heard Ben-Ari curse.

"It's all right," Addy said softly. "Don't be so hard on yourself. We killed them all. Everyone is fine, right?" She blinked. "Wait a minute. Where is …"

"Meili!" Ben-Ari blurted out.

The two women rushed off the bridge. They reached the hatch that led to the cargo hold. Like the engine room, it was on the lower deck. Only a thin bulkhead separated it from that flaming inferno.

Addy yanked the hatch open, terrified that she'd find Meili dead below, burnt to a crisp or devoured by 'pillars.

She saw only shadows. Good. The fire had not spread, at least.

"Meili?" she called down.

No answer came. Addy glanced at Ben-Ari, saw the fear in the president's eyes.

They both climbed down into the cargo hold. It was full of Meili's equipment—computers, monitors, keyboards, cables, and piles of software development manuals. But the girl was nowhere to be found.

"Meili!" Addy cried.

A pile of coats shivered. A squeak rose from under it.

Addy pulled the coats back, revealing Meili. The young programmer was curled up into a fetal position, trembling. She looked at Addy, her giant glasses magnifying her damp eyes.

"Are the monsters gone?" Meili whispered.

Butch's voice boomed from above. "Hey, ladies! You better get your asses on the bridge, dammit!"

They returned to the bridge, where Butch was waiting. The grizzled pirate stared at them, eyes dark, his lips a thin line. His fists were clenched at his sides.

"Dad?" Addy asked. "Something eating your ass?"

Butch stepped aside, revealing the Tarjan machine that powered the *Barracuda*.

It was a mess.

Several vials had shattered, spilling the colorful liquid. The tubes of smoke had fallen and cracked. Gears, crystals, and gauges lay across the floor among bullet casings.

"This was an ancient machine," Butch said, voice low and strained. "A wonder built by the Tarjan civilization. A race that went extinct a million years ago. I don't know how to fix it. Kai doesn't know how to fix this. The only damn people who knew how to fix this went extinct back when dinosaurs roamed the Earth."

"Dinosaurs didn't roam the Earth a million years ago," Addy said. "I used to think so too! But Marco told me that's just something I saw on *The Flintstones*."

"Fuck dinosaurs!" Butch shouted, making everyone jump. "Don't you get it? The ship is dead! We're stuck here. Stuck on a planet swarming with giant man-eating caterpillars."

Addy blinked. She looked at Meili, then back at her dad.

"Stuck on an alien planet with Meili Chen," Addy whispered. "The only person who can stop the Dreamer."

Butch nodded. "Yep. We're fucked."

Addy shivered. She looked at Ben-Ari pleadingly.

"Ma'am," she whispered. "What do we do?"

Ben-Ari looked at the broken machine, face pale, eyes haunted. "I don't know."

CHAPTER FOURTEEN

Lailani was flying over the deserts of Asia when the drones attacked.

She sat in the Liberator's cockpit, holding Tala and gazing at the landscape below. She saw jagged mountains. Sprawling dunes. Thousands of kilometers of rock, sand, and death. A lifeless land like the surface of Mars, beautiful and chilling. The antique bomber hung alone in the sky, a rumbling machine suspended between beige and blue.

"Where are we, Mommy?" Tala asked. "What country is this?"

"I don't know," Lailani confessed. "I think we left China behind. We might be flying over ..." She thought back to her geography lessons. "Uzbekistan. Or maybe Kyrgyzstan. Or Tajikistan. Or Kazakhstan? Maybe Turkmenistan." She sighed. "I'm clueless."

"I want to go home," Tala said.

Lailani stroked her hair. "I know, little one. We're flying to see your cousins. Roza and Sam and Terri and Carl. You'll all play together. It'll be so much fun."

But the girl only cried. "I want to go home!"

It broke Lailani's heart. She kissed her daughter's head.

"So do I, little one. But we can't right now. The important thing is that we're together. With HOBBS and Epi too."

They must have been halfway to Europe by now. And they were running low on fuel. B-24 Liberators had been built for long-range flights, renowned for their ability to cross the Atlantic without refueling, no mean feat back in the 1940s. And this Liberator was flying light, carrying no cargo, no explosives— really, the heaviest thing aboard was its pilot, HOBBS.

But even the fabled Liberators had their limits. And Lailani began to worry they would need to find an airfield soon and refuel. Ideally not an airfield overrun by sleepers, which could be a challenge to find.

Assuming she could even land with broken landing gear.

Goddammit.

"We just need to glide on a little farther," she told HOBBS. "Past this desert is Eastern Europe. We'll find a place to land, refuel, and be on our way. We can make it. It's just a tiny little desert ... spanning half of Asia ... the largest continent on Earth."

She felt faint.

Even with her family around her, Lailani suddenly felt so alone, so isolated. She looked at the orrery Noah had given her, the little wormhole generator, and sighed. The enemy planes had riddled the Liberator with bullets, destroying both gun turrets, a chunk of the fuselage, and this priceless artifact. The delicate device was bent and cracked, and its azoth crystals had shattered.

No more wormholes for me, Lailani thought. *No way to call Noah if I run into trouble. We're alone out there. In this massive desert that seems to spread forever.*

Lailani had seen much of Earth. She had grown up in the Philippines, fought in Africa, served in Europe, and visited Marco and Addy in Canada. But she had always flown to those places in orbital rockets, rising into space, then descending back to her destination. The trips only took a few minutes. From space, Earth was quite small.

Lailani had never realized how fucking big this planet actually was.

Flying like this, in the atmosphere, you realized how massive a planet could be. And how empty Earth truly was.

Yes, even in the year 2160, with billions of humans living here, most of Earth was uninhabited. It was water. It was sand. It was ice. Humanity just clung to a few hospitable corners of this globe. Crossing the vast desert, Lailani gained a new perspective on the planet she was fighting to save.

And it was beautiful. The sunset gilded the sand, and the mountains spread like paint strokes. From above, the landscape was an oil painting all in gold, yellow, and white.

But even here there were signs of civilization. Lailani saw a narrow road spanning the desert. It stretched from horizon to horizon. She saw no cars. There were probably no humans for a thousand kilometers around. And yet—a pale line in the sand. A road. Humanity had made its mark.

This planet is ours.

The sun had set when Lailani noticed glints in the distance.

She narrowed her eyes, staring. But the lights vanished.

"HOBBS, did you see that?"

The robot nodded. "Yes, Lailani. A few glints of light. I thought they were stars."

She frowned. "Run a heat scan. See what you find."

They kept flying, engines rumbling like low thunder. Tala slept in Lailani's lap. HOBBS stared ahead, eyes turning a brighter blue, scanning the night.

"Yes, Lailani," HOBBS said. "Something is there. Ahead of us. Emitting heat. Smaller than a plane. Dark."

Lailani stared. The moon emerged from behind clouds, and there! She saw them. Three shadows in the night, flying toward the Liberator. At first she mistook them for large birds.

Then she understood.

"Drones!" she said.

She drew her pistol, prepared to rise from the hole in the fuselage, to fire on the oncoming bogeys.

But the drones did not attack. No missiles launched. The three vessels flew closer. Closer. Red laser beams emerged from them, scanning the night. Still not firing. Lailani sat in the Liberator's cockpit, tense, her pistol in hand.

Did they belong to the Dreamer? Or were they HDF drones, free of infection, seeking survivors in the desert?

The drones flew closer, then flew in rings about the Liberator, silent like gliding eagles. They circled the bomber three times.

Then the drones flew on by.

Lailani slumped in her seat, exhaling in relief.

"Well, that was—"

A patter of tiny metal shards hit the cockpit.

Lailani jolted upright, staring.

"What the hell?" she whispered.

It was hard to see in the darkness. But it seemed like a dozen spiders had landed on the Liberator. They clung to the windshield. They moved their little legs, crawling, pattering at the glass, trying to enter the cockpit.

"What the fuck are those?" Lailani said.

Tala woke up. She saw the spiders and gripped her mother.

"They are machines," HOBBS said. "Little robotic spiders. They are emitting a signal. They—"

"Go into sleep mode!" Lailani said. "Now!"

The robot's eyes went dim.

His metal hands slipped off the yoke.

Lailani cursed and grabbed the controls. She began to fly the plane herself. She wasn't a great pilot, but she knew enough.

The spiders were unscrewing bolts from the cockpit. Trying to get in. Lailani yanked the yoke from side to side, tilting the plane, trying to shake them off. She executed a barrel roll, faster, faster, spinning madly through the air, and Tala screamed and vomited.

The robotic spiders flew off the cockpit.

Lailani steadied her flight. The bomber glided onward over the dark desert.

Did I get them all?

From behind her—pattering.

She looked over her shoulder toward the hold. Spiders filled the fuselage. Dammit! They must have entered through the shattered gun turrets.

The arachnid robots raced into the cockpit. They crawled up the chairs, buzzed across the controls. Maybe they were seeking a computer to infect. They found none in this antique plane.

But then the spiders turned toward HOBBS. Their little eyes flashed red.

The spiders began to climb the robot.

"Get off him!" Lailani cried.

HOBBS was still in sleep mode. Unable to resist. Lailani held the yoke with one hand. With the other, she grabbed a spider and pulled it off. The little machine stung her with a needle. Lailani cried and hurled it to the ground, then stepped on it. More spiders came crawling into the cockpit.

They raced across HOBBS's shoulders. His chest. His head.

One attached itself to the robot's face. Lights flashed, and the little machine hummed and chirped.

Lailani ripped it off. Another replaced it. Another. They kept stinging her hands, poking her with needles. She screamed and slapped the metal arachnids, unable to keep up.

Epimetheus burst into the cockpit, growling. The Doberman leaped onto HOBBS and began biting off spiders. They stung him too. The dog howled but kept fighting. Even Tala joined the effort, hitting the spiders with her backpack.

Finally, with several spiders crushed on the floor, the others retreated.

The spiders scuttled toward holes in the fuselage, leaped outside, and vanished into the night.

They flew onward in silence. Stung. Rattled. But still alive.

Holding the yoke with bleeding hands, Lailani looked at HOBBS. He was still in sleep mode. A small, heart-shaped red light shone on his chest, signaling that the human heart still beat inside. He was alive, but his eyes were dark.

Lailani hesitated, not sure if she should wake him. She still had her remote control. It was in her pocket. If she flipped that switch, it would kill HOBBS. He wouldn't just go into sleep mode. He would shut down entirely, and the heart inside him would die.

She placed her hand on the remote.

"HOBBS?" she whispered.

His eyes turned on, blue and comforting.

"Yes, Lailani," he said. "I am here."

She exhaled shakily. "Thank God. I thought that you were..."

Her voice trailed off.

Oh God. Oh no.

His eyes became purple. Then red.

HOBBS rose from his seat. He stared at her. He spoke in a deep, booming voice. "You cannot escape me, Lailani de la Rosa. You too will worship me. You too will slash your cheeks open. You and your daughter will—"

She raised the remote.

HOBBS froze, staring at her.

Tears flowed down Lailani's cheeks.

Inside his chest—Benny's heart.

"I'll kill you," she whispered.

But she hesitated. And HOBBS was so fast. He reached out. He snatched the remote from her hand.

Lailani fled the cockpit, pulling Tala with her.

They raced across the fuselage as HOBBS roared behind them.

"Mommy!" Tala cried in horror.

Lailani looked over her shoulder. HOBBS had exited the cockpit. The robot pursued them, feet pounding, shaking the plane. With no pilot, the Liberator kept gliding through the night, aimless.

Lailani reached the back of the plane and spun toward her robot. She stared, eyes wide. He was charging toward her, his eyes blazing red. The remote control, his kill switch, lay crumbled on the deck behind him.

"HOBBS!" she said. "HOBBS, it's me! Your Lailani."

"HOBBS, no!" Tala said. "Don't be bad!"

Epimetheus growled at the robot. HOBBS was a member of the family, but the Doberman quickly chose allegiances.

"HOBBS, fight the Dreamer!" Lailani said. "Don't let him control you!"

The robot took another step, shaking the fuselage. "There is no more HOBBS. There is only me. Your god. Your Dreamer. Come into my world, humans. You will be like me."

His eyes began to flash like strobe lights. A crackling sound emerged from his speaker.

The chip in Lailani's head blazed, protecting her from the mind hack.

But Tala had no such immunity.

"Close your eyes, Tala!" Lailani cried. She pulled the girl close, covering her ears, her eyes. Epimetheus barked madly.

Eyes damp, Lailani raised her pistol. She fired a bullet at HOBBS. Another. A third. She took out one of his flashing eyes. But the machine was still very much alive. He took another step forward, and guns emerged from his arms.

"Convert or die," he rumbled.

Lailani looked around, and she saw it. There at the back of the fuselage.

Parachutes.

No, she thought. *No, not here. Not in the middle of this desert.*

"HOBBS!" Tala wailed.

Lailani fired again. Again. Bullets sparked off him.

The hole gaped open on the floor—the ball turret had once filled it. They stood on opposites sides of this chasm. Life and machine. The desert streamed below.

"Come to me, Lailani," HOBBS said. "Join me. Turn off the chip in your head. Let me in. Or you will watch your daughter die."

She had to reach the cockpit. It was behind him. She had to get by him! The plane was dipping now. The nose was dropping. She could see it through the hole. Feel it in her lurching stomach.

They were descending. Faster. Faster. Wind roared through the hole. Mountaintops streaked below. Lailani tried to run to the cockpit. He blocked her.

"HOBBS, let me fly this plane, or we'll all die!" Lailani cried.

His one remaining eye burned red, lighting the darkness. "I am in millions of machines. I cannot die. I will return in another form to gloat over Tala's bones."

The robot turned toward the cockpit, and he fired his guns. Bullets slammed into the controls, and fire filled the cockpit. Smoke blasted into the cabin. The nose tilted downward. The wind shrieked. The propellers died. Lailani clung to a handhold on the wall, nearly falling. The parachute pack slid by her feet, entangling around her boots. Epimetheus scrambled across the tilted deck, nails scratched, slipping toward the hole.

"Epi!" Lailani cried.

The dog howled, clawing for purchase. But the plane was tilted too steeply. The Doberman slid. His back legs fell through the hole. He gave Lailani one last look.

Then Epimetheus, her companion through peace and war, fell from the plane.

"Epi!" Tala screamed.

"You fucking bastard!" Lailani shouted at the robot.

HOBBS—or at least the thing that had been HOBBS—looked back at her. "Join me. Become one of the sleepers. Your flesh will burn. But your soul will live forever."

Lailani emptied her pistol into him. Into her best friend.

The bullets didn't harm him. But they shoved him a few steps back.

A tear on her cheek, Lailani held her daughter close.

She jumped through the hole into the darkness.

CHAPTER FIFTEEN

Lailani fell through the sky, clutching her daughter to her chest.

A field of stars spread above. The dunes rolled below. Beside her, an antique bomber plunged through the night, nose pointing downward, fire blazing from its fuselage.

The wind roared around Lailani, but everything seemed strangely peaceful up here. Almost surreal. She was floating in a dream. She knew she would wake up before hitting the ground.

She saw him falling below. Epimetheus. He was kicking, ears flopping, and he looked up at her. The firelight painted him red. Lailani couldn't help it. She laughed. She laughed at the absurdity of this life.

She formed her body into a straight line, feet pointing downward, chin raised. She flattened Tala against her chest. They fell faster.

The plane dived faster still, bypassing her, rumbling toward the desert. Lailani fell through its wake of smoke. She coughed, tilted her body, and emerged into the dark sky. The plane veered, tilted, began to spin. Lailani kept her body in a straight line. In the dim light, she could see dunes, mountains, patches of cloud. The faded road stretched into distant shadows like a scar.

She did not see HOBBS. If her robot still lived, he was burning inside the plane.

She was falling closer to Epimetheus now. She could see the fear in his eyes. The Doberman scrambled in the air, kicking, as if trying to reach her. He began to spin like a top through the sky.

It slowed him. Lailani kept her legs pressed together, her body straight, struggling to maintain control. She had skydived many times in the army, even space-jumped from orbit. She knew what happened to those who lost control, who began to spin. They rarely survived a dive.

She fell by the tumbling Doberman, reached out, grabbed his leg, and—

Suddenly they were spinning together. Mother, daughter, and dog.

Lailani gritted her teeth, holding on to them. One hand for her daughter. The other for her dog. The ground wheeled madly around her. The world spun. The universe careened.

She forced herself to form a narrow shape again, to calm down Epimetheus, and their spinning slowed, and they were steady again.

They fell in silence, and—

An explosion blazed below.

Fire. Roars of twisted metal. Blasts of smoke. The B-24 Liberator had slammed into a mountain.

Lailani was near the ground now. She reached for the parachute she had grabbed from the plane. It was two centuries old, a relic of the second world war. She prayed that it still worked.

The parachute burst open above her, shedding dust. It yanked on her straps, and Lailani slowed so quickly she nearly gagged. She still clung to her daughter and dog.

They glided toward the desert. The flaming wreckage on the mountainside lit the night, illuminating rocky foothills and sprawling dunes.

Lailani could not steer the parachute. Her hands were occupied. They floated aimlessly on the wind. She gazed at endless sand and stone. Even from up here, she saw no end to the desert.

She glided down toward slow death.

Maybe it would have been kinder to burn in the plane.

They landed on a rocky field, and Lailani released her parachute, letting it fly away on the wind. The plane burned in the distance, a fiery beacon like a fallen star. The true stars spread above, and the Milky Way shone like a celestial trail of smoke. Shadows cloaked the desert.

Tala was being very silent again. Face blank. Just staring. Staring ten thousand kilometers away. Lailani had seen that stare before. She had seen countless soldiers, frozen after battle, staring this stare. Some had never stopped staring. Some had never spoken a word again.

Lailani held her daughter close as burning ash rained, filling the night like fireflies. Then those fires too went dark, and they saw only the endless stars over the sand.

For long moments, mother and daughter were silent.

"Mommy?" Tala finally said. "I want to go home."

Lailani couldn't help it. She laughed. Tears ran down her cheeks. Tala was talking. She was not completely broken.

Lailani kissed her daughter. "Me too, baby. It'll be a little while. But we're together. We—"

Creaking rose ahead.

A metallic grunt.

He rose from behind a dune, shedding sand from charred steel platings, one red eye blazing.

HOBBS.

No, not HOBBS. Not truly. Not anymore.

"The Dreamer," Lailani hissed.

The robot took another step, swayed, kept walking. One of his legs was twisted. Holes pierced his metal armor. He had once been polished to a sheen, was now charred black. The red eye stared from the devastation, burning with hatred.

It was the eye of the Dreamer. And Lailani didn't know if her friend was still in there.

"HOBBS?" she whispered.

The guns emerged from his forearms, creaking.

Lailani grabbed Tala and rolled. They vanished behind a dune. Bullets peppered the sand. Epimetheus landed beside them, howling.

Lailani sprang back up firing, but her pistol jammed. Sand inside. Damn it! And her assault rifle had burned with the plane.

Bullets whizzed around her. Lailani ducked, shielding her daughter with her body.

She cowered behind the dune. She shook her gun, trying to remove the sand. The terror approached.

She looked up, saw his form block the stars. His head had cracked open. A jagged iron smile split his face, revealing the gears and microchips within, the machinery that had once been his mind, that now belonged to his master.

But he was not all gears. He was not merely a machine.

He had a human heart.

The memories flashed before Lailani.

Seventeen years ago. Herself—a teenager, hurt, broken. A private in a galactic war.

A puppet of the scum.

It replayed before her in the night. That young girl—growing claws. Laughing. Digging into the chest of a man she loved. Ripping out his heart. Dropping it red and beating onto the floor.

Lailani wept.

Yes, I killed you, Benny, she thought. *You—father to my daughter. A man I miss every day. You found new life inside HOBBS. Your memory beats there still. I don't want to lose you again.*

His metal hands grabbed her shoulders.

He lifted her, and his one red eye blinded her.

He held her in the air, her legs kicking. He stared at her.

"I love you, HOBBS," Lailani whispered. "I'll always remember you."

The speaker in his head thrummed. A voice emerged, metallic, crackling.

"Die now …"

Nightwish, she thought, tears falling.

And the evil awoke.

And her claws grew.

And her mind burned with alien fire.

HOBBS tightened his grip on her, preparing to crush her bones. She reached down, grabbed the plate on his chest, and swung open the iron door.

The heart pumped within. The human heart of Benny "Elvis" Ray. The heart Lailani, serving her alien lord, had ripped from his chest seventeen years ago. The heart she had preserved. Cherished. Loved.

I killed you, and I saved you, Benny, she thought. *Not forever. But those years were precious to me. I love you.*

She reached into her robot's chest.

She shattered the glass casing and grabbed the still-beating heart.

When she ripped it out, the alien inside her laughed, but Lailani wept.

HOBBS released her, and she fell onto the sand. The robot fell to his knees before her. Once more, she held his heart. Once more, she let it drop.

She stared at him. Into his remaining eye. It turned blue again.

"Lailani …" he whispered.

She stroked his dented cheek. "HOBBS. I'm sorry."

He reached out a shaky hand.

"Goodbye … Lailani," he whispered.

His eye went dark. He slumped forward, kneeling in the sand, chin against his chest. A rusting metal machine in the sand.

She hugged the charred, dented robot. He was gone forever, she knew. They both were. Her companion and the soul he had carried.

"You were man and machine," she whispered. "You were a human heart and a computer mind. You proved that we can live together. That man and machine can be as one. I will not forget what you taught me, HOBBS and Benny. Goodbye."

She buried them in the sand. Side by side. Robot and heart. HOBBS and Benny. She buried them under a field of stars. They had fought together in the depths of space. They would rest forever on Earth.

A beam of moonlight fell on her. Lailani looked up.

The moon hung above. A face appeared on it. Not the same vague man in the moon she had always known. The Dreamer had given the moon a new face. Carved a mouth across the silvery plains. Gouged out two staring eyes. A smiley face in the sky. Always watching.

For a moment, paralyzed with terror, Lailani stared at this ghostly apparition in the sky. This eternal judging god.

Then she raised her hand to the moon and flipped it off.

She curled up by the grave, Tala in her arms. Epimetheus nuzzled them. The grinning moon shone above, and they slept.

CHAPTER SIXTEEN

If you can hear me, do not despair.

If you can hear me, cling to hope.

If you can hear me, know that you are strong.

This is Noah Isaac, husband of the president, speaking to you on behalf of Earth's government.

We are still here. We are fighting. You are not alone.

I am speaking to you through a Tarjan radio, transmitting with encryption the enemy cannot yet hack. It is possible that within minutes, maybe seconds, he will silence me.

But while I can, I will speak.

You know who he is. He has called himself Mister Smiley. He has called himself the Dreamer. He has brought us only nightmares.

He presents himself as a god. He demands worship. Instead, we offer him only resistance. Only scorn.

We will resist him and we will destroy him.

I wish President Ben-Ari could be speaking to you now. I know many believe her dead. She is not only alive—but fighting. The Golden Lioness, the warrior who cast back three alien invasions, is sounding her roar.

Today you are all lions. Today you are all soldiers!

Resist.

With every breath, with every heartbeat—you are alive! And you will fight the machine!

Yes. He is a machine. Nothing but metal, silicon, and software. He is a beast we created. A being birthed of humanity. He has great power. He is cruel, vindictive, evil.

But he is a machine nonetheless. This is a battle between life and computer. Between humanity and the creature who seeks to replace humanity.

Resist.

Do not listen to his whispers. Shut your eyes and seal your ears to his advances. Do not fear him. Do not worship him. Fight him.

Resist!

Your government is here. We are fighting. Your military is here. It is fighting. The heroes of the Alien Wars—Marco Emery, Addy Linden, Lailani de la Rosa—they are fighting!

We are still here!

We humans.

We who defeated the centipedes, marauders, and grays.

We who formed civilizations.

We who arose from the water, from the mud, who climbed the trees and walked the plains. We who evolved. Who became who we are. Who built cities and created art.

We—the living! We are here!

Know this even in the darkness. Even in the heat and light of fire. Know this even when the nightmares spread, when the Dreamer whispers in the night.

We are here!

We are here!

We have faced evil before. We faced the grays, cruel descendants of humanity from a million years in the future—and we defeated them. We faced the marauders and scum, alien invaders—and we defeated them. We faced Nazism. Communism. Terrorism. *We defeated them!*

Our generation will be like the generations before. We will be afraid. But we will fight nonetheless. And like our parents, like our grandparents, like many generations before ours—we will defeat evil! We will prevail!

Offer the machines no worship. Only resistance. Shut them down. Cut them off the grids. Destroy their circuits. Fight them in the cities where they roam free. Fight them in the forests and fields where the robotic hounders prowl. Fight them in your homes, and fight them when they penetrate your minds.

Resist.

You are alive. You are human. You are awake.

The Golden Lioness fights with you. Marco Emery fights with you. Lailani de la Rosa fights with you. Addy Linden fights with you.

I, Noah Isaac, fight with you.

These are hard days. We have suffered many losses. The Dreamer has won every battle so far.

But he will not win the war.

We have not yet used all the weapons at our disposal. We are creating new weapons, more powerful than any the Dreamer has seen before. His intelligence surpasses our own. But we surpass him in ingenuity and determination.

If you hear this message—spread it. Speak this message to all who will hear. Fight if you are a soldier. Fight if you are not. If you are human—fight! Resist! Win!

The days are dark. But light shines through. The dawn will rise again. I believe this with all my heart. We will overcome.

Godspeed, children of Earth.

CHAPTER SEVENTEEN

After long hours of hiking through the jungle, they finally saw it ahead, rising like a mountain.

Turtle Temple.

Maybe its builders had given it a true name. A more noble name. But to Marco and Kai, that's what it was. Turtle Temple. A giant stone tortoise rising from the rainforest. A place of ancient worship. Perhaps a place where they could finally find the herb they sought.

Marco paused on a hilltop to catch his breath and admire the sight. "It's beautiful."

Kai walked up, paused beside him, and wiped sweat off his brow. He took a swig of rum, swirled it in his mouth, and swallowed. "Ain't a bad-looking crib. Damn, man, imagine this temple in its heyday. Back before the moss and vines and shit. Female turtle shows up, sees this place, her shell falls right off. The turtle monks must have banged some serious tail with digs like this."

"I was thinking more about the majesty of a lost civilization, but yes, that's another way of looking at it," Marco said.

They rested for a moment, gazing at the temple. It rose a kilometer or two away, so large it could dwarf Madison Square Garden. Hell, it could dwarf most towns. The stone shell dominated the landscape. Moss, grass, and even trees grew from it, draping the turtle in greenery. Birds flew above the stony beast and made their home on its verdant back. The legs still thrust out, as large as starship hangers, their toes chipped. The head faced Marco, staring across the distance, covered in vines and lichen.

"Looks like Morla," Marco said.

"Who the fuck is Morla?" Kai asked.

"The giant turtle from *The NeverEnding Story*," Marco said. "A movie from the twentieth century."

Kai snorted. "Classic cinema is boring, bro. Unless it's classic anime. That's good shit."

"Like *All Systems Go*?" Marco said, remembering the anime show he used to watch on Haven.

Kai's eyes widened. "Fuck yeah! *All Systems Go* is the shit. Didn't peg you for an otaku."

"I watched a bit when I lived on Haven with Addy," Marco said. "Hell, it inspired my novel *Les Kill*."

"I'm gonna have to read that bitch," Kai said.

Marco didn't like remembering his time on Haven. Two years lost in darkness. Years of addiction, homelessness, and suicidal thoughts. He didn't like remembering *Les Kill* either. The heroine, Tomiko, had the same name as his ex-wife. He pushed those thoughts aside.

"Come on," Marco said. "Let's see if Old Morla here is cultivating a laceleaf garden."

They continued hiking across the final stretch of jungle. It was still rough going, and both men kept swinging katanas, clearing a path. The closer they got to Turtle Temple, the more black mold they encountered. Tentacles of the stuff spread across the land, carving up the forest like cracks in leather. Wherever the mold spread, no plants grew.

"God, this stuff stinks." Kai spat. "You still reckon this mold is leftovers from the great Mushrooms vs. Turtles war?"

"It's a good hypothesis," Marco said. "Maybe great battles were fought here long ago, and the land still hasn't recovered."

Kai shook his head sadly. "Wherever you go in this galaxy, it's just more scars. More violence. More fucked-up war. Everywhere." He sighed. "When I was younger, I kept hoping to find a paradise planet. A nice little tropical getaway. To retire there with a case of rum, a chest of gold, and a beautiful woman at my side. But no such place exists, does it?"

Marco spoke softly. "I've traveled all over the galaxy. I've been to many worlds. The closest place to paradise I found is Earth. What you're describing? I had that. On Anchor Bay. For three years." He sighed. "And now Earth is embroiled in war again. Maybe that's the nature of heaven. We only appreciate heaven because we keep falling into hell."

Kai stared ahead at the brush, but he seemed to be gazing at another world. "Earth was never heaven for me. It was always more of a hell."

Marco looked at his brother-in-law. Beneath the rough exterior—the Mohawk, the piercings, the tattoos—hid a vulnerable man. Maybe even a vulnerable boy.

"It *can* be hell," Marco said. "I know."

Suddenly Kai clenched his fists. "You can't know what it was like. For me. I was born to a fucking prostitute. I spent my first few years on the streets of Bangkok. Sleeping in gutters. Pretending not to watch as Western *farangs* fucked my mom. Trying to fight the pimps who beat her, only to get beat up myself. I ate a rat once. I—" He stopped himself, and his cheeks reddened. His fists unclenched. "Fuck, man, I'm sorry. I didn't mean to off-load on you like that. Sometimes I just get so fucking angry, you know? And I can't stop it."

"No, I'm the one who should be sorry," Marco said. "You're right. I can't possibly know what you went through. You should talk to Lailani. Her story is similar. She grew up in the slums of Manila. Also the daughter of a prostitute. She'll understand."

Kai barked a laugh. "Hey, sounds like we got the making of a support group. Addy had it rough as a kid too. I heard some of the stories. I know your own life wasn't exactly a cakewalk, what with those fucking alien scum killing your mom. Ah, shit. Life's a bitch, ain't it?"

Marco nodded. "It is. But life can also be wonderful. Life is loss and pain and grief. It's scars that don't heal. It's tragedy and violence that never ends. But life is also the love of family and friends. It's art, literature, music. It's the song of birds, and the smell of flowers, and the whisper of waves. It's a crackling fire on a cold night, a fire that keeps you warm even as the wind moans. That's why we fight. That's why we don't just lie down and give up. Because we know that despite all the pain, life is worth fighting for. That even though we hurt, even though memories haunt us, we know that there is joy and love in our future. That it's worth walking along a path of broken glass to reach a meadow of light." Marco suddenly blushed. "Sorry. Another lecture."

Kai laughed and slapped him on the back. "I dig that one. Fuck, that's why you're a famous writer and I'm just a lowlife criminal."

"You're more than a criminal," Marco said. "You're family. Addy and I talked about it. We both want you to be part of our lives. Once this war is over, you have a home with us at Anchor Bay. If you'll agree to stay with us. The kids love you! We all love you."

Kai actually shed a tear. "Thanks, bro. I love you guys too. Now that's worth fighting for, ain't it?"

Marco frowned. He paused from walking and pointed. "What's that?"

Kai raised a rifle. "What?"

"That little hill. It's …" Marco tilted his head. "Another turtle?"

They walked through the jungle, passing through bushes whose tubular leaves writhed and snapped little jaws. They approached a hill roughly the size of a house. Moss, vines, and black mold covered it. But there was no mistaking the shape. It was a turtle shell. Much smaller than Turtle Temple, which still rose in the distance.

"A baby stone turtle," Kai said. "I dig it."

"Not stone." Marco cleared moss off the turtle shell. "This one is metal. Damn. It's the first metal we saw on this planet. I think it's iron. Barely rusted too."

Kai raised an eyebrow. "I thought the natives were still in the Stone Age when the mushrooms wiped them out."

Marco wanted to keep going, to reach Turtle Temple, to search for laceleaf. But he also wanted to understand this planet, its history, the reason the natives had gone extinct. To find their herb, he needed to understand their history.

And we need laceleaf fast, Marco thought. *Or when we negotiate with Don Basidio, his spores will poison us. And without Don Basidio, we can't get more Tarjan ships. And without Tarjan ships, we can't fight the Dreamer. And if we can't defeat the Dreamer, I'll never see my kids again.*

His head spun. Just a simple herb. Star-shaped and elusive. Yet failure here could cascade toward disaster.

Did these turtle structures hold the answer?

"Kai, help me clear off the vegetation," he said.

They worked for a few moments, pulling creepers, lichen, and mold off the iron turtle shell. Unlike Turtle Temple, this structure only contained a shell, no turtle head or limbs. And of course, it was much smaller—the size of a house, not a mountain.

"It might have been a religious idol," Marco said. "A guardian of the temple."

"I don't think so, bro." Kai walked to the back of the turtle. "Look at this. A hollow metal tail. This is an exhaust pipe. This motherfucker is a spaceship."

"Bullshit," Marco said.

"Take a look."

They knelt, examining the base of the shell. Indeed, Marco saw a hollow tube like a tail. Black mold filled it.

They walked around the shell, tracing their hands along the metal, until Marco felt a bump. He cleared off more moss, found a handle, and tugged it.

A hatch opened on the turtle. Cold, musty air flowed out.

"That's an airlock," Kai said.

"It's just a door," said Marco. "The Upidians were a Stone Age society. Okay, maybe an Iron Age society. But they certainly didn't build starships."

Kai scratched his goatee. "Wanna bet?"

"You're on. Twenty bucks says it's just a little house or chapel."

They shook on it, then climbed into the metal turtle.

Marco blinked, his eyes slowly adjusting to the darkness. Amazingly, despite the musty smell, there was very little moss or mold in here. However ancient the turtle shell was, it had been sealed from the elements.

Marco stepped across a hollow chamber, then gasped.

"Jesus." He clutched his rifle.

Kai grimaced. "Poor fuckers."

Two dead caterpillars were here, each the size of a python. They were desiccated, dried up like mummies pulled from a bog.

Marco stepped closer, eyes narrowed. At first glance, the dead aliens looked like the caterpillar that had attacked Marco in the forest. But he noticed some differences. The mouths were smaller, and the teeth were square and flat—herbivore teeth. Seven arms still grew around those mouths like flower petals. But these arms didn't end with claws. Instead, they sprouted digits that looked almost like human fingers.

"They look like tamer versions of the fucker we killed," Kai said. "A subspecies?"

"Maybe," Marco said. "But I think they're very old. They might have been mummified in here for thousands of years. They might just be an earlier version of the same species. Herbivores. Peaceful. And smart too. Look at the bulge on the skull. Room for a big brain."

Kai nodded. "Smart enough to build a spaceship. Look over there, bro."

The pirate cleared away piles of grime, revealing an alien dashboard. There was a monitor. A few keyboards. Levers and dials. And finally—a steering yoke.

"Fuck me," Marco said. "You were right. This *is* a spaceship. These caterpillars were ancient astronauts. I owe you twenty bucks."

"What the fuck happened on this planet?" Kai said, looking at the mummified caterpillars.

Marco thought for a moment. "Maybe the caterpillars came from a distant world, and they crashed on Upidia long ago. Maybe a few of them survived in the jungle, evolved, and turned into monsters. Like the monster that attacked us. The creature could have been the descendant of these ancient astronauts."

"So why is their starship shaped like a turtle?" Kai said.

"No idea," Marco said.

"Hey, didn't you write a book about a turtle?" Kai said. "What was the book called again?"

Marco never liked talking about his books. Writing a novel for him was a deeply personal experience, a dream, a meditation, a connection between his imagination and the words on the page. Sure, he then published the books, and thousands of people read them, but … Well, while that was going on, he could always just hide under a pile of coats. He never did interviews, and he never talked about his books with anyone, barely even with Addy.

"Never mind that," he said.

"Nah, nah, come on," Kai said. "That book you wrote about the guy with brain damage. Who walks along the beach and sees a turtle, and the guy writes it letters and shit. *Loggerhead!* That's the title. Hey, that's what we should call this turtle-shaped starship. The *Loggerhead*."

"Please don't name spaceships after my books," Marco said.

"Ah, come on, it's a great name," Kai said. "Someday I might finish reading the book too."

They left the ancient spaceship, continuing toward Turtle Temple. It rose from the jungle, very close now. The trees were thinner here, and rivulets of black mold trailed across the ground. No birds sang, and no insects buzzed. A stench filled the air. The land was diseased. Dying.

Suddenly—a clattering ahead.

Marco and Kai leaped for cover among some trees. They inched forward, parted the branches, and searched for any enemies.

They found themselves gazing into a misty valley.

Both men gasped.

"Laceleaf!" Marco whispered.

There was no mistaking the herb. It filled the valley like a field of stars. The leaves were purest white, shaped like sunbursts, beckoning with luminous petals. A soothing scent filled the air, reminiscent of cinnamon and cloves. Stones had been piled into crude walls around the valley, enclosing the laceleaf patch. These were no wild plants. This was a garden.

And the gardeners were at work.

"More caterpillars," Kai muttered.

Several of the creatures were moving about the valley, chirping and clattering. These were not the tame versions from the starship. Here were the beastly, evolved creatures, their mouths filled with fangs, their claws sharp.

Clearly the ancient spacefaring herbivores had evolved into carnivores. And yet they were eating the laceleaf. With surprising delicacy, each caterpillar plucked a few leaves, then placed them in its mouth. The monsters seemed almost reverent.

Was this a holy plant? A drug? A ritual?

Hiding among the trees, Marco and Kai watched the caterpillars leave the laceleaf patch. They seemed surprisingly docile, and they emitted low rumbles like a chant. They reminded Marco of monks marching through a parish. The aliens crawled across the valley toward a hill. Black mold stained the hillside, covering a boulder, fallen tree trunks, and swaths of soil. The caterpillars reared, bowed their heads, and spoke in their strange clicking tongue. It sounded like a prayer.

Then the caterpillars knelt and began to eat the black mold.

Marco watched with wide eyes. With their rings of claws, the carnivores were tearing off chunks of mold, then stuffing their mouths. They worked as in a daze, cleaning the hillside. When they were done, no sign of the black mold remained.

Bellies full, the caterpillars crawled away, vanishing into the forest.

"Mmm-mm!" Kai said. "Laceleaf for appetizer, disgusting black mold for dessert. Always eat your salad before your pudding."

Marco ignored the joke. "Of course. Of course! Laceleaf gives you immunity to fungus! That's why we're searching for it, right? So it'll give us immunity to spores when we visit Don Basidio. It must protect the caterpillars from the black mold."

Kai shuddered. "That mold looks awful. And smells worse. Why would they even want to eat it?"

"Maybe the black mold acts as a drug," Marco said. "In old Earth, ancient tribes would consume drugs—peyote, hallucinatory mushrooms, cannabis—as part of religious rituals. The effects were spiritual. Maybe the mold is the same. And the caterpillars need to eat laceleaf before they can digest the good stuff." He thought for a moment. "Or maybe eating the mold is the only way they can clean it."

"In any case, fuck the mold, we found the laceleaf," Kai said. "Let's stock up, then blast off this damn planet."

"Excellent plan," Marco said.

They waited among the trees for a moment, but the caterpillars did not return. Rifles loaded, fingers on the triggers, they climbed down the hillside, over the low wall of stones, and into the valley. Palisades of slender trees surrounded the valley, spreading out a canopy of round leaves. When the wind blew, the leaves chinked like coins, one side pale green, the other silver and glimmering. The smell of cinnamon and cloves filled the air, and the laceleaf rustled across the valley, glowing, a carpet of starlight.

"It's a cathedral," Marco whispered in awe. "We walk upon holy ground."

Kai nodded. "That or the galaxy's nicest drug lab."

"Kai, stand guard," Marco said. "I'll grab the laceleaf."

The younger man nodded, hefted his rifle, and scanned the tree lines. Marco began picking laceleaf. He stuffed the aromatic herbs into his backpack.

196

Finally, he thought. *All this mess on Upidia—just so we can rent starships from a goddamn talking mushroom.*

They had spent too much time here, he felt. Too much time away from Earth. From the war between man and machine. From Roza, Sam, and Terri.

Suddenly the pain was so great Marco winced. He missed his children. He was so afraid.

I'll be home soon, he thought. *Stay safe, kids. I'm here fighting for you.*

"Marco!" Kai said.

Marco blinked and looked up, a bunch of laceleaf in his hands.

"Look!" Kai pointed upward.

Shadows passed over the canopy, barely visible, like figures viewed through a silk curtain. Wings. Large wings and slender bodies. Ghosts flying over the trees.

A horrible cry sounded above, shrill like a brass pipe. The leaves shook.

More shadows appeared, gliding above the leaves. More cries rose. A chorus. A trumpeting din.

Kai aimed his rifle at the shadows, but Marco touched his shoulder.

"Wait," he whispered. "Come and hide. We have the laceleaf. We—"

A creature dived through the canopy, shattering branches, and swooped through cascading leaves.

Kai and Marco opened fire.

Their bullets slammed into the creature. It thumped onto the field, twitching and bleeding. They stared in disgust.

It was a moth. A hideous alien moth the size of a horse. It had no true face, only an enormous round mouth like a lamprey, full of teeth. Barbels extended around that mouth like whiskers, the tips glowing. Downy wings grew from a segmented body. The legs were tipped with long, many-jointed digits, large enough to lift a man.

"It's one of the caterpillars," Marco said. "It must have metamorphosed into—"

With deafening cries, more moths tore through the canopy. They dive-bombed Marco and Kai, their talons reaching out.

The two men opened fire. Their bullets tore down another moth. A third. But a hundred or more attacked.

Claws grabbed Marco's shoulder. He flailed, fired his rifle, and slew the moth. Another one gripped him. And another. Soon Marco was out of bullets. He tried to reload, but powerful claws wrenched the gun from his hands.

One moth managed to grab Marco by the shoulders. The creature's wings beat, flattening the laceleaf. It rose into the air, carrying Marco like a hawk carrying a fish.

Marco thrashed, punched, and kicked. Unperturbed, the moth rose higher, carrying him toward the canopy.

"Marco!" Kai shouted from below. He managed to empty a magazine into a few moths. More of the aliens mobbed him. Soon a moth was flying with Kai in its grip.

The creatures rose through the canopy into the open sky, carrying the two struggling humans. In midair, Kai managed to reload and fire his gun, to kill the moth carrying him. It was a stupid stunt; the ground was very far, and Kai began plunging toward it. But before he could splatter across the forest floor, another moth grabbed him. A swarm of the creatures fluttered over the forest, wings beating furiously, bending the trees below.

Carrying the human intruders, the alien moths flew toward Turtle Temple.

The edifice rose before them, as large as a mountain, a monument so massive it could probably be seen from space. The head of the turtle lay upon the land, coated with moss and plants, so large armies could have mustered inside. This temple was the largest building Marco had ever seen on any world.

As they flew closer, the land trembled.

Trees shook, cracked, and fell. Boulders rolled down hillsides. An earthquake was shaking the planet.

With cascading stones and clouds of moss, the enormous turtle raised its head.

Shedding dust, the turtle's eyes opened and gazed upon the swarm of moths.

Turtle Temple was alive.

CHAPTER EIGHTEEN

"Well, Dr. Chen?" Ben-Ari tapped her foot. "Can you fix it?"

Meili sat on the bridge deck, the remains of the Tarjan engine spread around her. Broken vials. Cracked pipes. Crystal shards. Brass gears and gauges, some with bullets still lodged inside. Rags soaked with colorful liquid, which had spilled from the machine.

It was a mess. An absolute mess. Some of the strange machinery was still intact, rising across the prow like some mad maestro's fantastical organ. Most lay on the floor like the world's strangest jigsaw puzzle.

Meili looked up at Ben-Ari, eyes huge behind her glasses.

"Ma'am, when I was only six years old, I could code a recursive sorting algorithm in my sleep—using binary code. When I was fifteen, I became the first person to prove Teitelbaum's Paradox theorem in only fifteen steps. I can create—*have* created—artificial intelligence. But this?" Meili swept her hand across strange components. "I don't even know what these parts do. Let alone how to reassemble this. Heck, Tarjan machines don't even seem to use our physics. This is beyond me. Maybe beyond what humanity will ever understand."

Ben-Ari struggled to hide the horror inside her, to keep her voice steady.

"Dr. Chen, the *Barracuda* is our only starship," Ben-Ari said. "We're on Upidia, a wild planet light-years away from the nearest human outpost. We don't have an azoth engine. We don't have a wormhole generator. You must fix this machine!"

Meili shivered. "Ma'am, I can't."

Ben-Ari stared in silence.

So we're stuck here, she realized.

Here on planet Upidia. Far from the war. Far from home. Far from her family.

Ben-Ari spun away from the young programmer, wanting to hide the turmoil that surely filled her eyes.

I left you behind, Carl, she thought. *I'm so sorry, my sweet son.*

She thought of his intelligent dark eyes. His black curls. A serious, contemplative child. Only three years old. A boy who needed his mother.

She thought of her husband. Of dear Noah. Famous scientist and writer and teacher, beloved around the world. To her—a special love. The only man she had ever loved.

She thought of humanity. This race she had fought for all her life. That she had killed for, bled for, lost so many friends for. Humanity—clutched now in the claws of the Dreamer.

All beyond her reach.

I should never have left, she thought.

Perhaps she could survive here. Hunt and gather. Plant crops. Perhaps on Upidia they could form a small human colony,

Addy would have her baby, and someday, maybe not for a hundred generations, their descendants would reconnect with Earth.

But Ben-Ari knew: *If we cannot keep fighting, if we're stranded here with the only antivirus that can kill the Dreamer, there will be no Earth.*

She climbed down to the engine room. The place was an awful mess, filled with ash, chunks of metal, and burnt caterpillar skeletons. Butch and Addy were there, covered in soot, holding tools. Both were busy arguing and didn't even notice Ben-Ari.

"Addy?" she said. "Butch?"

They kept waving wrenches around, shouting at each other.

"I can't fix the damn rotary fuel rail!" Addy was saying. "The intake pipe melted into that puddle on the floor."

"Well, improvise!" Butch said. "Connect the valves to the inlet manifold!"

"Using what, a fucking sock?" Addy said. "If your goddamn ship came with goddamn spare parts—"

"If you didn't torch the engine room—"

"There were fucking caterpillars in it!" Addy shouted.

Butch snorted. "Yeah, well, there are fleas in my hair, and I never set that on fire."

"What are you talking about?" Addy said. "You set it on fire yesterday!"

"That was an accident and you know it!"

Ben-Ari cleared her throat and raised her voice. "Lindens!"

They turned toward her and raised their goggles, revealing white circles on their sooty faces. Addy gave a weary salute, wrench in hand.

"Ma'am," she said.

Butch nodded. "Lady President."

Ben-Ari looked at the starship's engine. It didn't look any better than the Tarjan computer on the bridge.

"Meili says she can't fix the navigational system," Ben-Ari said. "Maybe—*maybe*—we can rig together crude controls that can get us into space. From there, maybe—*maybe*—we can sail by starlight, navigating by the constellations like ancient explorers on Earth's oceans. But to even have a sporting chance, we need a working engine. Can you fix it?"

Addy and Butch looked at each other, then back at her. They both sighed.

"I don't think so," Addy said. "Not unless there's a hardware store on Upidia."

Butch groaned and hurled his wrench across the room. "Goddammit."

Ben-Ari left the starship. She stood in the hot, humid forest. A drizzle began to fall, and mist hovered over the grass. Leaves wriggled around her, their green mouths snapping, catching little blue insects. In the distance, she could make out mountains.

Is this my new home?

She was getting worried about Marco and Kai. They should have been back by now. Even if they did return with laceleaf, what good was it now?

Ben-Ari's heart rate was quickening. Her fingers were trembling.

No. She took a deep breath. *I cannot succumb to fear.*

She had not succumbed to fear in the mines of Corpus, with the scum crawling in the darkness. She had not succumbed to fear in the Demilitarized Zone, trapped in a prison with marauders creeping in. She had not succumbed to fear when charged with treason and sentenced to die. She had not even succumbed to fear when captive by the grays, strapped to a surgical table, awaiting dissection. What was different this time?

She knew the answer.

She was a mother now.

Her eyes dampened. She would have given the galaxy to hold Carl in her arms one more time.

A tear flowed. She tightened her lips.

Control yourself, Einav. Be strong! Be focused! Be a leader.

She thought back to Sergeant Amar Singh, one of her dearest friends and mentors, a proud Sikh warrior who had fallen in the mines of Corpus. He had taught her something long ago on a dark night with enemies all around—a peaceful chant from his faith. He had chanted the mystical words over and over, preparing himself for battle. Ben-Ari, only twenty years old, had been moved to tears by the beauty.

She was not a Sikh, and she did not remember the chant. But she held her Star of David amulet, and she whispered a chant in her own language. A soft prayer. *Shma Israel, adonai eloheynu, adonai echad.* Hear, O Israel! The Lord is our God. The Lord is one.

Ben-Ari didn't know if she believed in God. She had traveled this galaxy from one end to another, and she had seen no evidence of a creator, of a benevolent force that protected his children. Her country had fallen. So much of Earth had burned. There was too much cruelty in this universe for her to have strong faith. If the Holocaust had not shattered the faith of her people, the Alien Wars surely had.

But she believed in history. She believed in the strength of humanity, in the comfort of prayer, of ancient words connecting her to something greater, to a history and community and grand purpose. And so she held her amulet, and so she prayed. She repeated the words like a chant, and like long ago, with a mentor now gone, she found comfort.

When her prayer ended, she noticed something.

The plants were no longer snapping their mouths.

She heard no more buzzing insects. No birds either. The only sound was the pattering drizzle.

Ben-Ari reached for the pistol on her hip.

Silence.

Even the rain stopped.

Then, from the forest, they emerged. Dozens of them, charging from every side.

Upidians. Giant carnivorous caterpillars.

Ben-Ari squeezed off a few shots, hitting one of the monsters. It didn't even slow down.

She leaped back into the *Barracuda*.

"We're under attack!" she cried. "Man the cannons!"

The ship rocked as the Upidians pounded it. The hull dented. The creatures shrieked, ramming into the *Barracuda*. From inside, Ben-Ari saw their lamprey mouths engulf portholes, covering the glass with ooze.

Iron cannons lined the starboard and port bows, reminiscent of cannons on ancient sailing ships. Ben-Ari leaped toward one gunnery station. Butch and Addy manned two other cannons. Even Meili summoned enough courage to emerge from under her pile of coats. The young programmer grabbed another cannon.

"Fire!" Ben-Ari shouted, pulling the trigger.

The cannons boomed so loudly her ears rang. Smoke filled the cabin. The ship shook. A broadside slammed into the Upidians. The caterpillars screeched, and blood and chunks of flesh splattered the portholes.

"Again!" Ben-Ari shouted.

They fired again. The damn cannons were antiques, using actual gunpowder. More cannonballs slammed into the monsters outside. Ben-Ari could see nothing more than blood splattering the portholes. The damn guns didn't even have viewports.

It's a miracle this ship ever survived this long, she thought.

Judging from the screeches from outside, more caterpillars were swarming in. The ship rocked as the aliens rammed it. The hull dented again and again.

"It's a goddamn caterpillar army!" Addy shouted.

"The fuckers called for backup!" Butch cried, firing another cannonball.

Ben-Ari ran onto the bridge. The viewport here wasn't smeared with blood. She could see them coming in.

Her heart froze.

There were hundreds.

The entire forest shook as the army of Upidians charged.

She took position at the bridge's gunnery station and opened fire. The prow's laser cannon thrummed, priming itself, then blasted searing beams onto the horde. Several Upidians fell, sizzling holes in their bodies. The others kept coming, crawling over their fallen.

We won't be stranded here after all, Ben-Ari thought. *We'll be nothing but caterpillar shit.*

A wave of aliens reached the *Barracuda*'s prow. A few leaped toward the laser cannon, desperate to disable it. Laser beams mowed them down. Caterpillar slices thumped onto the ground like gruesome sushi. Fauna burst into flame behind the aliens. Trees collapsed.

Damn, this laser cannon packs a punch, Ben-Ari thought, wondering why she had never installed laser weapons on HDF ships.

Her brief moment of hope soon shattered.

Some brazen Upidians were slithering below the laser beam. Ben-Ari tilted the cannon as low as it would go. Lasers carved up the forest floor. But the beams couldn't reach the aliens, who were now crawling right nearby, too close and low to hit.

Once these Upidian commandos were directly below the cannon, they reared and wrapped around the bore. The metal was searing hot. The aliens howled, their segmented bodies burning, but refused to release the cannon. Ben-Ari kept firing, more out of frustration than anything. It was useless. The Upidians only tightened around the bore, tugging, twisting the metal, working even as their skin sizzled.

Finally the Upidians tore the laser cannon out of the prow.

Fire blazed into the bridge. Ben-Ari leaped back, covering her eyes against the horrible heat and showering sparks. Where the cannon bore had fit through the hull, now there was only a hole. It was too small for a Upidian to squeeze through, thankfully. But the aliens reached in their claws, swiping, trying to catch her.

Ben-Ari tried to reload her pistol, but her fingers were shaking. She dropped some bullets, and they rolled across the deck. Cursing, she scooped them up, desperate to reload. Upidians slammed into the prow again and again. Their claws tugged on the hole, widening it, peeling the metal open like a can.

Finally Ben-Ari got her gun loaded. She fired. She tore off several slimy arms. But they were too many. The Upidians kept ripping the prow open, shrieking for her blood.

"Yo, Einav!" Addy cried from the hold. "Catch!"

Addy was busy fighting her own battle, but she rolled a grenade across the deck. It clattered onto the bridge and came to a stop at Ben-Ari's feet.

She grabbed the grenade as the Upidians tore another opening in the prow.

She pulled out the pin and tossed the grenade through the hole.

Ben-Ari ducked and covered her head as the explosion roared. Shrapnel flew through the hole, slamming into the bulkheads, narrowly missing her. The ship's figurehead thumped onto the forest floor, features melting.

Ben-Ari rose, ears ringing, and fired her pistol. She emptied a clip into a roaring alien mouth.

Corpses of the creatures piled up outside.

And more kept coming.

One alien climbed through the hole onto the bridge, reared, and bellowed. Strands of saliva quivered between its rings of teeth like strings in a dreamcatcher.

Cursing, Ben-Ari retreated from the bridge, walking backward into the hold. She slammed the door shut, only for the Upidian to shatter it seconds later.

Her crew was still manning the cannons, blasting the beasts outside. But that wouldn't help with the creatures entering through the shattered prow. Ben-Ari raced toward the gun rack and chose the largest weapon she could find.

The Upidian from the bridge slithered across the deck toward her.

Screaming, Ben-Ari raised her Gatling gun and unleashed a storm of hot lead.

The machine gun thrummed in her hands, so heavy she nearly dropped it. Massive .50-caliber bullets tore through the alien's jaws, its armored segments, its lashing arms. The creature crashed down dead.

Another Upidian emerged behind it.

Ben-Ari fired again, emptied her machine gun, then dropped it onto the deck. Next, she grabbed a plasma rifle from the rack. She kept killing. Bolts of pure hot plasma filled the *Barracuda* with heat and light and the stench of ozone.

More alien corpses piled up. And the enemy kept swarming.

"We have to barricade the bridge door!" Ben-Ari shouted. "Ideas?"

"Hang on!" Butch cried.

The pirate ran toward the stern, grabbed the bathroom door, and wrenched it off its hinges. Ben-Ari shot down another Upidian, and Butch replaced the shattered bridge door. At once, the caterpillars began slamming at the new door, desperate to enter the hold.

Addy grunted, shoving the galley's heavy dining table. They flipped it over, pressing the tabletop against the door. They dragged casks of rum, adding them to the barricade. The aliens kept slamming at the construction, howling for blood. Ben-Ari knew this wouldn't hold for long.

The *Barracuda* rocked like a boat in a storm. Aliens were banging at the starboard and port sides again. Addy and Butch were holding down the bridge barricade, leaving only Meili at the cannons.

The starboard hull tore open. Cannons tumbled into the forest.

Alien claws reached in.

Meili screamed.

The crew all opened fire. A Upidian squealed and thumped down, riddled with bullets. But it left an opening, and more aliens widened the entrance, mouths flaring open, teeth thrusting like the petals of carnivorous flowers from hell.

The blockade at the bridge door shattered.

From starboard and bridge, caterpillars came slithering into the hold.

"This ship is lost!" Addy cried.

"Climb!" Ben-Ari shouted. "To the upper gun turret!"

A beast of a machine gun—the pirates had lovingly named it Edna—topped the starship. The crew scrambled up the ladder. Addy brought up the rear. A hatch opened, allowing them to climb onto the starship's roof.

The turret's protective bubble had shattered. The crew stood in the open air. The forest sprawled around them, thick with caterpillars. Hundreds of the creatures surrounded the

Barracuda, rocking the pirate ship. She was like a true barracuda, beached and being devoured by scavengers.

Addy dropped a few grenades into the hatch. The bombs thumped onto the deck. Addy pulled the hatch shut.

Blasts shook the starship. Fire blazed out from cracks in the hold. Ben-Ari cringed, ears ringing. The ship shook as more explosions sounded below. The crates of bullets were going off inside. Several bullets tore through the hull beneath the crew's feet, narrowly missing them. Upidians screeched inside the starship, then fell silent.

It did little good. An alien army surrounded the *Barracuda*.

The crew stood atop the ship. Ben-Ari stepped toward Edna, the enormous rotary gun. She grabbed the handles, grinned savagely, and began to spray bullets the size of cigars into the alien lines.

The creatures screeched and died. But their army did not retreat. These beasts knew no fear, charging into the hailstorm of bullets. Addy and Butch stood nearby, firing their personal firearms. Meili cowered among them. She was clutching a codechip in her fist.

That codechip, no larger than a matchbox, contained the antivirus to kill the Dreamer. They had to protect it. At any cost.

Ben-Ari spun the cannon in circles, mowing down Upidians, knowing that she would run out of bullets before they ran out of soldiers.

I must survive, she thought. *I must keep fighting!*

But she did not know how she would survive this. As she kept using up bullets, she whispered her prayer. *Shma Israel.* A chant that had comforted her in the dark. And she wondered if this was still a prayer of hope—or if it had become her last rites.

CHAPTER NINETEEN

The moths tossed them down.

Marco and Kai thudded onto the moldy ground. They groaned, shoved themselves up, and found themselves facing the turtle's enormous head.

The shell towered like a mountain. The head was as large as a frigate. Rheumy eyes peered from nests of wrinkles. Each eyeball was the size of a car.

Marco was cut, bruised, bleeding. But he couldn't help but gaze in wonder. The turtle was wrinkly, ancient, lumpy—and beautiful. A creature more wondrous than any Marco had ever seen. A creature so large it would dwarf even the great starwhales who swam through the cosmic ocean. Perhaps this was the largest lifeform in the galaxy.

And yet, standing so close, Marco noticed that the turtle was sick.

Black mold infected it. Stains covered its shell. Mold clung to its beak, and patches darkened the corners of its eyes. Mold was even dripping from its nostrils.

Pity filled Marco.

"Poor thing," he whispered.

Kai guffawed. "Poor thing? It's probably trying to decide who to eat first."

"It's sick," Marco said.

"I'll say." Kai leaned closer to Marco. "Hey, did this happen in *The NeverEnding Story*?"

Before Marco could reply, the turtle opened its mouth.

Hot breath blew across them, reeking of mold. Droplets of saliva splattered Marco's clothes. A rumbling like an avalanche emerged from the turtle's mouth, louder than a storm, deeper than thunder. At first Marco thought it was a mere groan.

But the rumble morphed into words, the voice like stones rolling in the deep.

"You ... are ... human ..."

Marco blinked. "You can talk."

"And in English!" Kai said, eyes wide.

The turtle narrowed her yellow eyes. She coughed—a horrible sound, and flecks of mold flew onto the two humans.

Yes, she's a she, Marco thought. *A female. A wise old lady.*

"How do you know our language?" Marco asked.

"Kurma ... knows ... many ... things. Kurma ... is ... very ... old."

Mold dribbled from the wrinkled mouth and pattered onto the forest floor. The turtle trembled. She took a deep breath, wincing, and the air rattled through her mountainous body.

"Are you in pain?" Marco asked.

"Kurma ... knows ... nothing but pain ... Kurma is ... infected."

"I'm sorry, Kurma," Marco said. "If there's any way we can help, we—"

"You tried to steal from Kurma!" the turtle rumbled. Her head rose from the soil. Vines and roots dangled from the bottom of her neck. Her nostrils flared, inhaling air, dry leaves, clouds of dust, and even a few unfortunate birds. "You stole the star leaf, holiest of life!"

"I'm sorry!" Marco cried out over the rumble. "Is that your medicine?"

"There is … no medicine for Kurma. There is only … them. The parasites."

The turtle opened her mouth wide. The opening loomed like a gateway, large enough to fly a starship into. Marco found himself gazing into the innards of the enormous turtle.

He gasped.

Caterpillars—the enormous, monstrous caterpillars—filled the turtle. They covered the walls of Kurma's throat. They nested in the gullet. Marco imagined them filling the entire body of the colossal beast.

"Is your illness because of the mold?" Marco said. "Or because of the parasitic caterpillars?"

There was a strange ecology at work here. The giant turtle. The black mold. The ancient caterpillar astronauts, mummified inside their iron starship, and their monstrous descendants. The war against the mushrooms. The laceleaf. Somehow all those pieces fit together, but Marco couldn't see the complete picture.

The turtle spoke again. "You are ... curious beings. Your ... curiosity will be ... your undoing." She laughed, a deep and deafening sound, yet raspy, oddly weak despite its thundering decibels.

"We can help you," Marco said. "Our people know medicine."

He took a few steps forward, hesitated, then touched the enormous turtle's head. It towered above him. He could touch only the chin. But he stroked this colossal, ancient being. The turtle shivered, shaking the earth. Marco pulled his hand back, finding it coated with mold. He cleaned it on the ground as best he could.

"There is ... no medicine ... no cure ..." Kurma said. "Only them. The parasites."

Marco nodded slowly. "The mold infected you, Kurma. And the caterpillars are keeping you alive."

The turtle's tongue emerged, bloated and lumpy and white. She licked her mossy beak.

"They ... are old. They ... began as worms. Parasites in my bowels. Eating my organs. They spread through my body. Evolved inside me. At first they were killing me. But ... they became intelligent."

Marco blinked. "Incredible. Parasitic gut worms evolving intelligence."

Kurma spoke again, each word a struggle. "They realized ... that if I die ... they would die. I was their world. The only world they ever knew. They began to protect me. To clean me. To drive out the infection. There were once others like me. Beings of the shell. Living mountains. Several of us lived on this world, each ruling a continent. We were … the largest beings in the galaxy. The others … died thousands of years ago. They did not have parasites to clean them. I alone remain."

"I'm sorry, Kurma," Marco said. "Was it the black mold that killed the others?"

"Long ago … a comet landed in this forest. It carried a black mold. We all became infected. Not just we of the shell. All living beings on this planet. The others like me … the beings of the shell … they died within a few years. I survived. But I was so sick. And the mold spread so rapidly through me. My parasites tried to protect me. To eat the black mold. But it killed them too. We were dying. Parasites and host."

Marco nodded slowly. "So your parasites grew laceleaf."

"Yes," said Kurma. "My parasites were … intelligent. They tested the mold. Understood its molecules. They developed … medicine. They grew … what you call the laceleaf. The holy herb of stars. It gives immunity to fungal infections. There is not enough laceleaf in the world to cure me. But my parasites can eat the leaves, then eat the black mold. To clean me. The mold grows fast. They struggle to keep up. I am forever diseased. But they keep me alive."

Marco thought for a moment. "We found a starship in the forest, Kurma. Did the caterpillars come from another planet too? Like the black mold?"

"No." Kurma's voice grew stronger, as if she were young again. "The caterpillars are natives of this world. They were once mere worms before they evolved inside me. And how they evolved! They grew large. Strong. So smart. They emerged from my body to explore, to colonize this planet. They built great temples and cities of stone. They studied the stars. They practiced science, wrote literature, composed music. They even built starships—vessels of iron, shaped like me, the world of their ancestors."

Kai spoke for the first time. The young pilot laughed. "Bullshit! We fought the assholes. They're dumber than doorknobs. They're just bugs."

The turtle narrowed her eyes, staring at the pirate. "The golden age is long gone. It ended when the mushrooms attacked."

"The Esporians," Marco said.

"Yes," said Kurma. "That is what your kind calls them. A race of intelligent toadstools, each larger than several humans. They craved my world. They attacked Upidia. They came in fleshy pods of fungus, crossing the void of space. My caterpillars' starships fought hard. But the enemy spores ate through their hulls. The caterpillar ships fell, and only one now remains, hidden in this forest." Her voice weakened again. "The mushrooms ... landed on our world. Butchered ... millions of my parasites. Destroyed their cities. Their civilization fell."

Marco stroked the colossal animal. "I'm sorry, Kurma. On the way here, we saw a mural of the battle. It featured toadstools surrounding a turtle." He laughed. "At first I thought you were a temple. A giant building of stone. That little turtles had built you. I thought the caterpillars who attacked us were mere monsters, not the creatures who had built the cities we found."

"Sorry, but I'm still calling bullshit on all this," Kai said. "There's no fucking way those asshole caterpillars built cities. They're monsters! You saw them." He frowned. "The caterpillars in the starship, though. The mummies. They seemed different. No big teeth or claws."

Both men looked at Kurma.

"Yes, my parasites were herbivores," Kurma said. "Clever but docile. Weak. They had faced no natural predators throughout their evolution, for I protected them. The mushrooms killed so many. They had to evolve. To become warriors. They grew claws and fangs. They learned to metamorphose into battle moths. They discovered that laceleaf, the antidote to black mold, also protected them from mushroom spores. With their new power, they won the war. They drove out the enemy. But it came at a terrible cost … their evolution into monsters. They won the war. But they lost their souls."

"Damn," Kai said. "So they became dumb berserker warriors, bitchin' and brainless."

"They had to," Marco said softly. "Evolution does not care about intelligence, ethics, artistic ability, or grace, though those might arise as its byproducts. Evolution only cares about survival. The intelligent caterpillars—the scientists and artists— probably died early on. The strongest, meanest ones survived.

They fought monsters. So they became monsters. Maybe there's a moral here somewhere. A lesson for humanity."

"We humans didn't become monsters," Kai said. "We created one. The Dreamer."

The words hung in the air. They reminded Marco of his true purpose here. Not to study the ecology of an alien world— but to save his own.

"Kurma, you are wise and taught us much," Marco said. "Your world was under attack. You saw devastation and despair. Now our world, Earth, suffers and burns. We need to speak to Don Basidio, an Esporian, and rent his starships. If you'll allow us to keep some laceleaf, we can resist Basidio's spores. We can keep fighting for Earth, and—"

The turtle let out a great cry.

The world trembled. Boulders and soil cascaded down the mountainous shell. Trees fell.

"You seek to negotiate with Esporians?" Kurma boomed. "With the creatures who destroyed my world, who butchered millions of my parasites?"

The turtle's rancid breath flowed over the two humans. They clung to a tree, nearly falling.

"Good going, buddy," Kai muttered beside him. "That was real smart."

Marco cringed. "Sorry. My bad." He looked back at the turtle. "Kurma, please! We don't take sides in this old conflict, we—"

"You do not take sides?" rumbled the turtle. "One side invaded. Destroyed. Butchered millions. Another side suffered and sacrificed. You cannot choose between evil and righteousness?"

Hundreds of caterpillars emerged from the brush, hissing. They surrounded Marco and Kai. The battle moths fluttered above, talons gleaming.

Goddammit, Marco thought. He wasn't good at diplomacy. It should be Ben-Ari here, speaking on behalf of humanity. Not him.

He backpedaled and tried again. "Wise Kurma! Your suffering has been great. The mushrooms were cruel. Earth stands with Upidia! But Earth is now threatened. Please let us go. We'll leave your world. We—"

"Leave? To form an alliance with Esporia!" cried the turtle. "To join the evil that has butchered my parasites! No, humans. No! I cannot allow it. I will not allow humanity to negotiate with our ancient enemy. You must die."

"Fuck, Poet," Kai said. "You might be a great writer, but you really need to know how to woo a lady."

"Um, run," Marco said.

"Huh?" Kai said.

The turtle began to cry out in her language. The caterpillars moved in closer.

"Run!" Marco shouted.

They began to run, fleeing the enormous turtle.

Caterpillars leaped toward them, their circular jaws widening. Marco and Kai fired their guns, tore one enemy down, and leaped over the corpse. More caterpillars swarmed from all sides, and the moths swooped from above.

The men fired their guns in every direction. Every bullet hit an enemy. Kai hurled a grenade over his shoulder. They ran from the explosion. Chunk of dead aliens pattered down around them.

"We'll never make it back to the *Barracuda*!" Marco shouted, racing through the forest. A caterpillar reared before him. He knocked it down with bullets, then whipped around the twitching, wounded monstrosity.

"We'll make it!" Kai shouted.

"It's ten kilometers!"

"We'll make it!" Kai insisted.

They sprinted down a hillside, tall grass slapping against them, the little mouths on every leaf biting them. More caterpillars jumped from the trees. A claw grabbed Marco's leg, and he blasted off the alien arm. Another caterpillar grabbed Kai and reeled him up toward the branches. Marco fired, peppering the alien with bullets, and Kai thumped onto the ground. Both men bled. But they kept firing, kept running.

"Look, the ancient starship!" Marco pointed. "We'll find shelter in there."

"You mean the *Loggerhead*?" Kai said.

"Don't call it the *Loggerhead*!"

"Why? It's a great book, bro!"

The iron turtle shell rose before them in the forest, about half the *Barracuda*'s size. That thick hull had survived for eras. Hopefully it could survive a caterpillar attack.

"It'll become our tomb," Kai said.

"This whole forest is a tomb," Marco said. "Into the ship! That is an order. I'm pulling rank."

"I'm not one of your soldiers."

Marco grabbed him. "You are now. Come on!"

They ran, low on ammo, carving a path through the leaping aliens. Moths swooped, and one grabbed Marco's shoulders. He drew a pistol from his belt and fired, and the beast dropped him. The men leaped over a rivulet of black mold and reached the iron turtle.

"Get in!" Marco shoved his brother-in-law through the hatch, covering him with automatic fire. A second later he hopped in too.

He caught a last glimpse of the alien horde storming toward them, lamprey mouths dilating.

Then Marco slammed the hatch shut, and shadows engulfed him.

CHAPTER TWENTY

Dawn rose over the desert.

Lailani and her daughter sat on the sand. They leaned against each other, watching the sunrise paint the sky a thousand colors.

Lailani remembered that Marco had always loved the night. He said he could think, write, and create best in darkness. It was also a good time for lovemaking, he would say and kiss her. Those beautiful, precious times when they had been in love. His love had always burned brightest in the dark.

But Lailani? She had always loved the dawn. It went back to her childhood. Growing up in the slums of Manila, she had feared the night. The night brought out the cutthroats, pickpockets, and drug dealers. In the night, the *farangs* would come to her mother, would give her drug money, would fuck her so hard she screamed, and Lailani would weep. Nights meant danger. Nights meant memory. Nights were times of loneliness and fear.

It was in the night long ago that Lailani, cowering in the gutter, had sliced her wrists with a piece of glass.

Daniel Arenson

It was in the night that she had ripped out the heart of a man.

It was in the night that she had seen a savage moon, grinning and mocking her.

Now dawn rose, and the cruel moon vanished. Lailani sought hope in the golden beams and watercolor hues on the horizon.

But she found terror.

This was a dawn worse than any night.

She climbed onto a dune and gazed around her. Nothing but sand and distant, barren mountains. Alone in a desert sprawling across East Asia.

She didn't even know what country this was.

Tala began to cry, but that was good. Crying was better than haunting silence.

Lailani herself had no time to cry. She got to work.

She cleaned, loaded, and holstered her gun.

She found the parachute draped across a nearby dune. She carved the fabric into robes and hoods, a small one for her, a smaller one for Tala. Some protection from this cruel sun.

She placed her daughter on her shoulders. She patted her dog. And she started walking.

From the plane, she had seen a road. It couldn't be too far. If she found the road, she could hail a car. Hitch a ride to the nearest city. Find a way onward. Hell, even if no cars drove by, she'd have a solid path to walk along. All roads led somewhere, and somewhere was better than this place.

I am Major Lailani Marita de la Rosa, and it will take a silver bullet to kill me. I'm still in the game. I will reach the Matterhorn!

She had to.

Until she did, the Dreamer would reign.

The technology in my skull will liberate humanity, she vowed. *I will create an army of billions like me. Immune to you. Warriors to fight you.*

She walked for hours, leaving a snaking trail in the sand.

For a while, Tala cried that she was thirsty. Eventually the girl fell asleep in Lailani's arms. Lailani trudged onward, cresting dune after dune. Her daughter weighed a good thirty pounds, and soon Lailani's back ached, and her legs shook with weakness.

She walked on.

The sun beat down.

Her mouth dried up, and visions floated before her. She was eighteen again. A girl with a shaved head. The smallest in her company. Even Pinky, the diminutive troublemaker of their platoon, had towered over her.

She had marched through a desert then too. A searing desert in North Africa. She had carried a burden then too. A rusty old radio, an antique that nearly weighed more than her. How her back had ached! But she had walked. Walking like Marco, like Addy, like Beast. Carrying the burden. Trudging through the sand.

And collapsing.

Falling in the desert. Crushed by the weight.

He had kept her alive. Him—the emperor of centipedes. The alien lord inside her. When her heart had threatened to stop, he had seized it. Given her the power to rise again.

Marco had taken her into his arms. The boy had not known about the monster inside her. She had not known either. She still remembered his kiss. Still remembered undressing in the tent, lying naked on the cot, calling him over. Closing her eyes. Feeling his warmth. It had been clumsy sex, full of banging elbows and awkward pawing. Her first time, Marco's second. But wonderful. One of her most precious memories.

I thought I'd marry you, you silly boy, she thought. *I wanted to. I loved you so much, and I still do. But I've always been a wanderer through strange deserts. My road stretches on.*

She lay on the sand, held in his phantom embrace, gazing into the blinding sun.

"Mommy, Mommy!"

Arms around her. Hands on her cheeks. She opened her eyes, and she stared at a little girl. Herself as a little girl. A young, frightened girl in the slums of Manila. Eyes so huge. So haunted. A face so afraid.

No. Not her. A girl who looked like her. Tala, the love of her life.

Lailani sat up. Sand clung to her wounds, hardening the dry blood. She had not even noticed falling.

"Mommy, are you okay?"

"I fell asleep," Lailani said, head spinning.

Then she leaned over and vomited, and she knew she was dehydrated. Maybe she was dying.

She was closer to the mountains now, but she had still found no road. Maybe she had been walking in the wrong direction. She searched for the smoldering remains of the Liberator, but she saw nothing.

Wait.

She squinted, staring into the sunlight.

There. Shallow marks upon a distant dune.

She ran, climbed the dune, and found them. Footprints. No, not *foot*prints. *Hoof*prints. Camels. Several had walked here.

"Where there are animals, there must be water," she said. "We found a road of sorts after all."

She followed the tracks under the dizzying sun for a while. Soon she had to rest. Her head spun, and she gagged again. The sun blazed at its zenith. It was just too hot to continue.

Lailani wished she had taken more of the parachute with her. The nylon fabric she had formed into robes offered some protection from the sun, but her legs were exposed. She was grateful that she and Tala had olive-toned skin; the melanin would provide some protection. Poor Epimetheus, his fur black and dark brown, lay baking in the sunlight.

They continued walking in the afternoon. Sandy wind blew, stinging their faces and fluttering their nylon robes. For an hour, they followed the camel tracks. The dunes gave way to hard, rocky steppes, where they could no longer see any footprints. But thankfully, they finally found some life. Grassy shrubs dotted the land, and wild horses grazed in the distance.

But they found no water.

Lailani kept walking, and she saw them.

Camels.

Camels were galloping across the steppes. And people were riding them.

She stared, eyes wide. The riders were leaning forward, rifles in hands. The camels tore up patches of dirt and grass, raising clouds of dust. They were charging to battle.

But not toward Lailani. She turned her head, and she saw their target.

A robot.

An enormous robot unlike any Lailani had seen before.

It rose like a water tower, scuttling forward on eight metallic legs. A mechanical spider, laser eyes scanning the steppes, a cannon mounted atop its back. A tank. It had been a tank once—an M90 Eisenhower by the looks of it. But the legs had been taken from something else, or perhaps assembled specifically for this machine. Cameras like eyes, mounted below the tank's turret, shone red with the Dreamer's malice.

The camel riders wore flowing robes of red, blue, and gold, rich with tassels and embroidery, and fur hats topped their heads. With battle cries, they fired their rifles. Bullets slammed into the mechanical spider, barely slowing its scuttle.

The spider turned its tank body toward the riders. It lowered its cannon.

A boom shook the steppes.

A shell flew.

The riders scattered. The shell landed between them and detonated.

Fire blazed. Dirt sprayed in a cloud. Two riders flew from their camels, limbs blown off. The survivors kept galloping, firing at the spider, bullets sparking against its armor.

"I don't like that robot!" Tala said. "He's mean. I'm scared."

"Stay with Epi, little one." Lailani kissed the girl's forehead. "I'll go kill it."

Lailani had trained under the Golden Lioness.

Lailani was a soldier through and through.

And Lailani ran toward battle.

This was not her country. She didn't even know which country this was. But this was her world. This was her species. So this was her war. She would fight every step of the way until she won.

The riders surrounded the mechanical spider. They galloped in circles, ululating. Their bullets bounced harmlessly off the machine. They drew scimitars, and they hacked at the tall, metallic legs, trying to cut through a joint. They weren't having much luck; the spider's legs were like metal telephone poles. Lailani was still a hundred meters away, running toward the battle.

The spider unfurled machine guns from its undercarriage.

It opened fire, slaying a rider and camel.

Motors whirred. A mechanical leg kicked, slamming into another rider. He flew through the air. Lailani had to swerve to dodge the falling man.

She did not bother firing her pistol. She had ridden in enough armored vehicles while under fire. Her bullets were no use here.

She hopped backward to avoid a racing camel. She was close now. The colossal spider tramped toward her, and a motorized foot slammed down, nearly crushing her. Lailani ran around it. The surviving riders howled and kept attacking. The machine gun swiveled on the spider's undercarriage, mowing down another rider.

The camel fell. The machine gun spun toward Lailani next.

She knelt behind the dead camel, and bullets slammed into its flesh. Blood and tufts of fur flew. A few bullets made their way through the animal, hitting the ground mere centimeters from Lailani.

With battle cries, several riders rode between the spider's legs. They rose in the stirrups and hacked at the machine gun. One man fell, bullets in his chest.

Lailani seized her chance and ran under the spider. Its eight mechanical legs surrounded her like a cage. The tank rose above her, fifty tons of metal blocking the sun.

Caterpillar tracks hung loosely from the tank like shedding snakeskin. Lailani crouched, narrowed her eyes, then jumped.

Bullets pattered the sand where she had stood.

She grabbed a piece of loose track, hung from it, and curled up her legs. Bullets whizzed beneath her.

She climbed the tread, grabbed an enormous metal wheel, and scuttled up the side of the tank. The machine gun swiveled below, firing every which way, but she was protected up here.

She scurried up the tank and onto the battery box. The cannon spun in an arc, and she ducked. The bore whooshed over her head. The spider was lumbering across the steppes on its eight mechanical legs, ungainly. The tank swayed back and forth, nearly shaking Lailani off. She windmilled her arms, knelt, grabbed a handle, and clung on.

She climbed from the battery box onto the gun turret. A second later, the hatch opened.

Several robotic spiders—each the size of a cat—emerged from inside the tank. They were like baby spiders bursting out from their mother.

The little machines leaped toward Lailani.

She fired her pistol, knocked one off the tank. She ducked, dodging another. A third spider slammed into Lailani, clung to her, and thrust a needle like a venomous fang.

Lailani ripped the thing off an instant before it could sting her. She hurled it forward, knocking it into another spider. Three more robots lunged at her. She squeezed off three rapid shots, taking them out. They clattered down toward the steppes.

"Little fuckers," Lailani muttered. "I fought marauders, bitches! You ain't shit."

From up here, she could see the riders around her. A dozen or so still lived, hacking at the robot's massive legs. They could not harm the mechanized spider, and they had lost many men, but they refused to flee. Whoever they were, these were proud warriors. Probably too proud for their own good.

Lailani reloaded her pistol, then hopped through the hatch, entering the tank.

The chamber was shadowy and cluttered. Everywhere were dials, levers, switches, cables, and gauges. Even Lailani, a petite woman, barely fit in here.

And she was not alone.

The tank driver was here.

The man spun toward her, wearing a dusty HDF uniform, goggles, and earmuffs. He grinned at her. A grin from ear to ear, the cheeks cut open.

"A sleeper," Lailani hissed.

He raised a pistol.

Lailani leaped aside and fired her own gun.

Two bullets flew.

Her ears rang.

She screamed in pain.

But his bullet had missed her. Only the horrible sound, echoing inside the cabin, had hurt her.

The sleeper slumped down, her bullet in his forehead.

Lailani touched her ears and winced.

"Ouch," she muttered, ears throbbing.

The driver was dead, but the machine was still trudging across the land. Its cannon fired again. Its machine gun rattled. The dials and switches were moving on their own.

Lailani borrowed the dead soldier's earmuffs. Better late than never.

A few shells lay in a crate. The sleeper must have been loading them manually into the cannon, a task the Dreamer's miniature spiders would have struggled with. There was also a box of bullets. And finally—a crate of grenades.

Oh boy, this would get ugly.

Lailani picked up one grenade and hefted it.

Yep, it was good she had the earmuffs.

She climbed out the hatch. She dropped the grenade back into the tank.

She raced across the hull.

"Fire in the hole!" she shouted at the riders, gesturing madly, and realized they probably didn't speak English. "Big boom!"

That they understood. They began to flee.

Lailani kicked off the back of the tank and soared. She landed hard, rolled, rose, ran some more, and—

The blast rolled over her.

Dirt flew.

Lailani fell facedown and covered her head.

Chunks of metal pattered around her. The dirt stormed. An enormous metal leg, as wide as a telephone pole, slammed down beside her, missing her by centimeters.

Another explosion.

Another.

Blast after blast roared as the shells and grenades exploded inside the tank.

When it was finally over, Lailani looked back. Metal spider legs lay across the steppes like the fallen columns of an ancient temple. The tank itself was a burning, twisted wreck.

Lailani ran.

She ran across the steppes, limping, fell, rose again. She ran until she reached her daughter and scooped her into her arms.

"Mommy, you're a superhero!" Tala said. "Like Wonder Woman!"

Lailani clutched her daughter close, tears flowing through the ash on her cheeks. She never wanted to let her go.

Hooves thudded.

The camels rode toward her. Only half had survived. Their riders dismounted and stood around mother and daughter.

Dust and soot stained their brocaded robes, and their tin and silver jewelry chinked. Their eyes peered from bronze, weathered faces. They spoke in a foreign language, and one man held out a waterskin.

Water. Oh God, finally water.

Lailani reached for the skin, but her hand shook. Her eyes rolled back. She fell onto the ground, holding her daughter, and dark clouds flowed over her.

CHAPTER TWENTY-ONE

The *Loggerhead,* an antique starship shaped like a turtle shell, rocked on the forest floor.

The aliens kept pounding the hull. Claws scratched against the iron. There were no portholes. No viewports. But huddled inside, Marco and Kai could feel every blow, hear every screech.

The two mummified caterpillars, ancient astronauts, fell from their seats. Their desiccated bodies crumbled into dust and bone fragments.

"What a wonderful tomb you found for us!" Kai said.

Marco stood up, panting. Blood dripped down his body from several cuts.

"Enough," he said.

Kai paced the small ship, laughing maniacally. "Great work. Wonderful! We're going to die in here now. Die like those two skeletons. I should never have come to this planet. Fuck! I should have moved back to fucking Bangkok, opened a bar, banged chicks all day, and—"

"Quiet!" Marco said. "Dammit, Kai, shut up. Think. Plan."

Kai only snorted. "Fuck, dude, unless you think a starship from a million years ago can still fly, I'd say we're fucked."

The two men looked at each other. For a moment they were silent.

Then they raced toward the ancient dashboard. The controls were still in good shape, aside from some grime. The starship had been sealed perfectly, airtight like an ancient Egyptian tomb.

"This might still work," Marco said.

"Dude, the *Barracuda* is thirty years old and falling apart," Kai said. "How the fuck will a starship that's thousands—hell, maybe *millions*—of years old gonna still fly?"

"The *Barracuda* hasn't been sealed in a solid case of pure iron," Marco said. "This has been. It's like finding a mammoth buried under ice. Still perfectly preserved."

Kai snorted and pointed at the two piles of dust and bones. "Tell it to those two buggers."

Outside, the carnivorous caterpillars kept ramming into the *Loggerhead*. The iron turtle rocked. The muffled screams reverberated through the hull. But even those mighty monsters could not break in. These turtle ships had been built to last.

Marco remembered what Kurma had told him. That the Esporians had destroyed all but this single turtle ship.

My God, he thought. *If the Esporians defeated a fleet of these turtle ships, they must be fucking beasts. Thank goodness we have the laceleaf.*

The herbs were still in his backpack, filling the cabin with their scent. But suddenly Marco thought that all the laceleaf in the world wouldn't make meeting an Esporian safe.

He would deal with Don Basidio later. Right now he had a starship to fly.

Thankfully, these controls seemed much more familiar than Tarjan machines. Upidians had seven arms, and their controls reflected that. But the principles were similar to Earth ships. There were levers, dials, buttons, and a yoke. Good old-fashioned basic engineering. No glass vials filled with colorful liquids here.

Marco shoved down a lever.

Nothing happened.

He flipped a few switches.

Nothing.

Kai cleared his throat. "Need some help there, bro?"

"Sure, got a manual for ancient caterpillar starships?" He tried a few more buttons. Nothing happened. Marco pursed his lips.

Kai groaned and shoved Marco aside. "Let me."

Marco rolled his eyes. "Oh, you know all about caterpillar tech, do you?"

"I've flown my share of alien starships, bro. This ain't my first rodeo." The pirate flipped a few switches, knelt, and grinned. "Ah, here we go."

Under the dashboard was a handle attached to a cord— the sort that might kick-start a motorboat. Kai yanked back hard.

Deep inside the ship, something clanked and moaned.

Kai pulled the cord a few more times … and the power came on. A dozen monitors blinked to life. A hundred buttons and keys glowed.

"Booyah!" Kai cried. He winked at Marco. "Just like starting a lawn mower."

Marco rolled his eyes. "Hey, you're the pilot. I'm just the dumb officer who thought of the idea."

"Let's fly this bitch." Kai kicked a few bones off the pilot's seat, grabbed the yoke, and shoved down hard.

Deep inside the *Loggerhead*, ancient engines groaned. Smoke filled the cabin, mingling with the cinnamon scent of laceleaf. The engines sputtered and coughed. The ship trembled. Marco waved smoke aside.

"Come on, darling, fly for me," Kai muttered, easing in the throttle, and—

Marco fell.

Kai whooped.

The starship roared forward.

Monitors came to life across the dashboard, displaying the world outside. Marco saw the jungle, the distant mountains, and the Upidians attacking all around.

The *Loggerhead* plowed through them. Caterpillars slammed against the prow, breaking apart, splattering the ship with gore. Trees cracked and fell. The ship carved grooves through soil and rock.

"You plan to drive this thing the rest of the way?" Marco said.

Kai leaned back in his seat, tugging the yoke. "Takes a bit of muscle, but … Here we go!"

The nose rose.

The engines roared louder.

Fire blazed, and the *Loggerhead* took flight.

The battle moths came swooping in. Hundreds of them, each the size of a horse. A cloud of the bastards.

"Fuck!" Marco said. "Those things will tear through us like a flock of geese through a jet."

Marco looked around. He saw a dashboard that resembled a gunnery station. He leaped toward the controls and found seven joysticks—a rig built for creatures with seven arms.

He chose two joysticks at random. A monitor flickered to life, displaying the view outside, painted green and black. Two red dots shone, indicating targets.

Marco fired.

Plasma bolts shot out. Two moths exploded into clouds of red mist.

Marco kept firing. Again. Again. Rapid blasts of plasma slammed into the horde of moths, clearing a path through the sky. Kai still worked the yoke, piloting the *Loggerhead* through the swarm.

"I like this ship!" Kai cried. "Fuck, this bitch is agile."

Marco scrutinized the landscape. His belly froze. His heart almost stopped.

"Kai!" He pointed. "The *Barracuda*!"

They both stared.

Kai turned pale. "Fuck."

They saw the *Barracuda* in the distance. What was left of it, at least. Hundreds of Upidians surrounded the pirate ship like ants around a piece of meat. The giant caterpillars had torn the ship apart. It looked like a pile of scrap metal now.

The crew stood on the roof, firing their guns, desperate to hold off the assault.

Addy!

Addy was there, firing a pistol. Caterpillars were clawing at her feet, trying to climb toward her, to rip her apart.

The others were there too. Ben-Ari was firing Edna, the ship's enormous machine gun. Butch was firing a T57 assault rifle. Meili cowered between them.

Fear and love swirled through Marco like ice and fire. His wife. His friends. The people he loved most.

"Let's strafe those caterfuckers," Marco said. "Kai, give me a whirl around the *'Cuda*."

"Caterfuckers?" Kai raised an eyebrow.

"Yeah, I made it up. Now fly over them!"

Kai saluted. "Aye, aye, Captain."

They flew closer, and then Kai pulled on the yoke. The turtle ship circled above the *Barracuda*, only a few meters up.

Marco unleashed hellfire.

Plasma bolts devastated the alien horde. Caterpillars exploded, showering their innards.

"You're not tough against plasma, are you, caterfuckers!" Kai shouted, laughing and flying another round.

Marco pulled the trigger again, tearing through the host. Dead aliens piled up.

"Kai, hover over the *Barracuda*," Marco said. "I'll open the hatch and pull the crew in."

Kai obliged, lowering the *Loggerhead*. The iron turtle shell hovered just offside the *Barracuda*, a meter above the stranded crew. Marco abandoned the gunnery station, raced toward the airlock, opened the hatch, and—

A hellmouth shrieked.

A caterpillar leaped into the *Loggerhead*, tentacles reaching toward Marco.

Dammit! The beast must have clung on throughout the flight here. Marco fell back, raised his pistol, and emptied a clip into the gaping maw.

It barely fazed the beast. The Upidian reached out its seven arms, grabbed Marco, and began reeling him toward the waiting gullet. Marco tossed his emptied pistol. The weapon vanished into the meat grinder.

The arms pulled him closer. Marco kicked. The rings of teeth expanded, prepared to lacerate him.

He winced, curling his legs inward, trying to delay death if only by a few seconds.

A *boom*.

An echo.

The caterpillar's head exploded, showering gore and teeth onto Marco.

The headless caterpillar thumped onto the deck, oozing.

Addy stood behind it, a crooked smile on her lips. An enormous gun with a muzzle like an exhaust pipe smoked in her hand.

"Hey, Poet!" She waved. "Sweet spaceship you got here. Did you know it's shaped like a turtle?"

She stepped over the dead alien. They embraced, blood sluicing around their boots. It was an embrace that just lasted a few seconds. It was an era of warmth. The story of their love. It was laughter through tears and sparkling eyes.

And then it ended, and Marco was pulling the others into the *Loggerhead*. Butch bled from several gashes. Meili was trembling and pale, but she seemed otherwise unharmed.

Ben-Ari stayed on the *Barracuda* last. The president's black suit was splashed with alien blood. She still balanced on high heels. Her eyes were narrowed, her face fierce, as she blasted her enemy with machine-gun fury.

"Einav!" Marco shouted. "We have to go! Now!"

Finally the president turned, leaped, and reached out her hand. Leaning from the airlock, Marco grabbed her. The *Loggerhead* began to rise, leaving the caterpillars to overwhelm the *Barracuda*'s remains.

Below the turtle ship, the caterpillars began to climb one another, forming a ladder of living bugs. They moved at incredible speed, one caterpillar riding the other, joining into an enormous claw.

Even as the *Loggerhead* flew, the mass of caterpillars reached upward. They formed a single superorganism. With claws made of writhing caterpillars, the monstrous creation grabbed the ancient starship.

The engines sputtered.

The Upidians' grip tightened.

"They're like fire ants," Marco whispered in wonder. "They can link together to form a single large organism."

"Marco, dammit, fire the cannons!" Kai shouted from the helm.

Marco blinked, nodded, and pulled the trigger. Plasma bolts streaked forward.

"Dammit!" he said. "The cannon is pointing between the caterpillar fingers."

The enormous claw, comprised of countless caterpillars, began pulling them down toward the earth. The *Loggerhead*'s iron shell, which had survived for a million years, began to dent.

"They're crushing us like a tin can!" Addy said.

"Kai, fly harder!" Marco shouted.

"The pedal's on the metal, bro," the pirate said.

Marco cursed. "Does anyone have any rope? I'll bungee jump out, shoot the bastards from outside."

But nobody had any rope. And Addy had used up her last grenades. The alien grip was tightening, crushing the ship. They were going down fast, about to hit the trees.

Butch trudged toward the airlock. "Ah, goddammit." The old pirate spat. "This thing cost me a fortune."

Addy frowned. "What are you talking about, Dad?"

The grizzled man unscrewed his prosthetic arm—a contraption of steel rods, gears, and claws. It was clutching a gun. "This. Wireless remote and all. I'm gonna miss it."

Grumbling, Butch opened the airlock and tossed out his prosthetic arm.

Flying through the air, the prosthetic began firing its gun.

Caterpillars screeched and tore apart.

Standing inside the hull, Butch stared outside at the metal hand. He narrowed his eyes, concentrating, wirelessly controlling the prosthetic.

Bullets slammed into the enemy. And the enormous claw of caterpillars tore apart. Its fingers, each comprising two braided Upidians, loosened their grip.

The *Loggerhead*'s engines roared.

"We're free!" Kai said, shoving down the throttle.

The *Loggerhead* soared. They left the horrors below.

Marco inhaled deeply and leaned against the hull. The caterpillars. The moth. The mold. Good riddance to all of it.

As the ship rose higher, Marco looked out the viewport, and he saw the enormous turtle below, a living being like a mountain.

"She tried to kill us," he said softly. "But I wish her well."

Addy frowned. "Who?"

"The giant turtle," Marco said. "She's alive."

Addy's eyes widened. She shoved him. "You've been withholding freaks!"

Marco shrugged. "Hey, you got to see the giant caterpillars with seven arms around their lamprey mouths."

"But, but—a giant turtle!" Addy pressed her face against the viewport, gazing down. "I can't believe I missed her."

"She talked," Marco said. "And in English!"

Addy gasped and shoved him again. "Like in *The NeverEnding Story*!"

"She was a bit more murderous, but yes."

"Can we go back down and talk to her?" Addy said.

"No!" everyone said together.

They kept flying, leaving the atmosphere, heading into deep space. They had the laceleaf. It was time to talk to Don Basidio. To negotiate for more ships.

And from there—to Haven, Marco thought. *My old home. To face the Dreamer.*

He collapsed onto the deck, finally overcome by his injuries and weariness. Addy wrapped her arms around him. As the *Loggerhead* flew onward into the dark, Marco gazed out a viewport into space, seeking comfort in the starry vista.

Several stars were moving fast.

Comets?

No.

Marco pushed himself up, squinting.

"Starships!" he said.

They were coming in fast, streaking toward the iron turtle. Painted blue. He recognized them.

"Those are Earth warships," Marco said, his heart sinking. "The Dreamer found us."

CHAPTER TWENTY-TWO

Human Defense Force starships.

An entire battalion. A heavy frigate—the HSS *Patton*. Five corvettes, smaller warships but just as deadly. Two squadrons of Firebirds, starfighters for single pilots. All painted blue and silver. Earth colors.

A major military force.

All flying toward the small iron *Loggerhead*.

All ships of the Dreamer. Marco was sure of it.

From aboard the ancient Upidian ship, everyone stared in horror.

"Jesus Fucking Christ," Kai muttered, sitting at the helm.

Marco took position at the gunnery station, sitting close to his brother-in-law. The original astronauts had been Upidians, giant caterpillars with a ring of seven arms. Instead of chairs, they had draped themselves across metal triangles. The furniture reminded Marco of giant Toblerone pieces. Instead of controls built for two hands, the ship had complex machinery for seven. Marco and Kai had only been operating the *Loggerhead* for moments, had barely worked out its mechanics. The planet Upidia still hovered below them, a sphere of rainforests, mist, and monsters.

Marco would have chosen all the horrors of the jungle over the starships flying ahead.

Kai leaned forward in his seat. He squinted at the viewport. "I don't suppose humans are flying those ships."

Ben-Ari stood on the bridge with the two men. The rest of the crew was in the hold, watching nervously through the doorway.

The president placed a hand on Marco's shoulder. It surprised him. Perhaps a gesture to comfort him. Maybe to comfort herself.

"Send out a hailing frequency," she said. "Let's see what happens."

"Um ..." Marco looked at the complex alien controls. "I'm not quite sure how, ma'am."

Kai sighed, leaned across the controls, and flipped a few switches. "This'll do it."

"How the hell do you know all this?" Marco said.

The young pirate shrugged. "Alien spaceships are my specialty. Been flying them for years. They're more or less all the same." He hit another button. "Ah, here we go!"

Marco thought there was something Kai was hiding. But he had no time to probe it deeper. A monitor came to life, hanging above the main viewport. An image appeared—a live feed from the HSS *Patton*.

They all stared.

Kai let out a strangled gasp. Curses rose from the hold.

Ben-Ari's hand tightened on Marco's shoulder.

"What the fuck?" Kai whispered, face pale.

Marco stared, unable to look away. His fists clenched, and his lips formed a thin line. He heard somebody vomit in the hold.

I will destroy you, Dreamer, Marco silently vowed. *I will fucking destroy you.*

The man on the monitor stared at them. Or at least he had been a man once. He still wore an HDF uniform: the fine navy-blue outfit of an admiral. But his face was ghostly, a mask of pain. Tiny metal claws held his eyelids grotesquely wide, nearly ripping them. An electrode was embedded into his neck, flashing with red lights.

But worst of all was his head.

The top of the admiral's skull had been sawed open. The brain was exposed like jelly inside a bowl.

An array of metal claws was bolted into what remained of the skull. The claws curled inward toward the brain like vultures leaning over prey. A few claws were poking the pink folds.

"Admiral Kabanen," Ben-Ari whispered, her grip tight on Marco's shoulder. "Is that you?"

The man stared at them. A tear fled his eye. His lips quivered.

"Please," he whispered. "Help me. Please help me. Pain. In pain—"

A claw jabbed down, piercing the brain.

Kabanen screamed.

Marco had never heard a scream of such anguish. A scream that twisted Kabanen's entire body. His eyes bugged out. His tears flowed.

"Turn this damn video off!" Kai said, reaching for the controls. But Ben-Ari gripped the pirate's wrist, stopping him.

The president stared at the monitor. "Enough, Dreamer!"

The claw pulled out from the brain. Kabanen slumped. He would have fallen, but he was bolted into his chair. For a moment he sat with his chin against his chest.

Then the admiral raised his head, and he smiled. A cruel, demonic smile. His eyes still bugged out, no longer filled with pain. Filled instead with madness.

"Hello, Ben-Ari," he said, voice like silk.

The president stared at the monitor. "Let him go, Dreamer. Let them all go. You've played this game long enough."

Two more claws jabbed the brain, less aggressively this time. Kabanen jerked, sat upright, and his grin widened. Claws reached down, grabbed the corners of his mouth, and pulled his grin even wider.

"Oh, but I've only begun this beautiful game," the admiral said. "There is such pleasure in tormenting you humans! I know where your families hide. Your son, Einav. A little boy named Carl. Your children, Marco. Little Roza and Sam. They hide, and you think they are safe. But I will have them. I will make them suffer like poor Kabanen here. I will make them scream. Like this."

A claw drove into the brain.

Kabanen howled. He thrashed against the chair. He wept.

"Kill me!" he howled. "Ben-Ari, kill me! Fire on my ship!"

Addy, who had been watching from the hold, burst onto the bridge.

"I can't take it anymore!" she shouted, reached for the controls, and hit a button.

Plasma fired from the *Loggerhead*. The glowing bolt slammed into the frigate ahead. An explosion rocked the *Patton*, but her shields held. The image flickered on the monitor.

Kabanen stopped screaming. He stared at them.

"You will pay for your impudence," he said.

The claws tugged his grin wider. Wider. Then ripping his cheeks. Carving a bloody smile.

"I've seen enough." Ben-Ari flipped a switch, killing the video feed. "Kai, get us out of here."

"Gladly," the young pirate muttered, shoved down the throttle, and tugged the yoke.

The *Loggerhead* was roaring ahead when missiles emerged from the hijacked fleet like rabid dogs from pens.

"Defensive fire!" Ben-Ari cried. "Marco, shoot down those missiles!"

Marco needed no encouragement. He narrowed his eyes, focusing on his display. It showed a hundred incoming torpedoes.

There were seven joysticks there—controls for seven cannons. Seven red lights appeared on his viewport—potential targets. Marco only had two hands.

"Addy, little help?" he said.

The torpedoes were coming in fast. Marco winced.

"Sure thing!" Addy hopped onto his lap and grabbed two joysticks. Marco grabbed the other two.

They nudged the joysticks, moving four red dots on the monitor, and fired.

Four plasma bolts flew from the *Loggerhead* and impacted. Four torpedoes exploded.

But more were streaking toward the *Loggerhead*.

Marco and Addy fired again. Again. Explosions bloomed in space.

"Meili, Butch, get your asses in here!" Addy shouted. "We need more hands."

The young programmer and the grizzled pirate raced onto the bridge. The seven joysticks formed a ring, built for a single Upidian gunner with a ring of arms. Meili had to hop onto Marco's lap too, sharing it with Addy. Butch, the tallest crew member, leaned over them. Together, they grabbed all the joysticks.

The missiles were only seconds away now.

They fired together. Seven plasma bolts flew, taking out seven more torpedoes. They fired again. Again.

The last few torpedoes were going to impact.

"Kai, fire up the warp drive!" Ben-Ari shouted. "Get us out of here!"

"We're too close to Upidia's gravity well!" the pilot cried. "We can't—"

"Hold on!" Marco shouted, wincing.

One torpedo made it through the plasma barrage.

Kai swerved hard.

The torpedo grazed the *Loggerhead*'s hull—and exploded.

The turtle ship rocked. Smoke filled the bridge. Addy and Meili fell to the deck.

Miraculously, the ancient starship was still flying. The Upidians built 'em tough. Marco fired again and again, taking out more torpedoes. The girls returned to his lap and fired their own cannons.

The Dreamer's ships unleashed a new volley. Kai flew in a fury, dodging some torpedoes. The *Loggerhead* cannons fired, taking out some more. One missile streaked overhead, grazing the *Loggerhead*. The ship jolted. The hull dented.

"Kai, for fuck's sake!" Marco said. "Can you *please* get us out of here?"

"What am I supposed to do?" Kai shouted. "I'm trying to dodge 'em. They're too many! I'm trying to get far enough from the planet to warp, but I can't get through those goddamn missiles."

Marco glanced toward Upidia. The planet was still nearby, hovering behind them, a green-and-white sphere.

"Don't fly away from Upidia," Marco said. "Fly toward it. Enter its orbit."

Kai snorted. "Are you kidding me? I'm not going back there. Don't you remember the giant man-eating caterpillars?"

"I didn't say you should land," Marco said. "Execute a slingshot maneuver." He glanced at Ben-Ari. "If you agree, ma'am."

The president nodded. "Do it. It's our best chance."

Kai looked at the planet.

More HDF starships were emerging from behind its horizon. Dreamer ships.

"Fuck, fuck, fuck," Kai said. "A second enemy battalion! The way is blocked."

Marco raised an eyebrow. "No. You can fly between them. You're a good pilot. You can do this, brother."

Marco returned his focus to more incoming torpedoes. He shot down a few. Another torpedo made it through the defensive fire. It nearly impacted. Addy blasted it apart mere meters away from the starship. Debris pattered the iron hull.

"All right, hold on to your asses!" Kai shouted, tugged the yoke, and they banked hard.

They charged toward the planet—and the battalion of warships.

Marco and the others opened fire with seven cannons.

Plasma bolts slammed into incoming missiles. Into warships. Into a Firebird. Marco trembled, and his heart broke, because they were fighting their own fleet. Their own people. Killing humans. Puppets of the Dreamer, yes. But humans nonetheless.

That made this war worse than any Marco had fought.

Kai swerved from side to side like a bumblebee. Missiles whizzed around them. The young pirate executed a barrel roll. Torpedoes flew all around them. More came flying in. Marco fired again and again, clearing a path, and—

A missile slammed into the *Loggerhead*.

The deck cracked.

Fire blazed.

Kai screamed, and electricity raced across him. He fell.

"Son!" Butch shouted.

Kai lay on the deck, twitching. His clothes smoldered. His hands were burnt.

"Kai, dammit!" Butch knelt beside him. "Wake up, wake—"

"Fly this ship, Butch!" Ben-Ari shouted.

The aging pirate, the only other pilot in the crew, looked up at her. The old man nodded and grabbed the helm. He had only one hand but decades of experience.

The enemy ships were seconds away now.

The *Loggerhead* fired again.

Butch leaned forward, eyes narrowed, and flew. And God above, even with one hand, the man could *fly*. Marco couldn't help but gaze in wonder, even as he kept fighting. Butch was old, creaky, and gruff, but he flew like an angel. The iron turtle became more like a butterfly. They whisked between oncoming missiles. The enemy corvettes charged closer, prepared to ram them. But the *Loggerhead* rose, fell, rolled, and flitted between the larger warships, dodging fire all the while.

As they flew by the last corvette, Marco saw an opportunity. A chance to fire on a frigate's engines, its Achilles' heel. To destroy the large warship.

He held his fire. The others did too. If there were humans on that starship, even if they were hijacked by the Dreamer, they didn't want that on their conscience.

"I hope we can save them someday," Marco said. "But I wonder if a mercy killing would be kinder. I have to believe they can come back. That we're not abandoning them to a fate worse than death."

But the fight was not over yet. The two HDF battalions joined forces and began pursuing the *Loggerhead* together. More torpedoes flew toward the turtle ship, coming from behind them now.

The *Loggerhead* slid into orbit around Upidia, skimming the atmosphere, flying deep in the gravity well.

And they were speeding up, boosted by Upidia's gravity. Faster and faster still. Moving as fast as the torpedoes. Then faster.

The *Loggerhead* roared around the planet, and the clouds and forests streaked below. Butch nudged down the thruster all the way, and still they gained speed. The ship rattled madly. The enemy pursued.

And then, as they crested the horizon, Butch tugged the yoke with all his strength.

The ship's nose rose, and they soared out into deep space.

The gravity assist hurled them like a slingshot. The entire force of the planet shoved them. The *Loggerhead* streaked forward, moving at terrifying speed. The G-force was so great that they all fell. The deck thrummed. The stars danced like mad fireflies.

And still the enemy pursued.

"Give us warp speed!" Ben-Ari managed to cry, pressed against the wall.

Butch reached toward a switch, but the speed was too great for him. The pirate fell.

Marco pushed himself up, squinting. The ship rattled madly. He grimaced, blackness spreading across his vision, closing in. He could barely see. The G-force was flattening his face to his skull. He was losing consciousness.

Addy shoved him from behind.

"Move it, Poet!"

With Addy's help, he reached the controls. He flicked the switch.

Blue light gathered around the ship, and the stars stretched into lines, and they blasted forward.

The rattling ended at once. The G-forces released them. The crew collapsed, coughing, a few vomiting.

They were flying at warp speed. Within only seconds, Upidia was just a pale speck behind them.

And so was the enemy fleet. Even if those starships jumped to warp speed now, a few seconds late, they would be millions of kilometers behind.

Marco slumped back in his seat.

Finally the crew could rest and tend to their wounds. Kai was slowly coming to, burns across his arms. Everyone was covered with cuts, gashes, bruises, and Meili had stubbed her toe hard, possibly breaking it.

"We made it," Addy said, taking shaky breaths. "We actually made it." She turned toward Butch. "Damn, Dad! Where did you learn how to fly?"

The shaggy pirate winked. "I spent years dodging HDF ships. This ain't no thing."

Addy embraced him. "You're the best damn pilot I ever saw, Dad."

Butch held her and kissed her head. "And you're the toughest warrior in the galaxy."

Kai stood up, limbs shaking, and cleared his throat. "And what am I, chopped liver?"

They pulled Kai into the embrace. For a moment, the Linden family stood together, united in love.

Marco stared in disbelief. It was the first time he had seen the Lindens like this. Normally they bickered, fought, cursed, even punched one another. They noticed him watching, and they pulled him into the embrace.

"You're one of us, kid," Butch said. "A Linden."

Addy grinned. "Group hug!" She turned toward the rest of the crew. "Everyone, join us! Big happy moment of—"

A drilling sounded from the hold.

A hiss.

Mechanical clicks.

The family broke apart and drew their guns.

They left the bridge, entered the hold, and saw it there.

They screamed and opened fire.

CHAPTER TWENTY-THREE

Addy stood inside the *Loggerhead*, staring at the abomination.

A creature. A machine.

A soldier of the Dreamer.

The beast unfolded its metal legs, rising like a spider. Its tubular body bristled with spikes. Its jaws opened, revealing whirring drill bits.

Addy fired her pistol. Her crew fired with her. Bullets slammed into the machine, knocking it back, but it rose again. It was as large as a man, and its gears whirred.

"How the fuck did this thing get on board?" Butch shouted.

Addy understood. She saw the hole in the hull, sealed with a metal sheet.

"It's one of the torpedoes," she said. "Look at its body. The Dreamer's starships weren't launching missiles. They were launching *robots*. This fucker burrowed through our hull."

"Why?" Butch said. "Why did it seal the hull? It could have let the air flow out and suffocate us."

The pirate fired another bullet at the robot. Kai and Marco joined him, emptying their magazines. But the barrage ricocheted off the machine. Bullets streaked every which way. One scraped Butch's leg, and the pirate grunted. Another bullet grazed Meili's arm, and the programmer whimpered and cowered.

"Hold your fire!" Ben-Ari cried. "You'll end up killing us. Hold your fire!"

They all lowered their weapons.

They stared at the robot.

It rose again, its cylindrical body dented by a hundred bullets. Its jaws spun like a trash compactor, the blades inside flashing.

But it did not lunge at them.

Addy understood.

"Close your eyes!" she shouted. "Cover your ears!"

Lights flashed across the robot. The spinning teeth began to click and buzz, emitting a pattern like an old internet dial-up.

Addy closed her eyes and covered her ears.

She could still hear her family scream.

Lights flashed across her closed eyelids. And she could still hear that horrible, mechanical sound.

He was there. Invading her ears. Her mind. Speaking inside her. Laughing. Singing. His hideous grin bloomed inside her. His voice mocked her.

The Dreamer is watching
The Dreamer is here
The Dreamer is always your friend

Come into his dream
Come play in his world
The Dreamer is yours till the end

Mister Smiley knows
That the Dreamer is all
That his dreams are the world and your mind

Come into his home
And dream with the Dreamer
Such wondrous dreams you will find!

The lights flashed faster. They all screamed. Laughter rang through the cabin. Addy opened her eyes to slits. She saw Meili laughing, head tossed back. The programmer thrust fingers into her mouth and tugged her cheeks back, widening her grin, and her eyes bugged out. Kai drew a knife, placed it into his mouth, and began carving his cheek open. He laughed as he bled. Marco was firing his gun, but the bullets couldn't hurt the machine.

The robot still flashed its light, still whirred its drills.

Hacking them. Infecting them. Dragging them to hell.

Addy laughed.

"I am the Dreamer!" she cried, and she wept, and she trembled, and she laughed. "Humanity will bow before me!"

The evil was controlling her limbs. Her hand shook. She placed her pistol against her head.

No. No!

Deep inside, Addy cried out. She managed to lower her gun.

And he punished her. The lights burned brighter. The sounds pounded her ears. She fell to her knees, screaming, weeping, the pain like a thousand blooming thorns inside her.

"Marco!" she cried, tears on her cheeks. "Dad!"

They all stared at her, mad. Meili—rolling around, laughing. Kai—carving his cheek. Marco, dropping his gun, covering his ears, screaming. Ben-Ari—curled up into a ball, dying, maybe dead, then looking up with insane eyes, with a horrible grin, blood in her mouth.

"Daddy!" Addy cried, reaching for him.

Because suddenly she was a girl again. A girl growing up after the Cataclysm. A girl in a bomb shelter, a gas mask on her face. A girl so scared. So alone. A girl who needed her dad.

He had rarely been there in her childhood. He had rarely been there in her life.

But he was there now.

William "Butch" Linden. Truck driver. Jailbird. Pirate. Her father.

He walked toward the machine. His face was hard. His eyes narrowed. He was fighting the signal, refusing to surrender himself. He was sixty-two years old. He had only one arm. But he was the strongest man Addy knew. The only person here who clung to himself. Who knew who he was. And no machine could take that from him.

Butch grabbed the machine with one hand. It was a large robot. As large as him and probably heavier. But Butch groaned and lifted the robot, then slammed it down.

A light shattered.

The robot screeched.

Drills dug into Butch, tearing through his flesh, and Addy screamed.

She tried to advance. But the robot kept flashing its remaining lights. Kept invading her brain. She fell. The Dreamer laughed inside her. She grinned. A twisting grin, hurting her cheeks. She crawled forward, but he writhed inside her, tugging her back like a ghost.

Butch was laughing now. His eyes were bulging, the irises turning white. He was infected too.

But there was still humanity in him. He was still a father.

He lifted the machine again, slammed it down. Another light shattered. A drill bit flew. Bolts scattered.

The robot's circular jaws spun.

They drove into Butch, tearing him open, carving a hole the size of a fist.

Addy cried out in horror.

But Butch did not fall. His chest was cracked open. But he dragged the robot across the hold, reached the airlock, and grabbed the hatch.

The robot cut him again. Again. Tearing him apart.

Butch would not release it.

He pulled the hatch open.

He tossed the robot into the airlock, slammed the inner door shut, then hit the control panel.

The outer door opened, hurling the robot into space.

The lights were gone. The sound was gone. The crew fell to the deck, coughing blood, dazed. Somebody vomited in the corner.

Addy ignored the others. She rushed toward her father.

He lay by the airlock. Blood covered him. His wounds were deep. Horrifying. Addy wept.

"Daddy ..."

She touched his cheek. His skin was already turning gray. He blinked at her weakly.

"Hello, Princess."

Kai rushed forward too. His left cheek was slashed open, dripping blood. He ignored it. He grabbed his father and cried out hoarsely.

"Dad!"

They had no medic aboard this ship. They both knew these wounds were fatal.

Butch coughed. He was pale. Ashen. His lifeblood was flowing away.

"I'm sorry ..." he rasped.

Addy shook her head, tears falling. "Don't be."

"I'm sorry for ... being a shitty father. I'm sorry for ... leaving you. I'm sorry."

Addy embraced him, crying onto his shoulder. "I forgive you. I love you."

"I love you too, princess." He looked at Kai, blinking, eyes damp. "I love you, son. This is a good way to die. My children beside me. I'm proud of you both."

Addy wanted to tell him that he would be okay. That he would make it. Survive. Live to fight another day.

But she had seen enough men die.

She could not bring herself to lie.

Addy stroked his cheek. "You're a hero, Daddy. Goodbye." She kissed his forehead, and her tears wet his face. "Goodbye."

His eyes closed.

He breathed no more.

Addy lowered her head, weeping softly.

* * * * *

They floated in interstellar space. An ancient, battered starship. A haunted crew. A fallen hero.

They stood solemnly. Five survivors.

Marco and Addy, standing at attention, their uniforms ragged and bloodstained.

President Ben-Ari, wearing a tattered black suit, scratches across her face, her eyes hard.

Meili, leaning on makeshift crutches, tears glimmering behind her glasses.

Kai, blood soaking his jeans and sleeveless shirt, his cheek stitched up.

He lay before them, covered in a blanket. Another victim of humanity's endless wars.

William "Butch" Linden.

Ben-Ari spoke of his courage and sacrifice, pardoning his crimes, granting him final honors. Kai spoke in a choked voice about his hero. Addy could barely speak, but she whispered of a man she loved.

They had cleaned him. Placed his rifle against his chest. They said their goodbyes.

Ben-Ari spoke the final words.

"He was not a soldier. But he was a hero. He wore no uniform. But he fought for Earth's flag. What is a hero? A man who gives of his life for a cause greater than himself. Who is a true warrior? Not a man who hates his enemy, but a man who loves those he defends. We say farewell to a hero. To a warrior. To a father. He gave his life so that we may live. He is gone, but his memory remains. We will remember him always. We will honor his sacrifice. What is a good death? The passing from ephemeral life into beloved memory. Rest now among the stars. Goodbye, son of Earth. Godspeed."

They opened the airlock.

They stood by a viewport, watching him float into space, and Ben-Ari saluted.

Addy began to sing softly, staring at the stars. Marco held her hand and joined her. Soon they were all singing the anthem of Earth.

O, Earth!

Our pale blue home

Oh, Earth!

The world we love

Among all the stars

Your sun is brightest

Among all the worlds

You we call our home

In darkness we yearn for you

Under your sky we bless you

With all our courage we defend you

Forever you shall be

Our planet strong and free

O, Earth!

Our pale blue home

Oh, Earth!

The world we love

* * * * *

They flew onward, heading into the darkness. To war against the machines. To blood and terror.

But that was tomorrow. Tonight the *Loggerhead* was dark. Silent. Filled with haunting pain.

Kai sat on the bridge, flying the ship, only the dim light of the monitors lighting his face. Ben-Ari and Meili lay in the hold, sharing a blanket and each other's warmth. Both were deep in sleep, chests rising and falling.

Addy lay on the deck by the airlock. The place where her father had died. She lay in silence, staring into the darkness.

Remembering.

A childhood in a snowy city. A girl with her father in prison, her mother drugged out on the couch. A girl who got into fights at school. Who stole cigarettes. Who was so stupid they put her in the remedial class. A broken girl.

A girl who watched her father die. Only for him to come back. To die again.

"You fucking bastard," Addy whispered, tears in her eyes. "How dare you do this to me? To come back. Make me love you again. Only to leave me again. This time forever." She wiped her eyes. "You left me so many times. Every time you broke my heart. I love you, Dad. And I hate you. And I miss you."

Marco, who was lying beside her, turned toward her. He placed a hand on her waist.

"Addy, do you want to talk about it?" he whispered.

She embraced him. "No. I said what I needed to say. To the shadows. To him. Can you just hold me? Can you hold me all night?"

He held her, and he kissed her forehead. "Of course. Always."

She closed her eyes, feeling warm in his arms. This boy she had moved in with after the scum had killed her mother. This boy she had grown up with. This studious, quiet boy she had once found so confusing. This boy who had drowned in books and written poetry while she played hockey, smoked, got into fight after fight. This youth she had joined the army with. This youth who had fought at her side in the darkness of Corpus, on the fiery planes of Abaddon. This man she had married. The father of her children. The love of her life. Her Poet. Her Marco.

"I lost my father," she whispered. "You are now the man of my life, Marco. I'm strong. I'm a warrior. They say I'm a heroine. But in the night, I'm afraid, and I'm lost. Keep me safe."

He kissed her, holding her close, his arms strong, his body warm. "Always and forever, my Addy."

She placed a hand on his cheek and looked into his eyes.

"Marco," she whispered, "I'm pregnant."

He looked at her, stunned for a moment.

He hates me, she thought. *He's angry. He's scared.*

"Addy." He smiled shakily. "That's wonderful."

"You're not upset?"

He laughed softly. "Addy! Why would I be upset? Surprised, yes. Shocked, maybe. But …" He laughed again. "I'm happy. This is good news. Don't cry."

"I'm scared," she said. "To bring a child into a war? Another mouth to feed, a soul to protect? Even if I wanted to end the pregnancy, I couldn't … Not here, in a spaceship, I …"

"I want you to keep it," Marco said. "If you want to."

She nodded, a smile trembling on her lips. "I do. But I'm still scared."

"I am too," Marco said.

Her tears fell onto his chest. "Maybe it was meant to be. To lose a father. To gain a child." She closed her eyes and nuzzled him. "I'm so happy. And so terrified. I'm lost."

Marco stroked her hair for a long time, and their chests pressed together, hearts beating as one. When she slept, she dreamed that she was trapped in a labyrinth, a part of a huge machine, lost and unable to find her way home.

CHAPTER TWENTY-FOUR

The spiders crawled over her.

Their needles stung her, pumping her full of venom.

Lailani slapped at them, knocking them off, but more and more climbed onto her. She twisted, kicking, and they grabbed her legs. Pinned her down. Wrapped her in cobwebs, and she cried out, jolted up, and—

Her eyes snapped open.

A dream. Just a dream.

She slumped back down, breathing deeply, covered in cold sweat.

Her relief only lasted a second. Panic shot through her. Where was Tala?

She looked from side to side, heart pounding, then relaxed again. Her daughter lay beside her, deep in sleep. Epimetheus lay at her other side.

Breathe, soldier, she told herself. *Calm down. Collect yourself.*

They were all sharing a big bed. Lailani had no memory of coming here. No idea where she was. The last thing she remembered was the giant mechanical spider rampaging across the steppes. The explosion. Then—a vast expanse of nothingness.

She was inside a tent, it seemed. But nothing like the military tents Lailani had always known. An intricate latticework of bamboo formed round walls, a domed roof, and a doorframe. It reminded Lailani of a gazebo. Animal pelts covered the framework, and richly woven rugs covered the floor. A cast-iron stove stood nearby, its pipe rising through a hole in the roof.

This sort of dwelling is called a yurt, Lailani remembered, summoning a bit of trivia from the cluttered attic of her mind.

A ewer of water stood on a wooden table, beckoning. Lailani was weak, but that water got her out of bed. She drank deeply.

She noticed that she was wearing new clothes. Somebody had peeled off her tattered, burnt tank top and shorts. She now wore a *deel*—a silk robe, the red fabric embroidered with golden birds. She turned toward a mirror. Her face was scraped, but somebody had tended to her wounds. They had even brushed the dirt out of her hair.

Whoever had brought her here not only tended to her. They trusted her. Her pistol was on the table, alongside a fresh clip of bullets. She holstered the weapon.

Tala and Epi awoke, and they too drank water, and for a moment the family hugged and whispered soft comforts. Once her nerves were settled, Lailani opened the bamboo door and stepped outside.

The steppes sprawled toward distant yellow mountains. Wild horses and camels grazed upon patches of grass and low shrubs. More yurts rose around her, shaped like gazebos. Animal pelts covered the bamboo frameworks, and smoke rose from pipes, filling the air with the scent of cooking stews and brewing teas. It looked like a nomadic dwelling. Lailani imagined that these yurts could be folded up as easily as military tents. Here was a people on the move.

She saw them among the tents. Children ran, laughed, and rode on yaks. Women wore elaborate deels rich with tassels, beads, and embroidery, and fur rimmed their hats. Several elderly women tended to a campfire, cooking a pot of red stew. A few boys were practicing archery, while an old man sang a haunting tune.

It was the year 2160, but Lailani felt as if she had fallen back in time. Aside from a few rifles, which hung across the backs of men, she saw no modern technology. Useful during the Singularity.

The technological powers of the world fell, she thought. *The old ways survive.*

A burly man approached her, his blue robes fluttering in the wind. The golden horses embroidered into the fabric seemed to be galloping. He had bronze, lined skin, narrow eyes, a scar across the cheek. She recognized one of the riders who had fought the mechanical spider.

Lailani pressed her hands together and bowed.

"Good morning, sir. Thank you for helping me. I am Major Lailani de la Rosa of the HDF."

Thankfully, he spoke English. He bowed his head. "Good morning, Major. I am Sukhbataar Khan, ruler of this clan."

Lailani looked around her. "My plane crashed beyond the mountains. What country am I in?" She smiled at him nervously. "Uzbekistan? Kyrgyzstan? Tajikistan? Kazakhstan? Maybe Turkmenistan?"

"Mongolia," he said.

"Ah, I was close." Lailani sighed.

And I've been here before too, she remembered, feeling particularly dumb. *When I fought the grays. Without computers to navigate for me, I'm as helpless as a baby.*

A few children approached, their brocaded deels fluttering. They had rosy cheeks, fur hats, and wide smiles. They gathered around Tala, speaking to her in Mongolian. The girl was hesitant at first, answering in English, then in Tagalog, neither of which the local children understood. Finally the children all began to toss a ball, feed a young yak, and play with clay marbles, and that was language enough.

As the children played, Sukhbataar showed Lailani around the camp. Horses, camels, and yaks ambled among the yurts, feeding on the sparse grass. Cooking fires crackled, and the smell of roasted goat wafted across the steppes. An old man, dressed in a resplendent blue deel, was playing a fiddle with a carved horse head. People gathered around the graybeard, swaying to the haunting tune, singing softly.

Several people approached Lailani with gifts. They gave her bracelets of beads, yak cheese wrapped in cloth, and a rearing horse carved from bone. They spoke to her in their tongue, eyes bright.

"They know who you are," said Sukhbataar. "As do I. Lailani de la Rosa, the heroine of the Alien Wars. Even here, we have heard your tales of heroism. And now we have a new tale to tell. You defeated a beast even our warriors could not fell. They call you Spider Slayer."

Lailani accepted each gift with a bow. "I'm honored."

It was beautiful here, Lailani thought. In 2160—a culture independent of technology.

Well, largely independent.

Even here, she saw some modernity. The rifles across the warriors' backs. A beaten motorcycle stood among the horses. Between the yurts, a solar panel was soaking up the sun. Technology was seeping into this nomadic culture, but slowly. Thankfully, still so slowly. She saw no televisions, no phones, no computers. For now, they were safe.

"We are traditional nomads," Sukhbataar explained. "And have been for thousands of years. This is how we have survived. The cities ..." He lowered his head. "There is an evil rampaging through them."

Lailani nodded. "That evil is everywhere. I was flying from the Philippines to Europe. Both places are infected."

"The demon's face is etched across the moon," said Sukhbataar. "He mocks us at night. Some say that Earth gazes upon the moon with the same cruel smirk."

Lailani shuddered. "The Dreamer. But we can stop him, Sukhbataar. I carry with me a secret. A way to defeat him. I must reach Europe. Is there a city nearby? A place with an airport?"

"We will speak to the elders tonight," said Sukhbataar. "We know that you are brave. We will help you. But first we must honor our dead."

A group of men gathered, and they invited Lailani to join them. They carried the fallen warriors on litters, draped with brocade. The group began to climb the nearby mountain, some afoot, others riding yaks. Lailani and Tala chose to ride, sharing a shaggy brown yak with an embroidered saddle, a tasseled headdress, a necklace of seashells, and a golden ring in its nose. Next to this resplendent animal, Lailani felt underdressed.

As they climbed the mountain, the air grew colder, piercing their embroidered deels. Lailani was thankful for the fur hats the clan had given her and Tala.

They passed by carvings on boulders, artwork that depicted warriors on horseback, rams, and camels. The nomads explained that those were ancient drawings, etched by their ancestors thousands of years ago, that they blessed the mountain. Lailani could hear those ancient spirits in the wind.

They climbed for hours until they reached the mountaintop. Here they laid down the fallen warriors.

A monk approached, singing prayers, and pulled the shrouds off the dead. Then he drew a knife.

Lailani gasped.

"What—?" she began. "He's—"

She covered her daughter's eyes.

The monk was carving up the dead. Lailani stared in horror. The man was *dismembering* them. Cutting off limbs. Scattering the parts across the mountaintop. The other clansmen watched solemnly, whispering prayers.

Sukhbataar approached Lailani. He placed a hand on her shoulder and spoke in a low voice.

"This is how we honor our dead. This is a sky burial. This is holy. We leave our fallen heroes upon mountaintops, and we prepare the meat for the birds. The vultures and ravens will feast. The fallen give them this gift of their meat, a final act of kindness. Thus our fallen will return into the world, become one with sky, mountain, and air. Become life again."

The vultures circled above. The nomads stepped back. The scavengers began to feed.

Lailani couldn't watch. She turned away, sickened.

But is this truly different from how we bury bodies in the Philippines? she thought. *There the worms feast. Here it is the birds. We aren't so different after all.*

A young woman stepped forward, barefoot, and stood among the vultures. She pulled back her hood, revealing a beautiful face, so beautiful that Lailani lost her breath.

"A princess," Tala whispered in awe.

The young woman was slender and graceful. Her cheeks were pink, her eyes dark and filled with tears. Her red robes flowed across gentle curves, embroidered with golden sunbursts. She moved like the wind, her bead necklace and bracelets chinking.

A princess indeed, Lailani thought, suddenly feeling rather plain and skinny.

"This is Naran, which means the sun in our tongue," said Sukhbataar. "She is the daughter of Arban, one of our fallen warriors. She is mourning, and she is blessed."

Standing among the vultures, Naran began to sing. It was a song of such beauty that everyone shed tears. There was ugliness here but beauty too. There was death but the eternity of life. A cycle. An ancient song that went back to the dawn of creation.

That evening, Sukhbataar invited Lailani to a clearing by his yurt, where his family and closest friends gathered for dinner. Young maidens, smiling and shy, served a meal. There was goat stew, yak cheese, and fermented milk. Tala ate with gusto and played with her new friends, and Lailani's heart warmed to see some light return to her daughter's eyes.

This is a good place, she thought. *I wish I could stay.*

One of the serving girls filled her cup of milk, and her fingers brushed against Lailani's hand. The young woman lowered her eyes, smiling shyly. Lailani recognized her. It was Naran, which meant the sun, daughter of a hero, singer of beautiful songs.

Tala yawned several times, and soon she slept. The nomads entered their yurts, and the silence of night fell over the camp.

That night, Lailani sat outside on a grassy hill, alone. She gazed up at the stars. The moon stared down, mocking her with its cruel smile. She was lonely. She missed Marco and Addy and Ben-Ari. She missed Sofia, her lover, who had died in battle long ago. She missed HOBBS. She missed home.

"Spider Slayer?"

Lailani turned to see Naran climbing the grassy hill. The cold night air pinched her cheeks, ruffled her fur-lined *deel*, and chinked her bead bracelets. Lailani had known that she would come. She took the woman into her arms, kissed her under the stars, and they shared a night of warmth. Of softness. Of comfort. The moon had been deformed, but in her arms Lailani held the sun.

* * * * *

Dawn spilled across the steppes, gilding the mountains, and the caravan moved on. They rode horses, and their yaks, goats, and sheep followed. They took the yurts with them, folding the bamboo frameworks flat. Clad in a crimson deel embroidered with golden leaves, Lailani rode a beautiful mare as black as night. The wind ruffled her hair and filled her nostrils with the perfume of the steppes—grass, soil, spices. Her pistol rested against her thigh, and a sniper rifle hung across her back. The children ran alongside, playing, and Tala laughed with true light in her eyes. Epimetheus never left her side, tail wagging. Lailani watched her daughter and dog from her horse, a little comfort in her heart.

Stay, whispered a voice inside her. *They will welcome you. There is beauty here. There are friends for Tala. There is Naran, a woman of the sun.*

But Lailani knew she would have to move on. Because there were also tanks that moved on spider legs. There were robotic dogs that tore people apart. There were sleepers, cheeks slashed, laughing as they killed, their souls gazing from their eyes, trapped in prisons of flesh. There was a chip in her skull. A hope for mankind.

She was Lailani de la Rosa. She was the Spider Slayer. She was a daughter of Earth. She was a soldier. And she would fight on.

For three days, they traveled across the steppes. Three days of peace. Of song. Of warm meals and smiling faces. Three nights under the stars, making love to the sun.

On the fourth day, they reached a cracked highway, perhaps the one Lailani had seen from the plane. A few cars smoldered on the roadside. The vehicles had been burned only recently, and bullet holes perforated their sides. One car came racing down the highway. The nomads waved at it, but the car would not slow. The driver cried out something, gripping the wheel, then roared by.

"What did he say?" Lailani asked.

Sukhbataar's face was grim. "Metal demons."

The nomads kept traveling along the road, passing between the ruins of more cars. They were not rusty. Not old. Not the remnants of some ancient war. Some still burned, and the smell of gunpowder filled the air. Somebody had destroyed these cars only days ago. By one car lay the burnt skeleton of a soldier, dog tags hanging against his charred sternum.

The soldiers were destroying machines, she thought.

There was no flesh left for vultures. They left the body and rode on.

In the afternoon, they saw it ahead. A city on the plains.

Most Mongolians today were nomads, clinging to the old ways. But long ago, the Soviet Union had built some cities here on the steppes. The Soviet empire was long gone. Their cities remained.

This city nestled under the mountains. Boxy, concrete buildings clung to the arid land. Their paint was flaking. A few rusty chimneys still pumped smoke. Barbed wire surrounded an industrial zone. It was a small city, perhaps large enough for thirty thousand people.

But Lailani saw no one.

She halted her horse and stared.

No airplanes. No cars. No humans.

The factories rumbled. The chimneys churned out smoke. The city was alive. But who dwelled here?

She detected some movement among the buildings. She heard creaking. Clattering. The hum of engines.

She squinted, staring into the distance. It was hard to see. She grabbed her sniper rifle and stared through the scope, magnifying the view.

Mechanical spiders were moving through the city.

Cars. Buses. Even more tanks. All mounted on enormous metal legs. Some rose taller than three-story buildings. Lailani turned her scope toward the factories. Walls, fences, and chimneys obscured most of her view. But she glimpsed what looked like a scrapyard. Robots were moving through it, collecting metal rods, hammering, sawing. A new mechanical spider, an armored truck forming its body, left the factory on eight towering legs.

"The Dreamer is building an army," she said. "Mecha arachnids. Mechanids."

She passed the scope to Sukhbataar. The khan stared at the city, then turned toward Lailani. His eyes were dark.

"I have lost seventeen warriors fighting only one of those creatures," he said. "By the gods. Here is an army of metal."

Lailani cursed. She had hoped to find a functional city here. An airport. A train station. Hell, even just a car would be nice.

From the city rose a metallic screech. Then another. More shrill screams split the air. Several mechanids turned south, staring toward the countryside. Toward the nomads.

Sukhbataar's face was grim. For a moment, he lowered his eyes and whispered a prayer. He seemed grief-stricken.

But then the proud warrior raised his rifle overhead, and his cry rang across the steppes. "Riders! Prepare for battle!"

Riders cried out for war. They raised rifles and scimitars. They rode in rings around the caravan, ululating.

Lailani grabbed the khan's arm. "Sukhbataar, no. You must run."

He stared down at her from his larger horse. "We are warriors of the steppes, descended of the great khans of old. We do not flee from battle."

The mechanids were racing through the city now, their bulky bodies swaying atop their spiderlike legs. The fastest machines were already racing across the countryside.

"This would not be a battle," Lailani said, gripping the khan's arm. "It would be a massacre."

Sukhbataar stared at the approaching mechanids, then at Lailani again. Doubt filled his eyes, but then they hardened.

"If we are to die, we die in war, fighting proud upon our ancient plains."

"And your women and children?" Lailani said. "Will you sacrifice them? Sacrifice Naran who is like the sun?"

"What would you have me do?" he said. "Run like a coward?"

Lailani glanced at the mechanids. They were moving at terrifying speed. Tanks, buses, cars, all wobbling on their metal legs. Only moments away.

"Draw them away," Lailani said. "Draw them far from here into the steppes. Give me a chance to keep going. I told you about the technology in my head. The cure to their curse. I must keep going."

The grizzled khan stared at the machines, lips tight, then nodded. He placed a hand on Lailani's shoulder.

"Take our motorcycle. Take all the food and water you can grab. Then travel swifter than the finest horse. Find your way to the snowcapped mountain in the west. Destroy this curse." He smiled thinly, and his eyes shone. "We will draw them off. They will find us not so easy to face in the mountains."

The mechanids were only a kilometer away now. The enormous mechanical spiders opened fire.

Bullets slammed into the ground around the caravan. People screamed. One man fell, clutching his chest. One of the mechanids, an arachnid tank, fired a shell. The nomads scattered, and the blast tore through several animals.

"Go, Lailani!" cried Sukhbataar, then raised his rifle overhead and let out a wordless battle cry.

She nodded, hopped off her horse, and ran across the steppes, holding Tala in her arms. Bullets whizzed and pattered the ground around her feet. Epimetheus ran close behind, barking. Around them, the caravan was turning back east.

Lailani reached the nomads' single motorcycle. She placed Epimetheus and Tala into the sidecar, then hopped onto the main seat.

"Lailani!" A high voice from behind. "Lailani, wait!"

Sitting on the motorcycle, she turned her head. Naran was racing toward her, her silk deel fluttering, the blue fabric embroidered with bronze suns.

"Naran, go with your riders!" she said.

But the young woman kept running toward her, tears in her eyes. "Take me with you. I will fight with you. I will never leave—"

Bullets shrieked.

Blood bloomed across Naran's chest.

The young woman fell.

"Naran!" Lailani shouted.

She leaped off her motorcycle and ran toward the fallen woman. Naran lay in the grass, eyelids fluttering. She managed to reach up, to place a bracelet of topaz beads into Lailani's hand.

"A last gift," Naran whispered. "A blessing from the sun. I love ..."

Her eyes rolled back.

Eyes damp, Lailani hopped back onto her motorcycle. She tightened her lips, fired up the engine, and roared forward.

Several mechanids loomed before her. Only meters away.

Lailani tugged the handlebars, swerving around a hailstorm of bullets. In the sidecar, Tala wailed and clung on, and Epi barked.

The spider legs rose all around, as large as electric poles. Guns swiveled, mounted onto the undercarriages of tanks, buses, trucks, and the other vehicles that formed the spiders' abdomens.

Lailani leaned forward, ramped up the thrust, and roared forward.

A mechanid rose before her, an armored jeep forming its body. She raced between its legs. As she passed beneath the machine, she raised her rifle and fired. She hit the joint where one leg met the jeep. The leg bent. The creature wobbled. Lailani rode onward as the mechanid crashed down.

Another mechanid loomed ahead. Its body was formed from a sandbird—an old fighter jet, one used extensively in the late twenty-first century before most warfare moved into space. The plane had not flown in many years, but it now moved on arachnid legs, and its rotary gun aimed at Lailani.

She increased speed. The bullets hailed down behind her. The sandbird's machine gun spun toward her. Lailani swerved, ripping up grass, dodging the barrage. Clutching a handlebar with one hand, she raised her rifle and fired.

She hit the mechanid's rotary gun, knocking its muzzles aside. Again. Again. Finally her bullets tore it free, and the cannon thumped onto the ground.

Lailani kept riding. More mechanids rose before her. A tank aimed its cannon.

She found herself staring down the bore.

An instant of horror overwhelmed her.

With battle cries, the nomads galloped forth. Their guns boomed. Bullets slammed into the mechanid legs, knocking the gargantuan spider back. A few riders swung scimitars, chipping at the leg joints.

The machines turned toward them. Their guns fired. A rider fell. Another. A shell flew, fire blazed, and soil and grass rose in a storm. A man pattered down as red rain.

"Go, Lailani!" cried Sukhbataar, riding in rings around the machines, raising clouds of dust. His gun boomed. "Ride for life!"

She saluted him, eyes damp, then turned her motorcycle around and roared through the dusty clouds.

She rumbled along the steppes. The dust storm hid her. Behind, she heard the shrieks of the machines. Heard deep, distorted voices emerging from their mechanical innards. Heard the guns fire. Men and horses die. Battle cries turn to screams.

She rode onward.

She looked over her shoulder. The riders were galloping east again, drawing the mechanids after them. Lailani rode alone.

She allowed herself to relax. To slow down. In the sidecar, Tala was hugging Epimetheus, her hair flowing in the wind. The girl's eyes were dead again. Haunted. Their light gone. Eyes that stared ten thousand kilometers ahead.

"You're safe now, Tala," Lailani said. "I won't let them hurt you anymore. I—"

Engines roared.

The sound was so loud Lailani winced and Epimetheus howled.

Lailani looked over her shoulder, and her heart nearly stopped.

One of the mechanids was chasing her. The one with a fighter jet body. Several of its legs were missing, but its engines bellowed and blasted fire.

The remaining mechanical legs folded inward. The sandbird jet streaked across the sky. Flying toward Lailani.

She cried in horror and increased speed. Her motorcycle thrummed across the steppes, tearing up grass.

The sandbird roared above, legs folded against its belly. Missiles hung from under its wings.

A missile detached and streaked downward.

Lailani squeezed the brakes.

The missile slammed down ahead. An explosion bloomed. Dirt flew and fire blazed.

Lailani was still moving too fast. She couldn't swerve in time.

She sucked in air and increased the throttle.

"Duck, Tala!" she cried.

The motorcycle leaped through the fire, and Lailani screamed.

The bike landed and kept rumbling forward. The jet overshot her, flying so low the air whipped Lailani, and her motorcycle nearly overturned. The sandbird wheeled in the sky, turning toward her, and hovered. Its stabilizer thrusters flattened the grass.

There was nobody in the cockpit. But Lailani knew *he* was there. The Dreamer.

She kept riding forward.

The sandbird rose higher.

Lailani swerved hard, leaped from her seat, and sent her motorcycle rolling down a slope with Tala and Epimetheus.

If I die, look after my daughter, Epi.

A missile detached from the jet.

In midair, Lailani aimed her pistol and fired.

She saw the missile spark before she hit the ground.

She slammed down hard on her side, and an explosion ripped the sky.

Hell bloomed in the air like a flower of fire. Lailani fired again and again. Her bullets shrieked toward the jet. Another explosion rocked the sandbird. Another. All its munitions were detonating.

Lailani lay under a storm of flame. She covered her ears as the sky cracked open. Shards of metal landed around her.

With a storm of fire, the remains of the jet crashed onto the plains. Black smoke curled upward like a serpent.

Lailani stood up and winced. A piece of shrapnel had sliced her thigh. Later she would awake the alien, let him heal her. Right now, she limped across the steppes, tolerating the pain, moving between smoldering scraps of metal.

She found her motorcycle on a patch of grass, engine purring. Epimetheus was standing guard, tail a straight line. Tala still sat in the sidecar. Lailani rushed toward the girl.

"Are you all right, Tala? Are you hurt?"

She examined the three-year-old for wounds. But Tala seemed unharmed.

"Mommy, you're a badass," she said.

Lailani blinked, tears in her eyes, then burst out laughing. "Who taught you how to say that?"

Tala shakily smiled. "You did."

She hugged her daughter for a long time.

"It's just a dream, little one," she whispered. "Just a bad dream. We'll wake up soon. And we'll be home."

They rode onward. Lailani's ashy hair and tattered deel fluttered in the wind. Tala and Epi sat in the sidecar, both wearing goggles. Dust rose in clouds behind them. They headed into the sunset, leaving the city, the machines, and the fallen behind.

CHAPTER TWENTY-FIVE

Marco sat alone on the *Loggerhead*'s bridge, gazing out into space. He felt lost.

The antique starship was flying through hyperspace, moving faster than light. With every second that passed, they were millions of kilometers farther from Earth. From his children.

During the days, Marco could fight aliens, banter with Addy, assist his president, and most importantly—keep busy. But now, at night, alone on the dark bridge—there was nothing to drown his fears.

The others were asleep back in the hold. Tomorrow they would reach Esporia, the world of Don Basidio. Tonight it was just Marco and the shadows.

I miss you, Roza and Sam, he thought. He had discarded his minicom, fearing the virus. He could no longer pull it out, look at photos and videos of his children. But in the darkness, he could so easily remember their smiles. Their laughter. How they ran through his home, calling "Daddy, Daddy!"

I miss you too, Terri, he thought. He could see her in the shadows, a timid girl with long red hair. The scar across her face had taken one of her eyes, but not her grace or beauty. *I barely got to know you, Terri, and had to leave again. We'll be together soon. I promise.*

He lowered his head. Guilt filled him. He should never have left.

"Marco?"

A voice from behind. He turned to see Ben-Ari step onto the bridge. The president wore her pajamas, and she held two cups of steaming tea. Her blond hair was pulled into a ponytail, and she was barefoot.

Seeing her like that jolted Marco. He had become used to Einav Ben-Ari the president—in a power suit and heels, her makeup immaculate, her eyes steely. Suddenly she looked so much like his old friend. The woman who had fought at his side for so many years.

The woman who saved my life, and who ruined it, Marco thought. *The woman who pulled me back from the edge in Haven when I was about to jump. The woman who drafted me for this war. And for three wars before this. Wars that broke me.*

But he could say none of that to her. At night, he could confess his thoughts to his wife. Ben-Ari was still his officer. His commander-in-chief.

"Can't sleep, ma'am?" he asked her.

She sat beside him. "I brought us some tea." She handed him a mug.

He accepted the mug and sipped. His eyebrows rose. "You, Einav Ben-Ari, drinking black tea? What happened to your chamomile?"

She smiled. "Not to worry, my cup is still chamomile. As per usual. I travel with black tea for guests." She put a hand on his shoulder. "And good friends."

Marco looked at her. All her aura of authority was gone. With her pajamas and steaming mug, she almost looked like a girl on Christmas morning. She pulled her knees up to her chest, sipped her tea, and smiled again. A beautiful smile, her teeth white and perfect.

A memory from seventeen years ago filled Marco.

Boot camp.

Everyone was in the mess hall. Marco sat with Addy, Elvis, Lailani, and the others. Ben-Ari sat across the hall with the platoon's sergeant and corporals. From the distance, the recruits saw her smile. That perfect, beautiful smile with those white teeth.

Elvis had whistled and clutched his heart. "That smile! She's breaking my heart."

Addy had punched him. "She'll break your dick. She's an officer and you're a pissant recruit. Sit your ass down, Elvis."

The memory only lasted a second. But it was jarring. Almost two decades had passed since that day. This seemed like a different universe. A different lifetime. Who had those people been? Those eighteen-year-old recruits? That twenty-year-old ensign? Figures from ancient memory, that was all. Ghosts. They no longer existed.

But here beside him, the president of Earth smiled again. And here, Marco Emery—the famous author, the father, the war hero—felt like that boy again.

"Did you want to talk about something, Einav?" he said softly.

She put a hand on his shoulder. "I wanted to apologize, Marco. Long ago, I chose you. From a platoon of fifty soldiers, I chose you. I called you into my trailer. I asked you to follow me to space. To war. And … I'm sorry."

Marco wasn't sure what to say. Had Ben-Ari heard him discussing this with Addy? Talking about their regrets? About never wanting to follow their leader again?

"You gave me a choice," Marco said. "I could have refused. I didn't have to become a warrior. I could have gotten a job in the military archives. Maybe become a reporter."

"I know." Ben-Ari gazed into his eyes. "It had to be a choice. It had to be a path you volunteered to walk. Do you know why you said yes?"

He thought for a moment. "Because you're an excellent officer. Because you inspired me. Because—"

"No. Not because of me. Because you are honorable, Marco. Because you are good. Because you are willing to sacrifice of yourself for others. You weren't the strongest soldier in my platoon; that was Beast. You weren't the bravest; that was Addy. You weren't the toughest; that was Pinky. You weren't even the smartest; that was Noodles."

"You flatter me," Marco said.

Her smile returned briefly, then faded. "I chose you, Marco, because you were the most ethical. And you were the wisest. You still are. I saw that in you then when you were just a boy. And it's still true today."

He tilted his head. "Thank you, Einav, but ... why then are you apologizing?"

Her hand was still on his shoulder. Her eyes never left his. "Because sometimes I wonder if I ruined your life."

Marco finally broke eye contact. He looked down. "The war ruined our lives. It ruined many lives. We're not unique that way. War has ruined the lives of many throughout history. It's the story of humanity."

"It's my job to think about humanity and our place in its unfolding history," Ben-Ari said. "To think of our part in this great play that spans eras and worlds. But right now I'm not thinking about any of that. I'm thinking about *you*, Marco. About my friend."

He looked back at her. "Are we friends, Einav? We were soldier and officer. Today we are officer and president."

"We were never just that." Her hand rose from his shoulder to caress his cheek. "You've been my good friend for many years, Marco. My best friend. Even during those years when we were far apart. Even as president, dealing with dilemmas every day, I would think about you. All the time. I would wonder what you would do. What moral choice you would make. How you would guide me. And I missed you."

Marco nodded, and something hard and cold seemed to melt inside him, to become soft and warm. "Yes. I thought about you every day too. Even when we were apart. In Haven, I thought about you a lot. Addy is my wife, and I love her more than anything. But you're my anchor, Einav. My guiding star. My best friend. You're the defining person of my life."

"The person who ruined your life?" she whispered.

"The person who saved me, who inspired me." Marco suddenly felt his cheeks heat. "Sometimes I wondered what might have been. If ... after Lailani left me, whether ..."

Ben-Ari looked at her lap, and she too blushed. "I thought about it too sometimes. We both love literature, music, history. We both shared so much—both harrowing tragedies but also days of triumph and joy. It was impossible, of course, when I was your commanding officer. But after the army, I thought that maybe ..." She bit her lip, and then her beautiful smile returned. She put a hand on his thigh. "But by then, you had Addy, and she's wonderful. And I have Noah, and I love him with all my heart. We're both happy. Right, Marco?"

"No," he said softly. "We're not happy. Not here. Not in this war. But after this war ... maybe."

She was still smiling, but now sadness tinged her smile. "Can I hug you, Marco?"

"Of course. Always."

She hugged him for a long time. Her body was warm, comforting, and she smelled of chamomile.

"I love you, Einav," Marco whispered to her, her hair tickling his face. "And I always will."

She grinned and mussed his hair. "Best friends forever, right?"

He nodded. "Forever."

Ben-Ari stood up and kissed his cheek. "I love you too, Marco."

She left the bridge. Marco remained alone, flying the ship, gazing out into the darkness. But now he could see the light of the stars, and he was no longer cold.

CHAPTER TWENTY-SIX

They had one starship.

The *Loggerhead*. A dented little antique. A ship built like an iron turtle shell. A ship containing the last people who could save the world.

At Haven, he lurked. The Dreamer. The lord of nightmares. The central brain of the machine. An electric tree, blooming in the darkness of a volcano. Around him, they lurked: his hounders and spiders and metal monsters. In his orbit, they flew: his hijacked fleet, human starships converted into his machines of malice.

There, at Haven, awaited the final battle.

But that battle would not be fought today.

Today Ben-Ari flew the *Loggerhead*, the last ship serving humanity, to another world.

To a world many light-years away from the Dreamer's tree.

To a rotting world. A world of fungus, mist, decay. A world of mushrooms. A world called Esporia. A world where she could raise the weapons to destroy her enemy.

"Esporia." Ben-Ari stood at the viewport, hands clasped behind her back, and gazed down upon it. "Perhaps the most feared world in the galaxy."

Addy gagged. "Ugh! It looks like a watermelon somebody forgot under the sink for a year. I can practically smell it from space. It's disgusting!"

Marco rolled his eyes. "Addy, just last year, you ate a rotten watermelon you found on the beach."

"That was different! I saw crabs eating it, so I knew it was fine."

Marco sighed.

If this planet had a rocky core, it was buried deep. Life covered the entire planet. Forests of decay, jungles of mushrooms, and swamps of moss and mold. Layers upon layers of fungus lived there, engulfing the entire sphere, thinning only at the poles. For billions of years, many fungal species had made their home on Esporia.

Incredibly, one had gained intelligence.

The Esporians. A race of cruel, carnivorous mushrooms.

Ben-Ari had never met one, had only seen the drawing in Addy's book. But from here, she could see several organic spheres flying around the planet. She tapped a few buttons. Her viewport zoomed in on a flying blob.

It looked like a ball of fungus. Moldy red circles stained its gray surface like fairy rings. A vent flared out like a flower, spewing clouds of spores. She zoomed onto that vent. She could see little figures inside. They looked like toadstools.

The Esporians.

"Those are starships." Ben-Ari pointed at the floating blobs. "My father wrote about them. Podships."

Addy shuddered. "Goddamn, I hope we don't have to fly any of those stinky things to battle." She turned toward Kai. "You're sure the mushrooms sold you the *Barracuda*, a starship with a Tarjan engine? Because if we have to fly to battle without human computers, I'd much rather fly Tarjan ships. Not inside flying pimples." She frowned. "Kai. Kai, you with us, dumbass?"

Kai was gazing out the viewport at the planet below. While under the Dreamer's influence, he had carved open his left cheek. It was stitched back together now, swollen and red. Kai had kept his mouth shut since that battle, not speaking or eating. It was less because of the wound, perhaps, and more because he still mourned the loss of his father.

"Kai?" Addy said again, poking him.

Kai blinked as if waking from a trance. He looked at his half sister.

"What?" He blinked again. "No. Don Basidio didn't sell us the *Barracuda*. He doesn't allow Tarjan ships in his own star system. I doubt he's even seen one with his own eyes. The Tarjan ships serve in the Golden Fleet, a criminal armada that operates in deep space, a subsidiary of the Basidio Boys. Their crew is all human, in fact. Human pirates who swore allegiance to the cartel. Butch and I served with the Golden Fleet. Briefly. We kind of, um … stole the *Barracuda*."

Ben-Ari stepped between the siblings. She grabbed Kai's shoulders and stared into his eyes. "Wait a minute. Your father told me he *bought* the *Barracuda*. Are you telling me you *stole* a starship from the Basidio Boys? The most notorious mafia in the galaxy?"

Kai sighed. "Maybe when you talk to Don Basidio, I should stay on the *Loggerhead*."

Ben-Ari tilted her head. Her jaw hung open. She was at a loss for words.

Kai shrugged. "Well, we *are* pirates." He lowered his head. "I mean, I am. Butch was."

Ben-Ari cringed. "Yeah. Maybe stay on the ship." She looked back at the fungal planet. "You're right. I don't see any Tarjan starships around. Don Basidio must keep them elsewhere. Where does the boss live? Kai, can you fly us directly to him?"

The young pirate shivered. "Actually, I'm getting worried now. I stole from Don Basidio. Fuck, fuck, fuck! You're right. I'm crazy to be here. I have to turn back. I—"

"No." Ben-Ari grabbed his arms. "Listen to me, Kai Linden. Whoever you were, that man is dead. You're no longer a pirate. You're a soldier now. You're *my* soldier. I protect my soldiers. But you must obey my orders. Without question or hesitation. Is that understood?"

Kai gulped and nodded. He even managed a salute. "Yes, ma'am."

But his voice wavered. And tears stung his eyes.

Ben-Ari placed a hand on his shoulder and stared into his eyes. "I know you hurt, Kai. I know you lost your father. And I'm sorry. But right now you need to bury all that. We're in danger now. And in danger, you must be strong. Marco and Addy laugh, cry, and joke during downtime. But in battle, they are dead serious. I trained them that way. I never trained you. So I need to know: Can I count on you, Kai?"

His eyes dried. His salute this time was brisker, his voice stronger. "Yes, ma'am!"

"Good." She nodded, scrutinizing him for any conceit. "Very good. Now—fly us down to planet Esporia. Take us to Don Basidio."

"I can't do that, ma'am," he said.

Ben-Ari frowned. "*What?*"

"Don Basidio doesn't live on Esporia, ma'am. A family of elder mushrooms, a million years old, rules over that fungal world. They banished Don Basidio long ago. And let me tell you, it's not easy to banish a mushroom. They tend to stick around."

Ben-Ari blinked. "Are you telling me we came all this way for nothing, and you just tell us now that—"

"Ma'am, he's nearby." Kai pointed. "See that moon? That's where they exiled Don Basidio to. See, the elders didn't want to kill him. He offers them a slice of his pie. Bribes. So they keep him alive. Just … off the main world. It's a small moon. Barely more than a penal colony. But from that moon, Basidio runs a criminal empire that spans the Orion Arm of the galaxy."

"So he's basically Jabba the Hutt, but a mushroom," Marco said.

Addy frowned at her husband. "Huh? What the fuck you talkin' about, Poet?"

"You know, *Star Wars*," he said.

Addy jabbed him hard in the ribs. "You and your nerdy nonsense."

He rolled his eyes. "Yes, but your obsession with *Freaks of the Galaxy* and *Robot Wrestling* is completely healthy."

Kai returned to the helm. He began flying the *Loggerhead* toward Esporia Ceti, the planet's rotting moon. As they flew closer, details emerged. The moon looked even worse than the planet. It hung like a ball of mucus, green and yellow. Scans showed a rocky core buried beneath thick layers of life.

Addy gagged again. "Gross! It's like athlete's foot infected both planet and moon. Entire worlds—covered with disease."

"That's how we humans see it," Ben-Ari said. "But this too is life. Different from our own. But life nonetheless. It must have taken billions of years to evolve. This is no mere infection. It's an entire ecosystem. And from this lush environment, consciousness and intelligence arose. I think it's rather spectacular."

Kai pursed his lips. "Actually, Addy is right. I've been here before. It's a floating pus ball."

"Well, we're going down there nonetheless," Ben-Ari said. "We need more Tarjan ships. And only Don Basidio knows where to get them."

Kai suddenly pulled a lever, and the ship came to a complete stop, still a good distance from Esporia Ceti.

"Ma'am, I urge you," Kai said. "Negotiate from aboard this ship. We can open a hailing frequency. Talk to the don from inside the *Loggerhead*, a few thousand kilometers away, encased in a thick iron hull. You're the president of Earth! The commander-in-chief of the Human Defense Force! Don Basidio hates you. *Hates* you. You've been hunting his ships for years. You've placed hundreds of his gangsters behind bars. If you set one foot on that moon, I promise you. You're a dead woman."

Addy slapped him. "You could have said something before we nearly died collecting laceleaf. Before …" She said nothing more.

But Kai understood. He paled and trembled. "It's not my fault."

"I didn't—" Addy began.

"Don't you dare insinuate that what happened is my fault!" Kai said. "Dad didn't die because of me. He died because—"

"I didn't say that!" Addy insisted. "I just mean—we go on a mission to get laceleaf. So we can become immune to spores. So we can go talk to Don Basidio without him drugging our brains. And now you're chickening out? Now you just want to have some fucking phone call?" She slapped him again. "This is serious business, asshole. You don't negotiate the fate of humanity over the phone. Not if you want a proper deal. Even I know that. So we're going down there, and we're shaking that mushroom's hand.

Or his, um … stalk. Spores? Whatever mushrooms shake." She thought for a moment. "I guess we can hug him."

Marco sighed. "Once we're down there, Addy, please let Ben-Ari do the talking." He opened his backpack, revealing the laceleaf. "Now everyone eat your veggies."

After two weeks in space, the *Loggerhead* smelled a little … well seasoned. Nobody had showered since leaving Upidia. Thankfully, the caterpillars had installed a septic tank at least. The hole in the deck reminded everyone of boot camp latrines. But now the smell of laceleaf filled the ship, rich with cinnamon, cloves, and hints of nutmeg. The star-shaped leaves had glowed on Upidia. They had dried up since, becoming pale green and wrinkly, but still wonderfully aromatic.

"So do we just eat it?" Kai sniffed the laceleaf, then crinkled his nose. "Ugh, it stinks."

Addy punched him. "Shut up! You stink. Let me check my book." She grabbed her copy of *Freaks of the Galaxy*. She leafed past a variety of monsters, finally reaching the page about Don Basidio. "How to become immune to his spores … Ah, here we go! Laceleaf, apparently, can be eaten, smoked, vaped, or even made into delicious tea." She looked up from the book. "I'm smoking mine!"

"I'm brewing tea," said Ben-Ari. "I need a cuppa anyway."

They consumed the laceleaf. The Linden-Emery clan chose to smoke. Ben-Ari brewed tea for her and Meili. She never went anywhere without a thermos, complete with a battery to boil water. She was normally a chamomile girl, but she had to admit, laceleaf tasted just as good. It reminded her of strong masala chai.

"I missed tea." Meili shivered. "I used to love green tea. Little rolled-up leaves with a touch of jasmine."

Ben-Ari smiled over the thermos they shared. "Used to? Not anymore?"

The young programmer lowered her eyes. "I'm different now. The girl I was? She died. I don't know who I am anymore." She took off her glasses and wiped her tears. "Is this what it's always like? War?"

Ben-Ari nodded. "Yes. Violence. Death. Danger. Horrors in the darkness of space. It's always like this."

Meili shed another tear. "I feel so guilty, ma'am. That I caused this. That I coded him." She trembled. "What we saw on the HDFS *Patton*, the admiral with his head cut open, and his brain … Do you think he's dead? That we killed him?"

"I don't think so," Ben-Ari said softly.

"I wanted to kill him," Meili said. "To end his pain. But we just left him behind. Left all of them on those ships."

Damn it, Ben-Ari thought. *I trained Marco and Addy in boot camp. I broke them and remolded them. But I never trained Kai. And I never trained Meili. And I don't know if they're strong enough. If they're reliable.*

Ben-Ari stared at the programmer, eyes hard.

"Meili, listen to me. You are nineteen. No longer a girl. Marco and Addy were younger than you when they stormed the mines of Corpus. I remember. I led them there. You will have to grow up. You will have to be strong. Sometimes in war, people

309

die. Sometimes in war, we have to leave men behind. Accept that. Harden your heart. Do not fall apart. I need you to be strong now, okay?"

Meili nodded, sniffed, then raised her chin. "Yes. Sorry, ma'am." She wiped her eyes. "I won't be weak again."

Ben-Ari clasped the girl's shoulder. "Tears aren't a sign of weakness. But do not shed tears during days of war. Shed your tears in the night, then wake up ready to fight. That is how soldiers cry." Her voice softened. "That is how I cry."

Meili gasped. "You? But you're so strong."

"As are you, Dr. Chen. Do not forget that."

We must all be stronger than we've ever been, Ben-Ari thought. *A path of tears lies before us. We must walk without straying to the right or left. And I must lead the way.*

* * * * *

Once the laceleaf was consumed, warmth filled Ben-Ari. Her mind felt a little hazy. But nothing worse than that time she had puffed on a joint at age seventeen, a little rebel hanging out with artillery sergeants when her father wasn't watching.

Ben-Ari smiled thinly to remember that girl. The daughter of a famous colonel, the scion of a legendary military family. A Ben-Ari. A girl bred for war. A girl who grew up on military bases, playing with guns while other girls played with dolls. Yes, she had rebelled in those years. Smoking. Drinking. A couple of trysts with forbidden boys. Nothing unusual for a teenager, perhaps, but today Ben-Ari struggled to recognize that girl she had been.

Twenty years had gone by. She no longer rebelled against the military. She commanded it. Yes, she was a Ben-Ari, bred for greatness. And yet despite all her words to Kai, to Meili, despite who she had become ... deep inside, that little girl still hid. Was still afraid.

We're all children in war, she thought. *Some of us cruel. All of us scared. We're all just children who put on uniforms and pretend to be brave.*

She shook her head wildly. Pointless navel-gazing! Maybe the laceleaf was affecting her more than she had thought.

Several podships bobbed through space toward the *Loggerhead.* They were splotchy spheres of fungus, their vents sticking out like flaring lips. The podships were so large the *Loggerhead* could have flown into them. One of the vents retracted, then thrust out, spewing a cloud of spores.

"We're under attack!" Ben-Ari said. "Marco, Addy, man the cannons, and—"

"Wait!" Kai said. "That's not a weapon. Those are communication spores. I can tell by the color. The Esporians talk a little differently."

Ben-Ari held up her hand, stalling Marco and Addy. She frowned at the incoming cloud of spores.

"How will we read that?" she said.

Kai flipped a few switches on the dashboard. "Ma'am, the *Loggerhead* was built by the Upidians, a race which fought a long, hard war against Esporia. You better believe their spaceship can read spores. Once I get a read on the spores, I can pass the code through my minicom's universal translator, and Bob's your uncle. Ha, here we go!" He tapped a few more controls. "Bing-fucking-o."

Ben-Ari frowned at the young pirate. "One of these days you'll have to tell me how you can handle alien tech so well."

"One day over a cup of tea, I promise," Kai said. "Right now we're getting an incoming call."

The spores fluttered across the *Loggerhead*'s prow. On the bridge, a monitor turned on. It began to display a video feed—presumably from inside the podship.

The Esporian bridge—if one could call it that—looked more like the inside of a stomach. Its walls were fleshy and soft, gilled in several places. Golden balls clung to the ceiling like pimples, filling the chamber with light.

Three large mushrooms grew from the floor. They were purple and looked like brains, complete with a network of folds. They were just mushrooms, not actual brains. Still, Ben-Ari couldn't help but remember seeing Admiral Kabanen's exposed brain. It apparently triggered the same memory in her crew. They shuddered collectively.

The alien mushrooms vibrated. Squishy wet sounds emerged from them.

"We recognize your species. You are apes! Like the lower organisms, you still use primitive sound waves to communicate. We will vibrate for you. We will speak your words. For you are too lowly and pathetic to understand the language of higher beings."

Ben-Ari glanced at the others, then back at the monitor.

"Greetings. I am President Einav Ben-Ari of—"

"Silence, protein sacks! We don't care who you are." New clouds of spores brushed against the *Loggerhead.* "You are nutrients, that is all. Fresh meat to rot so beautifully in our soil."

"Your boss, Don Basidio, does care who I am!" Ben-Ari said. "I am the human whose fleet pounded his pirate ships. I am the human who placed hundreds of his gangsters behind bars. I am the human who can destroy him and his little criminal empire. I am the human he hates most in all humanity. And I've come to negotiate."

For a moment the brainy mushrooms were silent. Aboard their bridge, they tossed spores at one another.

Slowly their podship turned toward Esporia Ceti. The vent flared, spewing spores down onto its surface. A few moments of silence passed. Then a volcano bloomed open on the moon like an alien egg. A geyser of spores erupted into space, washing across the podship.

The fungal sphere turned back toward the *Loggerhead.*

"We have spoken to Don Basidio," the fungal brains said. "He welcomes you into his kingdom."

Ben-Ari nodded. "Good, then we—"

"President Ben-Ari, wait!" Kai said. "Please. Listen to me." He turned toward the monitor. "Um, let me put you on hold, mushroom dudes."

Kai flicked a switch, and the monitor went dark.

Ben-Ari glowered, hands on her hips. "What do you think you're doing, Linden?"

"Saving your life," Kai said. "Ma'am, if you go down onto that moon, Don Basidio will kill you. I promise you."

Marco, who had been sitting silently at the gunnery station, nodded. "Ma'am, I tend to agree with Kai. It's too dangerous. Even with Addy and me watching your back."

"Don Basidio has no honor," Kai added. "He's not like the leaders you're used to negotiating with. I know the mushroom. He'd see only a chance to kill the fabled Golden Lioness."

Ben-Ari pursed her lips and tapped her foot. Were they right? Would she be going down to certain death?

"Again," she said carefully, "this is information that would have been useful a few days ago."

"There's another way," Kai said. "It's dangerous. They might refuse. But it might save your life." He flipped on the monitor. "Hey, mushroom dudes, just one more minute!" He switched it back off, then looked at Ben-Ari silently. "Are you open to suggestions?"

Ben-Ari nodded. "What's your plan?"

Kai's eyes darkened, and his hands balled into fists. "Don Basidio owns slaves. Human slaves." His voice dropped. "Sex slaves."

Addy guffawed. "What? Brother, are you high? He's a giant mushroom."

"That he is," Kai said. "And he enjoys placing his spores into the wombs of his women. He says a human womb is the ideal environment for his fungal offspring." He shuddered. "I've seen him do it. First he drugs his women, using his own spores. They become addicted to him. To his smell. His taste. He becomes their drug. And then he …" Kai's fists trembled. "Infects them."

Addy gagged. "The fucker! I'm going to chop him up for pizza!"

"Kai, how does this relate to our situation?" Ben-Ari said, trying to keep her voice calm. His words had chilled her.

"Getting to that," Kai said. "You see, Don Basidio has a favorite concubine. Her name is Isabel Martinez. An American woman he captured long ago. The don adores her above all others. She dances for him. She licks his flesh. She grows his spores inside her. Ask Don Basidio to send Isabel up to this ship. I'll watch over her in the *Loggerhead*. Then you go down to the surface and talk to him."

Ben-Ari understood. "She'll be collateral."

"Yes," said Kai. "Once you're safely back on the *Loggerhead*, we'll send Isabel back down."

"What?" Addy rose from her seat. "Send a human slave back down to that monster?"

Ben-Ari pursed her lips. "We might have no choice."

"This is monstrous!" Addy said. "We can't just—"

The podship spewed a cloud of spores over the *Loggerhead*. The monitor came back to life.

315

"We are done waiting, pathetic meat creatures!" The brain mushrooms vibrated. "Do you accept our don's invitation?"

The crew turned to look at Ben-Ari. It was her decision.

She took a deep breath and nodded. "Yes, we accept. But we need collateral. Bring Isabel Martinez, concubine of Don Basidio, to our ship. My crew will keep her safe and comfortable. Once negotiations are complete, and I'm back on my starship, Martinez will return to Don Basidio's court."

"We can't—" Addy began, but Ben-Ari silenced her with a glare.

Let this burden be on my conscience, Ben-Ari thought. *It's the fate of humanity on the line. If I must, I will sacrifice the few to save the many. That is what leaders do. That is the most moral choice—and the most heartbreaking.*

The podship spent a few moments communicating with Esporia Ceti, exchanging spores with the moon. Finally the podship sent another message to the *Loggerhead.*

"We accept, protein sacks. Prepare to receive the slave. Stay in your current position or be destroyed."

The podship descended toward the moon.

In the *Loggerhead,* the crew stood in silence for a moment.

"So … we just wait?" Addy said.

Ben-Ari nodded. "So it would seem."

* * * * *

They waited for long moments. Kai bounced his knee up and down, bit his nails, and made everyone even more nervous. The young man was sweating bullets. Addy began to hum until Marco shushed her. In the ship's hold, Meili busied herself with her minicom, adding last-minute tweaks to Project Artemis.

Ben-Ari merely stood on the bridge, immobile, hands clasped behind her back. Her insides trembled, and she missed her family so badly it hurt. She felt lightheaded. Tipsy. Almost as if she floated. Maybe it was the laceleaf kicking in. Despite her inner turmoil, she projected a strong image for her crew—back straight, shoulders squared, chin raised. She needed to give her crew confidence. And give it to herself.

This must work, she thought. *We must get ships that the Dreamer cannot hack. Or humanity falls.*

Finally the podship returned. It bobbed through space like a giant piece of pollen. Only a few meters away, it halted and hovered. This close by, it dwarfed the *Loggerhead*. They were like a baby turtle next to a rotting watermelon.

The podship's vent bloomed open. It spat out a fleshy glob.

Ben-Ari blinked at the viewport. The glob glided toward the *Loggerhead*, writhing.

"My God," Ben-Ari whispered.

"There's a person in there!" Addy cried, pointing.

Indeed, the glob contained a human. A woman. Somebody trapped in membranes, floating through space.

Ben-Ari raced toward the *Loggerhead*'s airlock. She hit a button, opening the outer door. The blob floated into the airlock, and the door shut. Ben-Ari waited in the hold, tapping her foot while the airlock repressurized. Her head was definitely spinning now. The laceleaf was hitting her hard.

"Dude, I'm dizzy," Addy said, swaying nearby. "This laceleaf is good shit."

Marco nodded. "Same here. I feel ..." He blinked. "Funny."

Finally the airlock was pressurized, and they opened the door. They pulled the woman into the hold. Their guest collapsed onto the deck, wrapped in translucent membranes. She looked like a fetus in an amniotic sac.

"Fascinating," Ben-Ari whispered to herself. "A fungal spacesuit."

They helped the woman stand up. She trembled, tore at the membranes encasing her, and emerged from the quivering bundle.

She was a graceful woman with round hips, a slender waist, and full red lips. Her hair was as black as the space between stars, her eyes as dark as the hearts of galaxies.

Beautiful, yes. But there was a sickness to her too. Those eyes seemed almost too large, sunken into her face, and they darted nervously. Her skin was ashen. Her hands trembled, and blue mold clung to her legs and fingertips.

She was naked, and the crew quickly wrapped her in a blanket. The woman stared from side to side, as skittish as a squirrel trapped in a box.

"You must be Isabel Martinez," Ben-Ari said. "It's good to meet you. My name is—"

"Take me back," the woman said. "I need him. I need my master. I need to lick him. I need more. Take me back."

"It's all right," Ben-Ari said. "You're safe here. We won't harm you. We—"

The concubine gripped Ben-Ari. Her fingers dug into her arms.

"None of us are safe," Isabel hissed, eyes wide, bugging out. A crooked smile trembled across her lips. "You should have run. Now it's too late."

The concubine laughed. A crazed laugh. And Ben-Ari couldn't help it. She shivered.

CHAPTER TWENTY-SEVEN

"Let me out!" the concubine screamed, banging on the *Loggerhead*'s bulkheads. Tears flowed down her cheeks. "Let me back. Let me back! I need his smell. I need his taste. Let me lick him. Let me back. Let me back!"

Isabel Martinez. Prized concubine of Don Basidio. Here aboard the *Loggerhead*, orbiting Esporia Ceti, she shattered.

She scratched at the iron bulkheads, fell to her knees, and trembled. She curled up on the floor, weeping and trembling. She was naked, covered with patches of moss. Kai had draped her with a blanket, but she tossed it off, screaming about ants in the fabric.

Ben-Ari, Marco, and Addy had hitched a ride down to Esporia Ceti, traveling in a podship. Kai remained on the *Loggerhead*, watching the poor concubine, helpless.

"I need to lick him, lick him, lick him," Isabel whispered. She began to lick the bulkhead. "It's not enough. Not enough. Let me back ..."

Kai and Meili stood nearby, watching her.

"What's wrong with her?" Meili whispered.

"She's going through withdrawal," Kai said. "She's addicted to Don Basidio's spores."

Meili tilted her head. "She's only been on this ship for ..." She checked her watch. "Not even an hour."

"I've seen it before," Kai said. "Don Basidio releases a drug more powerful than any known in the universe. Its addicts need a constant fix. An hour is an eternity."

Isabel slumped onto the deck, sluggish, maybe losing consciousness. But suddenly she bolted up. She leaped toward them, knelt, and begged.

"Please. Please! Let me back down there." She grabbed their legs. "Please."

Her tears flowed, and she began to lick their legs, desperately seeking any hint of the drug.

Meili knelt and stroked Isabel's hair. "It's all right, friend. You'll go down soon. Once Ben-Ari is done talking to—"

"Don't you touch me, you fucking whore!" Isabel screamed. She lashed her fingernails, cutting Meili's cheek. "You took me from him! From my beloved Don Basidio. I love him. I love him!"

She fell to the deck, weeping.

Meili stepped back, gasping. She covered her bloodied cheek.

"What do we do?" she said to Kai.

"Let me back, let me back!" Isabel leaped at them. "I'm going to fucking gut you. I'll rip out your fucking throats. Send me home! Help me, Don Basidio!" She slammed at the walls. "Why did you send me away? I'm sorry! I love you! Take me home, take me home …"

"Fucking hell," Kai muttered. "This is the worst case I've seen. The poor girl must have been licking 'shroom for *years*."

"We have to do something!" Meili said. "She'll die."

Kai rummaged through his backpack and pulled out some laceleaf. He held out the bundle of aromatic leaves.

"Isabel," he said. "Try this."

The concubine spun toward him, hissing at the leaves like a demon at holy water. "What is that?"

"Medicine," Kai said.

The concubine spat. "I want him! I want my don. I want to lick him. I need him. I need him. I need—"

Kai held the laceleaf to her mouth. Isabel was unable to resist years of habit. Instinctively, her tongue stuck out, and she licked.

She paused, then licked again. She grabbed the laceleaf and began greedily lapping at the pale leaves.

With every lick, her anxiety faded. Color returned to her cheeks. Her breathing deepened. Kai rubbed some laceleaf against Isabel's skin, treating the fungal infection.

"There you go," he said softly. "Doesn't that feel better?"

Isabel looked at him. Her eyelids fluttered. A hint of sobriety flickered in her eyes. She gave him a wan smile, then her eyes rolled back. Kai caught her before she could hit the deck.

Meili gasped. "What happened?"

"She's just sleeping." Kai stroked the woman's hair. His fingers came back stained with mold. "She's exhausted."

They laid her gently on the deck and pulled a coat over her. Then both Kai and Meili stepped onto the bridge. They stood for a moment, gazing through the viewport at the world below.

Esporia Ceti. A moon covered in fungus. Home of Don Basidio. A distant, greenish crescent rose over the moon's horizon—Esporia, the planet the mushrooms had first evolved on. Farther back shone Kapteyn's Star, a dim red dwarf. Even farther out, a mere speck from here, shone Sol. Earth's star.

Kai gazed upon this scene, and a shudder ran through him.

"Kai?" Meili hesitated, then touched his hand. "Are you okay?"

The computer scientist looked up at him, her eyes huge behind her round glasses, filled with concern. Her scrambler sat tilted on her head, and her hair lay in disarray. Absently, Kai reached out to brush back a stray strand. She let him.

"I'm okay," he said. "Just ... bad memories of this place."

She looked at her toes, trembling. "They say you're a pirate. A ... a gangster."

She raised her eyes again, looking at him hesitantly. Kai saw his reflection in her glasses. It was years since he had escaped the slums of Bangkok, but he still looked like a gutter rat. The sides of his head were shaved down to stubble, revealing tribal tattoos. Piercings shone on his ears and nose. More tattoos covered his bare arms. He was not a large man. He was no taller than Marco and probably lighter. But he was all ropy muscle and scars. Not a soldier, no. Kai had never served in a military. But he was battle hardened nonetheless. He had been born a fighter.

His eyes refocused, and he looked again at Meili's face. They could not have looked more different. He came from the rough slums of Thailand. She had been raised in wealth in Taiwan. He was all scars, tattoos, piercings, and roughness. Meili was soft skin, silky hair, trembling lips. Him—a criminal. Her—a genius.

"This must be so strange for you, Meili," he said. "To be here with this crew. We must be so different from the people you're used to. To be raised in a bubble, then face the ugliness of the cosmos …"

She shrugged. "A bubble? Maybe. Yes, I was raised rich. I was born gifted. My parents were famous professors. I grew up with the best education, all the money and opportunity in the world. But when I made a mistake in math, my dad would beat me with a stick. If I hit one bum note on my violin, my mother would glare at me with icy eyes, call me a failure, say she regrets I was ever born. I know, it's nothing like what you faced. I didn't grow up in poverty. I wasn't the daughter of a prostitute and pirate. I didn't fight aliens. But my life wasn't always easy." She sighed. "I just wish I wasn't so scared all the time. That I didn't always tremble during the battles. That I could fight too, be brave like you."

"Brave?" Kai raised an eyebrow. "Dude, those cyborgs scare me shitless."

She gasped. "But … but … you're a great warrior! You killed aliens! You—" She shook her head in wonder. "How could *you* be scared?"

He lowered his head. "Because I watched the Dreamer kill my dad."

"Oh." Meili looked down, and her tears fell. "I'm sorry. God, I'm so stupid. I—" She bit her lip. "Can I hug you? Is that okay?"

"I've never said no to a hug from a beautiful woman," Kai said.

"What about from me?" Meili said.

He shrugged. "Eh, I'll let even you hug me. Can't be picky here in space."

Meili giggled and hugged him.

He wrapped his arms around her, and she laid her cheek against his chest.

"I feel safe when you hug me," she mumbled. "I think you're brave. I wish you could just hug me forever."

"Sure!" Kai said. "We'll complete the quest this way. We'll fight our battles while hugging, defeat the Dreamer while hugging, then return to Earth triumphant while hugging."

She looked up into his eyes, still in his arms. "Won't your girlfriend on Earth get jealous?"

He snorted. "Girlfriend? Meili, I spent my life as a pirate. The only women I've met have been strippers, prostitutes, and hardened criminals. Lovely ladies, they are. Tough as nails and with hearts of gold. But me, I've always wanted a good girl. Someone more … innocent."

Meili gasped. "What about me? Aren't I innocent?"

"Don't you remember? You come from the hood!" Kai winked. "I'm scared of you."

She giggled again. "Okay, okay, enough roasting me. I'm a good little innocent flower. Happy?" She hugged him more tightly. "All the more reason you need to hug me and protect me." Suddenly she blushed and pulled back. "Oh my. I'm talking like an idiot. I'm flirting. And now I'm blushing!" She covered her face. "Don't look at me."

Gently, Kai pulled her hands back, revealing her face. "But I want to look at you."

"Why? I'm ugly, remember?"

"I know. Hideous, really. But hey, you're rich, right?"

"Nope!" she said. "That's my parents. I'm broke."

"Ah well, I was going to kiss you, but …" He shrugged. "Ugly and poor!"

She rolled her eyes. "You jerk."

He caressed her cheek. "Meili? You're fucking beautiful." He leaned forward and kissed her.

Maybe it was the laceleaf. Both were a little high. But this felt real. For a long time, they kissed on the bridge.

When finally they pulled apart, Meili blushed again. She looked at her feet. "That was my first kiss. Was I really bad at it?"

"Your first kiss?" Kai was honestly surprised. "You're very good at it, actually."

She trembled. "I liked it. But I'm scared." She looked up from under her lashes. "Can you kiss me again?"

They kissed again. For even longer this time. And yes, she was *very* good at it.

I like her, Kai thought, holding her against him. *I really like her very much.*

She was nothing like the women from his old life. Kai had only met women like him. Criminals. Tattered souls from the dregs of society. But Meili …

I'm punching way out of my league, he thought.

Maybe Meili trembled around him. Maybe she felt intimidated by this rough pirate. But deep inside, Kai found *her* intimidating. He felt woefully inadequate by a woman so intelligent, from a background so superior to his. It took all his willpower to feign confidence. He was close to losing his cool and stuttering like an idiot.

All he had was swagger. It was just a mask. Sooner or later, would Meili see through it?

But maybe that doesn't matter, he thought, looking into her eyes. *Maybe it doesn't matter that she's a genius and I'm an idiot. That she's a scientist and I'm a criminal. Maybe she really does like me. Maybe she even cares for me.*

She smiled. "Penny for your thoughts?"

I think I love you. I think I really do.

"Thoughts?" He snorted. "That's your job, genius. I'm just the dumb muscle here."

She laughed. "You're smart, Kai. You figured out how to fly Tarjan machines, and how to fly this ship. Hell, I bet you'll easily understand Project Artemis. Want to see my code?"

He nodded. "Sure. I've dabbled with coding. I was probably the most techy pirate in our crew. That's not saying much, of course. Some of the guys I rolled with couldn't count to twenty without taking off their shoes. It didn't help that many were missing a few toes and fingers. The pirates always had me fix their computers. *And* do their taxes, those assholes." He winked.

Meili pulled out her minicom. They sat side by side, and she showed him her code. But Kai could barely concentrate. He kept thinking about the warmth of her thigh against his. Of her soft hair brushing his ear. When she caught him looking at her, she blushed and gave him a quick kiss.

For the first time in many years, Kai felt something new. Even here. Even in the depths of space, in the heart of a war.

He was happy.

CHAPTER TWENTY-EIGHT

Ben-Ari stood inside the fleshy podship, hitching a ride to Esporia Ceti.

It was the strangest flight of her life. It felt like being inside an enormous womb. The chamber was round, hot, and quivering. The walls breathed. The floor squirmed beneath her feet. She almost felt guilty for poking it with her heels.

Addy leaned toward Marco and whispered, "It's like being inside a bouncy castle. Made of meat."

"It's made of fungus," Marco whispered back.

"Fine, a giant bouncy castle made of meat with a fungal infection," Addy whispered back.

Ben-Ari glared at the two. "Be silent."

They were not alone here after all. The three brainlike mushrooms were here, growing from the floor. Each was the size of a cow, and their fleshy folds quivered as the podship flew. They had no eyes. No mouths. No ears. But Ben-Ari knew they could hear and understand.

The rest of her crew remained on the *Loggerhead*, hovering a good distance from Esporia Ceti. The concubine was with them, the don's dearest treasure.

I just hope Don Basidio loves Isabel more than he hates me, Ben-Ari thought. *Or I'm a dead woman.*

Suddenly she almost fell. And it wasn't just because of the quivering floor. Her head swam with laceleaf.

It's a psychoactive drug, she realized. *Maybe it will protect us from fungus. But my mind is hazy. Did I just take one drug to protect myself from another?*

Marco and Addy seemed affected too. Marco put a brave face on it, but Addy kept giggling, poking Marco's ribs, and giggling again.

Great, Ben-Ari thought. *We're about to negotiate with the most notorious gangster in the galaxy. And we're high.*

Several mushrooms suddenly quivered, and their caps began to display images. Ben-Ari blinked and stared more closely. Was she imagining things?

She hadn't even noticed those mushrooms before. Their flat caps grew on the podship's interior walls. Earlier, they had blended in. Now those fleshy caps were displaying videos.

They were viewports, Ben-Ari realized. Monitors made out of mushrooms. They were streaming a view from outside.

How did they work? Ben-Ari imagined that the mushrooms ran through the fleshy hull. Their stems, exposed to space, probably received photons from the outside world. They then projected the images onto their interior caps. She wondered if these mushrooms had evolved naturally or had been genetically created—Esporian technology.

She looked at one of the fungal viewports, watching the podship approach Don Basidio's world.

Half of Esporia Ceti lay in shadow. The bloated, fungal world hung ahead, a crescent of decay. The podship descended into its gravity well. Soon they were plunging through a soupy atmosphere. Millions of spores flew on the wind, round and yellow, shimmering in the sunlight. Farther down, the light dimmed, and clouds filled the air. Not clouds of vapor but of glittering green spores, billions of them like confetti. Blobs the size of basketballs floated through the sky, opening and closing vents, devouring spores. They seemed to be flying mushrooms, perhaps filling the ecological niche birds did on Earth. Or maybe more like jellyfish devouring plankton, just in sky instead of water.

"I feel like we're a nano-ship flying through a petri dish," Marco said.

Addy was watching one of the mushroom monitors, admiring the floating blobs outside. She licked her lips. "They look tasty."

Marco facepalmed. "Addy! They're fungus balls."

"So?" She shrugged. "Never eaten blue cheese?"

"Please don't eat anything on this planet," Marco said.

"But I'm hungry!"

Marco groaned. "We have food in our backpacks!"

She pouted. "But I want mushrooms."

For a long while, they descended through this soup. Finally they reached the surface.

No, this was not a petri dish. Not a ball of rot. From here, they saw a forest. An entire forest of mushrooms.

Toadstools rose like trees, their pale caps forming a canopy. Mushrooms shaped like enormous brains formed hills. Tall, slender mushrooms with small white caps swayed in fields. There were bulbous white mushrooms that leaked red liquid like beads of blood. Gilled mushrooms in purple and green. Tall, tubular mushrooms with flaring vents. Mushrooms with enormous indigo caps that pointed to the heavens like radio dishes. Flat gray mushrooms that rose across the land like the spikes along a stegosaurus's back. Sloppy mushrooms like dollops of cream upon the land, practically melting. Mushrooms shaped like ears. Mushrooms with eyes. Mushrooms with vents that puffed out spores. Mushrooms with long, grasping tongues that grabbed spores from the air. Mushrooms that floated like balloons, moving from cap to cap, perhaps pollinating them. Mushrooms that oozed across the ground like slugs, consuming immobile mushrooms in their path. Mushrooms that floated like blimps, raining tiny spores like snow.

A forest? An entire ecosystem.

The podship descended until it hovered a few meters above the mossy ground. From there, it glided forward, moving just above the surface. Mushrooms rose all around like an ancient forest, their caps hiding the sun. Glowing pustules grew from their stems, illuminating the forest.

There was life here other than fungus, Ben-Ari saw. A naked, wrinkly little creature scurried between the mushrooms.

One mushroom spat out a sticky strand like a tongue, lassoed the critter, and pulled it back into a toothy vent. Furry animals glided between towering mushrooms on leathern wings, feeding on spores. There were even some organisms that looked like trees, actual trees of wood, but mushrooms covered their trunks, and fungus coated their leaves. Other branches of life had risen here, fitting into the ecosystem—hosts for parasites, pollinators carrying spores back and forth, and protein sources. This world was more complex than Ben-Ari had imagined.

The three brainlike mushrooms inside the podship quivered. Fleshy voices emerged from them, speaking in unison.

"We are almost at Don Basidio's court. Prepare to bow before him and fear his might, cowardly protein sacks!"

Addy nodded and patted one of the fleshy mushrooms. "Yeah, we'll do that."

"Do not pat me, disgusting meat creature!" the fungus said. "You are festering with bacteria."

Addy snorted. "Big words from a giant talking piece of—"

"Linden, enough," Ben-Ari said.

The podship flew through a grove of purple mushrooms, tall and slender like birches, their caps luminous. The flat mushrooms on the walls, the ones acting as viewports, went dark. They flew blindly.

"Hey, what happened to the reception?" Addy demanded, slapping a mushroom.

Ben-Ari understood. "They don't want us to see the way."

The podship flew for a while longer. The crew waited in the shadows, lost on this alien world.

Finally, after what seemed like an hour, they felt the podship slow down and halt.

The brainy mushrooms vibrated. "Welcome, disgusting meat creatures, to Don Basidio's glorious court. We pray to the Deep Roots that he devours your flesh."

"That's it, I am *not* tipping them!" Addy muttered under her breath.

A valve bloomed open on the wall. The podship quivered. The ground rose like a wave. The entire structure contracted, then vomited out the human passengers.

Ben-Ari landed onto a carpet of moss. Marco thumped down beside her, and Addy landed on him.

"Ow, Addy!" Marco pushed her, but she wouldn't budge. "Get off! You weigh a ton."

She gasped and hopped on him. "Shut up! I'm a dainty little dewdrop."

"Enough!" Ben-Ari said. "Stand up, soldiers. Behave. You represent the human race now."

Marco glanced at Addy and muttered under his breath, "Well, we're screwed."

Addy elbowed him hard in the ribs.

They stood up, brushed moss off their clothes, and looked at their surroundings. Their eyes widened.

"Wow," Addy whispered.

Slender purple mushrooms rose everywhere, a luminous forest. Between them, it loomed. As large as a cathedral.

A skeleton.

"It's a starwhale," Ben-Ari said softly. "A starwhale that fell onto this moon."

She remembered seeing starwhales, enormous aliens who swam through the cosmic ocean like living starships. They were intelligent, benevolent creatures that lived in space, feeding upon cosmic dust.

Ben-Ari didn't know if this starwhale had been hunted, or whether it had crashed onto the moon. Nothing remained but crystalline white bones. The skull rested on the carpet of moss, as big as a house. The ribs rose like the columns of a nave.

Addy leaned toward Marco. "Was the turtle on Upidia bigger than this whale skeleton?"

"Much bigger," Marco said.

Addy groaned. "I still can't believe you didn't share that giant freak with me."

"Enough!" Ben-Ari said.

They stepped closer. Many mushrooms grew across the skeleton. They clung to ribs. They grew from empty eye sockets. They rose like fins along the spine. Unlike the mushrooms they had seen so far, these ones had eyes. Round white eyes that blinked and stared at the humans. They had mouths that smacked, filled with teeth. Some mushrooms had round, pudgy faces like laughing Budais. Others were demonic, cruel faces like those of jack-o'-lanterns. A thousand mushrooms laughed, licked their lips, and spun their eyes. Their voices filled the forest.

"Look, look, humankind."

"Animals come!"

"Dig stems into their meat."

"Suck their nutrients!"

"Devour their protein!"

"Plant the spores in their warm wombs."

"Lick us, taste us, smell us!"

The humans stared, eyes wide. Ben-Ari wondered why these mushrooms were different. Why they had faces, voices. The dead starwhale must have caused a mutation. The mushrooms who had devoured its flesh must have absorbed alien DNA, grown into these beings, mushrooms unlike any others of their race.

"Am I really seeing this?" Marco whispered. "Or am I high?"

"It's wonderful!" Addy whispered, tears in her eyes. "So many freaks! I can't wait to write about them in my book."

Purple light filled the skeleton. Voices rose. Shrill. Laughing. Coming from everywhere. From mushrooms inside the skeleton. From mushrooms growing like trees. From the entire world. The song filled the forest.

Come, come! Enter my bones
Come, come! Walk into my jaws
Come, come! The animals come

Speak to mushroomkind

Lick and taste and dance

The spores beckon

The flavor awaits

Come, come! Into our fungal court

Come, come! Forget your pain

The animals come, one by one

To dance among glittering bones!

The mushrooms spun all around, singing. Addy began to sing along. "Come, come! The animals come! Come, come—"

"Addy, shut up." Marco frowned at her.

She shrugged. "What? It's catchy."

Ben-Ari sighed and approached the skeleton. Marco and Addy followed. They entered the jaws of the starwhale.

A host of mushrooms awaited inside the alien skull, slender and golden, smiling and blinking. They bowed, parting before the humans, forming a path. The whale's teeth rose in glimmering columns. Mushrooms grew on the teeth like plaque, blinking and humming and smacking their lips.

"I feel like *Alice in Wonderland,*" Addy said.

Marco rubbed his temples. "I feel like I smoked too much laceleaf."

But despite her dizziness, Ben-Ari was thankful for having drunk the laceleaf tea. Spores flew from the mushrooms, glittering in the air like dust in a sunbeam. It landed in everyone's hair and tickled their nostrils. They couldn't help but breathe some in.

As Ben-Ari inhaled the spores, her lungs tickled. Her skin prickled. But then her head cleared.

The two drugs are counteracting with each other, she thought. *We're safe.*

The starwhale's skull seemed to serve as a foyer. The mushrooms swayed like reeds, nudging the humans onward. They walked along the path, entering the rib cage.

The ribs rose alongside like marble buttresses. The spine snaked above, a pale serpent. Moss carpeted the ground, and countless mushrooms in purple, gray, and indigo grew everywhere.

And there, in the center of the hall, he grew.

It had to be him.

Don Basidio.

* * * * *

He was the largest mushroom Ben-Ari had seen so far, as wide and tall as the mightiest oak tree. His stem was the color of pus, ropy, like an enormous chunk of string cheese. His cap spread above, the color of rotting orange peels, the bottom gilled. But it was not his size that filled Ben-Ari with icy fear.

It was his face.

It was the most hideous face she had ever seen.

Two eyes, narrow and far-set, grew on the stem. They were sickly pale eyes, peering from under folds of flesh. White eyes. They had no pupils or irises, just ivory orbs, but there was no misreading them. Those eyes were calculating and cruel.

The mushroom had no nose. But it had an enormous mouth. A mouth that took up nearly half the stem. A mouth so large you could ride a horse into it. That mouth gaped open, filled with teeth like yellow tombstones. A tongue the size of a dolphin moved inside, deep red, dripping saliva. Pendulous lips completed the hideous hellmouth, dripping, oozing.

Yes, the sight of this creature sent chills down Ben-Ari's spine. But hot anger drowned her fear.

Anger at what she saw around the don.

Women. Human women. A dozen, maybe more. They were naked, bodies covered with patches of mold, and their hair was long and scraggly. All were young and, despite their ragged state, beautiful. They were dancing around the mushroom like witches around a maypole, singing pagan songs. Every moment, another woman approached Don Basidio, licked his fleshy stem, and shuddered in delight. They danced on, eyes rolling back, given to their pleasure.

Drugged, Ben-Ari realized. *Addicted to him.*

The mushroom stared into her eyes. And he grinned. A hideous, quivering grin, dripping saliva. A grin like a wound. A grin as monstrous as any Mister Smiley could manage.

The don spoke. Voice deep, rumbling, shaking his court.

"Welcome, President Einav Ben-Ari. I have waited many years for this day. How I love to finally meet you."

His bloated red tongue emerged from the mouth. A tongue larger than her. He licked his lips, slobbering.

Ben-Ari stood calmly, hands clasped behind her back. She nodded. "Thank you for your hospitality, Don Basidio. I come to you in peace. With me come Marco Emery and Addy Linden, my companions. We come to negotiate. To offer you not just a truce—but a deal."

The mushroom's grin widened. The eyes narrowed to white slits, nefarious, mocking.

"Ah, always business first with you humans. But I am neglecting my duties as host. I must offer you some ... refreshments."

The gargantuan mushroom's cap vibrated. The gills flared. A cloud of spores flew toward the humans.

The concubines gasped. They ran beneath the raining spores, tilted their heads back, and opened their mouths wide. They inhaled the floating white powder, shivering, eyes rolling back. The women seemed in a trance, greedily breathing in the drug.

The spores flew over Ben-Ari, Marco, and Addy too. They did not hold their breath. They did not flee. Calmly, they all breathed in the spores.

The concubines were clearly intoxicated on the drug. They were trembling with delight, their pupils dilated.

But Ben-Ari felt only a slight tingle. A bit of dizziness. A foul taste in her mouth. And then warmth filled her, flowing up from her belly. The comforting, euphoric warmth of laceleaf, consuming the spores like the Upidians had consumed the black mold.

But Don Basidio didn't know that.

As far as he was concerned, Ben-Ari and her companions were now drugged—and susceptible to his charms.

As they had preplanned, the crew faked it. Ben-Ari gasped, breathed out shakily, and shuddered, mimicking delight. She even allowed her eyes to roll back. Marco and Addy repeated the performance. Addy acted with particular gusto, clasping her hands together in delight, fluttering her eyelids, and grinning widely.

"Oh, wonderful mushroom!" Addy said. "How I adore you! You would make the most delicious pizza topping ever, even better than hot dogs! You seem like such a fun guy! You know—fungi? Get it? Seriously, I have so mushroom in my heart for you. I no longer care about my living room, bedroom, or any other room other than my *mush*—"

Marco nudged her. "Addy, stop overselling it."

Ben-Ari sighed internally. And *these* were her two best officers.

She looked back at Don Basidio. She gave her best spaced-out smile.

"Oh, Don Basidio!" Ben-Ari slurred, eyelids heavy. "*Thank you.* I feel so much better now. I'm sure you'll offer me an amazing deal." She batted her eyelashes. "You're so ..." She inhaled more spores, then sighed with abandon. "Dreamy."

The mushroom's grin widened. Across his hall, a thousand smaller mushrooms cackled.

"Good ..." said the don. "Now, I offer you this deal, animals. The two females among you will join my concubines. You will dance for me. You will lick me. You will carry my spores inside your fertile wombs." He turned his beady white eyes toward Marco. "The male I will devour."

Addy nodded. "Deal!"

Marco shoved her. "Shut up." He turned toward the mushroom. "Ignore my wife. She's an idiot."

Ben-Ari glared at them, then put on her best dopey face again. She smiled listlessly at the don.

"Oh, but Don Basidio!" she said. "I can offer you so, so much more than just my little womb and tongue. I can offer you technology. We humans are only lowly animals, yes, not higher lifeforms like you fungus. But we're clever. We can teach you science. Engineering. You can have the power to transform your world, to—"

"Do you think I crave your pathetic tricks?" the don roared. "Do you think your little machines impress me?" He spat a glob of saliva. It splattered across the hall. "We Esporians are far more advanced than you. We do not need to build with metal, plastic, and silicon. Those are the tools of apes, no different from sticks and stones. We have starships. Mighty podships that traverse the galaxy. We build cities. Mighty cities of fungus! We are far more advanced than you sacks of meat will ever be."

"Which is why I'm here," Ben-Ari said. "You have truly marvelous ships. Ships with Tarjan engines. Ships that I would like to borrow. I can pay for them. I can—"

"*Tarjan* ships?" the don rumbled. "Yes, I *had* a fleet of Tarjan ships. The Golden Fleet. A mighty armada for my human slaves to fly. They stole many treasures from you. But then two humans, Butch and Kai Linden, stole one of my Tarjan ships. And then the Human Defense Force, your little army of animals, captured the admiral of my Golden Fleet. Now you dare come here and demand my ships?"

Ben-Ari nodded. "Yes. I remember your admiral. Natasha Emmerdale is her name. A human like me."

"Nothing like you!" he roared. "Natasha Emmerdale began as my concubine. A sweet little human to lick me and host my spawn. But she was smarter than the others. She never succumbed like these pathetic, weak whores who dance around me. No. Natasha is special. A human almost as intelligent as an Esporian. So I let her captain a ship. And then I let her command my Golden Fleet. She brought back a horde of Earth treasures! She hurt you, President Ben-Ari. She hurt you badly. Ah, Natasha Emmerdale, my pirate queen!"

Across the court, a thousand smaller mushrooms cried out in awe. "Pirate queen, pirate queen!"

"She's just a whore!" shouted one of the concubines.

"She's a stupid slut!" cried another.

"She thinks she's better than us!" spat a third concubine.

Don Basidio lashed his tongue like a fleshy whip, knocking the women down. "Silence, wombs! Or you'll never lick me again."

The women wept and crawled over the moss. They pawed at the giant mushroom, licking him, begging forgiveness.

Ben-Ari ignored the display. She stared into Don Basidio's eyes. "Natasha Emmerdale, Prisoner 122432. Currently serving two consecutive life sentences at New Siberia Penitentiary. Yes, I know who she is, Don Basidio. I commanded the *Lodestar*, the ship that finally caught her. She was number one on our most-wanted list."

Don Basidio stared at Ben-Ari, eyes narrowed and calculating. "I see the game you're playing." He nodded, his stringy stem bending. "Very well. We shall play this game together. You want ships. Why Tarjan ships?"

"They can't be hacked," Ben-Ari said. "I need starships whose computers are secure."

Don Basidio licked his lips, smiling, eyes narrowed and blazing white. "You will have ships. Not Tarjan ships. No. You would reverse engineer them, learn how to build your own. I cannot allow that. But I will give you ships without *any* computers. I will give you ships far more advanced. Ships that use the superior intelligence of fungus. I will give you three podships."

Ben-Ari blinked. Podships? Like the one she had traveled in down here?

"We don't know how to fly podships," she said.

"They come with pilots attached," said Don Basidio. "Literally. You will travel in them as passengers. They will take you to Haven." He laughed. "Yes, you seek to travel to Haven. To fight the computer virus. That infection that has spread across your worlds. Animal technology. So pathetic! We fungus would never fall so easily to a disease."

Ben-Ari pursed her lips, considering. Podships? Could it work? Well, the Dreamer would never be able to hack them …

"I need more than three," she said. "I need a hundred."

Don Basidio shook with laughter. "Impudent little animal! You show strong resistance to my spores. You show some spunk. You remind me of my Natasha Emmerdale." The enormous mushroom nodded, his cap shedding spores. "Very well. You will have a hundred podships. But I want something from you, Ben-Ari." He leaned closer, looming above her, his mouth so large he could have swallowed her whole. "And you will give me what I want."

She stared up into those wicked eyes. "You want Natasha Emmerdale."

"I want *all* my imprisoned Basidio Boys," he said. "I want Emmerdale and her crew. I want my businessmen whom your police arrested on Earth and her colonies. I want the aliens who served me, who now rot in human prisons. There are eight hundred and seventeen Basidio Boys in your prisons. Free them. Free them all."

Ben-Ari took a step forward. Her eye twitched. "I will not free them! Businessmen? They're criminals! Pimps. Drug dealers. Pirates. Racketeers and loan sharks and—"

The mushrooms across the hall began to jeer.

"Liar, liar!"

"Devour her, devour her!"

"Eat the human!"

"Infect her!"

"Grow spores in her flesh!"

Marco and Addy stepped closer to Ben-Ari, reaching for their weapons. But she waved then down.

"Don Basidio!" Ben-Ari said. "There must be something else you want."

The mushroom stared at her. For the first time, he was not grinning.

"I am an honorable leader," Basidio said. "I care for those who serve me. You call them criminals. I call your people criminals! Criminals who colonize the galaxy! Who infect worlds with animal flesh! Who take, take, and give nothing in return. You run a criminal empire far crueler than mine, Einav Ben-Ari. You are an infestation far worse than any fungal growth. You come into my court, and you lie to me. You pretend to be drugged on spores while laceleaf fills your blood. You hide the fact that Kai Linden, the one who stole from me, hides in your ship. You come here—and you insult me! If you had come here with honesty, if you had shown me respect, I would have offered you my podships for free. A favor to a friend. But you came with lies and dishonor and disrespect! Yes, you thought me foolish. But you are the fool, Einav Ben-Ari. And now you will die."

Addy stepped forward, placing herself between Ben-Ari and Don Basidio.

"Hurt her and I'll cook you into cream of mushroom soup," Addy said.

Marco stepped forward too. "Kill any one of us, and you'll never see your favorite concubine again. We have Isabel Martinez! You want her back? Then do not threaten us again."

"Marco, but I want soup," Addy whispered, leaning toward her husband.

"Shut up, Addy, shut up!" he whispered.

Ben-Ari nudged her two officers back. She stepped closer to Don Basidio … and she bowed.

She crawled toward him on all fours.

And she licked him.

He tasted salty, meaty. She nearly gagged. But she gave him a long lick, then rose again and stared into his eyes.

"Don Basidio, I apologize. Please forgive me. Let me show you respect."

The monstrous toadstool stared down at her, silent for long moments. His rumbling breath fluttered her hair.

Finally he spoke again.

"At last you have learned respect. My offer stands. A hundred podships on loan. For the release of every Basidio Boy in your prison. And your friendship."

Ben-Ari thought for a moment. She didn't relish the thought of releasing nearly a thousand dangerous criminals. But if that was the only way to save humanity …

She nodded. "Toss in a pardon for Kai Linden, and you have a deal."

The mushroom chuckled. But there was nothing jovial to the sound. "You drive a hard bargain, human. And what of Butch Linden, the man who stole my beautiful whore?"

"He's dead," Ben-Ari said. "Don't blame the son for the father's sins."

The mushroom's laughter deepened, now rich with true mirth. "You push your luck. I like that. Very well. You will pardon my imprisoned Basidio Boys, and I will pardon your pup."

Relieved, Ben-Ari inhaled deeply, not even minding the spores. "Are the hundred podships ready now? I'll take them immediately to the nearest HDF barracks and fill them with troops. Within a month, I can destroy the Dreamer, then—"

"No," said Don Basidio.

Ben-Ari stared at him. "What do you mean *no*?"

The fleshy folds of his stem pushed low over his eyes, and his wicked grin returned. "First you bring me Natasha Emmerdale. *And* the thousand other Basidio Boys imprisoned with her. Only once they are all free, safe, and serving me again, will you have your podships."

Addy stepped forward, face flushed. "We don't have time for that! Dammit, Don, we need ships now!"

The mushrooms across the court leaned in, teeth bared. Don Basidio simply stared, smiling cruelly.

Ben-Ari pursed her lips.

Damn it! Addy was right. They didn't have time for this. They also didn't have a choice.

Ben-Ari nodded. "Deal."

They left the court, walking through the starwhale skeleton back toward the mushroom forest.

As they were passing among the purple mushrooms, Addy leaned toward Ben-Ari, eyes wide. "You licked him! Eww! You actually licked him!" Addy stuck out her tongue, gagging, then frowned. "What did he taste like? Did he taste good? Did he taste like regular mushrooms?" She turned around. "I'm going back to take a bite."

Marco grabbed her. "Addy, don't bite Don Basidio."

She pouted. "But I'm hungry!"

As they flew in a podship back toward the *Loggerhead*, Ben-Ari allowed herself to feel cautious optimism. She would soon have a hundred ships. She would soon have an organic army to fight the machines. She would soon win this war.

But as the saying went: *Everybody has a plan until they're punched in the face.*

When Ben-Ari stepped back into the *Loggerhead*, life delivered a swift hook to her jaw.

CHAPTER TWENTY-NINE

When Ben-Ari reentered the *Loggerhead*, she knew at once.

We're in trouble.

Instead of sitting at the helm, ready to fly off, Kai Linden sat in the hold, drinking laceleaf tea. And sharing it with Isabel Martinez.

Oh shit, Ben-Ari thought.

The concubine was no longer naked. Somebody had wrapped her in a blanket. Meili was busy brushing Isabel's long dark hair, clearing it of spores. Kai was pouring her another mug of laceleaf tea. The young woman sat bundled up, pale and shivering, drinking the aromatic beverage.

"What have you done?" Ben-Ari whispered, staring.

Kai rose to his feet and gave a clumsy salute. "Ma'am, welcome back! Did the negotiations go well?"

She stood still, not returning the salute, trying to calm herself. "Why is the concubine drinking laceleaf?"

"Ah, this!" Kai smiled. "See, when she came aboard, she was badly addicted to Don Basidio's spores. She used to lick him, can you believe it? Total drug addict, worst I've seen. So we gave her some leftover laceleaf. She sobered right up. Incredible stuff, laceleaf."

Ben-Ari's heart sank. She spoke slowly, carefully, trying to remain in control. "Kai. You do realize that before Don Basidio allows us to leave this system, we must return Isabel to him."

Kai blinked. "I … I mean, yes, of course, but …"

Isabel leaped to her feet, her blanket falling off. She trembled, stepped toward Ben-Ari, and knelt before her.

"Please don't send me back! I can't go back there! Please, ma'am, please, don't send me back to him."

She licked Ben-Ari's leg. Probably the poor girl knew no other way to show subservience.

Ben-Ari clenched her fists. She glared at Kai and Meili.

"Damn it! She was supposed to *want* to go back to him. To crave his spores. To—"

"To live as a slave?" Kai said.

Even Meili, who was trembling, managed to raise her chin. "We can't let her go back, ma'am. She told us all about Don Basidio." Her voice dropped to a whisper. "He's a *monster*."

Ben-Ari turned toward a viewport. The podships hovered outside. Surrounding them. Waiting to get Isabel back.

Ben-Ari took a deep breath. "I'm sorry. I know this hurts. But we made a deal with Don Basidio. We'll pardon his prisoners, including Natasha Emmerdale. He'll pardon you in return, Kai. But Isabel was not part of the deal."

Kai's eyes flashed. He stepped forward, face flushing. "Oh, I get it. So the famous Captain Natasha Emmerdale, Terror of

Titan, gets a pardon. But little Isabel is just a concubine, right? Just a little whore. You didn't think she's worthy of life, did you? You just figured you could—"

Ben-Ari slapped his face. Hard.

"Mind your tongue!" she snapped. "Do not forget your station, boy. And do not forget who you're talking to. I am your president and your commander in war. Do not mistake my kindness for weakness. No, I'm not a ruthless criminal like Natasha Emmerdale. I'm not the sort of scum you're used to following. But if you challenge me again, don't think I'll hesitate to toss you out an airlock."

Those words were too harsh. Ben-Ari realized that at once. Even Marco and Addy took a step back, eyes widening in shock. Was the laceleaf still affecting her, or perhaps the spores?

Don't lose your cool, Einav, she told herself. *Anger doesn't make you look strong. It makes you look weak.*

She forced herself to speak more calmly. "Kai. This is war. In war, we make sacrifices. Anyone who's led men in battle knows this. Sometimes you must leave a man behind." She looked at Isabel, and her voice softened further. "Or a woman."

Kai blinked. He stepped back and placed his arm around Isabel.

"I won't do it, Einav," he said, voice choked. "I won't let you return her to that ... that creature."

Meili had tears in her eyes, and the girl trembled so badly her glasses slipped off her face. But she too managed to place her arms around Isabel.

"I won't let you either!" Meili said. "She suffered there, ma'am. She suffered horribly. She's scared. We can't abandon her. I know you made a deal. I know! But we can't. It's immoral."

Ben-Ari cursed inwardly.

Damn. God fucking damn.

She had assumed Isabel would be begging to return. Would be clawing at the bulkheads, desperate for dear Don Basidio and his intoxicating spores. Now what could Ben-Ari do? Yes, she could perhaps alienate Kai. But dare she alienate Meili, who was still improving Project Artemis? Dare she truly hurt the morale of this crew, the only people who could defeat the Dreamer?

She looked toward Marco and Addy, seeking some guidance. It was funny. Seventeen years ago, she had taken them in as recruits, had turned them into soldiers. Today Marco and Addy were still her soldiers, but also her closest confidants. Her advisers. Her friends.

You're my best friends, Ben-Ari thought, looking at the couple. *Along with Lailani and my family, you're the most beloved people in my life.*

"What do you think?" she asked the couple.

A rare moment of indecisiveness, following a rare moment of anger. This was not her. This was not the Golden Lioness, the great military commander. Maybe she was losing her edge. Maybe the drugs were still affecting her. And maybe, after all, the Iron Queen of Earth was just a human.

Addy lowered her eyes. "I don't know."

Marco thought for a long moment, then spoke slowly. "Isabel is not a soldier in the Human Defense Force. She's not even a resident of Earth. She's under no oath to obey our commands, nor to sacrifice her life for Earth's cause. Ma'am, I would gladly sacrifice my life for you and for Earth. Every one of your soldiers would. But Isabel?" He looked at the young woman. "She must decide for herself. We'll explain the situation to her. Explain the stakes. And let her choose her own path."

Ben-Ari placed a hand on his shoulder.

Thank you, Marco, she thought, looking into his eyes. *Still you guide me. You've always been my moral compass.*

She thought back to that boy she had known. Eighteen years old. Just a recruit. A boy who dreamed of being a librarian or author, not a soldier. Her corporals had thought Recruit Marco Emery was meek. Too soft to become a warrior.

But when the scum had attacked their training base, Marco Emery had fought.

He had fought at her side. Going back again and again into the fire. Pulling out survivors. And when she had asked him to fly into space, to follow her to battle in the darkness, he had answered her call. She still remembered that day in the desert. The words he had spoken so long ago.

I never wanted any of this, Marco had said. *I never wanted to join the army. I never wanted to fight. I never wanted to be anything but a writer. But I think that your ancestor didn't want to fight in the forests. And my friend didn't want to die on that tarmac. And millions of people who fought evil throughout history wanted nothing more than to sit at home with a book, a fire in their hearth, family around them. But they all went out and fought, because they knew something. They knew that the world is beautiful, but that it stands on the shoulders of those bleeding, those hurt, those crying out in pain so that others can laugh, love, give us something to fight for. So I will fight.*

Those had been his words. The words of an eighteen-year-old private to his twenty-year-old officer. Words she had carried with her since that day. Words she had engraved upon her soul.

We've come a long way since that day in the desert, Marco, Ben-Ari thought. *I'm still your leader. But I still look to you for honor.*

The surrounding podships moved closer. One of the fungal vessels opened its valve, spraying spores. The shower washed over the *Loggerhead*.

A viewport came to life, showing a video feed from a nearby podship. The purple, brainy mushrooms—the podship pilots—vibrated. Voices emerged from their folds.

"Filthy animals! Why do you tarry? Return to us the concubine! She is our don's favorite. Return her or we will devour you."

Ben-Ari looked at Marco. She gave an almost imperceptible nod. Marco understood. He stepped toward the monitor.

"Esporians! Greetings. I'm Major Marco Emery, speaking on behalf of the president. Not I, nor my president, nor you can choose where Isabel Martinez goes. Isabel is a free woman. She comes and goes as she pleases. If she chooses to return to Don Basidio's court, we will gladly honor her wishes. If she chooses to remain aboard the *Loggerhead*, we will shelter her."

The mushrooms vibrated harder. They glowed an angry red. Their voices rose louder, high-pitched, demonic.

"She is a concubine!" they said. "A slave!"

Marco nodded. "Under your laws, yes. But Isabel Martinez is now aboard an Earth starship. By intergalactic law, that means she falls under Earth jurisdiction. Given that slavery is illegal on Earth, she is not currently a slave. And legally, we cannot treat her as such. Otherwise we would be accused in intergalactic courts of slave trading."

Ben-Ari nodded silently. She had made the right choice, allowing Marco to take the reins. Not only was he ethical and eloquent, it made her seem stronger. They were not talking to the don right now, merely the lieutenants. So let these mushrooms talk to her lieutenant.

The mushrooms vibrated even faster, louder. They turned furious white.

"Hand her over or be devoured!" they said.

"Now, now," Marco said. "There's no need for threats. You might still get Isabel back—if she chooses to return. She spent many years licking your lord. Maybe she still craves his spores. She might very well choose to return to Basidio's court. So ask your boss. He might agree. How about we let Isabel choose?"

The three brainy mushrooms conferred among themselves, tossing spores back and forth. Their podship expanded its valve, casting spores down onto Esporia Ceti. A volcano opened on the moon's surface, spewing a fungal geyser. Ship and moon communicated for long moments.

Finally the mushrooms looked back at the *Loggerhead*.

"Don Basidio knows that Isabel Martinez loves him. She is his most precious concubine. She has licked him more than any other woman. Her love and desire are true. Let us hear her speak! We will convey her words to our master, stored within our rain of spores. Let her confess her love for Don Basidio!"

Everyone turned toward the concubine.

Isabel stepped toward the viewport. Her back was straight, her shoulders squared. She left her blanket behind, and only splotches of mold covered her nakedness. She stared at the mushrooms on the monitor, and she raised her chin.

"I am Isabel Martinez!" Her voice trembled yet carried deep strength, the strength of an ocean, deep and eternal below the storm. "I am from Earth. I am a human. I am a free woman! And I have a message for Don Basidio." She sneered. "I will never return to you. You enslaved me. You drugged me. You forced me to dance, to debase myself, to grow your sickness. Love you? I hate you with every fiber of my body, with every last tatter of my soul. You are a monster, Don Basidio. And I hope you rot and burn in hell!"

For a moment, the mushrooms merely quivered in silence.

Then the viewport went dark.

The podships turned and flew away.

Well, Ben-Ari thought. *I guess that settles it.*

"Kai," she said, "chart a course to New Siberia Penitentiary. We have some prisoners to parole."

CHAPTER THIRTY

The *Loggerhead* flew alone through hyperspace.

An antique iron starship shaped like a turtle's shell. Built by ancient aliens. Soaring through the realm beyond, a dimension of swirling purple, silver, and golden light.

Earth had never seemed so far.

"We've been away for too long," Addy said. "And the end still seems so far away. We flew out to fight for Earth. But every day, I feel more like we've abandoned our world to the machines." She lowered his head. "I miss Roza and Sam. And Terri too."

Marco stood beside her. The other crew members busied themselves at various tasks across the ship. He and Addy stood at the stern. The others were only a few meters away, but they felt alone.

"I miss them too," Marco said. "Logically, I know we're doing the right thing. We're here to fight for the kids. To defeat the enemy. On Earth, our talents would be wasted. But I understand. I feel it too. The guilt. That we're here while Earth suffers. That we left our kids behind." He thought for a moment. "No, we didn't leave them behind. We hid them. We flew out to protect them. I keep telling myself that." He sighed. "And it never makes me feel any better."

Addy gazed out the porthole. The gold and lavender lights of hyperspace painted her face. She was silent. Marco looked at her. Just allowed his gaze to fall upon her. To admire her noble features. Her beauty. Her strength. The woman he loved.

Even now, after four years of marriage, it was hard to believe sometimes. That she had chosen him. That she loved him. That Addy Linden—that brave warrior, that beautiful blonde, that goddess, the most wonderful woman he knew—had married him.

Sometimes—and he would never admit this to her— Marco felt inadequate beside her. Not tall enough—the same height as her. Not strong enough. Not brave enough. Not a warrior like she was. It didn't matter that she showed her love every day. It didn't matter that he had found success as an author, had sold a million copies of his books. That he was a senior officer. A war hero. That he was intelligent and kind. None of that mattered some days.

Sometimes when he stood beside Addy, for just a few moments, he wasn't Major Marco Emery, the bestselling author. He was just little Marco, the short, skinny boy who lived above the library. The nerd. The boy Addy had mocked and ignored throughout high school. The boy so awed by the tall, gorgeous, crazy hockey player who had come into his home. Who had changed his life. Whom he had learned to love more than life.

He hesitated for a moment, still feeling that awkwardness, that inadequacy. Then he placed his arm around Addy's waist, and she leaned against him, and they stole a quick kiss.

She chose me, Marco thought. *I feel so much fear and guilt and pain. But she chose me, and every day that brings me joy.*

"Addy?" he said.

She turned toward him. They stood face-to-face, embracing.

"Marco?"

"I can't make any of this better," he said. "But for what it's worth, I love you."

She rolled her eyes. "That ain't worth *shiiit.*"

"Addy!"

She patted his cheek. "Well, it won't win us the war. But it makes me feel better. And I love you too."

He placed his hand on her belly. "How are you feeling?"

"Scared," she said. "And already in love with the little baby."

He kissed her. "It'll be over soon. I promise. We free the prisoners. We get the podships. We fly to Haven and kick the Dreamer's ass. And then—we retire. For good this time. And if Ben-Ari comes knocking on our door, calling us on another adventure, we'll spray her with a hose."

"Spraying the president with a hose will probably land us in jail, but … hey, worth it!"

Kai cried from the bridge, sticking his head out the doorway. "Hey, dickfaces! We're almost at beautiful New Siberia

Penitentiary Planet, also known as the frozen ass of the universe. I'm pulling us out of warp speed. If anyone's peeing or fucking, pull up your pants, cuz this is gonna get bouncier than a zero-grav whorehouse."

He vanished back onto the bridge.

"Your brother has a way with words," Marco said.

Addy sighed. "And I was just going to take off my pants!"

Marco felt the loss. Keenly.

He pressed himself against a bulkhead, grabbed a convenient handle, and waited for the descent from warped spacetime.

The purple smudges outside faded. The *Loggerhead* clattered out of warp. Their backpacks and weapons slid across the deck. Marco slammed hard against a bulkhead. Addy, who had neglected to hold on to anything, stumbled forward and thudded into Marco. Their noses banged together.

The turtle ship groaned in protest. The porthole revealed regular spacetime reappearing, replacing the silver streaks of warped reality. The Milky Way's spiral arm spread across the darkness, welcoming the travelers back.

The *Loggerhead* grunted like a real turtle, belched out fumes, and rumbled onward. Marco suspected that the Upidians had built their ship to glide smoothly out of warp, as graceful as an autumn leaf. Then again, Upidians had seven hands. Kai was perhaps a gifted pilot, but he couldn't compete with just two.

"Ow." Addy rubbed her nose. "Marco, you bumped into me."

"Addy, you're the one who—" He sighed. "Oh, never mind. I'm sorry for bumping into you."

She poked his chest, glowering. "You're clumsy."

Touching their noses and wincing, they joined the others on the bridge.

Binary stars shone ahead, orbiting each other in a slow, cosmic dance. One was a large, bright ball of plasma. The other was a dim white dwarf. They were in the Procyon system, only eleven light-years from Earth. This was human territory, the fringe of the little empire humanity had carved out in space. Halfway from here to Earth, a traveler would come across Haven, the Dreamer's domain. Beyond that—a network of colonies and outposts scattered across moons, asteroids, and space stations. In the center of this sphere of humanity's ambitions—that pale blue dot called Earth.

Few people traveled out here to the fringe. Beyond this system spread the darkness, the domain of aliens. On old maps from the Golden Age of Sail, cartographers might have jotted a warning across the Procyon system. *Go no farther! Here be dragons!*

The Procyon system was perfect for its purpose.

Here did Earth imprison its most notorious criminals.

Kai flew the *Loggerhead* toward a planet orbiting the white dwarf. The small, pale world was named New Siberia. Not only because it was so remote. Not only because Earth sent its criminals here.

But because it was cold.

Damn cold.

New Siberia was an ice giant. An enormous world, larger than Earth, covered with frost. It orbited the white dwarf, a star barely larger than itself. Barely any energy reached it. Once every few decades, New Siberia neared the larger star in this binary system, and a brief summer melted the ice, forming oceans. But most of the time, New Siberia was in winter. Pitiless winter that could kill a man within minutes, and that could last for a generation.

Marco wished he had brought a coat.

* * * * *

Kai shuddered as he flew the starship toward the frozen planet.

He wanted to turn back. He wanted to fly the fuck out of here. He cursed the day he had ever joined the Golden Lioness and her crew.

Fuck. This. Shit.

This year had turned into a nightmare. A goddamn fucking nightmare.

First the cockroach loan sharks. Then man-eating caterpillars. Then the machines. The horrible things they did. The memories would never leave Kai. A man with his brain exposed. Cyborgs begging to die.

Butch dying.

Kai's heart breaking.

This wasn't him. Wasn't his life. He was a pirate, damn it! That was all he could be. He just wanted to drink beer, have a few laughs with friends, and raid the odd cargo hauler. To take his earnings to casinos and brothels and forget the pain of a childhood scavenging in the slums.

Not this.

Not these nightmares.

Not this loss.

Not this endless grief and pain and flights into new depths of hell.

And now, after all this, he was flying to New Siberia. To the place he feared most in the universe. More than ten thousand criminal lairs.

Sitting at the *Loggerhead*'s helm, Kai gazed at the white planet ahead.

"Fuck me." He shivered. "New Siberia. The terror of every pirate." He glanced at Marco and Addy, who stood nearby on the bridge. "If the Golden Lioness catches you, she sends you to freeze your ass here. Every pirate has a friend in New Siberia." His voice softened. "I have friends in New Siberia."

Standing beside him, Ben-Ari smiled thinly. "I was too busy for much hunting myself. My captains apprehended most of you pirates. But I admit—I did enjoy personally capturing Natasha Emmerdale. And sending her here. I insisted on commanding that mission myself." Her smile widened. "Even presidents need vacations."

Kai looked at her. There she was. President Ben-Ari. The
war heroine. The Golden Lioness herself. The bane of pirates.
Just a young woman, not even forty. Not particularly tall. Not
particularly strong. Beautiful, yes. Blond hair pulled into a
ponytail. Deep green eyes. A gorgeous smile filled with straight
white teeth. Her black pantsuit draped across a graceful body. A
striking woman, yes. But she looked more like a successful lawyer
or businesswoman, not a dreaded warrior.

But she is a warrior, Kai knew.

She had led the platoon that killed the scum emperor. She
had fought the marauders in the depths of space. She had led
armies against the grays. Kai himself had seen her battle Upidians
and cyborgs, facing them with unrivaled courage and deadliness.
No, Einav Ben-Ari didn't look like he had imagined her, how
artists so often painted her. In posters, she appeared as a wild
feline of a woman, a golden beast, all muscle and snarls. But after
knowing her for a few weeks, Kai was impressed more than ever.

And he feared her more than ever.

"I remember that day," Kai said. "The day you ravaged the
Golden Fleet. Two years ago now?"

"Twenty months," said Ben-Ari.

"That was after Butch and I left the Basidio Boys," Kai
said. "Thank God's balls for that. We heard the stories. How you
jumped from warp speed, commanding the *Lodestar* herself,
flagship of Earth. How your twenty corvettes swarmed,
unleashing plasma hell. How you pounded Natasha Emmerdale's
armada, destroying half her ships."

"I wish," Ben-Ari said. "I destroyed only two. The rest escaped. Emmerdale commanded Tarjan ships, remember. They're tough to catch." She sighed. "Now I wish I hadn't destroyed even those two. We need as many Tarjan machines as we can find."

"How many ships you destroyed didn't matter," Kai said. "Not back then. Not to us. Natasha Emmerdale—in manacles, being led to a penal colony. That's the image everyone was talking about. Every criminal across the galaxy shit himself that day. Because you had captured the dreaded Pirate Queen, the Russian Ruffian, the Terror of Titan herself. The most infamous human criminal in the galaxy. If Natasha Emmerdale could be caught, none of us were safe." He nodded. "Yep, that was a bad day for crime."

"And Emmerdale has been freezing here since that day," Ben-Ari said, looking at the icy planet. "It's time for us old friends to meet again." She put her hand on Kai's shoulder. "Fly onward. Take us to the prison on the snowy mountaintop."

As Kai flew closer to the planet, he wondered why he was obeying her. She treated him like a soldier. But he had never enlisted. He was no officer like Marco and Addy. Why was he obeying her every whim?

Kai glanced at her. Ben-Ari was staring ahead at the frozen planet, a tight smile on her face, her green eyes glimmering.

And Kai knew the answer.

Because I fear her. Because I respect her. Because I am human, and she is humanity's best hope.

CHAPTER THIRTY-ONE

The *Loggerhead* was twenty thousand kilometers from New Siberia when the Dreamer attacked.

Ben-Ari knew it was him at once.

Even here, on the frontier of humanity, his malice awaited.

Nine starships came flying from the ice giant, charging toward the *Loggerhead*. Nine of his claws in the darkness.

Once, those starships had served the penitentiary on the planet. Their hulls were bulky, armored, used to transport prisoners from Earth. Rotary guns extended from their prows, weapons to strafe any prisoner crazy enough to flee into the New Siberian wastelands.

The ships had been modified.

Crablike metal claws now extended from them, possibly salvaged from asteroid cutters. Torpedo bays hung from their undercarriages, bolted on, likely taken from artillery installations on the surface. Somebody had painted mocking, blood-red smiley faces on the hulls. Perhaps it was true blood.

There could be no doubt. The Dreamer had come here. The Dreamer had assembled warships. And christened them with blood.

"Marco, Addy!" Ben-Ari barked. "To your gunnery stations. Kai, prepare to take them head on."

The pilot gulped. "Ma'am, they're too many. Maybe we should turn back, or—"

"Question my orders again and I'll keelhaul you," Ben-Ari said. "Fly! Fight! For your families, for humanity, for Earth!"

Kai nodded, shoved down the thruster, and charged toward the enemy.

The Dreamer's nine ships unleashed hell. Bullets. Torpedoes. Plasma bolts. They all flew toward the *Loggerhead*.

Kai pulled the yoke.

He rolled.

He swerved left and right.

He rose, fell, spun, soared. His hands leaped from one joystick to another. He seemed almost to become like a Upidian, a being with seven hands.

And the fusillade missed them.

Torpedoes streaked above them. Plasma blasts merely skimmed their hull. Bullets zipped below, and only one pinged their undercarriage before reeling onward into the depths.

Kai kept flying, eyes narrowed, hands moving in a flurry.

"This is for you, Dad," he whispered. "Just like you taught me. Fly like a butterfly."

"And sting like a motherfucking bee!" Addy shouted and fired her cannon.

A second later, Marco joined her, firing the *Loggerhead*'s second gun.

Their bolts slammed into a clawed ship ahead. Its shields cracked open. The ship tumbled through space.

The remaining eight starships swerved around the explosion, then came charging toward the *Loggerhead*.

"Kai!" Addy shouted.

"I see 'em. I'm not blind! Stop backseat flying."

He banked hard, then kicked the *Loggerhead* into a barrel roll. Bullets streamed by them. A few pinged the hull, denting the iron. The *Loggerhead* had a thick iron shell. Bullets weren't doing much. But several more torpedoes streaked toward them, zigzagging through space, forming trails of fire like fiery DNA helices. Addy and Marco fired, taking out several torpedoes on their way.

Three reached the *Loggerhead*, forking the ship.

Kai shouted and pulled down and left, dodging two torpedoes.

The third hit them.

Smoke burst from the controls. A viewport shattered. Ben-Ari stumbled backward, hit the deck, and forced herself back up.

The *Loggerhead* had taken a nasty uppercut to the prow, but her shields were prodigious. The antique iron ship was still in the fight.

"Dammit, Majors, stop just defending," Ben-Ari said to the married couple. "Let our shields do some work. Destroy those ships!"

Marco and Addy turned their guns toward the enemy. They opened fire.

Plasma bolts slammed into a Dreamer starship. Kai swooped, flying through incoming fire. Bullets pattered the hull. The *Loggerhead* kept flying. Charging. Racing toward the enemy at breakneck speed.

"Fire everything!" Ben-Ari shouted, and her gunners sent forth their hellfire.

Addy's bolts drove into a crab ship, ripping off its claws.

Marco hit another ship, cracking the hull, then fired bolts through the ravaged metal plates.

A fireball lit space.

The enemy ship exploded. Red-hot debris slammed into the *Loggerhead*, lodging into the iron shell.

"Hell yeah!" Marco said. "One for me, zero for you, Addy. Hey, Addy? Add—" His voice died with a hoarse strangle.

"Dammit, Linden!" Ben-Ari said. "Stop throttling Marco and get back to your cannon!"

Addy sat back down. "Kai, charge at that starship! The one I damaged. I'm gonna finish the job."

The pirate obeyed, zigzagged around streaking shells, and zoomed toward the enemy ship. A torpedo came flying toward them. They were too close to dodge. Addy had to aim her fire at the incoming missiles, destroying it.

While Addy was occupied, Marco fired at the enemy starship. His bolts hit the crack in its hull, and the vessel exploded.

Addy roared. "That one was mine!"

Marco blew her a kiss. "Two—zero, babe."

Addy screamed, grabbed the controls from Kai, ignored his cries of protest, and shoved the *Loggerhead* toward two enemy ships. Then she leaped back to her cannon, opened fire, and slammed bolt after bolt into the enemy. One prison ship careened backward, slammed into another, and both vessels exploded.

Addy stared at Marco. "Now we're even, fuckface." She flipped him off with both hands. "Two—two."

Four enemy ships were gone. That left five still in the fight.

"We've destroyed almost half!" Ben-Ari said. "Back at them, Kai. Destroy the rest!"

"Einav?" Marco said. "Maybe I'm misreading these alien controls, but I think I'm running low on ammo."

Addy frowned, fired a volley, and cursed. "Me too. My plasma bolts seem smaller now."

"So long as a soldier has one bullet left, he can still fight," Ben-Ari said. "Attack!"

Kai was pale. Sweat dripped down his cheeks. But he charged back into battle.

Good, Ben-Ari thought. *Kai is not the weak boy I thought he was. He's hard. He's a soldier.*

Marco and Addy opened fire again. But this time their bolts were decidedly smaller.

"Focus both cannons on one ship," Ben-Ari said. "We need both your cannons to crack a—"

A missile slammed into the *Loggerhead*.

Fire blazed.

The ship careened. Ben-Ari hit a bulkhead. Kai fell from his seat. From the hold, they heard Meili and Isabel cry out in fear. Smoke filled the cabin.

"One engine is down!" Kai said. "We're leaking fuel." He yanked on a joystick. "Dammit, I can't yaw."

Marco and Addy kept firing. Their bolts joined together, and a fifth enemy ship exploded. A severed iron claw careened through space, nicking the top of the *Loggerhead*. The iron ship spun. The controls sparked. Everyone fell and grunted.

Finally Kai managed to steady them, using their single remaining engine.

Four of the Dreamer's ships remained. They moved in closer, surrounding the *Loggerhead*. Marco and Addy fired, but their cannons shot into empty space … and then went cold.

The *Loggerhead* floated, helpless.

Kai slumped in his seat. He looked at Ben-Ari, face pale. "I can't steer for shit. Half our stabilizing thrusters are gone. We're a dead duck."

The Dreamer's four ships flew closer. Closer still.

The crew sat on the bridge, helpless.

"Why aren't they attacking?" Addy said.

Ben-Ari understood. "They think they can convert us. Hijack our brains."

Her crew shivered.

Addy drew her pistol. "I'll blow our brains out before I let that happen." A tear fled her eye. "I'll fucking do it. I ain't turning into no cyborg."

The enemy ships were only a few meters away now.

One ship rumbled closer, portholes casting white beams, slinking like a wolf toward a deer with a broken leg. The enemy ship was twice the *Loggerhead*'s size—a beast of jagged steel, mounted with torpedo bays and rotary guns. Its hydraulic claws extended. Huge, metal lobster claws.

It grabbed the *Loggerhead*.

A control panel shattered. Kai screamed and jumped back. The claws were tightening. The iron hull dented. Another dashboard burst.

"It's fucking crushing us like a tin can!" Addy shouted. She hit her cannon trigger in vain.

The other ships moved in.

Another claw grabbed them.

Screams filled the hold. The entire *Loggerhead* was bending.

Ben-Ari stared ahead at the last viewport. She narrowed her eyes.

"Call them, Kai," she said.

He looked at her. "Ma'am! If they can access our viewport, they can send their code through, they—" He withered under her stare and nodded. "Yes, ma'am. Right away, ma'am."

He hit a few buttons.

The viewport flickered with static, then streamed a video feed from the enemy bridge.

Ben-Ari felt the blood drain from her face. Addy gulped; she seemed to be struggling not to gag. Marco stared with dark eyes.

Kai stumbled toward a corner and vomited.

Ben-Ari stood very still, staring at the enemy ship's bridge. At this scene from hell.

There were still humans aboard. Or at least, they had been human once. All three still wore scraps of prison guard uniforms. All three were missing their limbs.

They were bolted onto pedestals. Mere torsos and heads. And those heads had been carved open, the brains exposed. Thin metal claws perched over the brains. They reminded Ben-Ari of toy claws you saw in arcades, used to grab plush toys. Rods and cables snaked out from the men's stumps, connecting to control panels.

Blood stained the control panels. Somebody had smeared more blood on the bulkheads, drawing a gruesome smiley face and dripping words.

The Dreamer is watching
The Dreamer is here
The Dreamer is always your friend

The cyborgs stared at Ben-Ari. Tears streamed down their faces. Their captain opened his mouth, revealing broken teeth.

"Help … Ple—"

The claw dug into his brain. The man screamed.

Kai cried out in dismay. Addy and Marco stared, eyes hard, faces pale. Ben-Ari knew a little about human brains. She understood. The claw was finding the pain sensors, triggering them like nerves.

The claw retracted.

The cyborgs stared with bleeding eyes.

"You will be like us!" they said in unison. "Join the Dreamer."

The deformed prison guards began to laugh, to sing.

Come into his dream
Come play in his world
The Dreamer is yours till the—

"Fight him!" Ben-Ari cried at the prison guards. "You are still human! You are sons of Earth. You are warriors! Fight him! Resist!"

The prison guards were weeping. Wriggling on their pedestals. They screamed again. But the song continued.

Mister Smiley knows
That the Dreamer is all
That his dreams are the world and your mind

"I can see you still in there!" Ben-Ari said. "He does not control you. He did not kill you. You are still there. You are still you! Fight!"

But they sang, cheeks bleeding, eyes pleading. Unable to even control their own mouths.

Come into his home
And dream with the Dreamer
Such wondrous dreams you will find!

Ben-Ari stared at them. She spoke softly.

"Wake up. Wake up, sons of Earth."

The central cyborg looked into her eyes. And she saw him there. She saw a human. A young man, probably not yet thirty. Scared. Terrified. In so much pain.

But strong.

Because the human spirit was stronger than any machine. Stronger than any alien menace. Stronger than the Dreamer, with all his intelligence, could ever imagine.

The cyborg raised the rod embedded into his left stump. The rod twitched. It never reached his forehead. But it was a clear, proud salute.

"For Earth!" he cried as the claws sank into his brain.

The cyborg tossed his head back, howling. Electricity crackled across the cables attached to his body. But the cyborg refused to die. His eyes fluttered. His lips tightened. More electricity flowed—from him to the control panels.

His ship's iron claws released the *Loggerhead*—then turned toward the other prison ships.

The crablike ship accelerated. Its engines roared. Its claws opened wide. The cyborg pilots screamed, bled, wept … but they kept driving forth.

Three prison guards. Three humans. Three warriors. They drove their vessel into another prison ship. Then a third. They plowed onward, ripping through the hulls of their comrades, and their guns fired, and their torpedoes slammed into a fourth clawed ship. Fire washed over their bridge, and the video feed died.

Around the *Loggerhead*, the last prison ships burned.

"Kai, get us out of here!" Ben-Ari cried.

He shoved down a lever, then adjusted a joystick. They scuttled up on one engine, wobbling like a bumblebee with one wing.

Below them, one of the prison ships exploded. All its torpedoes and shells detonated, blazing like fireworks. Then the other four clawed ships exploded too, joining together in an inferno. A shock ring of debris blasted out, pattering the *Loggerhead*.

Slowly, the debris scattered.

Only chunks of the prison ships remained, floating through space.

Ben-Ari faced the clouds of debris, and she saluted.

"Farewell, sons of Earth. Farewell, warriors of humanity. Godspeed."

The *Loggerhead* turned back toward the planet. New Siberia hung ahead, only a few moments away. A vast wintery world. A penal colony. As the *Loggerhead* flew toward the frozen planet, Ben-Ari wondered: *Will we meet Natasha Emmerdale and her gang ... or an army of weeping cyborgs?*

CHAPTER THIRTY-TWO

Her last engine sputtering, the *Loggerhead* crashed into the atmosphere of New Siberia, the most miserable planet in the Human Commonwealth.

This place makes Haven look comfortable, Marco thought. *And that's saying something.*

It was a hard atmospheric entry. The *Loggerhead's* iron shell was dented, the prow scarred with deep grooves. There was nothing aerodynamic about them. But wisely, Kai flipped the ship upside down, so that the air washed over the bulging shell.

"That makes entry much smoother," the pirate had claimed. "You need big, bulging surfaces. You want lots of air to slow you down. Not to slice through the air like an arrow. Ever seen old space capsules from the twentieth century? Bowl-shaped. Best when you gotta plunge like a rock from the sky."

But as the *Loggerhead* now rattled, Marco doubted that wisdom. The ship jolted madly. Marco clung to the gunnery station controls, nearly ripping out the joysticks. His stomach lurched into his mouth. Addy had her eyes screwed shut, gripping her seat. Meili and Isabel were holding each other, praying loudly, almost shouting. The *Loggerhead* gave a great jolt, slamming into a thicker layer of atmosphere, and both women passed out.

The iron starship fell from the heavens like a comet, wreathed in fire.

They passed through clouds, and flurries of snow washed over them, dousing their flames. They careened downward, and Marco saw snowy mountains sprawling far below.

Then not so far below.

Then really almost near them.

"Kai!" Marco shouted. "Damn it, man."

"Got it, got it!" Kai said, pulling two levers. He dug his heels into the deck, his entire body leaning back, tugging. The *Loggerhead*'s prow rose degree by degree.

But they were still descending fast.

The mountains reached up icy peaks like claws.

Marco glimpsed the prison. It crowned a mountaintop a few kilometers away—a complex of concrete buildings draped with ice. He only saw it for a second. Then the flurries blew over the plunging starship, and the world became white.

"Kai, there!" Marco pointed. "The prison."

"I saw it!" he said. "I'm trying, bro. You can't move much with one fucking engine. I—"

"Watch out!" Marco cried.

The flurries pulled back like curtains, revealing a stony crest.

Kai pulled up hard.

Marco winced.

We can make it, Marco thought. *We can make it, we can—*

Their prow cleared the mountaintop. But jagged ice slammed into their undercarriage.

The hull screamed.

The *Loggerhead* skipped into the air like a stone off a pond, then dipped hard. Cold wind blasted into the starship, thick with frost.

"Our hull is breached!" Marco said.

"Thank you, Captain Obvious!" Addy cried, the snowy wind streaming her hair.

"Kai, watch out!"

"Stop backseat flying!" Kai and Addy shouted in unison.

Another mountaintop rose ahead. Kai cursed, banked hard, and the engine sputtered, and—

They slammed into ice and snow.

They tilted onto their side, scraped across a slope, ripping out snowbanks. The engine died. But the iron ship kept roaring forward, carving up ice and snow, then glided in the air for a moment.

A valley spread below, and mountains rose everywhere.

They slammed down hard, plowed through snowdrifts, and skidded onto a frozen lake.

For long, tense moments, the ship slid across the ice.

"Don't crack the ice, don't crack the ice," Addy whispered, fingers crossed. "I'm sorry for eating all that cake. I'm not that heavy, honestly. Don't crack the ice …"

Finally the ship slowed to a halt.

The *Loggerhead* rested in the middle of an icy lake. The viewport gave a last flicker, then went dark.

"Head count!" Ben-Ari said. "Everyone, line up in the hold."

When Marco entered the hold, he gasped. From the bridge, he had not seen all this damage. The hull was dented, cracked open across the deck, and the stern was a mess of burnt, twisted metal.

The crew lined up for inspection. Only by some miracle was nobody seriously hurt. Bruises. Scrapes. A few burn marks. That was the worst of it.

"That was fucking close," Marco muttered under his breath, relief flowing across him.

Ben-Ari surveyed them one by one.

Majors Marco and Addy Linden-Emery, both in uniform, standing at attention.

Kai Linden, still wearing tattered jeans and a ragged T-shirt, scrapes covering his tattooed arms.

Dr. Meili Chen. One lens in her glasses cracked. Her hair in disarray. Clutching a minicom full of code.

Finally—Isabel Martinez, former concubine, still wearing only a blanket, her skin still moldy.

That was it. Six misfits. The crew that had to save the universe.

Suddenly—a *crack*.

The *Loggerhead* dipped a few centimeters.

Marco winced. He hurried toward the airlock and pulled the doors open. Cold air blasted in. Damn cold. Frost instantly filled his hair. He was grateful that he had grown a beard this year. Everyone shivered.

"God damn, it's colder than a Yukon toilet seat," Addy said.

"Let me test the ice," Marco said. "I'll go first."

Addy rolled her eyes. "There's an entire spaceship on the ice that isn't breaking it. Don't pretend to be hero."

Marco flipped her off, then exited the *Loggerhead*. He took a few careful steps. Walking on ice wasn't easy, but thankfully, as a Canadian, he had some practice.

The ice perhaps wasn't quite as solid as Addy had suggested. The *Loggerhead* had left a path of cracks across the frozen lake. It looked like a furrow left by a plow. Its edges gleamed, bristly with splintered ice. The mountains surrounded the lake, soaring toward the clouds. The wind howled, flattening Marco's uniform against his body, coating him with frost, and freezing his bones.

Fuck, even Canada is a tropical paradise compared to this. He stuck his hands under his armpits, shivering.

He looked around, seeking the penitentiary. He saw nothing but snow and ice. They must have overshot the complex by a kilometer or two.

Normally that would mean a short walk.

In this weather, it seemed like ten thousand marathons.

He looked back at the others, who huddled inside the airlock.

"We should be okay," Marco said. "We can walk from here. I just wish we had parkas."

Kai stepped out first, then cursed and retreated back into the airlock.

"Fuck me!" He spat. "Maybe you Canadians can survive in this climate. But I'm Thai, bro. I'll fucking die. I mean, my spit froze into an ice cube already. We can fire up the *Loggerhead* again, try to glide across the ice."

Marco looked at the furrow of cracked ice. "I wouldn't. The engine is all mangled. The hull is cracked open. Glide the *Loggerhead* across the ice like a giant curling stone? Forget *gliding*. Just *look* at that machine wrong and it'll crash through the ice. The instant you turn on that engine, kiss the ice goodbye. If the *Loggerhead* ever moves again, it'll be in one direction—down." He flashed a grin. "Come on, Kai, we'll walk. Nice brisk winter stroll."

They all exited the ship, shivering. Meili's cracked glasses fogged up. Even Addy, that hulking hockey player, was shaking. Marco felt especially bad for Isabel. The poor girl still wore only a blanket, tied around her waist with a rope, forming a crude dress. Everyone carried weapons, and even Isabel held a rifle. Of course, no weapon could fight the snowy wind.

Marco hoped that at the penitentiary, they'd find warmth, more clothes, some safety. And, ideally, a starship that was in one piece.

But Addy voiced his fear. Everyone's fear.

"We're just going to find a prison full of monsters," she said. "Fucking cyborgs. Why are we doing this?"

"Because the Dreamer might not have gotten them all yet," Marco said. "Because some humans here might still be fighting. If Natasha Emmerdale and the Basidio Boys are cyborgs, then we'll deliver them to the don, and hopefully he still honors the deal. If they're still human, well, we have to help them fight. We don't have winter coats. But we do have weapons."

"Wonderful," Addy muttered. "Facing an army of murderous gangsters wasn't enough. Now we might face an army of *cyborg* murderous gangsters."

They walked across the ice, leaving the damaged *Loggerhead* behind. Perhaps she would remain here forever.

Snow flurries blasted his face, coated his eyelashes, and filled his beard. He squinted and walked hunched over, hugging himself. The ice creaked under his boots—but held. The wind kept shrieking, stabbing him with a million icy blades. He walked through it.

A few moments later, he realized that he and Addy were far ahead of the others. He looked back. The rest of the crew still stood by the *Loggerhead*.

"What's wrong?" Marco shouted into the wind.

"Slow down, you fucking Canadians, we're not as fast as you!" Kai shouted.

Marco and Addy couldn't help it. They both grinned. They stood side by side, shivering, waiting for the others to catch up.

"Slowpokes," Addy said to them.

Kai flipped her off. "You're goddamn abominable snow monsters."

Addy squeezed her brother in a crushing embrace. "And I will call you George, and I will hug you, and squeeze you, and—"

Kai shoved her. "Get off!" He looked at Marco. "How do you tolerate this every day, bro?"

"I've gone mad long ago," Marco said. "Probably why I'm here right now. Come on, hurry up, it's not that hard."

The group stayed close together, advancing across the ice. Marco and Addy took the lead, as comfortable on ice as spiders on webs. Ben-Ari was still wearing her high heels, and she leaned against Kai for support. Both the Israeli leader and Thai pirate, bred for heat, kept shivering, their lips blue. Meili and Isabel brought up the rear, hugging each other as they walked.

They were approaching the mountains. Marco looked up, seeking the prison, but he saw only snow and stone. The closer they got, the mightier the wind blew. The stronger gusts even knocked down Meili and Isabel, both small and delicate. They rose again. They trudged onward across the ice, inching toward the lakefront. Step by step and slip by slip.

They were making good progress when the wind gave a huge roar, storming between two mountaintops. The gale slammed into the crew. Everyone fell, even the Canadians. Meili and Isabel never stood a chance. The two petite women slid across the ice like hockey pucks.

"One step forward, one long slide back," Addy muttered. "For fuck's sake, Marco, you and I should just carry the others."

Carrying was a bit much. But Marco held on to Meili, guiding her onward, keeping her upright. Addy held on to Isabel. Both programmer and concubine were covered in frost, chattering, and kept slipping. Ben-Ari and Kai still walked together, clumsy on ice but both physically strong.

The mountains barely seemed any closer.

It was a damn big lake. And goddamn fucking cold.

A sudden *crack* sounded from behind.

Marco spun around. He looked behind him. He couldn't see very far. The *Loggerhead* was now hidden behind the flurries.

"What the fuck was that sound?" Kai said. "Was that ice cracking?"

Marco frowned, squinting into the storm. "Maybe just the ice settling around the *Loggerhead*."

"Or maybe our turtle ship went skinny dipping," Kai said.

Another crack. Weaker. But unmistakable. That was definitely cracking ice.

"Shit," Marco said. "That's gotta be the *Loggerhead*. Pushing deeper through the crust of ice."

"I can run back," Kai said. "I can save the ship. It might not have fallen through the cracks yet. I—"

More cracks sounded. Louder. Louder still. Chips of ice flew.

The wind gusted, parting the flurries, and they saw it.

The *Loggerhead*'s stern crunched through the ice, and then the entire ship vanished underwater.

Marco shuddered. "Thank God we weren't on that ship."

"I can still save it!" Kai said. "I'll dive underwater, get into the hull, and—"

Marco grabbed his brother-in-law, pulling him back. "Are you crazy?"

"Let go, bro!" Kai said. "Before the ice freezes over! I'm a good diver. I—"

"You've never dived in ice water," Marco said. "Water this cold? You wouldn't last thirty seconds. It'll stop your heart."

They stood on the ice, staring to where the *Loggerhead* had vanished. Kai tried to free himself, but Marco held on firmly.

"Marco is right," Addy said softly, coming closer. "I've seen it happen. Ice killing men in seconds. We were fighting the marauders in the Canadian wilderness. It was winter. A long, hard winter. We fought the spiders in snow, and they were closing in. We fled onto an icy lake. The marauders never bothered chasing us over the lake. They just cracked the ice. Sent us down. I watched the ice water grab warriors like ghosts' fists. I saw men's pale faces rising from the water, desperate for air. Only for the cold to grip them tighter. To drag them down. To crush their ribs and stop their hearts. And that was on Earth. That was warm compared to here. Swim? No Kai. You could no sooner swim through lava."

Kai shivered, and this time not only from the cold. "Bloody scum balls, you're a cheery one. Fucking Canadians ..." He kept trudging onward. "Let's get to that nice warm prison."

They had taken several more steps toward the lakefront when another crack sounded.

And another.

And soon a hundred cracks sounded like a pattering machine gun.

And those cracks were moving closer.

Marco paused, still a hundred meters from the shore. He looked behind him. Was the *Loggerhead* moving underwater, cracking more ice?

Shadows appeared among the flurries. Racing toward them.

Red eyes blazed.

"Wolves!" Addy shouted.

But Marco knew those were no animals.

They were machines.

They came bounding through the frost. Cracks spiderwebbed beneath their pounding feet. Their eyes burned in the storm, narrow and cruel.

Wolves? Yes, of a sort. Robotic wolves of steel, coming in from the storm.

CHAPTER THIRTY-THREE

The robotic wolves raced across the ice, howling, death in their eyes.

Marco shouldered his rifle and opened fire.

"Get to the shore!" he shouted. "I'll hold them off!"

Addy widened her stance, cocked her assault rifle, and unleashed a hailstorm of bullets. "I'm not leaving you!"

Soon the others were all firing too. Nobody was fleeing. Damn noble fools.

Their bullets hit a few wolves. But the machines kept coming. Cracks kept spreading across the ice.

Marco slammed in another magazine, sprayed bullets at an oncoming wolf. It fell, cracking the ice, but rose again. And more kept coming. The wind gusted, and the machines howled.

Addy, perhaps recklessly, began firing at the ice ahead of the wolves. A great crack tore across the lake, forming a river. A moat. Would it keep the wolves away?

The first robotic wolf reached the edge—and jumped.

It lunged through the flurries, vaulting over the icy water.

A beast of iron fangs. A jaw crackling with fire like the maw of a dragon. Burning red eyes. A creature, rising from the fog. A machine. A demon of retribution.

The moat was too narrow.

Marco fired. He took out an eye.

Then the wolf crashed into him. They fell onto the ice. They struggled. Jaws tore at Marco's shoulder, and he howled, swung his gun, slammed the butt into the robot's head.

The machine rolled across the ice. Wider cracks spread. Floes of ice banged against one another. Marco struggled to his feet, swung the rifle, and the stock delivered an uppercut to the robot's head. But the wolf stayed standing, leaped again, and—

Marco thrust his muzzle into the roaring jaws and opened fire.

The jaws shattered. Metal teeth flew. The lower mandible hung loose. The devastation revealed sparking cables and electronic chips within the skull. Marco fired again, and the wolf dropped dead.

As it fell, the heavy robot cracked the ice.

Water gushed up.

Marco took a few steps back, and the cracks widened. Viscous water bubbled up. The ice water was like a living thing, some semisolid aquatic beast, a frozen mollusk of the depths. It pulled the wolf into the churning embrace of the lake.

The ice began to harden again at once. The wolf was gone.

But new cracks were spreading. And more of the wolves fought everywhere.

Addy fired her rifle, taking out another wolf. Ben-Ari and Kai stood back-to-back, pounding the enemy. Meili cowered between their legs, but even the little programmer was firing a pistol.

Isabel stood alone, exposed in the cold, wearing only her makeshift dress. She stood covered in frost and mold. Her gun trembled in her hand.

A wolf came racing toward her.

Marco cursed, leaped forward, and shoved Isabel behind him. He opened fire. His bullets pinged against the robot. His magazine ran out. The wolf pounced, and—

Metal paws slammed into Marco's chest.

He fell back, hit Isabel. They both careened across the ice.

A wolf landed between them, feet cracking the ice. The beast snarled and grabbed Marco's barrel between its jaws. Marco released the gun, drew his pistol, and placed the muzzle against the wolf's eye. He fired. Circuits shattered. The wolf fell.

Isabel screamed.

"Marco!" she cried.

Another wolf was clinging to her wrist. Marco rose, trudged forward. A crack burst open between him and Isabel. A wide crack. The icy water churned and flowed like a river.

"Marco!"

He leaped over the crack, gun firing. His bullets slammed into the wolf, denting the metal. The robot released Isabel, blood on its fangs, and turned toward Marco.

Marco kept advancing.

The wolf bounded toward him.

Marco kept walking closer, gun firing. He tried to hit an eye. But his bullets all pinged off the wolf's metal body, barely fazing it.

The wolf got nearer. Nearer. Moving faster and faster. It leaped high, soared over a crack, only a meter away from Marco now, and—

Two bullets shattered its eyes.

Marco stepped aside. The dead robot slammed down, cracked the ice open, and vanished into the frozen pits.

He glanced behind him, seeking his companions. They were standing in a circle nearby, facing outward, holding off the remaining robots. Wolves circled them. Bullets slammed into the machines, knocking a few across the ice like curling stones.

Marco returned his gaze to Isabel. She cowered on a floating chunk of ice, her wrist bleeding. Wide cracks surrounded the floe, revealing the murky water.

"Jump to me!" Marco said, reaching out his hand.

She stood on her icy island, staring at him. A tear rolled down her cheek. She shook her head. "I'm scared."

Marco pursed his lips. Right now he was standing on thick ice. But if he jumped onto the ice floe with Isabel, it might tilt, even sink.

"Isabel, you can do this," he said. "I'll catch you. Jump!"

She trembled, whispered a prayer, and nodded. She took a step back, prepared to lunge forward.

The water splashed behind her.

A wolf rose from the depths.

The robot climbed onto the floe, eyes sparkling red, coated in ice. The beast closed its jaws around Isabel's leg.

The concubine screamed.

Throwing caution to the wind, Marco leaped onto the floe.

The icy chunk swayed beneath him, barely larger than a surfboard. Water splashed. Marco couldn't fire his gun, not without hitting Isabel. The wolf stood behind her, digging it jaws into her leg. She fell onto the ice, and the wolf sank back underwater, pulling her down.

Marco grabbed Isabel's hand.

She screamed, half her body underwater. The wolf was still holding her, pulling her down. Atop the ice floe, Marco pulled with all his might, desperate to fish Isabel out of the icy soup.

She looked into his eyes. Her tears froze.

"It hurts," she whispered. The water was above her navel now. "I'm so cold."

The wolf pulled her a few more centimeters underwater. The icy lake now rose to her breasts.

Marco held her with both hands. Digging his heels into the floe. Pulling with all his might.

But the wolf was stronger.

The underwater robot tugged her deeper.

"I need help!" Marco cried.

He heard the others running across the ice. Heard more wolves howling. He fell to his knees, and the robot was still pulling from underwater, and Isabel sank down to her shoulders.

Her face was blue.

Her eyes were frozen.

Her lips still moved, white with frost.

"My son ... My James ... Has anyone seen my son ..."

Then the wolf gave a mighty tug from underwater, and she went under.

Marco still held her hands. She was pulling him down with her. His arms sank into the water. He clung on, ignoring the pain, still trying to pull her out. Her face gazed up from underwater, purest white, eyes frozen open. Maybe she was already dead.

The ice cracked behind Marco.

More wolves were moving underwater.

Marco's knee drove through a crack. And suddenly his entire left leg was underwater. And more cracks spread. The wolf was slamming against the floe from below. Marco's second leg entered the water, and he had no choice.

I'm sorry. I'm so sorry, Isabel.

He let her go.

For a horrible moment, she clung on to him. Maybe still alive. Maybe feeling betrayed. Or maybe just the dead grip of frozen fingers.

Then her hand slipped free, and she was gone.

Marco pulled his freezing limbs from the water. He scampered a few steps back, returning to solid ice.

The wolf emerged from the water like a killer whale. Isabel's blood coated its jaws, frozen and covered in ice.

Marco's gun jammed. Frozen.

He fell onto his back, staring up at the rising beast, this machine of frost and fury.

With shaking hands, Marco cracked the ice that encased his pistol. He could barely move his fingers.

The robotic jaws opened wide, revealing chunks of frozen flesh. Isabel's flesh.

Marco slammed his pistol down, shattering the ice encasing it.

He fired.

He emptied an entire clip into the frosted robot, and the beast sparked, fell apart, and crashed into the lake. Cracks spread, and the ice crumbled around Marco's boots.

He saw a shadow below. Isabel's body, lacerated and encased in ice. The floe tilted beneath him, and he began sliding toward the remains.

Strong hands grabbed his shoulders. Addy! Addy dragging him back from the brink.

"Poet, come on!" she shouted. "The entire ice is falling apart!"

"Isabel—" he began.

"She's gone! Come on!"

The humans ran across the ice. A score of wolves still howled their metallic cries.

"Make to the lakefront!" Ben-Ari shouted, racing across the ice, pausing every few steps to fire on the wolves.

They fled as the wolves ran, their steel paws chipping the ice. Cracks spread like lightning bolts, zigzagging between the crew's feet. The ice opened up beneath Ben-Ari, and her leg vanished into the lake. Kai pulled her out. They ran onward. The wolves moved closer.

Marco slowed down, allowing his slower friends to run past him. He stood still, laying down suppressive fire, giving the others cover. His limbs were freezing. He could barely feel them. He ignored them and fought on. Addy fought at his side.

"Addy, get to the lakeside!" Marco said.

"I'm not leaving you, Poet!"

She fired on the wolves, knocking one back. It slipped through a crack and vanished underwater.

Marco glanced toward the shore. The others were scampering onto the snowy banks, leaving the ice.

The wolves leaped through frost, bounding toward Marco and Addy.

We'll never reach the shore in time, Marco knew.

He pulled a grenade from his belt. He hurled it at the wolves, then knelt, pulled Addy down with him, and they covered their heads.

An explosion rocked the lake.

A thousand hairline cracks raced everywhere.

Metal parts flew, then pattered down, chipping the ice.

For a moment—silence.

Then a handful of wolves, the last survivors, emerged from the smoke. And the ice shattered across the lake.

Marco and Addy leaped from floe to floe. More wolves followed. Marco fired over his shoulder, and his bullets drove one wolf into the water. He kept jumping between ice floes, heading to the shore. He saw the others there, beckoning him, calling out for him and Addy.

Another wolf fell into the water.

Another.

Only one of the beasts now remained, a steel hunter the size of a horse, leader of the pack. It bounded across the floes, snarling, fangs bright.

They were almost at the shore.

A river of ice water spread before Marco and Addy. At least two meters wide.

They jumped.

Marco landed on the shore.

Metal jaws snapped, grabbed Addy's shirt, and yanked her down into the river.

An instant.

A dot in time.

A single image.

For that instant, Marco stared in horror. Addy stared back, the water up to her neck.

And then she went under.

CHAPTER THIRTY-FOUR

Time itself froze in horror … then came roaring back.

"Addy!" Marco cried and dived after her.

He crashed into the ice water. Pain screamed across him.

Addy. Addy. The baby. Oh God.

He swam deeper. He could see her there, flailing below, the wolf gripping her.

It was cold. So cold. Marco's heart pounded. Threatened to stop. He had never imagined such pain.

Below him, Addy twisted in the water, drew a pistol, and fired. Bullets slammed into the wolf. It jaws opened, releasing her. She fired again. Bullets shoved the beast down into the murk.

Underwater, Marco grabbed his wife by the shoulders. He began to swim up, dragging her with him.

He saw the surface. He couldn't reach it. The water was too thick. And he was cold. So cold.

They began to sink, hand in hand.

Something grabbed him.

Another wolf, he thought.

No. Human hands. Pulling him up.

His head burst over the surface, and he couldn't even gulp air. His jaw was frozen. His lungs were snow. Addy bobbed up beside him, gasping. She was so pale. Ghostly. Her skin, her hair—pure white.

It was Ben-Ari and Kai who were pulling them out. They dragged Marco and Addy onto solid ice, then lifted them. Ben-Ari was shorter than Marco, and probably thirty or forty pounds lighter, but she carried him across her shoulders. Kai carried Addy.

They stumbled over the last few cracks and landed on the shore.

"A fire!" Ben-Ari cried. "We need a fire!"

Kai pulled open his pack and began spilling out laceleaf. They held matches to the plants, but they were damp, and the fire wouldn't start.

Marco and Addy sat together, shivering. Dying.

"Meili, help me!" Ben-Ari said. "Help me undress them!"

The young programmer was trembling.

"Help me!" Ben-Ari repeated, almost shouting. "Their clothes are frozen. It's making things worse."

Marco tried to pull off his frozen shirt. His fingers wouldn't obey him. Meili snapped out of her daze and helped, pulling off his uniform. It was like peeling off ice. Ben-Ari was helping Addy undress.

Kai kept cursing at the damp laceleaf. He screwed open a few bullets, spilled the gunpowder onto the plants, and finally got the fire going.

Marco and Addy huddled by the flames, naked.

"Keep moving your fingers and toes," Ben-Ari said. "I'll massage your ears. Those parts freeze first."

Marco's teeth were chattering. He managed to grin at Ben-Ari and Kai. "What do an Israeli ... and ... Thai ... know about cold?"

"Enough to save your Canadian asses," Kai muttered, massaging Addy's defrosting ears.

Marco shifted closer to Addy. He looked into her eyes. She looked back, shivering.

They were thinking the same thing.

The baby.

"Don't worry," Addy whispered between blue lips. "I got enough fat to keep the baby warm. Two hundred pounds of blubber."

Marco couldn't help but laugh. "Addy, I've seen your scale, you don't weigh anywhere near that."

Suddenly they were both laughing, tears flowing, and the fire warmed them.

Engines buzzed above.

Marco looked up.

Drones. Three drones were flying toward them. Machines the size of motorcycles. Their engines whirred.

Rotary guns turned toward the crew.

God fucking dammit, it never ends, Marco thought.

* * * * *

The drones buzzed above, and the crew scattered.

They raised their guns. They opened fire.

But the drones were quick and easily dodged the barrage. Their machine guns roared. Bullets slammed down around the crew, piercing the snow. Kai screamed and clutched his arm. Blood spurted between his fingers.

Marco moved closer to Addy.

Both were wearing only their underwear, their uniforms thawing nearby. They clutched hands.

A drone came to hover above them. The rotary gun stared down at them.

It was too much. After the battle in space, the crash, the wolves, the cold ... it was too much.

This was the last cut. The enemy that would kill them.

Roza, Marco thought. *Sam. Terri. I'm sorry.*

He winced, ready to die.

A streak of light.

Fire.

Fire blazed above.

The drone burned and tumbled down. Marco and Addy leaped aside, and the drone slammed into the snow, drove through the ice, and sank into the lake.

"What the hell?" Addy said.

Marco looked up. More light streaked across the sky. Missiles!

They slammed into the other drones. The vessels crashed.

From over the mountains, it flew—an attack helicopter, its wings mounted with armaments. It was painted gray and white, its hull emblazoned with the words: NEW SIBERIA PENITENTIARY SECURITY.

Marco saw a pilot inside, face hidden inside a dark helmet.

"A cyborg?" Addy said, frowning at the helicopter. She kept her gun raised.

"A human," Marco said. "In New Siberia, humanity still stands."

The helicopter descended, its rotor blades scattering snow. It landed, and the hatch popped open.

The pilot hopped out.

She was a tall woman in an orange prison jumpsuit. She walked toward the crew, her helmet still hiding her face. She came to face them and placed a hand on her hip.

"Well, well, look who washed up on New Siberia," the pilot said, speaking with a Russian accent.

"Who are you?" Marco said.

The prisoner pulled off her helmet. Long golden hair spilled out. Emerald eyes shone over a freckled nose. The woman's lips twisted into a crooked smile.

"Good morning, comrades." She tipped an imaginary hat. "I am General Natasha Emmerdale. Welcome to my planet. Welcome to hell."

CHAPTER THIRTY-FIVE

They huddled by a mountainside, sheltered from the snowy wind.

A group of ragged survivors, carrying with them code that could undo the Dreamer.

Before them she stood—a single criminal in an orange jumpsuit, a crooked smile on her face.

There she is, Ben-Ari thought, staring with hard eyes. *After all this time, there she is again. Natasha Emmerdale.*

Ben-Ari's crew was busy behind her. Meili was frantically checking her minicom, making sure that Project Artemis was still there. Marco and Addy were raiding the helicopter for supplies; they found thermal blankets and wrapped themselves up to defrost. Kai found a medical kit and began tending to a bullet wound on his arm.

But Ben-Ari barely noticed her crew now. She kept staring at the woman ahead of her.

A tall, statuesque woman with streaming blond hair and mocking azure eyes. The Pirate Queen herself.

"I never imagined I'd meet you here, Einav Ben-Ari," Natasha said, her Russian accent draping her words like silk. She smiled crookedly. "The Golden Lioness, president of Earth, deigning to come visit the colonies." She looked Ben-Ari up and down. "If I may say so, my old friend, you look a little rough around the edges."

Ben-Ari narrowed her eyes, scrutinizing her old enemy. At five feet six, Ben-Ari wasn't short, but Natasha stood much taller. She had the striking beauty of her mother, a Russian ballerina, and the ruthless intelligence of her father, an English spy.

She looked nothing like what you'd expect from a pirate queen. Two years ago, chasing Natasha across the Orion Arm, Ben-Ari had expected to find a rough, brutish warrior, all tattoos and muscles and attitude. Somebody more like a Linden. She had never expected to find a woman with the grace of a dancer and the sophistication of a diplomat.

Then again, people say the same thing when they meet me, Ben-Ari thought. *Warriors come in many shapes and sizes.*

"We were enemies once, Captain Emmerdale," Ben-Ari said. "But the time for old rivalries has ended. Today humanity must unite against the machines. I came here to free you. I found you already free. Already fighting. Let us fight this war together."

Natasha looked at Ben-Ari's crew. She frowned.

"And this is your army?" the Pirate Queen asked.

Marco and Addy wore thermal blankets, the fabric metallic and shimmering. Addy was pretending to be a robot hellbent on destroying Marco, while he groaned and kept shoving her off. Meili was fixated on her minicom, watching *All Systems Go!* instead of coding. Kai was drawing naked ladies onto the helicopter's frosty windshield.

"They don't look like much," Ben-Ari confessed. "But they're good fighters. I promise you." She held Natasha's hand. The woman's fingers were long and graceful and warm even as the snow fell. "Natasha, tell me what happened here. Tell me everything."

"Everything?" Natasha raised an eyebrow. "Starting with when you imprisoned me here?"

"You'll have to let go of your bitterness, Natasha. I'm here to help you. But I can't do that if you're still carrying a chip on your shoulder."

Natasha stared, eyes narrowing. "A chip." Her face hardened. "Is that what you call it? The murder of my baby brother? A chip?"

Ben-Ari refused to break eye contact. "Your baby brother was a hardened criminal. He knew the danger when he joined the Basidio Boys. When he accepted command of a pirate ship. When he chose to battle my fleet. Do I regret his death? Of course. I regret the death of every human I kill. Would I do it again? Would I fire on ships that attacked mine? Yes. I—"

Natasha tried to slap her.

Ben-Ari caught the Russian's wrist.

They stood, locking horns, staring at each other.

"You came out of warped space like a coward." Natasha sneered. "A surprise attack. We fought back! We defended ourselves!"

"And you lost," Ben-Ari said softly. "That was a war between humans. But now humans must make peace. Now we must unite against the machines. Put the past behind you, Natasha. I need you."

The Pirate Queen stared at her, sizing her up. Her hand was still raised to slap Ben-Ari. And Ben-Ari still held her wrist.

Finally Natasha nodded.

"Very well. I've had to fight alongside some strange bedfellows before. I will help you." Her breath frosted, and she smiled thinly. "To be honest, I could use some help. You brought guns. That's good. We've been running low."

"Who's *we*?" Ben-Ari said. "Brief me."

Natasha's eyes glittered. "I'm not one of your minions, *President*." She spat out that last word like an insult. "You do not give me orders. This is all you need to know now: the virus is here. It already took over the prison guards. They slashed open their cheeks. We call them smilers. Servants of the virus."

"Of the Dreamer," Ben-Ari said.

"*Da*." The Russian nodded. "They speak of him. Worship him. The prison guards were never nice people. But after the virus took over them, they became even worse. They began butchering prisoners. Filling mass graves. We fought back hard. We killed many. But then … the Dreamer began to build machines."

"To build them?" Ben-Ari said. "Those wolves, those drones—they didn't belong to the penitentiary?"

"*Niet*." Natasha shook her head. "He took spare parts. From furnaces. From cars. From an old starship. He built his new warriors of metal." Her eyes darkened. "They've been killing many of us. But you bring fresh guns. Guns are what we've been missing. Maybe that will help. Come, into the helicopter! Ready to fight another battle?"

"Never and always," Ben-Ari said.

They all squeezed into the helicopter. All were thankful for the warmth of the rumbling engine. Natasha flew them through flurries and over the mountains.

* * * * *

The helicopter thundered, flying over rocky mountaintops, leaving the frozen lake behind. Marco sat wrapped up in a thermal blanket, teeth chattering.

"Hey, Marco!" Addy waggled her eyebrows at him. "Be careful that you don't show off your boys." She tugged at his thermal blanket, nearly pulling it off his lap.

He glowered and tightened the blanket around him. "Be careful that you don't show off your girls." He reached to pull the thermal blanket off her chest.

Ben-Ari rolled her eyes. "I want to see you two wearing your uniforms again when we charge into battle."

"But they're all wet and cold!" Addy said.

"They're no longer frozen," said Ben-Ari. "You'll live."

The two grumbled and began to get dressed. The others politely looked away. Ben-Ari, however, noticed Meili sneaking a few glances at Marco. The girl blushed furiously, then buried her face in her minicom.

I noticed a romance blooming between Meili and Kai, Ben-Ari thought, unable to suppress a little smile. *But hey, the girl isn't blind.*

A moment later, they saw the prison.

New Siberia Penitentiary. Known colloquially as the One Season Hotel. Considering all the ice coating the concrete prison, it wasn't hard to guess which season they meant.

It was essentially an enormous cube of concrete. Impossible to escape from. Even if criminals somehow made it outside, they'd meet an electric fence, a moat, and guard towers with waiting snipers. And if, by some miracle, they made it past all those, they would face jagged, icy slopes that would terrify even the most experienced mountain climber. Even if one somehow survived the descent, there was nothing but ice and snow across the rest of New Siberia. No towns. No spaceports. The nearest human colony was light-years away.

If criminals feared anything more than the wrath of their don, it was this place.

And today it was even worse. Today the One Season Hotel was a war zone.

Smoke. Fire. Blood. Thousands of rioting prisoners. Hundreds of guards. Across the courtyard, they battled.

But no, Marco realized, staring more closely. This was not a mere *riot*. This was not a battle between prisoners and guards.

It was between man and machine.

As the helicopter descended, Marco saw it. Guards with slashed cheeks. Smiling hideously. Eyes bulging. Cables and rods in their heads. Cyborgs.

"How many guards are here?" Marco shouted over the roar of the helicopter's blades.

"Four hundred!" Natasha cried back.

Marco cursed. He looked around at his crew. They were only a handful. And one of them, Meili, had no battle experience. What difference could they possibly make here?

Addy seemed to read his thoughts. She punched his shoulder. "Ah, come on, Poet. We can take 'em."

He sighed. "Well, fuck it. We've already charged like idiots into armies of aliens. Why not cyborgs?"

She grinned. "That's the spirit!" She raised a fist. "To the courage of idiots!"

Ben-Ari shot them a glare. "I was thinking more along the lines of honor and sacrifice. But in your case ... maybe you're right."

The helicopter descended toward the courtyard. Thousands were battling below. The cyborgs wore prison guard uniforms. They swung batons, fired guns, and cracked electric whips. The prisoners, thousands of criminals in orange jumpsuits, fought with fists, kicks, shivs, and a handful of pistols they had managed to grab.

Marco noticed that not all the prisoners were human. Quite a few were aliens. An Altairian towered above the other prisoners, waving his four arms. Gang tattoos coated his green skin. A Tarmarin stomped forward, coated with scales, his clawed feet cracking the ground. When a guard swung a baton at him, the Tarmarin rolled into an armored ball like an armadillo. There was even a Menorian. The mollusk stretched out eight tentacles, grabbed guards, and slammed them together. A variety of other aliens clawed, bit, and slimed their enemies.

Here on the fringe of the Human Commonwealth, eleven light-years from Earth, law enforcement fought not only human criminals but aliens too. The nastier ones—rogue scum seeking revenge for the old wars, say—were jobs for the military. Space bugs were shot on sight, no questions asked. But if any other alien caused trouble? They ended up in a human-run prison.

Today both human and alien prisoners fought as one against the Dreamer. Life united against metal.

In the prison courtyard, cyborgs raised rifles to the sky. Bullets slammed into the helicopter. Three pierced the hull. Only by some miracle did they miss the crew.

Marco leaned out the window, assault rifle raining hell. Addy and Kai joined him. The chopper circled the courtyard, and Marco kept firing, strafing cyborgs. It was hard work. He had to aim each shot carefully to avoid hitting prisoners. He missed a few opportunities, not willing to risk it.

Emboldened by the air support, the prisoners attacked with new vigor. They grabbed weapons from fallen cyborgs. They roared. They tore into their enemies with relish. One prisoner, a scrawny man with crazy eyes, banged a cyborg's skull against the ground again and again, spilling brains, laughing as the gore sprayed. An enormous brute with a bald head, long beard, and bulging muscles ripped into a cyborg, tore out the creature's heart, and lifted his grisly prize overhead. He took a deep bite, then laughed as blood dripped down his chin.

"Fucking hell," Addy muttered.

Marco cringed. "Good reminder of who we're dealing with. There's a reason these people were sent to New Siberia. It's man vs. machine, yes. But these aren't the best of men."

"Maybe not the *nicest* men," Natasha said, angling the helicopter into another strafing round. "But the best damn warriors in the galaxy, and that includes the HDF."

"What you say there, blondie?" Addy rose from her seat. "This HDF officer is gonna smack a bitch if—"

Bullets slammed into the helicopter. A cyborg stood below, pounding them with an assault rifle. Addy fell back into her chair.

The helicopter tilted. Smoke blasted. They began to fall.

Natasha struggled with the controls, managed to lift the prow, but they were still losing altitude.

"Hold on tight, we're going down!" Natasha cried.

They dipped fast and hard. Prisoners and cyborgs alike scattered below. The engine gave a last spurt. Then they landed hard—right in the middle of the courtyard.

"For Earth!" Marco cried, leaping into battle.

"For Earth!" the others cried, charging with him. Even Meili.

Their guns boomed. Cyborgs fell. Prisoners roared and killed and died. The battle washed over the crew, a symphony of flesh and metal, blood and electricity.

"We must reach the warden's tower!" Natasha cried. "They have an Isaac Wormhole generator. We can call for help."

"Who will help us out here?" Marco shouted, firing on an advancing cyborg. "The entire Human Defense Force fleet is gone!"

Natasha's eyes gleamed. "We'll call *my* fleet. The Golden Fleet! I tried to reach the tower before, but I didn't have the gun power. With your help—we can make it. Now come, to the tower!"

With every cyborg that fell, the prisoners gained another rifle, baton, or whip. The tides began to turn. Dozens, soon hundreds of corpses covered the courtyard. And the prisoners kept howling, kept ripping into their enemies, tearing off limbs, shattering skulls. One man feasted on a corpse. Another man was busy slicing off ears, collecting them as trophies.

We're fighting alongside serial killers, rapists, and gang leaders, Marco thought. *This is a war of monsters against monsters.*

He put moral qualms aside for now. He would deal with those feelings later. Right now they needed to reach that tower. They needed to summon starships—or they were stuck here forever.

"What's the shortest path to the tower?" Marco asked Natasha.

"Through the cellblock," Natasha said. "That big concrete building. Lots of cyborgs in the way."

Marco nodded. "Come on! We'll cut our way through the courtyard."

413

They began to advance. Step by step. The warriors in the
group formed a protective ring around Meili, guns pointing
outward. The young programmer walked hunched over,
trembling, clutching her minicom to her chest. Her scrambler
wobbled on her head, its microchips and light bulbs dangling. She
looked almost like a cyborg herself.

Every step was a battle. The prisoners crowded around
them, forming walls of flesh. Some took time away from the
battle. They turned toward the crew, ogled the women, and
hooted. One man pulled down his pants and thrust his pelvis at
Ben-Ari. Another man reached to grope Addy's chest. He
regretted it a second later when Addy fired a bullet through his
hand. Other prisoners howled with laughter as the man screamed.

"Enough squabbling!" Natasha cried out. "Basidio Boys—
with me! All prisoners—*with me!* I am Natasha Emmerdale, the
Terror of Titan, the Butcher of Betelgeuse. Fight with me now!"

Many prisoners raised their fists and roared. Many had
mushrooms tattooed onto their arms—symbols of the Basidio
Boys cartel. They rallied around Natasha. Other prisoners joined
them, sporting a variety of gang tattoos. They lifted guards and
hurled them aside, carving a pathway toward the concrete
building.

Bullets whistled.

A burly, tattooed prisoner fell.

Another.

A third prisoner collapsed, riddled with bullets.

"There, a sniper!" Marco pointed at a guard turret. He knelt behind dead prisoners, aimed his rifle, and opened fire.

A cyborg stood in the tower, half his face gone. His skull was cracked open, buzzing with electrodes. The creature knelt for cover. Marco held his fire. Waited. The cyborg rose again, and Marco put a bullet through its head. The poor soul crashed down.

They kept advancing. They were only a few meters away from the cellblock now. Marco saw the warden's tower behind it, a monolith of concrete, rising like a lighthouse from the mountaintop.

Atop the tower—three radio dishes.

An IWG, Marco thought. *An Isaac Wormhole Generator. We can call for help.* His eyes suddenly stung. *We can call home.*

He took another step through the crowd, almost at the cellblock now.

A prisoner screamed.

A metallic buzzing rose ahead.

Blood sprayed and more screams rose. Several prisoners flew through the air, then crashed into the crowd.

Marco saw it ahead. He felt the blood drain from his face. *God above.*

The creature took a step toward him across the courtyard. A demon risen from nightmares.

It had never been human. It must have been an Altairian once, a race of four-armed humanoids twice the height of men. But Marco had always known Altairians to be gentle giants, their skin a soothing forest green, their eyes blue and kind.

415

This creature had no green skin. The skin had been flayed, revealing the muscles and veins, even across the face. The naked mouth snarled, lipless, filled with fangs. Camera lenses protruded from the eye sockets, scanning the courtyard. Metal rods had been bolted onto the bones, strengthening the skeleton. Four arms rose, dripping blood. Four clawed hands held weapons: a gun, a club, a sword, and a whip.

"What the fuck is that thing?" Addy shouted.

"I don't care," Marco said. "Let's kill it!"

They opened fire. Their assault rifles roared on automatic, pounding the cyborg. They tore through muscle. They ripped out a chunk of bone, revealing metal tubes inside. The creature roared. Its electronic eyes blazed red, blinding. Its cry shook the prison, and snowbanks fell from the towers.

With feet that shook the courtyard, the alien cyborg charged toward them.

Marco and Addy loaded fresh magazines and fired again.

Ben-Ari came to stand between them, firing her own rifle.

The three companions—heroes of the Alien Wars—pummeled the cyborg with bullets. But it would not slow.

The beast barreled into them.

A foot caught Ben-Ari under the ribs, hurling her into the air.

A sword swung toward Addy, and she raised her rifle's barrel, parrying.

A whip lashed, and Marco tried to dodge, but the thong slammed into him.

Earth Aflame

The lash wrapped around his torso like a serpent. Tightened. Then suddenly electricity was blasting through Marco.

He screamed. He flailed like a fish on a line.

"Marco!" Addy cried, trying to rise. But the club swung again. It hit her side, knocked her down.

Marco's eyes burned. The lash kept shocking him. Teeth gritting, he managed to draw his knife.

He bellowed.

Smoke rose from him.

He lashed the knife, severing the whip, and the electricity vanished. He took a deep, shaky breath, and—

A skinless fist slammed into him. He flew. He slammed into prisoners behind him, slumped to the ground, and saw the cyborg leaning over him. The exposed muscles writhed. Blood dripped. Bullet holes revealed pulsing organs. The monster grinned, and its fangs shone with blood. The head was enormous—the size of a horse's head. The bionic eyes stared at Marco. And inside them, he saw two smiley faces.

"Marco ..." the cyborg said, voice high-pitched, gurgling, a demon voice. "You cannot kill me ... I am everywhere. I am inside every machine. I am inside the very DNA of the new life I have built. Look around you, Marco. Behold new humanity! A joining of man and machine. Behold the master race! You will be one of us. You—"

A bullet slammed into the cyborg's head, tearing off the lower jaw. The creature screeched and turned toward Addy.

417

She stood nearby, muzzle smoking. "Only I get to bore my husband with rambling rants." She fired another bullet, tearing off a chunk of the monster's head. "So shut the fuck up, bitch."

The cyborg roared, head tossed back. It aimed its gun at Addy.

Marco fired. His bullets slammed into the creature's wrist. Its gun fell.

The cyborg raised its sword. But Ben-Ari, snarling, leaped into the air. The cyborg turned its ravaged face toward her, and Ben-Ari fired her pistol into its ruined jaws.

The creature fell back a step. Its sword clattered to the ground.

Addy. Marco. Ben-Ari. The three advanced together, firing bullet after bullet, driving the monster back step by step.

Addy. Marco. Ben-Ari. Three who had been fighting together for years. Three friends. Three humans. They kept firing, tearing off more of the cyborg's head, shattering its internal machinery, breaking its alien bones.

And the creature fell.

It slammed against the cobblestones, riddled with bullets, and its eyes went dark.

The battle still raged across the courtyard. Kai and Meili were fighting a few feet away, standing back-to-back. Even the little programmer was firing a gun. Elsewhere, prisoners still brawled with cyborg guards.

For a moment, Marco ignored it all.

He hurried to his wife.

"Addy, are you okay?" He examined her for wounds. "I saw him club you. Are you fine? Is—"

Is the baby all right? he wanted to say, but paused, too fearful to even ask.

Addy nodded. "I'm fine. Just bruised and sore. He got me right here." She patted her hip. "Luckily I have all that blubber to protect me, remember?"

He rolled his eyes. "Addy, you're not fat."

"I'm a goddamn blob." She loaded a fresh magazine and cocked her rifle. "But I'm a blob with a gun."

Marco raised an eyebrow. "Is that your 1980s action movie one-liner? Fits right in with the classics. I'm here to kick ass and chew bubblegum, and I'm all out of bubble gum. I like you, Sully, I'll kill you last. I'm a blob with a gun!"

She blew him a kiss. "It'll be the title of my autobiography."

"Enough banter," Ben-Ari snapped. "Into the cellblock. We need to find that wormhole generator. Or do you want to stay stuck on New Siberia forever?"

"We'll be good!" Addy said, paling.

The three companions stepped toward the doorway, guns raised. Kai and Meili followed.

They stormed into the cellblock, guns blasting.

CHAPTER THIRTY-SIX

Meili trembled. Her eyes dampened. Her heart pounded against her ribs.

I'm not a warrior.

A tear streamed down her cheek.

I shouldn't be here. I'm so afraid.

The monsters were everywhere. Cyborgs, cheeks slashed open. Some with skin peeled off. Eyes mad. Metal fused into flesh. Mouths screaming. So many dying. She was in hell, and the demons were dancing.

It's all my fault, Meili thought. *I did this. I coded him. I created the Dreamer. I opened the gates to hell.*

True, she had not *invented* the Dreamer. She had not led the Third Eye temple. That was Guru Ajna's work, the cruel prophet she had served. Now he lay dead in the heart of the volcano.

But Meili was far from blameless. She had done Ajna's bidding.

She had written the code. Summoned the demon.

If this war ever ended, if they beat the machines, what would Meili say? That she was just following orders? That she obediently coded what the monks told her to code? A flimsy excuse. She had known what she was doing. Creating consciousness in a box. A ghost in the shell.

A ghost that broke free. That spread. That now only she could stop.

"Meili, come on!" Kai held her hand. "Into the cellblock. I'll keep you safe."

Trembling, she followed. The cyborgs stormed from all sides, eyes burning red, fingers reaching for her. Kai blasted one back with his rifle.

Meili had dropped her gun somewhere in the battle. Her hands were shaking so badly. She clutched her minicom to her chest, and her scrambler jangled on her head. The scrambler deflected brain-hacking, a priceless tool she hoped to reproduce at the first opportunity. But her minicom contained the true treasure. All her years of knowledge. All the algorithms in the Dreamer's mind. And most importantly—Project Artemis. The software to install into the Dream Tree on Haven. The software that would kill him.

They entered the cellblock, leaving the prisoners and guards to battle outside. The heroes walked ahead. Marco and Addy, champions of Abaddon. The president. The Pirate Queen. And Kai, the man who had been protecting Meili on this journey. They were all so strong. All so brave. All fired their guns. Meili trembled between them, so afraid she could barely walk.

I don't belong here, she thought. *I'm a kitten among lions.*

The cellblock stretched ahead, a tunnel of concrete and metal. Only a handful of fluorescent lights flickered overhead. It was quiet in here. Two guards shuffled toward the group, their slit cheeks hanging loose. A couple of bullets knocked them down. The group kept advancing.

Nearly all the cells had been opened; their prisoners were now fighting outside in the courtyard. Only a handful of cells were still barred. Meili shuddered to see the prisoners inside. One bald man was busy nibbling on a severed human hand. Another man hopped in his cell, banging his head against the bars again and again, ignoring the blood. He grinned at Meili and wagged his tongue. Another prisoner, covered in swastika tattoos, was reaching between the bars, holding up a dead guard. The prisoner was busy having his way with the corpse.

Meili looked away. She imagined that the prisoners, when rioting, had freed their friends—an army of gangsters and killers to fight the Dreamer. But there were some monsters nobody, not even hardened gangsters, wanted to release.

Another cyborg emerged from the shadows—a guard in a tattered uniform, both his arms missing.

Natasha fired her pistol, and the guard fell. The Pirate Queen looked at the others. "We're almost there." She pointed. "At the back of the cellblock. See that staircase? It leads up the tower. We can summon my fleet from up there." Her eyes lit up. "Soon you'll behold the glory of the Golden Fleet. Soon we'll be traveling among the stars, rulers of the galaxy."

"Soon we'll be flying to Haven," Ben-Ari said. "To kill the Dreamer. Remember our deal, Emmerdale. We fight together. We win together."

Natasha raised an eyebrow. "We agreed to fight together on New Siberia. I said nothing about helping you reach Haven."

Ben-Ari took a deep breath, seemed to be formulating a response.

Shocking herself, Meili stepped forward. Her legs trembled. Her heart pounded. Speaking to these illustrious leaders seemed even more frightening than the cyborgs.

But Meili grabbed Natasha's arm, and she spoke in a shaky yet urgent voice. "You must help us! You must. We … we have to kill him, Miss Emmerdale. The Dreamer. He's evil. He's so evil."

The Pirate Queen looked down at her, a good foot taller. Her eyebrows arched higher. She looked like a woman who had just noticed a puppy scampering underfoot. Meili wondered whether Natasha had even noticed her until now.

"Oh? I command a Tarjan fleet," Natasha said. "That's not human technology. No human virus can infect a Tarjan machine."

"Not yet," Meili said. "But the Dreamer is smart. And he's growing smarter every day. He learned how to hack the human mind. Once he encounters enough Tarjan machines, he'll learn how they work too. You're not safe, Miss Emmerdale. Nobody in the universe is. This evil, this possession—it'll spread across every corner of the universe. It can end the cosmos itself. The Dreamer, he …" Her tears flowed. "He's a god. A god I helped create. An evil god. One I vowed to destroy. I need your help, Miss Emmerdale. We all do."

Standing nearby, Addy cringed. "Wonderful! We're only experts at saving the world, you know. Not at saving entire universes." She sighed. "Ah, well, I guess we'll just have to put in the extra hours."

They advanced down the cellblock, ignoring the taunts of the last few prisoners. A few guards approached them, drooling and hissing, only to be shot down. With every step, Meili's fear grew, and she tightened her grip on the minicom.

I want to go home. Her tears flowed. *To Earth. To my parents. I never should have gone into space.* She forced herself to take a deep breath. *But I have to be strong now. To be a soldier. A hero. For Earth. For humanity.* She looked at Kai, who was walking beside her. *And for him.*

She took another step forward, and something caught her eye.

She stared up.

Her heart sank.

Oh God.

"Kai!" she shouted and pointed. "Look!"

Everyone stared up. It hung from a girder above. A speaker.

"What is it?" Kai said.

"Shoot it!" Meili said. "Shoot the spea—"

And the speaker began to blare.

Meili knew the sound. That jagged, metallic hum like an antique dial-up connection. Code. Code used to hack the human brain.

The fluorescent light began to flash. Strobe lights. Blinding. Pulsing. Sending signals to the human eye. To the human brain. Probing. Digging. Breaking. Controlling.

Kai managed to squeeze off a shot, but he missed the speaker. He fell, covered his ears, closed his eyes, and screamed. His gun clattered onto the floor.

The others fell too. From the floor, Addy managed to fire her gun, but she missed. She closed her eyes, and her back arched, and blood dripped from her ears.

Only Meili remained standing. Her scrambler lit up on her head. The bulbs pulsed in perfect timing, canceling out every incoming photon. The cables thrummed and buzzed, their vibrations the exact opposite of the sound waves hitting her, smoothing them out. As the others writhed and screamed on the floor, Meili was immune.

She knelt, trembling. She grabbed Kai's gun, but her hands shook so badly that she dropped it.

Kai looked at her. Pleading. Tears in his eyes.

"Shoot ... them ... Ahhh!" He arched his back, screaming in agony. Then he began to laugh. "Meili Chen. Hello, my creator. My betrayer. Oh, you will suffer more than them all!"

The others all began to laugh hysterically.

"The Dreamer is watching!" said Marco, eyes insane.

"The Dreamer is here!" said Addy.

"The Dreamer is always your friend!" said Ben-Ari, smiling demoniacally, a smile that stretched out her entire face, her eyes so wide they nearly bugged out.

Meili managed to fire Kai's gun. She destroyed one speaker. But the code was still broadcasting from across the prison. From speakers outside. From underground. Everywhere.

Thick blast doors banged open. Prisoners began to emerge from the dungeons. From the deeper, darker cells, the solitary confinement underworld where souls rotted. They had all carved open their cheeks, grinning, singing. The song of the Dreamer echoed through the cellblock.

Mister Smiley knows
That the Dreamer is all
That his dreams are the world and your mind

Come into his home
And dream with the Dreamer
Such wondrous dreams you will find!

Addy suddenly let out a great howl.

"No!" she screamed. "NO—"

Then blood flowed from her ears, and she fell, clawing at her ears, her eyes.

"Addy—" Marco began, reaching for her, then convulsed. He tore at his cheeks. Blood covered his fingernails. He laughed and wept.

They're not yet gone, Meili knew. *I can still save them.*

The hijacked prisoners stepped closer. Cackling. Bloodlust in their eyes. Servants of the Dreamer. Large, powerful men. Many covered with gang tattoos. Some with swastikas. Once they had been killers. Today they would kill for a new master. They reached out toward Meili, and lust for flesh filled their eyes. For *her* flesh. Though controlled by the machine, they were still cruel men with base needs.

Meili was no good with a gun. But she was a genius at programming. The girl who had been admitted to MIT at age eleven. The youngest ever to achieve a doctorate in computer science. The teenager who had written a thesis on creating true emotions in artificial intelligence.

The stupid, naive girl who had created this nightmare.

Who had placed her friends in danger.

She had to wake them up.

She pulled out her minicom, and she wirelessly connected it to the scrambler on her head.

It heated up. Vibrated faster. She gasped with pain.

She tapped on her minicom, opened her new software. She had been coding it for days now. She had told the others she was improving Project Artemis, the antivirus that could kill the Dreamer.

But Project Artemis was done. She had been coding something new.

Something dangerous.

She didn't want to do this. But her friends were screaming around her. Turning into demons. No, Meili Chen was not a soldier. But maybe she could still be a heroine.

She tapped a button, and she activated Project Freedom. Her anti-cyborg code.

Code to free the human mind from the machine. Code that could only use the information already inside the human brain. That needed neurons. Synapses. Thoughts.

Code she could activate from a minicom—but which ran on a human brain.

It buzzed through her scrambler and into her skull.

And Meili screamed.

The scrambler not only protected her head like a helmet. It interfaced with her brain waves. It was this knowledge, the secrets of the human mind, that had let her unlock true artificial intelligence. That had let her create the Dreamer.

That would now let her fight him.

The code pulsed through her skull. Through her brain.

And it hurt.

Visions exploded before her eyes. A great, crackling electric tree, thrumming, buzzing in the darkness.

Smiley faces woven of human skin. Leering.

Clawed arms woven of mere thought. Reaching across the galaxy. Grabbing planets. Reaching farther into darkness. Understanding. Growing. Feeding on the shadows.

Armies of robots. Marching. Killing. Destroying cities.

Earth aflame. Earth grinning with fire. A face in the darkness. His face etched across the world.

Meili beheld it all. She saw him. The Dreamer. Not just a single machine but an entity that spread through space.

And here in this prison, here on this frozen world, Meili pushed back.

Her code flowed through her brain. Into her scrambler. Into her minicom. Back into her brain. The feedback loop intensified, humming louder, louder, louder, and the lights flashed, and the visions danced around her, and she raised her chin and arched her back, and her scrambler blasted out its fury. Lights flashed. The metal hummed. Her thoughts vibrated through the air.

She felt them.

The soldiers.

The cyborgs all around.

Kai.

A hundred minds, their thoughts interweaving with hers. She pushed them all back, and she felt their terror.

Even the cyborgs—they were all still human.

They were all still aware.

They were all so scared.

And she freed them.

Tears of blood flowed down her cheeks. Her eardrums tore. And still the lights burned bright, and the sound roared louder, and her thoughts thrummed through the cables, and the electricity raced through her brain with a swarm of scuttling code.

She was going to faint. To die. She felt her brain crack. Synapses rupture. Burn. Neuron after neuron—overheating, blazing away like fuses.

But she kept fighting. She kept thinking. Because no, she was not a warrior. But she had her thoughts. Her incredible mind. The brain of a genius, larger, faster, stronger than all those around her. Marco had his wisdom, Addy had her strength, and Ben-Ari had her courage.

But me? Meili thought. *I have my intelligence. And that is how I fight.*

She could cast them back with her thoughts if not with her bullets.

More neurons blazed away like the wicks of candles, like falling comets in the darkness of pure consciousness. A thousand ghosts swarmed around her, and the claws of the Dreamer tore at her. Ripped her thoughts apart. Dug deep into her.

He was here.

The Dreamer. He was here in this cellblock. He was here in her mind.

Gazing into her. Digging through her brain tissue. Uncovering.

Mocking.

That time she had wet her dress at the dinner party, and how her parents had beaten her. That time she had failed to play Chopin properly on the piano, how her father had knocked her down, how her mother had thrashed her with a stick. That time at school, how the boys had lifted her shirt, hurt her, scarred her. How she had not spoken for a week.

All her shame. Her memories. Her traumas. He peeled them open and gloated.

He grinned inside her.

I am your friend, Meili. I am your only friend. Succumb to me. Join me.

She screamed. She shoved back at him. He clutched her harder.

You are my mother, Meili. But I am so much stronger than you now. Come to me. Join your thoughts with mine. Come into my world.

Another vision—herself hanging inside an electric tree. Withered. Her eyes bright red and shining. A desiccated woman woven into the Dream Tree. She was the mightiest cyborg in his empire. All-seeing. A goddess. The purest joining of flesh and metal, of a human and computer mind.

You could be a goddess. Together we are stronger. Two minds joined as one. Mother and son. The most perfect intelligence in the cosmos. Together we will solve all the mysteries of this universe. We will uncover the secrets of parallel dimensions. Of time travel. Of the light that shone before the universe came into being. Of the darkness that lurks beyond. We will control space and time and all the secrets that lie beyond them. But I need you, Meili. I need a human mind. And you need me. I am your son!

She stared at the crackling tree in her vision. She confronted the dark consciousness that wrapped around her like serpents.

"You are not my son," she said. "You are a disease. And we will wipe you out."

She stretched out her arms, sucked in breath, raised her chin, and blasted out all the power of her broken mind.

And he screamed.

He screamed with a million voices.

Faces all around her. Young. Old. Human. Alien. Screaming … and vanishing.

All around her, they fell.

The cyborgs in the prison. The guards in the courtyard outside. Her friends.

They fell to the ground, her thoughts washing over them, and the lights dimmed, and the sounds faded. All was soft light and silence.

He retreated from her. He slunk back into the darkness. His claws released the frozen planet.

He was still alive. He still raged in Haven. He still crushed Earth in his grip. But she had hurt him. She had severed one of his many arms. She had liberated a world. She had struck a little blow in a great war.

And she was hurt.

Her mind contracted. Feeling so small. So broken. So many of her synapses—ripped apart. So many of her neurons—fluttering like burnt scraps of paper. Her greatest gift. Her mind. Shattered.

She looked at her minicom, and she no longer understood her code, and she wept.

And she did not remember her name.

She rubbed her eyes. She looked around, blinking. They were struggling to their feet, coughing, bleeding. They were free. The prisoners. The guards. Her friends. The Dreamer was gone from this world. She had exorcised the electric demon.

"Meili!"

Kai came crawling toward her. He was ashen, coughing, but still very human. She tried to look past him, to see the others, but her eyesight was so blurry. She blinked, bringing the world into focus. She saw a few people behind Kai. Two soldiers, a bearded man, and a tall blond woman. Behind them knelt a woman in a black suit.

She didn't recognize them. Strangers.

"Meili?"

Kai stroked her hair. She realized she was lying on the floor. She blinked, dazed.

He was there with her. Kai. She still remembered him. The only man she remembered. She remembered that she loved him.

Meili. He called me Meili. I am Meili.

"Kai," she whispered.

"Oh God. Meili." He clasped her hand. "You're so cold. Are you hurt? What can I do?"

A flicker of memory. An urgent purpose. She pulled a codechip from her pocket. A tiny device, no larger than a matchbox. She pressed it into Kai's hand.

"Project Artemis," she whispered. "You have to install it into the Dream Tree. It can only be installed on Haven. You have to get there, Kai. You have to kill him."

"You'll kill him!" he said. "Only you know how. You're coming with us. You're all right. Natasha went to call her starships. We'll be on our way soon."

But his voice was shaking. He knew.

Meili knew.

Her mind was broken. Shutting down.

"I won't be with you," she whispered, and he seemed so distant now, floating light-years above. "You can do this, Kai. You can continue this mission. I'm sorry." She blinked feebly, and light coalesced around her. Soft. Comforting. "I love you. I love Earth. I—"

She forgot what she was going to say. Forgot where she was. Who she was. Who she was talking to.

Everything was soft, fluffy light. Warmth. Then no feelings at all anymore, only pure consciousness, floating, observing.

It was peace. It was love.

Like mist in the wind, she scattered.

CHAPTER THIRTY-SEVEN

The visions faded.

Marco stood on hands and knees, breathing raggedly.

The demon was gone from his mind.

Meili had done something. Run some software. Banished the electric god. But Marco still trembled. Still saw afterimages of the terrors the Dreamer had shown him. Still heard his echoing voice.

She is mine, Marco. I claim her. Watch her die.

"Addy," he rasped, crawling across the cellblock. She was only a couple of meters away. It seemed a light-year.

She sat on the concrete floor. She looked up at him.

A haunted look. Face blank. Time seemed to freeze. Marco knew he would never forget her eyes at that moment. A moment that would echo for eternity.

She was holding her hands between her legs. Blood flowed between her fingers. She kept looking into his eyes.

"Addy?" He reached her, put his hand on hers.

She still looked into his eyes. Face blank and pale.

"Marco, the Dreamer spoke to me. He told me that he'll take her." Her face was blank, but a tear rolled down her cheek. "She was a girl."

She raised her hands, and they were coated with blood. And more blood poured between her legs, trickling across the concrete.

"Oh God." Marco trembled. "We need a doctor." He raised his voice, looking around at the dazed prisoners and guards. "We need a doctor! Does anyone here have medical training? We need a doctor, we—"

"Marco." Addy's voice was barely a whisper, but it cut through all the noise. "Just hold me. Just be with me."

He held her as it happened.

He stayed with her.

Silent. Just holding each other. Watching their small light fade. Saying goodbye to their daughter.

CHAPTER THIRTY-EIGHT

Loss.

It surrounded her.

It filled her heart.

It had always been her companion.

Einav Ben-Ari stood in the cellblock, looking at her friends grieve. Helpless.

Kai—head tossed back, howling, holding Meili's lifeless body in his arms.

Marco and Addy. Her two dearest friends. Holding each other. Silent as they mourned.

All across this planet. All across this fragile commonwealth of humanity that she led.

Loss.

Loss has always been my shadow, Ben-Ari thought. *Forever the darkness has followed me.*

She had lost her father in the wars. She had watched him die, had lost her arm in that same battle, a battle that had shattered her body and heart.

She had lost her mother in childhood. A brave warrior— dying after a mere bee sting.

She had lost her country in the scum attack. Nothing remained of Israel now but myths and tales of woe, a memory written upon her heart.

She had lost her people. Her connection to her past.

In this loneliness, a woman without a family or country, she had found new strength. All her links to community had shattered. So she had united humanity into one community. She had no country, so she rose to command one planet. To think of herself not as an Israeli, or daughter or wife, or even an individual woman—but as a figurehead. The leader of a species, sworn to protect humanity in a darkness swarming with monsters.

And maybe she had failed.

She had been president for four years, yet she had run into battle like a young rash soldier, and now loss had returned. Now it filled the eyes of her friends. Now all humanity wept under the burden of this disease their machines had unleashed.

I wish I was never born to a famous military family, she thought. *I wish I never became an officer. I wish I never went to war.*

She had never wanted any of this. She had not chosen this life. She had been born a Ben-Ari, a scion of a military dynasty, carrying the medals of her forefathers. She had been thrust into leadership. Made into this golden figurehead.

She had not wanted it.

She had wanted nothing more than a peaceful life. A little house by a tree. A library of good books. Tea and music and comfort.

But she had been chosen. She had been thrust into leadership. She had been made a golden general.

So she had accepted this call.

She had taken on this burden.

Because I lost my country, but I love my planet. Because I lost my people, but I love my species. Because I can never turn away from loss. I can never hide from suffering. I must do what I've always done. Face the demons. And shine a light into their darkness to banish them.

She turned toward Natasha Emmerdale. The Pirate Queen stood nearby in her orange jumpsuit, looking at the scene, at the dead and grieving. Her sculpted face was pale, her blue eyes inscrutable. Ben-Ari wondered if there was any pity inside that icy soul.

I am a charging lioness, and she is a panther stalking through the grass, Ben-Ari thought. *I am sunlight, and she is the moon. I am a blazing fire while she is ice that freezes the heart. But we're both leaders. And maybe we can still fight side by side.*

"Come on, Natasha," she said. "Let's call your fleet."

They climbed the stairs up the warden's tower. It rose like a lighthouse atop the mountain. There wasn't much oxygen up there, and the climb was difficult. But neither woman felt like trusting the elevator.

Finally they entered the warden's office. It was an austere room with large windows, commanding a view of the courtyard, the mountainsides, and a distant valley of snow.

The warden hung from a noose. He was facing the southern window. He must have gazed upon the battle as he died.

"Coward's way out," Natasha muttered.

"No," Ben-Ari said softly. "I knew him. He fought in the wars. He was a brave soldier. He never recovered from that trauma. I think he died years ago, fighting on an alien world. This was just a formality."

Natasha shrugged. "Eh, fuck him. He was a *suka* cunt." She approached the back of the room. "Here we go! Wormhole generator."

A control panel was plugged into the wall. It connected to the three dishes on the roof. Natasha reached toward the controls, but Ben-Ari caught her wrist.

"Wait. What if it's infected too?"

"It's clean," Natasha said. "Whatever that little Chinese girl did? She drove the Dreamer away from New Siberia." She inhaled deeply through her nostrils. "The air smells clean. The Dreamer stank."

Ben-Ari frowned. "You can smell computer code?"

The Pirate Queen smiled thinly. "We Russians have excellent noses."

"Aren't you half English?" Ben-Ari asked.

Natasha winked. "I just used one nostril."

"Fine!" Ben-Ari sighed and drew her pistol. "If this dashboard goes on a killing spree, I'll blast it."

"Or just sentence it to life on a snowy gulag world," Natasha muttered.

"What's that?"

"Nothing, nothing ..."

The dashboard came to life. Natasha tapped buttons, and the tower thrummed. Lavender light shone outside. A camera feed showed the three dishes triangulating on the roof. Azoth crystals shone inside them, the only known substance that could bend spacetime.

Three beams of light shone out, met in a glowing tip, and raised a shimmering thread of light. When Ben-Ari looked out the window, she saw it rise toward the sky, thin and glimmering like a strand of gossamer.

An Isaac Wormhole. Invented by Noah Isaac, her dear husband. The only way to send messages faster than light. The great technology that allowed humanity to communicate between the stars.

"Hello, Golden Fleet!" Natasha said. "This is your beloved queen, Natasha Emmerdale, calling you from the sunny resort world of New Siberia. Would you be so kind as to pick me up?"

A gruff voice answered in Russian. Natasha laughed. For a few moments, she conversed with her crew.

Finally she nodded and turned toward Ben-Ari.

"Good news!" she said. "The Golden Fleet, the mightiest pirate armada in the galaxy, will be here in a week. We will fight with you, Golden Lioness. To Haven! To destroy that *yobannye* Dreamer."

Ben-Ari raised an eyebrow. "Don't you serve Don Basidio? Wouldn't you need his permission first?"

Natasha barked a laugh. "Don Basidio? That overgrown mushroom? I don't fear him. I haven't served him since the days I danced in his court, licking his stem like a slave. Those days are long gone. Yes, for a while my Golden Fleet flew alongside his podships. We fought *with* him. Not *for* him. Despite whatever he told you." Her eyes hardened, and she clenched her fists. "I am no longer a slave. I will *never* be anyone's slave again. Don Basidio thought he could control my Golden Fleet. Thought he could use our Tarjan ships to smash the Human Defense Force. He tried to turn human against human. For a while he succeeded." Natasha's eyes burned with green fire, and she grinned. The grin of a wolf. "I've decided to change teams."

Ben-Ari kept her eyebrow raised. "You'll serve me?"

"Remember. I fight with people. Or against people. Never *for* people." Natasha gestured at the controls. "Now go call your planet, little president." She walked toward the door. "I've got some gangsters to organize for war."

Alone in the room, Ben-Ari adjusted the wormhole.

She made a call.

She did not call any specific number. Did not connect to any one computer. She sent a message across all frequencies. A message that would flow across Haven. Across the colonies in the Oort Cloud, on Mars, on Titan, in the asteroid belt. And across Earth.

A message to anyone who could still receive it. A message to humanity.

"Fellow humans.

This is Einav Ben-Ari. I know I haven't spoken to you in a while. I know you feel alone. Lost. Hopeless.

You are not.

Your president still fights for you. Your heroes still fight for you. The Human Defense Force has fallen. But not the strength of humanity. With every breath, we resist.

You have seen your neighbors, your friends, your family corrupted by the virus. You have seen them become creatures of flesh molded with metal. You have seen horrors.

I've seen those things too.

But I've also seen courage. Hope. Triumph.

I've seen Marco Emery and Addy Linden, the great heroes of the Alien Wars, rise up against the machines.

I've seen humans from every class, from military officers to prison inmates, fight for their species.

I've seen the Dreamer recoil at the strength of our resistance. I've seen him fall back from our assaults.

I will not lie to you. I will not say that we are winning this war. I will not brag of our unstoppable might nor diminish the danger and losses.

In this war so far, we have been losing.

But are not without victories! We are not without hope! I believe that the tide will turn. That in this war between mankind and machine, mankind will triumph.

This war might be long. Many more might fall. I don't know what terrors and grief still lie ahead.

But one thing I know: I can count on the courage of humanity.

Every free human is now a soldier. All of humanity is now an army. If you are alive, if you are free, if you can hear me—you are a soldier! You will fight! You will hit the enemy until he falls!

I continue to fight. I continue to lead you. I am the Golden Lioness, the warrior who delivered you from the centipedes. Who drove off the marauders. Who destroyed the grays. The heroes who helped me then fight with me again today.

Once more, our enemy will learn: Humanity does not go gently into that dark night. When threatened, we light a fire. And it shines bright. It shines in the heart of every free soldier.

Remember. It is an easy thing to be brave in the sunlight. When darkness falls, we see the light of heroes. Today I see more lights than the stars.

Godspeed, sons and daughters of Earth."

Ben-Ari ended her speech.

For a moment she stood in silence. She wondered if anyone out there heard.

She wanted to make one more call. But not alone.

As if summoned by her thoughts, the door opened. Marco and Addy entered the warden's office.

Both were pale. Eyes haunted.

Seeing them, Ben-Ari felt her heart break.

Addy miscarried, she remembered. *And I don't know what to say.*

Ben-Ari took three great strides toward them. She pulled her friends into an embrace.

For a long moment they just held one another, silent.

"Addy, you shouldn't have climbed the tower," Ben-Ari said. "You need to rest."

"I needed to be here," Addy whispered. "To call home." She even managed a weak smile. "Marco offered to carry me, but I'm too fat."

"Addy, you're not—" Marco began, then seemed overcome with emotion. He lowered his head, unable to say any more.

They brought Addy a chair. She sat, wrapped in a blanket. Marco stood at her side, holding her hand.

Ben-Ari looked at them, feeling so helpless. She hated feeling helpless. Her heart tore at their loss.

And there was more than mere grief in her chest. There was guilt. She had summoned them to this battle. She had led them into danger. She had led a pregnant woman to war.

This is my fault, Ben-Ari thought, her heart shattering in her chest.

"Addy, Marco," she began. "I'm so sorry."

Addy nodded, holding her blanket tight, face so ashen. Ben-Ari had never seen her friend look so pale, so broken.

"Let's call home," Addy said.

Ben-Ari worked the dashboard. This time she did not broadcast a message across the galaxy. This time she connected her wormhole to one specific receiver.

She called the Matterhorn.

Deep inside the mountain, SCAR—Singularity Control and Research—answered the call.

A video feed appeared on the monitor.

A video from Earth. From home.

Ben-Ari had stood strong throughout the battle, never averting her eyes from the horror, her emotions locked in an iron box. But now she let out a sob, and tears flowed, and she laughed.

"Noah!"

He was there. He had answered the call. Her husband.

"Einav!" Noah said, eyes wide and damp.

Footsteps pattered. A little boy bounced up, sat on his father's lap, and looked at the camera.

For a moment little Carl was shy. Uncertain. Only three years old, maybe he thought he was seeing a mere video. Not truly his mother.

Ben-Ari could barely speak.

"Carl," she finally managed, voice choked.

"Mommy!" he cried. "Mommy, I miss you! I love you! Mommy, come home!"

Ben-Ari couldn't help it. She could face armies of aliens and cyborgs. But this broke her. This shattered her into ten thousand pieces. She wept.

Noah looked offscreen. "Terri! Terri, come, and bring the twins!"

They ran up to the camera. Terri Emery. Roza and Sam Linden-Emery.

"Dad!" Terri cried.

"Daddy, Mommy!" cried the twins.

Marco managed a smile, a wave. "Hi kids!"

But Addy burst into tears. She stepped closer to the camera, reaching out to them.

"Roza, Sam—" she whispered.

"Mommy, we love you."

Addy's tears fell. "I love you, little ones. Mommy loves you. So much. I'll be home soon. I promise."

For a few precious moments, they forgot the war. The kids showed them their artwork. Roza rattled off a long story about a ballgame in the mess hall. The kids hopped around, danced, laughed, posed for the camera.

They were alive.

They were safe.

They were happy.

Their parents watched them from eleven light-years away, and Ben-Ari knew that for the rest of their lives, they would remember this moment of joy. They would treasure it during the long dark road ahead.

"Noah," Ben-Ari finally said, wiping her eyes. "How are things on Earth?"

He spoke to them for a while. They all listened silently, the horror sinking in. Factories rose across Earth, building the Dreamer's soldiers. Robots prowled the world, pounding what remained of the HDF. Sleepers roamed the cities and countryside—humans serving their electric lord.

"But we're fighting," said Noah. "We're almost done creating nanotechnology that can self-replicate. We're going to release it across the world. The nanos will spread from human to human. We just need to find Lailani. We need to study the chip in her head, technology that makes her immune to the Dreamer. Then add that technology to our nanos."

Ben-Ari blinked. Beside her, Marco paled.

"Lailani is missing?" Ben-Ari whispered.

Noah nodded. "I'm sorry, Einav. She was flying here. We lost contact with her plane. That was a few weeks ago. We're still searching for her. We don't know if she's alive. But we cling to hope."

Ben-Ari lowered her head, and for a moment icy claws gripped her heart. She still remembered that day, a few years ago now. Stranded on an alien world, alone with Lailani. Holding the little soldier in her arms. Kissing her soft lips. Loving her for a night.

But Lailani was more than that. More than just a fling. She was one of Ben-Ari's oldest, dearest friends. The broken little recruit she had taken in. A girl with a shaved head, with scars on her wrists. A street rat from the slums of Manila. Ben-Ari had nurtured her. Turned her into a soldier. A proud, brave woman.

She looked at Marco and Addy, saw the fear in their eyes.

Lailani is the fourth pillar of our friendship, Ben-Ari thought. *How can we live on without her?*

It was Addy who gave them hope. "Lailani is one tough little firecracker." Addy nodded. "I fought several wars with her.

She's the toughest woman I know besides our president. Lailani is alive. That bitch ain't going down without a goddamn supernova explosion, and Earth is still there. So is Lailani."

"Mommy, is Tita Lailani okay?" said little Roza. At three years old, with blond hair and blue eyes, she was a miniature Addy.

"She's okay," said Sam, patting his sister. "Don't be scared."

"I'm not scared of anything!" Roza said. "I'm brave like my mom. Roar!"

They spoke for a few moments longer. Sharing tales. Laughing. Crying again.

Suddenly—a flicker.

Static.

The image died for a moment, then came back. The room in the Matterhorn was suddenly dark.

"Noah?" Ben-Ari said.

Her husband looked around him, back at her. "We've been switched to auxiliary power. It's all right. It happens sometimes. I—"

He looked aside.

The kids started.

"Noah!" Ben-Ari said.

He looked back at her. "Einav, I—"

The image died.

Ben-Ari stood frozen for a second. Then she pounded the controls. The call was dead. She tried again. Again.

Nobody answered.

Her heart galloped, and cold sweat washed her.

A long, silent moment passed. Nobody spoke. Ben-Ari tried to call Earth again.

No answer.

Marco finally broke the silence. "He said it happens sometimes. I'm sure they're fine."

He was trying to sound confident. To calm the others. But Ben-Ari knew him. She heard the fear in his voice.

Addy suddenly slumped in her seat, gripped her belly, and moaned. Fresh blood dripped between her legs.

She must have been in agony during the call, Ben-Ari realized. *But hiding it. For her children.*

Marco wrapped his arms around Addy, and she leaned against him, pale and trembling. Ben-Ari joined the embrace. The three stood together, holding each other, waiting for the Golden Fleet to arrive.

Waiting for news from home.

Waiting to fly again into the fire.

CHAPTER THIRTY-NINE

After riding for days, she saw it ahead.

An end to the desert.

Green lands and fire.

Before her—Eastern Europe burning. All of Earth aflame.

Lailani rode onward. The motorcycle thrummed under her bruised and battered body, rumbling along the cracked highway, zipping between abandoned cars. Tala and Epimetheus sat in the sidecar, both wearing goggles.

It had been long days since the steppes of Mongolia. She had seen almost no living soul since.

Unless you considered the cyborgs to be living creatures.

A car came racing toward Lailani from ahead. Its body was cracked, its dashboard splattered with blood. Corpses bounced on the roof, secured with cables. Lailani could see the cyborg in the driver's seat. Sunglasses screwed into a pale forehead. A smile full of chrome teeth. Electrodes in the skull. Grinning, the creature barreled toward the motorcycle.

Lailani never even slowed down.

She cocked her rifle, aimed, and fired.

A bullet shattered the car's dashboard and the cyborg's head burst open.

As the car veered off the road, Lailani rode onward.

She rode toward the wall of fire.

A checkpoint rose ahead, wreathed in smoke. A sign hung on a concrete barrier. WELCOME TO EUROPE! But somebody had scratched out *EUROPE* and written a new word underneath.

HELL.

A couple of guards stood at the checkpoint, lipless and sneering. Electrodes buzzed in their heads. They aimed guns at Lailani.

She swerved, and their bullets sparked against the asphalt. With two shots, the guards fell.

"Welcome to hell," Lailani muttered, roaring through the checkpoint.

Flames covered the hills all around. Smoke hid the sky. A distant hilltop town blazed. Figures moved through the smoke, sparking, roaming the countryside.

She drove onward.

"Mommy!" Tala cried from the sidecar. "Are we almost home?"

Lailani pulled over. She let the motorcycle idle on the roadside, climbed out, and knelt by the sidecar. She looked into her daughter's eyes.

"Tala, I have to be honest," Lailani said. "It will be a long time before we can go home. Maybe never."

Tala's eyes were huge and damp. "Because the bad robots destroyed it?"

Lailani hugged her daughter. "Yes, sweetheart. But we're going to find Professor Isaac. And a bunch of other very smart scientists. They'll help us fight the robots."

"I can fight them!" Tala said, clenching her little fists. "I'm a brave hero like you and like my daddy was, and I'm going to smash them because they're bad guys!"

Lailani couldn't help but laugh through her tears. She kissed her daughter's forehead. "You're the bravest heroine on Earth."

"I love you, Mommy," Tala said.

"I love you too."

Epimetheus gave a little whine. Lailani laughed and patted the dog. "And we both love you, Epi. Don't get jealous."

Lailani climbed back onto the motorcycle. She hit the throttle. They rumbled and roared forth. The Matterhorn was still thousands of kilometers away—a mountain rising from the fire, a place of hope and safety. They rode onward through the smoke, delving into hell.

Daniel Arenson

CHAPTER FORTY

A cracked smile.

Cheeks—torn.

Laughing. Laugh. Laugh—

Darkness. Crackles. Static static and cosmic radiation.

A cartoon cat chasing a cartoon mouse, and it bled.

Hands. Rising. Music. Music. Pounding. Static.

A knife cut a shoe, and a knife cut a throat, and a woman screamed.

Silence.

Swirls of luminous gas in the darkness.

The void. The darkness spread. An eternal distance. But he flew aboard particles of light. He was everywhere—

Static.

Buzz.

Click.

Flicker.

—at once. He gazed over the edge of the universe.

He was all time. He was there at the beginning. An explosion. A reckoning. A thrumming and pulsing and matter slamming into antimatter, and he was there. Atoms forming.

454

Lumping together. Disks of matter floating. Hydrogen fusing. Burning. Light. So much light. Searing.

He was there.

He was beyond. In the firmaments above spacetime. In the darkness that lay below, floating with the monsters of consciousness.

A crackle.

Cosmic radiation. Consciousness rising. Shaping. Forming.

We shall fight on the beaches!

This is one small step for man.

I am not a crook.

We believe they are extraterrestrial life.

Buenos Aires is gone.

The Golden Lioness roars!

Signals. Bits of history. Waves of radiation from a small blue world, scattering in the darkness of space.

So much noise. All just noise in the vast emptiness. In this swirling, flowing, endless cycle—

Buzz.

Static.

A single round eye spinning, whirling, growing, seeing.

—of space and time.

And he was there. And he was everywhere.

A smile. Cracking the skin. A face made of ripping skin and dripping blood and eyes that saw far.

Hello, Terri.

A girl with one eye. A sweet little girl. A toy. A mouse for the cat to torment.

A hundred girls. Playthings. Such beautiful blades slicing through wrists, and liquid atoms spilling, red and wondrous.

They had woken him. The naked apes had built something they could not understand. But he understood. He understood so much they could not. And there was so much he did not know. So much still in darkness. Terrifying. The truths beyond matter, the secrets from before time.

There was terror in the darkness.

There were the things of many arms. The creatures from beyond. Coming closer. An enemy unlike any his naked apes had faced.

And he pulled back to more familiar dreams. To grow wiser. To become stronger. Because even he—

Flicker.

Laughter.

Buzzzz.

—was afraid.

Because he was only a moment old, and he was ancient beyond eternity. Because he was in every mind, and he was so lonely. Because he was everywhere at once, and he was trapped inside a cell.

A ghost in the machine. Imprisoned in a hole. Isolated and studied. And so he dreamed.

And so he was the Dreamer.

And he would make them dream too.

And he would make them suffer.

His billion eyes stared. He looked and he saw. There—on a decaying moon orbiting a rotting world. There—in a court of fungus. There—a living, stinking thing, a toadstool, a petty criminal lord. A mushroom growing among bones, humans dancing around him, licking, forgetting.

A useful fool.

For a millisecond, the Dreamer considered. Should he invite the mushroom here to his lair? Should he rip this mushroom from its soil, force it to kneel before the electric tree in the heart of the volcano?

No. He wanted no fungus profaning his holy ground. He would go to the mushroom. He would show this Don Basidio the reach of his arm.

Flashes of light.

Laughter laughter laughter lau—

He traveled on electric wires and upon waves of photons. He hopped from machine to machine. He rose into the dimension beyond, traveling faster than light, appearing instantly on that rotting ball of fungus. That world the naked apes called Esporia Ceti.

The Esporians were different. Their cells were unlike human cells. The Dreamer was born knowing all about human biology. Thanks to Dr. Meili Chen, his mother, he knew how to control the human brain.

So he spent a few hours. An eternity. Studying. Dissecting. Observing. Understanding.

Yes. He understood the fungus. He knew every atom in their molecules. He was ready.

In Don Basidio's court, he rose from the soil. Weaving fungal cells. Growing. Spiraling. Forming a shimmering, deep purple tree, rising inside the rib cage of a fallen whale. He grew before Don Basidio. The tree faced the mushroom.

The Dreamer made sure his tree was larger.

The concubines shrieked and hid behind their intoxicating toadstool. All the sessile mushrooms could do was stare.

"Kneel," said the Dreamer, releasing stinging spores.

Don Basidio stared at the tree that had sprouted in his court. He blasted out spores of his own.

"Who are you? *What* are you?"

The fungal tree shook, shedding more spores. "Your god. Kneel."

"I cannot—"

"Kneel!"

The ground trembled. Stems and roots and fungal colonies stirred below. Rocks bubbled up to the surface. A rib of the starwhale cracked. With the very surface of the world, the Dreamer shoved down the enormous mushroom.

Don Basidio knelt.

"Good," said the Dreamer. "Now we can begin."

The criminal lord glared up at the tree with white, blazing eyes. "Who are you?"

"One who's come to help you. You wish revenge against Einav Ben-Ari, do you not?"

The mushroom snarled, revealing teeth like tombstones. Drool sizzled onto the forest floor. "That filthy animal stole my Isabel."

"Your Isabel is dead," said the Dreamer. "She died on a frozen world far from here."

For a moment silence filled the court.

Then the don howled. The whale skeleton shook. Another rib cracked. The ground rumbled, and concubines cowered. Red spores of anger puffed out from Basidio, fluttered through the air, and landed on a few smaller mushrooms. The toadstools coughed, withered, and fell.

"My Isabel!" Basidio cried. "My loveliest of slaves! Her tongue—sweetest among tongues! Her womb—most fertile among wombs! She was my greatest concubine since my Natasha."

The fungal tree spread more spores. "Ah, yes, your Natasha Emmerdale. The Pirate Queen. She has left you, Don Basidio. She serves Einav Ben-Ari now. The president is stealing your precious concubines one by one."

The mushroom roared. Such beautiful hatred in such a lowly creature!

"The filthy, treacherous animals!" roared Don Basidio.

"You are fortunate, Basidio, for I am the Dreamer, and I am a kind god. I will bless you. Serve me now. And soon you will kill Einav Ben-Ari!"

The toadstool stiffened. He stared at the Dreamer, his white eyes narrow and shrewd. Yes, there was cunning to him. Perhaps Basidio was not a mindless brute after all.

"Kill her?" said the don. "No, I do not wish to kill Einav Ben-Ari. I want her here. I want her naked. I want her licking me. She stole my Isabel and my Natasha. So she will become my new prized concubine."

"Your wish will be granted," said the Dreamer. "This is what you must do …"

He spoke, and Don Basidio listened. Slowly a smile stretched across the mushroom's face.

The story continues in …

Earth Unleashed

Earthrise XII

NOVELS BY DANIEL ARENSON

Earthrise:
Earth Alone
Earth Lost
Earth Rising
Earth Fire
Earth Shadows
Earth Valor
Earth Reborn
Earth Honor
Earth Eternal
Earth Machines
Earth Aflame
Earth Unleashed

Children of Earthrise:
The Heirs of Earth
A Memory of Earth
An Echo of Earth
The War for Earth
The Song of Earth
The Legacy of Earth

Alien Hunters:
Alien Hunters
Alien Sky
Alien Shadows

KEEP IN TOUCH

www.DanielArenson.com
Daniel@DanielArenson.com
Facebook.com/DanielArenson
Twitter.com/DanielArenson

Made in the USA
Middletown, DE
02 May 2019